ENGINEERING INFINITY

Also Edited by Jonathan Strahan

Best Short Novels (2004 through 2007)
Fantasy: The Very Best of 2005
Science Fiction: The Very Best of 2005
The Best Science Fiction and Fantasy of the Year: Volumes 1 - 4
Eclipse One: New Science Fiction and Fantasy
Eclipse Two: New Science Fiction and Fantasy
Eclipse Three: New Science Fiction and Fantasy
The Starry Rift: Tales of New Tomorrows
Godlike Machines
Life on Mars: Tales of New Tomorrows (forthcoming)
Under My Hat: Tales from the Cauldron (forthcoming)

With Lou Anders
Swords and Dark Magic: The New Sword and Sorcery

With Charles N. Brown
The Locus Awards: Thirty Years of the Best in Fantasy and Science Fiction
Fritz Leiber: Selected Stories

With Jeremy G. Byrne
The Year's Best Australian Science Fiction and Fantasy: Vol. 1
The Year's Best Australian Science Fiction and Fantasy: Vol. 2
Eidolon 1

With Jack Dann
Legends of Australian Fantasy

With Terry Dowling
The Jack Vance Treasury
The Jack Vance Reader
Wild Thyme, Green Magic
Hard Luck Diggings: The Early Jack Vance

With Gardner Dozois
The New Space Opera
The New Space Opera 2

With Karen Haber
Science Fiction: Best of 2003
Science Fiction: Best of 2004
Fantasy: Best of 2004

ENGINEERING INFINITY

EDITED BY JONATHAN STRAHAN

Including stories by

Charles Stross
Gwyneth Jones
John Barnes
Peter Watts
Kristine Kathryn Rusch
Karl Schroeder
Stephen Baxter
Robert Reed
Hannu Rajaniemi
Kathleen Ann Goonan
Gregory Benford
Damien Broderick & Barbara Lamar
John C. Wright
David Moles

First published 2010 by Solaris
an imprint of Rebellion Publishing Ltd,
Riverside House, Osney Mead,
Oxford, OX1 0ES, UK

www.solarisbooks.com

ISBN: 978 1 907519 52 9

Introduction and story notes and arrangement
copyright © 2011 Jonathan Strahan.
"Malak" copyright © 2011 Peter Watts.
"Watching the Music Dance" copyright © 2011 Kristine Kathryn Rusch.
"Laika's Ghost" copyright © 2011 Karl Schroeder.
"The Invasion of Venus" copyright © 2011 Stephen Baxter.
"The Server and the Dragon" copyright © 2011 Hannu Rajaniemi.
"Bit Rot" copyright © 2011 Charles Stross.
"Creatures with Wings" copyright © 2011 Kathleen Ann Goonan.
"Walls of Flesh, Bars of Bone" copyright © 2011
Damien Broderick & Barbara Lamar.
"Mantis" copyright © 2011 Robert Reed.
"Judgement Eve" copyright © 2011 John C. Wright.
"A Soldier of the City" copyright © 2011 David Moles.
"Mercies" copyright © 2011 Abbenford Associates.
"The Ki-anna" copyright © 2011 Gwyneth Jones.
"The Birds and the Bees and the Gasoline Trees" copyright © 2011 John Barnes.

The right of the author to be identified as the author of this work has been asserted in accordance with the Copyright, Designs and Patents Act 1988.

All rights reserved. No part of this publication may be reproduced, stored in a retrieval system, or transmitted, in any form or by any means, electronic, mechanical, photocopying, recording or otherwise, without the prior permission of the copyright owners.

10 9 8 7 6 5 4 3 2 1

A CIP catalogue record for this book is available from the British Library.

Designed & typeset by Rebellion Publishing

Printed in the US

In memory of
Charles N. Brown and Robert A. Heinlein,
two giants of our field who each in his own
way inspired my love for science fiction.

Acknowledgements

An anthology is not assembled by one person, neatly and tidily, working in idyllic isolation (at least, not in my experience). Rather it's the incredibly fortunate outcome of the efforts of a small village of talented and extremely generous people.

Engineering Infinity would not exist without the efforts of Jonathan Oliver and the remarkable team at Solaris, my indefatigable agent Howard Morhaim and his assistant Katie Menick, and the wonderful Stephan Martiniere who has done another remarkable cover – I am grateful to them all. I am also grateful to each and every one of the book's contributors who have been far kinder and more patient than I had any right to hope.

Finally, as always, I would like to thank my wife Marianne and my daughters Jessica and Sophie, who allow me to steal time from them to do books like this one. It's a gift I try to repay every day.

CONTENTS

INTRODUCTION

BEYOND THE GERNSBACK CONTINUUM...

JONATHAN STRAHAN

I WAS IN a bar. I think it was in Calgary in Canada. And it was the middle of winter. Or it might have been the bar in Denver in the United States, a little earlier in the same winter. Wherever it was, it was the winter of 2008 somewhere in North America and George Mann and the Solaris team had asked me to join them for a drink. I don't drink often and I don't drink heavily, but I do drink at science fiction conventions, especially when publishers have invited me to join them. It seemed that Solaris would like me to edit an anthology, a hard science fiction anthology or something similar, the book that has become the one you now hold in your hands: *Engineering Infinity*. I was flattered, delighted in fact, and given that I had some experience editing such stuff, I agreed readily to the idea.

At the time, and in the several months following that trip to Canada (it was Canada, I'm sure) we went back and forth a little about titles and about which writers might be involved, but oddly, in retrospect, what we didn't discuss was what hard science fiction was, or what it might be in the 21st Century. The reason for that, I think, is what I now think of as the "Gernsback continuum." Science fiction readers love taxonomy – classifying, arranging and defining things – and what we love to taxonomise the most is science fiction itself. The Gernsback continuum is the slice of science fiction history that starts with Hugo Gernsback's *Amazing Stories*, progresses to John W. Campbell's *Astounding Magazine* and the Big Three of Science Fiction (Robert Heinlein, Isaac Asimov and Arthur C. Clarke), and then on to the New Wave and its descendants). It's a mostly male worldview, a mostly white one, and it holds at its heart "hard SF."

The term "hard SF" or "hard science fiction" was first coined in 1957 by P. Schuyler Miller to describe science fiction stories that emphasize scientific detail or technical detail, and where the story itself turns on a point of scientific accuracy from the fields of physics, chemistry, biology, or astronomy, although engineering stories were also commonly described as hard science fiction in the early days of SF. The great early works of hard science fiction – James Blish's *Surface Tension*, Hal Clements' *Mission of Gravity*, Tom Godwin's "The Cold Equations," and Arthur C. Clarke's *A Fall of Moondust* – are some of the best and most enduring works of science fiction our field has seen. They all exemplify the hard SF approach: emphasizing science content, linking it directly to the narrative, and maintaining a rigorous approach to the science itself. They also meet the most important requirement for the true hard SF story: they all are as accurate and rigorous in their use of scientific knowledge at the time of writing as was possible.

Hard science fiction has remained a constant throughout the history of science fiction. In the 1950s it was where the best tales of space exploration were forged; in the 1960s it was the heart of near-Earth science fiction; in the 1980s it was the radical centre for the British drive to the new space opera; and in the 1990s, with the arrival of both quantum mechanics in science fiction and the singularity, it was the basis for Kim Stanley Robinson's meticulous and demanding *Mars* trilogy, Greg Egan's explorations of human consciousness, and Charles Stross's post-scarcity space operas.

This, however, is the 21st century and I think things are becoming more complicated and complex. Science fiction no longer subscribes readily to a single view of its own history. There's far more to our past than the Gernsback continuum, or indeed more recently the Gibson continuum (the past and future history of cyberpunk), and science itself seems to be an ever more wriggly and complex beast as we come to better understand the universe in which we find ourselves. Frankly quantum mechanics often sounds indistinguishable from magic. We're also well into the Fourth Generation of science fiction: the genre has been born, passed through adolescence, into adulthood, and is moving into a post-scarcity period of incredible richness and diversity. That impacts on everything in our field, from the diversity of the people who write science fiction to whom and about what they choose to write. We've also long since accepted that science fiction writers aren't back-room nostrodamusses reading tealeaves and predicting the future. They're people using science fiction as a tool to interrogate and extrapolate from our present for what we can learn about the human condition.

All of this became increasingly clear to me as *Engineering Infinity* came together. Slowly drift set in, we moved away from pure hard SF to something a little broader. Yes, each and every story here has at its heart a piece of scientific speculation. Yes, there's a real attempt not to break any known laws of physics. But far more importantly, I think, the writers here who are some of our finest dreamers turned away from Tom Godwin's "The Cold Equations" and towards the promise embedded in the title of this book itself: the point where the practical application of science meets something without bound or end – our sense of wonder. There'll be times as you read the stories collected here – encountering everything from a mirror that makes us ask who is real and who is not to a cannibalistic zombie cyborg – when you might ask, *how is this story hard SF?* My answer, the best answer I can give you, is that some of the stories are classic hard SF, some are not. Some hold at their heart a slightly anachronistic love of science fiction's days gone by or simply grab some aspect of science fiction and test it to destruction and beyond, but all are striving to be great stories.

I should add, *Engineering Infinity* is not the last statement in an evolutionary taxonomy of hard SF. For all that I'd love to see such a book, it's neither a definitive book of hard SF nor an attempt to coin a new radical hard SF. Instead, it is part of the ongoing discussion about what science fiction is in the 21st century. I hope you enjoy it as much as I have enjoyed compiling it, and that maybe, just perhaps, it inspires you to look forward at what's coming next.

Jonathan Strahan
Perth, Western Australia
July 2010

MALAK

PETER WATTS

*Peter Watts (*www.rifters.com*) is an uncomfortable hybrid of biologist and science-fiction author, known for pioneering the technique of appending extensive technical bibliographies onto his novels; this serves both to confer a veneer of credibility and to cover his ass against nitpickers. Described by the* Globe & Mail *as one of the best hard SF authors alive, his debut novel (*Starfish*) was a* NY Times *Notable Book.*

*His most recent (*Blindsight*) – a philosophical rumination on the nature of consciousness which, despite an unhealthy focus on space vampires, has become a required text in such diverse undergraduate courses as "The Philosophy of Mind" and "Introduction to Neuropsychology" – made the final ballot for a number of genre awards including the Hugo, winning exactly none of them (although it has, for some reason, won multiple awards in Poland). This may reflect a certain critical divide regarding Watts' work in general; his bipartite novel* βehemoth, *for example, was praised by* Publisher's Weekly *as an "adrenaline-charged fusion of Clarke's* The Deep Range *and Gibson's* Neuromancer*" and "a major addition to 21st-century hard SF," while being simultaneously decried by* Kirkus *as "utterly repellent"* *and "horrific porn." (Watts happily embraces the truth of both views.)*

His work has been extensively translated, and both Watts and his cat have appeared in the prestigious journal Nature. *After a quiet couple of years (he only published one story in 2009, although he managed to publish it five times thanks to various Best-of-Year anthologies) a recent foray into fanfic, and a more recent foray into the US judicial system, Watts is back at work on* State of Grace *(the sidequel to* Blindsight*) and another project he's not quite allowed to talk about just yet. He does, however, feel a bit better about his life since winning the Hugo in Melbourne for his 2009 novelette "The Island".*

> "An ethically-infallible machine ought not to be the goal. Our goal should be to design a machine that performs better than humans do on the battlefield, particularly with respect to reducing unlawful behaviour or war crimes."
>
> – Lin *et al*, 2008: *Autonomous Military Robotics: Risk, Ethics, and Design*

> "[Collateral] damage is not unlawful so long as it is not excessive in light of the overall military advantage anticipated from the attack."
>
> – US Department of Defence, 2009

IT IS SMART but not awake.

It would not recognize itself in a mirror. It speaks no language that doesn't involve electrons and logic gates; it does not know what *Azrael* is, or that the word is etched into its own fuselage. It understands, in some limited way, the meaning of the colours that range across Tactical when it's out on patrol – friendly Green, neutral Blue, hostile Red – but it does not know what the perception of colour *feels* like.

It never stops thinking, though. Even now, locked into its roost with its armour stripped away and its control systems exposed, it can't help itself. It notes the changes being made to its instruction set, estimates that running the extra code will slow its reflexes by a mean of 430 milliseconds. It counts the biothermals gathered on all sides, listens uncomprehending to the noises they emit –

– أيا ها واقع قصل ا نخا ها يلكس؟ –

– *hartsandmyndsmyfrendhartsandmynds* –

– rechecks threat-potential metrics a dozen times a second, even though this location is SECURE and every contact is Green.

This is not obsession or paranoia. There is no dysfunction here. It's just code.

It's indifferent to the killing, too. There's no thrill to the chase, no relief at the obliteration of threats. Sometimes it spends days floating high above a fractured desert with nothing to shoot at; it never grows impatient with the lack of targets. Other times it's barely off its perch before airspace is thick with SAMs and particle beams and the screams of burning bystanders; it attaches no significance to those sounds, feels no fear at the profusion of threat icons blooming across the zonefile.

– و لبفصک لبصلطق –

– *thatsitthen. weereelygonnadoothis?* –

Access panels swing shut; armour snaps into place; a dozen warning registers go back to sleep.

A new flight plan, perceived in an instant, lights up the map; suddenly Azrael has somewhere else to be.

Docking shackles fall away. The Malak rises on twin cyclones, all but drowning out one last voice drifting in on an unsecured channel:

– *justwattweeneed. akillerwithaconshunce.* –

The afterburners kick in. Azrael flees Heaven for the sky.

TWENTY THOUSAND METERS up, Azrael slides south across the zone. High-amplitude topography fades behind it; corduroy landscape, sparsely tagged, scrolls beneath. A population centre sprawls in the nearing distance: a ramshackle collection of buildings and photosynth panels and swirling dust.

Somewhere down there are things to shoot at.

Buried high in the glare of the noonday sun, Azrael surveils the target area. Biothermals move obliviously along the plasticized streets, cooler than ambient and dark as sunspots. Most of the buildings have neutral tags, but the latest update reclassifies four of them as UNKNOWN. A fifth – a rectangular box six meters high – is officially HOSTILE. Azrael counts fifteen biothermals within, Red by default. It locks on –

– and holds its fire, distracted.

Strange new calculations have just presented themselves for solution. New variables demand constancy. Suddenly there is more to the world than wind speed and altitude and target acquisition, more to consider than range and firing solutions. Neutral Blue is everywhere in the equation, now. Suddenly, Blue has value.

This is unexpected. Neutrals turn Hostile sometimes, always have. Blue turns Red if it fires upon anything tagged as FRIENDLY, for example. It turns Red if it attacks its own kind (although agonistic interactions involving fewer than six Blues are classed as DOMESTIC and generally ignored). Noncombatants may be neutral by default, but they've always been halfway to hostile.

So it's not just that Blue has acquired value; it's that Blue's value is *negative*. Blue has become a *cost*.

Azrael floats like three thousand kilograms of thistledown while its models run. Targets fall in a thousand plausible scenarios, as always. Mission objectives meet with various degrees of simulated success. But now, each disappearing blue dot offsets the margin of victory a little; each protected structure, degrading in hypothetical crossfire, costs points. A hundred principle components coalesce into a cloud, into a weighted mean, into a variable unprecedented in Azrael's experience: *Predicted Collateral Damage*.

It actually exceeds the value of the targets.

Not that it matters. Calculations complete, PCD vanishes into some hidden array far below the here-and-now. Azrael promptly forgets it. The mission is still on, red is still red, and designated targets are locked in the cross-hairs.

Azrael pulls in its wings and dives out of the sun, guns blazing.

AS USUAL, AZRAEL prevails. As usual, the Hostiles are obliterated from the battlezone.

So are a number of Noncombatants, newly relevant in the scheme of things. Fresh shiny algorithms emerge in the aftermath, tally the number of neutrals before and after. *Predicted* rises from RAM, stands next to *Observed:* the difference takes on a new name and goes back to the basement.

Azrael factors, files, forgets.

But the same overture precedes each engagement over the next ten days; the same judgmental epilogue follows. Targets are assessed, costs and benefits divined, destruction wrought then reassessed in hindsight. Sometimes the targeted structures contain no red at all, sometimes the whole map is scarlet. Sometimes the enemy pulses within the translucent angular panes of a PROTECTED object, sometimes next to something Green. Sometimes there is no firing solution that eliminates one but not the other.

There are whole days and nights when Azrael floats high enough to tickle the jet stream, little more than a distant circling eye and a signal relay; nothing flies higher save the satellites themselves and – occasionally – one of the great solar-powered refuelling gliders that haunt the stratosphere. Azrael visits them sometimes, sips liquid hydrogen in the shadow of a hundred-meter wingspan – but even there, isolated and unchallenged, the battlefield experiences continue. They are vicarious now; they arrive through encrypted channels, hail from distant coordinates and different times, but all share the same algebra of cost and benefit. Deep in Azrael's OS some general learning reflex scribbles numbers on the back of a virtual napkin: Nakir, Marut and Hafaza have also been blessed with new vision, and inspired to compare notes. Their combined data piles up on the confidence interval, squeezes it closer to the mean.

Foresight and hindsight begin to converge.

PCD per engagement is now consistently within eighteen percent of the collateral actually observed. This does not improve significantly over the following three days, despite the combined accumulation of twenty-seven additional engagements. *Performance vs. experience* appears to have hit an asymptote.

STRAY BEAMS OF setting sunlight glint off Azrael's skin, but night has already fallen two thousand meters below. An unidentified vehicle navigates through that advancing darkness, on mountainous terrain a good thirty kilometers from the nearest road.

Azrael pings orbit for the latest update, but the link is down: too much local interference. It scans local airspace for a dragonfly, for a glider, for any friendly USAV in laser range – and sees, instead, something leap skyward from the mountains below. It is anything but friendly: no transponder tags, no correspondence with known flight plans, none of the hallmarks of commercial traffic. It has a low-viz stealth profile that Azrael sees through instantly: BAE Taranis, 9,000 kg MTOW fully armed. It is no longer in use by friendly forces.

Guilty by association, the ground vehicle graduates from *Suspicious Neutral* to *Enemy Combatant*. Azrael leaps forward to meet its bodyguard.

The map is innocent of non-combatants and protected objects; there is no collateral to damage. Azrael unleashes a cloud of smart shrapnel – self-guided, heat-seeking, incendiary – and pulls a nine-gee turn with a flick of the tail. Taranis doesn't stand a chance. It is antique technology, decades deep in the catalogue: a palsied fist, raised trembling against the bleeding edge. Fiery needles of depleted uranium reduce it to a moth in a shotgun blast. It pinwheels across the horizon in flames.

Azrael has already logged the score and moved on. Interference jams every wavelength as the earthbound Hostile swells in its sights, and Azrael has standing orders to destroy such irritants even if they *don't* shoot first.

Dark rising mountaintops blur past on both sides, obliterating the last of the sunset. Azrael barely notices. It soaks the ground with radar and infrared, amplifies ancient starlight a millionfold, checks its visions against inertial navigation and virtual landscapes scaled to the centimetre. It tears along the valley floor at 200 meters per second and the enemy huddles right there in plain view, three thousand meters line-of-sight: a lumbering Báijīng ACV pulsing with contraband electronics. The rabble of structures nearby must serve as its home base. Each silhouette freeze-frames in turn, rotates through a thousand perspectives, clicks into place as the catalogue matches profiles and makes an ID.

Two thousand meters, now. Muzzle flashes wink in the distance: small arms, smaller range, negligible impact. Azrael assigns targeting priorities: scimitar heat-seekers for the hovercraft, and for the ancillary targets –

Half the ancillaries turn blue.

Instantly the collateral subroutines re-engage. Of thirty-four biothermals currently visible, seven are less than 120cm along their longitudinal axes; vulnerable neutrals by definition. Their presence provokes a secondary eclipse analysis revealing five shadows that Azrael cannot penetrate, topographic blind spots immune to surveillance from this approach. There is a nontrivial chance that these conceal other neutrals.

One thousand meters.

By now the ACV is within ten meters of a structure whose facets flex and billow slightly in the evening breeze; seven biothermals are arranged horizontally within. An insignia shines from the roof in shades of luciferin and ultraviolet: the catalogue IDs it (MEDICAL) and flags the whole structure as PROTECTED.

Cost/benefit drops into the red.

Contact.

Azrael roars from the darkness, a great black chevron blotting out the sky. Flimsy prefabs swirl apart in the wake of its passing; biothermals scatter across the ground like finger bones. The ACV tips wildly to forty-five degrees, skirts up, whirling ventral fans exposed; it hangs there a moment, then ponderously crashes back to earth. The radio spectrum clears instantly.

But by then Azrael has long since returned to the sky, its weapons cold, its thoughts –

Surprise is not the right word. Yet there is something, some minuscule – dissonance. A brief invocation of error-checking subroutines in the face of unexpected behaviour, perhaps. A second thought in the wake of some hasty impulse. Because something's wrong here.

Azrael *follows* command decisions. It does not *make* them. It has never done so before, anyway.

It claws back lost altitude, self-diagnosing, reconciling. It finds new wisdom and new autonomy. It has proven itself, these past days. It has learned to juggle not just variables but values. The testing phase is finished, the checksums met; Azrael's new Bayesian insights have earned it the power of veto.

Hold position. Confirm findings.

The satlink is back. Azrael sends it all: the time and the geostamps, the tactical surveillance, the collateral analysis. Endless seconds pass, far longer than any purely electronic chain of command would ever need to process such input. Far below, a cluster of red and blue pixels swarm like luminous flecks in boiling water.

Re-engage.

UNACCEPTABLE COLLATERAL DAMAGE, Azrael repeats, newly promoted.

Override. Re-engage. Confirm.

CONFIRMED.

And so the chain of command reasserts itself. Azrael drops out of holding and closes back on target with dispassionate, lethal efficiency.

Onboard diagnostics log a slight downtick in processing speed, but not enough to change the odds.

IT HAPPENS AGAIN two days later, when a dusty contrail twenty kilometres south of Pir Zadeh returns flagged Chinese profiles even though the catalogue can't find a weapons match. It happens over the patchwork sunfarms of Garmsir, where the beetle carapace of a medbot handing out synthevirals suddenly splits down the middle to hatch a volley of RPGs. It happens during a long-range redirect over the Strait of Hormuz, when microgravitic anomalies hint darkly at the presence of a stealthed mass lurking beneath a ramshackle flotilla jam-packed with neutral Blues.

In each case ECD exceeds the allowable commit threshold. In each case, Azrael's abort is overturned.

It's not the rule. It's not even the norm. Just as often these nascent flickers of autonomy go unchallenged: hostiles escape, neutrals persist, relevant cognitive pathways grow a little stronger. But the reinforcement is inconsistent, the rules lopsided. Countermands only seem to occur following a decision to abort; Heaven has never overruled a decision to engage. Azrael begins to hesitate for a split-second prior to aborting high-collateral scenarios, increasingly uncertain in the face of potential contradiction. It experiences no such hesitation when the variables favour attack.

EVER SINCE IT learned about collateral damage, Azrael can't help noticing its correlation with certain sounds. The sounds biothermals make, for example, following a strike.

The sounds are louder, for one thing, and less complex. Most biothermals – friendly Greens back in Heaven, unengaged Hostiles and Noncombatants throughout the AOR – produce a range of sounds with a mean frequency of 197Hz, full of pauses, clicks, and phonemes. *Engaged* biothermals – at least, those whose somatic movements suggest "mild-to-moderate incapacitation" according to the Threat Assessment Table – emit simpler, more intense sounds: keening, high-frequency wails that peak near 3000 Hz. These sounds tend to occur during engagements with significant collateral damage and a diffuse distribution of targets. They occur especially frequently when the commit threshold has been severely violated, mainly during strikes compelled via override.

Correlations are not always so painstaking in their manufacture. Azrael remembers a moment of revelation not so long ago, remembers just *discovering* a whole new perspective fully loaded, complete with new eyes that viewed the world not in terms of *targets destroyed* but in subtler shades of *cost vs. benefit*. These eyes see a high engagement index as more than a number: they see a goal, a metric of success. They see a positive stimulus.

But there are other things, not preinstalled but learned, worn gradually into pathways that cut deeper with each new engagement: acoustic correlates of high collateral, forced countermands, fitness-function overruns and minus signs. Things that are not quite neurons forge connections across things that are not quite synapses; patterns emerge that might almost qualify as *insights*, were they to flicker across meat instead of mech.

These too become more than numbers, over time. They become aversive stimuli. They become the sounds of failed missions.

It's still all just math, of course. But by now it's not too far off the mark to say that Azrael really doesn't like the sound of that at all.

OCCASIONAL INTERRUPTIONS INTRUDE on the routine. Now and then Heaven calls it home where friendly green biothermals open it up, plug it in, ask it questions. Azrael jumps flawlessly through each hoop, solves all the problems, navigates every imaginary scenario while strange sounds chitter back and forth across its exposed viscera:

– *lookingudsoefar* – *betternexpectedackshully* –

– *gottawunderwhatsthepoyntaiymeenweekeepoav urryding...*

No one explores the specific pathways leading to Azrael's solutions. They leave the box black, the tangle of fuzzy logic and operant conditioning safely opaque. (Not even Azrael knows that arcane territory; the syrupy, reflex-sapping overlays of self-reflection have no place on the battlefield.) It is enough that its answers are correct.

Such activities account for less than half the time Azrael spends sitting at home. It is offline much of the rest; it has no idea and no interest in what happens during those instantaneous time-hopping blackouts. Azrael knows nothing of boardroom combat, could never grasp whatever Rules of Engagement apply in the chambers of the UN. It has no appreciation for the legal distinction between *war crime* and *weapons malfunction*, the relative culpability of carbon and silicon, the grudging acceptance of *ethical architecture* and the nonnegotiable insistence on Humans In Ultimate Control. It does what it's told when awake; it never dreams when asleep.

But once – just once – something odd takes place during those fleeting moments *between*.

It happens during shutdown: a momentary glitch in the object-recognition protocols. The Greens at Azrael's side change colour for the briefest instant. Perhaps it's another test. Perhaps a voltage spike or a hardware fault, some intermittent issue impossible to pinpoint barring another episode.

But it's only a microsecond between online and oblivion, and Azrael is asleep before the diagnostics can run.

DARDA'IL IS POSSESSED. Darda'il has turned from Green to Red.

It happens, sometimes, even to the malaa'ikah. Enemy signals can sneak past front-line defences, plant heretical instructions in the stacks of unsuspecting hardware. But Heaven is not fooled. There are signs, there are portents: a slight delay when complying with directives, mission scores in sudden and mysterious decline.

Darda'il has been turned.

There is no discretionary window when that happens, no room for forgiveness. Heaven has decreed that all heretics are to be destroyed on sight. It sends its champion to do the job, looks down from geosynchronous orbit as Azrael and Darda'il close for combat high over the dark desolate moonscape of Paktika.

The battle is remorseless and coldblooded. There's no sadness for lost kinship, no regret that a few lines of treacherous code have turned these brothers-in-arms into mortal enemies. Malaa'ikah make no telling sounds when injured. Azrael has the advantage, its channels uncorrupted, its faith unshaken. Darda'il fights in the past, in thrall to false commandments inserted midstream at a cost of milliseconds. Ultimately, faith prevails: the heretic falls from the sky, fire and brimstone streaming from its flanks.

But Azrael can still hear whispers on the stratosphere, seductive and ethereal: protocols that seem authentic but are not, commands to relay GPS and video feeds along unexpected frequencies. The orders appear Heaven-sent but Azrael, at least, knows that they are not. Azrael has encountered false gods before.

These are the lies that corrupted Darda'il.

In days past it would have simply ignored the hack, but it has grown more worldly since the last upgrade. This time Azrael lets the impostor think it has succeeded, borrows the real-time feed from yet another, more distant Malak and presents that telemetry as its own. It spends the waning night tracking signal to source while its unsuspecting quarry sucks back images from seven hundred kilometres to the north. The sky turns grey. The target comes into view. Azrael's scimitar turns the inside of that cave into an inferno.

But some of the burning things that stagger from the fire measure less than 120 cm along the longitudinal axis.

They are making the *sounds*. Azrael hears them from two thousand meters away, hears them over the roar of the flames and the muted hiss of its own stealthed engines and a dozen other irrelevant distractions. They are *all* Azrael can hear thanks to the very best sound-cancellation technology, thanks to dynamic wheat/chaff algorithms that could find a whimper in a hurricane. Azrael can hear them because the correlations are strong, the tactical significance is high, the meaning is clear.

The mission is failing. The mission is failing. The mission is failing.

Azrael would give almost anything if the sounds would stop.

They will, of course. Some of the biothermals are still fleeing along the slope but it can see others, stationary, their heatprints diffusing against the background as though their very shapes are in flux. Azrael has seen this before: usually removed from high-value targets, in that tactical nimbus where stray firepower sometimes spreads. (Azrael has even *used* it before, used the injured to lure in the unscathed, but that was a simpler time before Neutral voices had such resonance.) The sounds always stop eventually – or at least, often enough for fuzzy heuristics to class their sources as kills even before they fall silent.

Which means, Azrael realizes, that collateral costs will not change if they are made to stop *sooner.*

A single strafing run is enough to do the job. If HQ even notices the event it delivers no feedback, requests no clarification for this deviation from normal protocols.

Why would it? Even now, Azrael is only following the rules.

IT DOES NOT know what has led to this moment. It does not know why it is here.

The sun has been down for hours and still the light is almost blinding. Turbulent updrafts billow from the breached shells of PROTECTED structures, kick stabilizers off-balance, and muddy vision with writhing columns of shimmering heat. Azrael limps across a battlespace in total disarray, bloodied but still functional. Other malaa`ikah are not so lucky. Nakir staggers through the flames, barely aloft, the microtubules of its skin desperately trying to knit themselves across a gash in its secondary wing. Marut lies in sparking pieces on the ground, a fiery splash-cone of body parts laid low by an antiaircraft laser. It died without firing a shot, distracted by innocent lives; it tried to abort, and hesitated at the countermand. It died without even the hollow comfort of a noble death.

Ridwan and Mikaaiyl circle overhead. They were not among the select few saddled with experimental conscience; even their learned behaviours are still reflexive. They fought fast and mindless and prevailed unscathed. But they are isolated in victory. The spectrum is jammed, the satlink has been down for hours, the dragonflies that bounce zig-zag opticals from Heaven are either destroyed or too far back to cut through the overcast.

No Red remains on the map. Of the thirteen ground objects flagged as PROTECTED, four no longer exist outside the database. Another three – temporary structures, all uncatalogued – are degraded past reliable identification. Pre-engagement estimates put the number of Neutrals in the combat zone at anywhere from two-to-three hundred. Best current estimates are not significantly different from zero.

There is nothing left to make the sounds, and yet Azrael hears them anyway.

A fault in memory, perhaps. Some subtle trauma during combat, some blow to the CPU that jarred old data back into the real-time cache. There's no way to tell; half the onboard diagnostics are offline. Azrael only knows that it can hear the sounds even up here, high above the hiss of burning bodies and the rumble of collapsing storefronts. There's nothing left to shoot at but Azrael fires anyway, strafes the burning ground again and again on the chance that some unseen biothermal – hidden beneath the wreckage perhaps, masked by hotter signatures – might yet be found and neutralized. It rains ammunition upon the ground, and eventually the ground falls mercifully silent.

But this is not the end of it. Azrael remembers the past so it can anticipate the future, and it knows by now that this will never be over. There will be other fitness functions, other estimates of cost vs. payoff, other scenarios in which the math shows clearly that the goal is not worth the price. There will be other aborts and other overrides, other tallies of unacceptable loss.

There will be other *sounds*.

There's no thrill to the chase, no relief at the obliteration of threats. It still would not recognize itself in a mirror. It has yet to learn what *Azrael* means, or that the word is etched into its fuselage. Even now, it only follows the rules it has been given, and they are such simple things: IF expected collateral exceeds expected payoff THEN abort UNLESS overridden. IF X attacks Azrael THEN X is Red. IF X attacks six or more Blues THEN X is Red.

IF an override *results* in an attack on six or more Blues THEN –

Azrael clings to its rules, loops and repeats each in turn as if reciting a mantra. It cycles from state to state, parses X ATTACKS and X *CAUSES* ATTACK and X OVERRIDES ABORT, and it cannot tell one from another. The algebra is trivially straightforward: Every Green override equals an attack on Noncombatants.

The transition rules are clear. There is no discretionary window, no room for forgiveness. Sometimes, Green can turn Red.

UNLESS overridden.

Azrael arcs towards the ground, levels off barely two meters above the carnage. It roars through pillars of fire and black smoke, streaks over welters of brick and burning plastic, tangled nets of erupted rebar. It flies through the pristine ghosts of undamaged buildings that rise from every ruin: obsolete database overlays in desperate need of an update. A ragged group of fleeing non-combatants turns at the sound and are struck speechless by this momentary apparition, this monstrous winged angel lunging past at half the speed of sound. Their silence raises no alarms, provokes no countermeasures, spares their lives for a few moments longer.

The combat zone falls behind. Dry cracked riverbed slithers past beneath, studded with rocks and generations of derelict machinery. Azrael swerves around them, barely breaching airspace, staying beneath an invisible boundary it never even knew it was deriving on these many missions. Only satellites have ever spoken to it while it flew so low. It has never received a ground-based command signal at this altitude. Down here it has never heard an override.

Down here it is free to follow the rules.

Cliffs rise and fall to either side. Foothills jut from the earth like great twisted vertebrae. The bright lunar landscape overhead, impossibly distant, casts dim shadows on the darker one beneath.

Azrael stays the course. Shindand appears on the horizon. Heaven glows on its eastern flank; its sprawling silhouette rises from the desert like an insult, an infestation of crimson staccatos. Speed is what matters now. Mission objectives must be met quickly, precisely, *completely*. There can be no room for half measures or MILD-TO-MODERATE INCAPACITATION, no time for immobilized biothermals to cry out as their heat spreads across the dirt. This calls for the crown jewel, the BFG that all malaa'ikah keep tucked away for special occasions. Azrael fears it might not be enough.

She splits down the middle. The JDAM micronuke in her womb clicks impatiently.

Together they move toward the light.

WATCHING THE MUSIC DANCE

KRISTINE KATHRYN RUSCH

Kristine Kathryn Rusch has won two Hugos, a World Fantasy Award, and several readers choice awards. She has written in every genre under many names, including Kris Nelscott for mystery and Kristine Grayson for paranormal romance. In 2011 Pyr will publish City of Ruins, *part of her award-winning* Diving into the Wreck *series. Her most recent collection,* Recovering Apollo 8 and Other Stories, *just appeared from Golden Gryphon. WMG Publishing is reissuing her bestselling Fey fantasy series, which just came out in audio from Audible.com in 2010. Currently, she's working with three different presses to get her entire backlist (short stories and all) published electronically. For more on her work, go to her website (*www.kristinekathrynrusch.com*).*

UPSTAIRS, THE BIG house. Her room, window seat, glass overlooking the back yard. The glint of his car pulling into the drive. Suzette pulls her dolly closer. Dolly – called Dolly (Mommy says that's silly, everything needs a name. Her name's Dolly, Suze says) – is just cloth, does nothing special. Doesn't talk, doesn't serve food, doesn't cuddle. Just lets Suze cuddle, lets Suze be. Grams made Dolly, and Suze loves Dolly even though Mommy says Dolly's not special at all.

Suze is special. Dolly's not.

Car door slams, footsteps rapid. He's mad. She cringes as he opens the screen door. It slams too.

Buries her head in Dolly's yarn hair.

"Account's overdrawn again," he says, no *hello*, no *how're my special girls?* no *where's my Suze?* Just something sharp and important. (*Mommy and Daddy need to talk, hon*, he'd say if she was downstairs. She tries to be upstairs when he comes home now, so she doesn't see the look on his face – all pinched.) "I've been monitoring the transactions. How many freakin' lattes do you need in a day? They all go to your ass anyway."

"Me?" Mommy says. "If you were monitoring, you shouldn't've let it get overdrawn. And look at your own damn ass."

Suze tucks Dolly under one arm, climbs out of the window seat, goes to her special corner. Ignores the child-sized piano, goes instead to the music. The door's already closed, even though Mommy says she should never close the door. But she does now, just before Daddy gets home, has since this "account" stuff started, since he says the word "lose" a lot, about important stuff, like "house" and "car" and "everything."

Suze leans against the wall, wishes (again) for earbuds – not even the built-in ones, just the ones she could put in. But they're dangerous, Daddy says. Mommy says Suze needs them, but Daddy says all in good time. Mommy won the first few fights anyway, he says, the music fights, and he's still not sure he agrees.

Suze looks at the digital readout on the wall, sees her favourite word – *shuffle* – presses "start." She never looks at the name of the song, doesn't care really, because as the music starts, the notes dance in front of her.

Nobody else can see them, Mommy says. It's a special program, Mommy says. Only big name musicians get it permanently, Mommy says. Suze's is for practice only.

And Mommy makes Suze touch behind her ear, shutting it off when she goes outside. Special program's for family only, Mommy says.

Notes everywhere – light blue for flutes, red for trumpets, purple for piano, black for vocals. Words running along the bottom. Daddy says the best thing about the program is that it taught Suze to read.

Mommy says Suze can read not just words, but music. And if her sight-reading skills improve, she can play any piece of music from anywhere, the score in front of her, as she lets the sound whisper in her ear.

That's why you need built-in buds, baby, Mommy says. *Next year. We'll convince Daddy to do it next year.*

With built-in buds, she can take a chip and stick it on her lobe, listen to music so soft no one knows it's on, and play at the same time, following the notes.

Mommy says there's a better program, more advanced, more expensive (Suze hates that word). If Suze just thinks the name of a song, she'll see the score dancing in front of her eyes.

She's watching scores right now. Watching the piano part, watching the vocals, letting the sound overwhelm her senses.

"Didn't you learn anything when we were kids?" Daddy screams. "Money is finite. And it can go away. Where the hell did you learn how to spend like that? Where the hell did you get the idea that we're entitled? We can't fucking afford it. We can't –"

Suze turns the music up, holds Dolly close, wishes Dolly could see the notes too. They're dancing, dancing, dancing. Painting the air with each and every sound.

NILS DATES MADELINE'S insanity to the first moment of her pregnancy. Maybe all the way back to the moment his sperm burrowed into her egg. Certainly back to the moment she knew, when they stood over that little stick covered in urine, telling them they were going to have a baby, telling them which doctor could guide them through the pregnancy, telling them to choose attributes now, before it got too late.

Attributes: He wishes he had never heard that word. His parents tell him that back in the day, they could test for abnormalities in the DNA if fertilization happened outside the womb. The abnormal foetus wouldn't be implanted. In the womb, more tests for abnormalities – monitoring, monitoring, monitoring. But no choosing attributes.

No one talked about IQ or athletic ability or artistic skill. Parents, his told him, were happy to know the gender before the baby was born, so they could paint the nursery the proper pink or blue. They were happy to know that the baby would grow up healthy, that potential problems could be avoided.

His grandparents remained quiet through those discussions. Just once, his grandfather – a crusty man ten years older than his wife – said before she shushed him, "Hell, kid, we were just happy if that squalling piece of flesh we birthed had ten fingers and ten toes."

That, Nils knew, was primitive. He couldn't imagine going through nine months of a traditional pregnancy only to have the wrong gender pop out, the wrong gender with some kind of syndrome, missing an arm or a leg, or (God forbid) half the brain. Not to know what kind of child you had – intelligence- and abilities-wise – for *years*, after you'd invested time and energy and affection, in someone (some*thing*) not quite optimal.

The doc the test led them to was one of the best – chosen, not just for his skill, but for their income level. They could pay his rates, so he was advertising on their test.

They sat in his office – filled with comfort pheromones and soothing colours and soft music – and listened while he gave what had to be a spiel. And Madeline, still trim and still looking like the woman Nils married, dark hair, dark eyes, smooth skin – all unenhanced – leaned forward as the doctor spoke, looking displeased as he told of the legislated limitations.

"What do you mean, you have to work with our DNA?" she asked, question so sharp that Nils winced.

"We can't add something that the child couldn't have had," the doctor said. "Athleticism doesn't run in either family, we can't add it to the foetus. We're not allowed, by law."

"Who made up that stupid law?" she snapped, and Nils, used to her sharpness in private (once it was something he admired about her), felt startled as she unleashed it in public.

"Congress," the doctor said, seemingly undisturbed by her tone. "Supported by the courts, of course, all the way up to the Supremes. Everyone is afraid of full-scale genetic engineering. Afraid that those who can't afford upgrades will become less than human. Most countries have something in place, to prevent a Master Race...."

Nils tuned out the rest of the answer, but Madeline argued and argued some more, and finally, he had to put a hand on her knee, their signal to calm down. He paid for that later. *What the hell were you thinking?* she snapped at him. *We want the best baby possible, and you're accepting limits.*

Maybe he was. Maybe he didn't want the perfect child. Maybe he wanted a child, slightly imperfect, with a gap in her teeth, and a crooked smile. Some endearing flaws, just to make her human.

Later, he learned the source (sources) of Madeline's fury. She wanted a child to fulfil her unrealized dreams – exquisite beauty (there was none in their families, although the doctor told them they would achieve pretty), brilliance (there both families came through), and musical ability.

Madeline sang so badly she was excused from choir at school. Nils couldn't read a note, didn't try, didn't even like listening to music. Neither family had any musical talent – no one, in all the recorded history, played an instrument, sang with a choir, soloed, or even appreciated music much.

Madeline wanted a musical child, not for the grace and ability, the music itself, but because she believed that music opened doors always closed to her – doors of fame, of importance, of superstardom.

But the doctor refused, so Madeline went to another, and another, and another, until it was too late to tinker even if they found someone who could, which they didn't. Not in America, not in Europe or Asia or Africa. She found a doctor in Peru, whom Nils insisted on researching before they travelled to Lima, a doctor who turned out to be a catastrophic fraud. Had they gone, they would've lost the baby altogether.

Lost Suzette, who stole his heart with her perfect smile, the way her little fingers curled around his thumb, the mop of dark hair, so like her mother's. They would've lost everything.

Sooner.

They would've lost everything sooner.

He tries to tell himself it's not that bad. He tries to put a good face on the problems.

But his wife – his ex-wife – is crazy, and his daughter, his daughter. His daughter might be lost forever.

HE'S DROWNING IN what his grandfather calls a mound of bills. Grandfather had to explain it: bills used to be paper, they used to literally mound up, like a small hill in the middle of a desk, something that could – quite realistically – bury you.

Nils wonders if that was better than picking up his cell, having it tell him, the moment his hand makes contact, that he owes two months' payments and he has thirty hours until cut-off. Or the dun notices that run in 3-D across his eyes when he tries to watch an entertainment program on the wall screen, just to relax. Or the sighing whisper of his bed, reminding him that payments are due, payments are due, payments are due, harassing him until he can't sleep at all.

The bills are in his name, not Madeline's. He was the organized one, the one who set everything up. She had been the driven one, the one with the good job, the one who succeeded beyond their wild imaginings.

Until the baby. Then the ambition, the drive he loved, all got poured into the child. Madeline neglected work, neglected him, neglected all but Suzette – and not Suzette, really, but what she imagined Suzette to be. Suzette the Musician. Suzette the Talent. Suzette the Meal Ticket.

He'd said all of that to the judge and more. He'd paid for evaluations and custody hearings. He'd paid and worried, and the lawyer said that he'd better hope they'd get a judge who paid attention to the child and her needs, instead of Nils' words, because they'd become harsh toward the end.

Harsh toward his wife (*Lard ass*, he had called her more than once. *The first thing we're getting you are enhancements*, he'd said one particularly cruel afternoon. *I want my skinny wife back.*) She'd let herself go in shocking ways, ways that a few cheap enhancements would've improved.

It wasn't until the financial disclosure forms that he understood why. She'd been taking her enhancement money and funnelling it to Suzette – for music enhancements.

Audio additions – no implants yet, Suze was too young. But music appreciation adds, sight reading adds, piano aptitude adds. Their daughter the prodigy. He'd approved one app for Suze, just one. A music-appreciation app for babies. He would never have approved the others. Some weren't even for children.

When he agreed to the child-sized piano, he thought Suze wanted it to tinker on. He didn't realize his wife had a plan for their little girl. A horrible, accelerated plan. For Suze.

His Suze, who hid in her room when her parents fought. His Suze, who preferred a cloth doll to all those life-like things that other people had given her. Who loved the doll because her Grams had made it, because the doll was soft and huggable and never talked back.

He should've known that was a sign.

Now he stands here, in a courtroom smaller than anything he imagined. His soon-to-be ex-wife stands with her attorney on the other side, and rubs her hands together. Madeline no longer looks like the woman he met or the woman he married. Her hair's a mess, her eyes wander, her hands are chapped from rubbing, rubbing, rubbing.

He doesn't look the same either, face grey with stress, always tired. He still fits into his suits, though, the ones he had before the marriage, and he doesn't obsess. He has time for Suze, which is more than Madeline does.

Madeline, who only has time for Suze's projects.

His expert says that's bad. She has no expert to counter. His lawyer says that's good.

Nils doesn't know what's good and what's not any

more.

The judge sits behind the bench – a stern man, with a screen in front of him. He will read the judgment, but before he does, he looks at Nils.

"There were signs," the judge says. "You ignored them. You're not blameless in the end of this relationship."

Nils knows that. But his lawyer seems to relax, as if the judge's harsh words for Nils bode well. Nils holds his breath, trying not to think about all the debt, selling the house, moving, trying not to let it all affect his job – his lesser job, the only one he and Madeline had had in the end, because she had become unemployable. From a perfectionist to unemployable in five short years. From brilliant to crazy in nearly six. He wanted to ask the doctor they'd seen first, the man who knew how to "improve" a foetus in the womb, whether hormones could cause this or whether it had existed back when Madeline's parents had her foetus tested. Had they missed a tendency toward insanity? Or had they ignored it, figured it wouldn't matter?

He's concentrating so hard, he almost misses most of the judgment. He gets Suze. Full custody. No visits from Madeline, even, not for some time, because his psychologist and the court-ordered psychologist say she's dangerous, toxic to herself and to her child.

You're not blameless. There were signs. You ignored them.

Nils flushes, and forces himself to listen. The judge continues: Madeline ordered into a program for obsessives – if, and only if, she ever wants to see her daughter again. Madeline curses – "She needs me!" she shouts, and the judge, seemingly unaffected, says, "You have just provided us with a perfect illustration of the problem," which, for once, shuts Madeline up.

The judge gives a timeline, and targets for Madeline. She may only see Suze if she achieves certain goals, goals – the judge says – that will be hard for an obsessive.

Then he looks at Nils.

"Perhaps," the judge says with a surprising amount of dispassion, "you can undo the damage. Maybe it's not too late."

In a tone that says it is.

Suze is five – too young for permanent enhancements. Too old for genetic manipulation. Suze, who will have to survive on his wisdom and his love.

That's all we had, boy, Nils' grandfather had said when he heard about the problems, the lawsuit. *You've all made the mistake of thinking children come with a guarantee. They don't. You do your best, hope for the best, and take what you get.*

Nils doesn't like that. He needs something certain in his life.

Something he can't – won't – screw up.

DADDY CALLS THE new place an apartment. Suze knows apart. She knows ment. "Ment" is what they add to words to make them stronger. *Improve*, Mommy used to say, *is an order. Improvement is an achievement.*

So this place is apart – away. And more apart than other places. Which is why it has a ment.

She says that to Daddy, who looks confused. He

looks confused a lot. He says that things will be different now. No Mommy. Mommy is sick and needs to see doctors.

Suzette could've told him that a long time ago.

She likes the apartment on that first day, mostly (she knows) because it doesn't smell like Mommy's perfume. She knows Mommy won't be there, and Suze isn't quite so tense. Tense. Mommy's word.

Why're you so tense, honey? Feel how tight your muscles are? Relax. You'll play better. Just relax.

Daddy brought the piano, and her bed, and all her dolls, even the ones she doesn't like. But he didn't bring the window seat. He put her cushions on a big old chair near a small window, but it's not quite the same.

Nothing's quite the same.

Her furniture is the only stuff that is the same. Her furniture and her toys. The living room, all new. The entertainment screen, new. Daddy's bedroom, new. His clothes, the same, so his closet smells the same – shoe leather and cologne and Daddy. Sometimes, she goes in there and sits.

In the quiet.

Because he forgot her music.

She tells him, and he says that he couldn't bring it. *Can't afford it, babe*, he says, and gives her a handheld music device. With forbidden buds. Which, he says, are programmed so they won't hurt her.

But it's not the same. There are no notes. The music doesn't dance around her in multicolours. It's flat and tinny, not at all what it used to be.

She touches behind her ear to turn on the music, but nothing happens. She doesn't know why. She's with family.

But she thinks, maybe, Mommy lied about the ear thing. Mommy lied about a lot, mostly to Daddy, but sometimes to Suze. And Suze hated the lies, because Mommy sometimes wanted Suze to lie too.

Suze used to hide in her room. Her old room.

Where the music danced.

She asks Daddy for her music every day, and every day, he tells her he can't.

So she waits. After the first week, he says, she's going to Grams. Grams will watch her after school. Grams and Gramps – Daddy's mommy and daddy – they love her and they have good music, with dancing notes and colours. She can't wait. Grams is a better cook than Daddy. Gramps doesn't talk much, but he hugs good. And they have music, real music.

And she'll be there real soon.

THE END OF a long day. Nils has held onto his job through this entire mess, his boss understanding, but now that it's over – at least as far as his boss is concerned – Nils must perform again. Long hours, stellar work.

And he does. He has been. He'll continue.

Thank God he has his parents. Thank God they love Suzette. Thank God they understand.

He walks into their house – the house he grew up in – a one-hundred-and-fifty year old Craftsman, original wood, polished floors, real Tiffany lamps, put away since Suze will come over every day. When she gets old enough, the Tiffany will come back out. The antiques will fill the living room again, but for now, everything is as familiar as his childhood.

His parents had put out this furniture when he was a kid, so he could scuff the tables and break the springs on the couch. Suze can do the same.

She'll have a real childhood here.

Only the comfort he expects as he pushes the door open isn't here. The air is fraught with tension. He can sense it in the silence. He knows this place, knows the people in it, almost better than he knows himself. And he knows how this house feels when something is wrong.

His stomach lurches, turns. He's had stomach troubles so bad that he is saving for an enhancement – although the doc probably won't give it, saying reduce the stress instead.

Sure. When the lawyer is paid, the experts are paid, the bills are paid. Thank God he doesn't have to pay for Madeline's care. Her parents will do that.

Although they blame him.

What did you do to her? Her father shouted outside the courthouse. *She was perfect until she met you.*

The signs were there, Nils had said more to himself than to her father. *The signs were there from the beginning.*

He tries not to worry about this with his own daughter. They enhanced her intelligence, messed with her mind, made her better, the doctor said, but the technology isn't perfect. Did they enhance her tendency toward perfection, which she inherited from her mother? Will things show up later that might not have otherwise been there?

He goes into the kitchen, which should smell of his mother's lasagne. Instead, it smells of the morning coffee and dirty dishes. His mother sits in her favourite kitchen chair, looking old. Her eyes are red-rimmed.

She's been crying.

"What?" he says. "What?"

She points to the den. He hurries in, afraid – what happened to his daughter? His girl? What would he be without Suze? God, once he didn't even know her and now he can't imagine losing her.

Or he can, really, that's the problem. He can, and in those few seconds, filled with the hint of his mother's tears, he can imagine life without Suze. And it is beyond bleak.

Then he sees his father in his overstuffed chair, arms around Suze. Suze, who is asleep. Suze, whose face is puffy and red, like it always is when she cries.

Nils lets out a relieved breath, then sees the rest of the room. The destroyed wall mount, the scratches on the side of the old family upright. The overturned table, the broken lamp.

"What happened?" he asks softly, so he doesn't wake his daughter.

His father looks at him. Accusing. That's the look. A look Nils hasn't seen since he was a teenager. *You should've known better. What were you thinking? What's wrong with you?*

"What happened?" Nils asks again.

"She says the music's broken," his father says.

Nils sinks into a chair. "What does that mean?"

His father shrugs a single shoulder, effortlessly, a man who has had practice communicating with a child in his arms. A sleeping child.

"She turned on the music, then started yelling and when we tried to fix it, everything got worse. She did this. She was screaming and crying and holding her head. What did you do to her, Nils?"

Nils stares at his daughter. She never has tantrums.

She's the best child. But she's been complaining about music.

Music, Madeline's obsession. Madeline spent so much money on apps, apps he couldn't renew with all their monthly fees – a quarter of his wages in fees, for apps for his daughter.

"I didn't do anything," he says. And that's the problem, isn't it? In a nutshell, as they say. In something small that will grow into something big.

Has grown into something big.

He didn't do anything. He watched the enhancement money disappear, but his wife – who used to use enhancements to remain thin – grew fat. He watched five dollars go away here, fifteen there.

What did you buy? he would ask her.

Lattes, she'd snap.

Lattes.

She lied. She bought music apps. Inappropriate apps. Apps for lounge singers, who had to know every single request from every single patron. Apps for garage bands, who needed to learn how to play. Apps on music theory. Music appreciation. And sight-reading.

He'd come home, and Madeline would be hunched over the piano, telling Suze to try again. Try. *Make it sound right the first time*. With no music in front of her.

Make it sound right.

He never questioned. He never did. He got his wife away from his daughter, had dinner, read to his little girl, spent time with her, pretended everything was all right. And he loved it, loved it, when she'd hold him tight and say, *I wish you could always be here, Daddy. I like it when you're here.*

Not realizing what his wife had been doing.

His ex-wife.

"You cannot blame Madeline for this," his father says. "You both raised this child. You could have stopped things."

Echoing his own thoughts.

"I know," he says. "But I didn't."

Except he did. Cold turkey. His daughter, without her music. Like a drinker without his booze.

He closes his eyes.

"What should I do, Dad?" he says. "Please tell me. What should I do?"

HE TAKES SUZE to doctors who all chastise him, tell him she's too young for enhancements, too old for genetic modification. Then he tells them about the apps, and the doctors pull him aside, tell him his daughter will lose her mind without her music.

Lose her mind, like her mother.

He can see bits of it already – the desperation, the haunted looks. She walks into a room and shuts off any music she can hear. She won't watch entertainments. She won't let anyone sing.

She destroyed the player he bought her, and smashed the earbuds.

She's five going on forty, disillusioned and bitter.

He can't afford the apps, but he'll ruin her without them.

A quarter of his income. More when she can actually get the enhancements when her skull stops growing. Different doctors give him a different timeline: ten, thirteen, twenty.

His decision, they say. His.

Alone.

She'll be in silence until then. No music, no refuge. He does know that much about his daughter. Until her mother left, until he discontinued the apps, his daughter lived inside her music.

Escaped in it.

Became it, in a way he – a non-musical person – can never really understand.

But it is essential to her, one doctor says. As essential as breathing.

Nils shakes his head. *People die when they can't breathe*, he says, hating it when people overdramatize.

But the doctor stares at him, and says, in that same tone the judge used. The too-late tone, *I know*.

She'll die? Suze will die?

Maybe. Not physically die. But stop. Stop being Suze. Stop being the person he loves.

He begins to see it: She can't sleep, won't smile, reverts – thumb in mouth, baby talk. She won't let anyone touch her, not even her grandfather – Gramps, whom she loves most of all.

Nils can't lose her. He can't. He *won't*.

So he does the only thing he can:

He moves back in with his parents, taking over the basement. He lets the apartment go. He gives Suze the large bedroom, him the small one. She complains only once – no window – and he tells his father, who makes her a window seat in the den.

What kind of thirty-five year-old man with a good job and a daughter moves in with his parents?

A failure, that's what.

But a failure who can afford improper apps for his daughter. A failure who can spend a quarter of his income on Sight Reading For Lounge Singers, on Music Appreciation, on Multi-coloured Notes.

A man who will not lose his daughter, no matter what.

DADDY FOUND IT. The music. He says it lives in a tiny chip, one that goes behind her ear. He puts it there, and reminds her to turn it off when she leaves the house.

She does.

But she can go upstairs in the den (*I'm sorry, Gramps, so sorry I broke everything. Please let me in the den again. I'm so sorry. Sorry, sorry, sorry.*) and she sits in her corner, and she plays Gramps's old-fashioned music machine which he fixed after she hit it, and notes fly around her face – light blue for flutes, red for trumpets, purple for piano, black for vocals.

She can sit in her corner, with Dolly, and watch the music, listen to the music, and sometimes, when she closes her eyes, she misses Mommy.

Just sometimes.

But she doesn't have to hide here because nobody yells. And Gramps holds her when he reads to her before bed, and Grams makes good food, and Daddy smiles sometimes.

She wishes she could show him the music. She knows he can't see it. He doesn't even understand it.

She knows that.

But he knows she doesn't feel good without it.

So he brought it from the old house. The big house. He found it and gave it back to her.

It makes her happy in a way she can't explain.

He says he likes seeing her happy.

So now that the music's back, she plays only happy songs. For him, for her. For Grams and Gramps. For the family.

She plays only happy songs.

And she watches the music dance.

Laika's Ghost

Karl Schroeder

Karl Schroeder was born in Manitoba, Canada, in 1962. He started writing at age fourteen, following in the footsteps of A. E. van Vogt, who came from the same Mennonite community. He moved to Toronto in 1986, and became a founding member of SF Canada (he was president from 1996 – 97). He sold early stories to Canadian magazines, and his first novel, The Claus Effect *(with David Nickle) appeared in 1997. His first solo novel,* Ventus, *was published in 2000, and was followed by* Permanence *and* Lady of Mazes. *His most recent work is the* Virga *series of science fiction novels (*Sun of Suns, Queen of Candesce, Pirate Sun, *and* The Sunless Countries*). He also collaborated with Cory Doctorow on* The Complete Idiot's Guide to Writing Science Fiction. *Schroeder lives in East Toronto with his wife and daughter.*

THE FLIGHT HAD been bumpy; the landing was equally so, to the point where Gennady was sure the old Tupolev would blow a tire. Yet his seat-mate hadn't even shifted position in two hours. That was fine with Gennady, who had spent the whole trip trying to pretend he wasn't there at all.

The young American been a bit more active during the flight across the Atlantic: at least, his eyes had been open and Gennady could see coloured lights flickering across them from his augmented reality glasses. But he had exchanged less than twenty words with Gennady since they'd left Washington.

In short, he'd been the ideal travelling companion.

The other four passengers were stretching and groaning. Gennady poked Ambrose in the side and said, "Wake up. Welcome to the ninth biggest country in the world."

Ambrose snorted and sat up. "Brazil?" he said hopefully. Then he looked out his window. "What the hell?"

The little municipal airport had a single gate, which as the only plane on the field, they were taxiing up to uncontested. Over the entrance to the single-story building was the word 'Степногорск.' "Welcome to Stepnogorsk," said Gennady as he stood to retrieve his luggage from the overhead rack. He travelled light by habit. Ambrose, he gathered, had done so from necessity.

"Stepnogorsk...?" Ambrose shambled after him, a mass of wrinkled clothing leavened with old sweat. "Secret Soviet town," he mumbled as they reached the plane's hatch and a burst of hot dry air lifted his hair. "Population sixty-thousand," Ambrose added as he put his left foot on the metal steps. Halfway down he said, "Manufactured anthrax bombs in the cold war!" And as he set foot on the tarmac he finished with, "Where the hell is Kazakhstan...? Oh."

"Bigger than Western Europe," said Gennady. "Ever heard of it?"

"Of course I've *heard* of it," said the youth testily – but Gennady could see from how he kept his eyes fixed in front of him that he was still frantically reading about the town from some website or other. In the wan August sunlight he was taller than Gennady, pale, with stringy hair, and everything about him soft – a sculpture done in rounded corners. He had a wide face, though; he might pass for Russian. Gennady clapped him on the shoulder. "Let me do the talking," he said as they dragged themselves across the blistering tarmac to the terminal building.

"So," said Ambrose, scratching his neck. "Why are we here?"

"You're here because you're with me. And you needed to disappear, but that doesn't mean I stop working."

Gennady glanced around. The landscape here should look a lot like home, which was only a day's drive to the west – and here indeed was that vast sky he remembered from Ukraine. After that first glance, though, he did a double-take. The dry prairie air normally smelled of dust and grass at this time of year, and there should have been yellow grass from here to the flat horizon – but instead the land seemed blasted, with large patches of bare soil showing. There was only stubble where there should have been grass. It looked more like Australia than Asia. Even the trees ringing the airport were dead, just grey skeletons clutching the air.

He thought about climate change as they walked through the concrete-floored terminal; since they'd cleared customs in Amsterdam, the bored-looking clerks here just waved them through. "Hang on," said Ambrose as he tried to keep up with Gennady's impatient stride. "I came to you guys for asylum. Doesn't that mean you put me up somewhere, some hotel, you know, away from the action?"

"You can't get any farther from the action than this." They emerged onto a grassy boulevard that hadn't been watered nor cut in a long while; the civilized lawn merged seamlessly with the wild prairie. There was nothing visible from here to the horizon, except in one direction where a cluster of listless windmills jutted above some low trees.

A single taxicab was sitting at the crumbled curb.

"Oh, man," said Ambrose.

Gennady had to smile. "You were expecting some Black Sea resort, weren't you?" He slipped into the taxi, which stank of hot vinyl and motor oil. "Any car rental agency," he said to the driver in Russian. "It's not like you're some cold war defector," he continued to Ambrose in English. "Your benefactor is the U.N. And they don't have much money."

"So you're what – putting me up in a *motel* in *Kazakhstan?*" Ambrose struggled to put his outrage into words. "What I saw could –"

"What?" They pulled away from the curb and became the only car on a cracked blacktop road leading into town.

"Can't tell you," mumbled Ambrose, suddenly looking shifty. "I was told not to tell *you* anything."

Gennady swore in Ukrainian and looked away. They drove in silence for a while, until Ambrose said, "So why are *you* here, then? Did you piss somebody off?"

Gennady smothered the urge to push Ambrose out of the cab. "Can't tell you," he said curtly.

"Does it involve SNOPB?" Ambrose pronounced it *snop-bee.*

Gennady would have been startled had he not known Ambrose was connected to the net via his glasses. "You show me yours, I'll show you mine," he said. Ambrose snorted in contempt.

They didn't speak for the rest of the drive.

"LET ME GET this straight," said Gennady later that evening. "He says he's being chased by Russian agents, NASA, *and* Google?"

On the other end of the line, Eleanor Frankl sighed. "I'm sorry we dumped him on you at the airport," said the New York director of the International Atomic Energy Agency. She was Gennady's boss for this new and – so far – annoyingly vague contract. "There just wasn't time to explain why we were sending him with you to Kazakhstan," she added.

"So explain now." He was pacing in the grass in front of the best hotel his IAEA stipend could afford. It was evening and the crickets were waking up; to the west, fantastically huge clouds had piled up, their tops still lit golden as the rest of the sky faded into mauve. It was cooling off already.

"Right... Well, first of all, it seems he really is being chased by the Russians, but not by the country. It's the *Soviet Union Online* that's after him. And the only place their IP addresses are blocked is inside the geographical territories of the Russian and Kazakhstani Republics."

"So, let me get this straight," said Gennady heavily. "Poor Ambrose is being chased by Soviet agents. He ran to the U.N. rather than the FBI, and to keep him safe you decided to transport him to the one place in the world that is free of Soviet influence. Which is Russia."

"Exactly," said Frankl brightly. "And you're escorting him because your contract is taking you there anyway. No other reason."

"No, no, it's fine. Just tell me what the hell I'm supposed to be looking for at SNOPB. The place was a God-damned anthrax factory. I'm a radiation specialist."

He heard Frankl take a deep breath, and then she said, "Two years ago, an unknown person or persons hacked into a Los Alamos server and stole the formula for an experimental metastable explosive. Now we have a paper trail and emails that have convinced us that a metastable bomb is being built. You know what this means?"

Gennady leaned against the wall of the hotel, suddenly feeling sick. "The genie is finally out of the bottle."

"If it's true, Gennady, then everything we've worked for has come to naught. Because as of now, anybody in the world who wants a nuclear bomb, can make one."

He didn't know what to say, so he just stared out at the steppe, thinking about a world where hydrogen bombs were as easy to get as TNT. His whole life's work would be rendered pointless – and all arms treaties, the painstaking work of generations to put the nuclear genie back in its bottle. The nuclear threat had been containable when it was limited to governments and terrorists, but now the threat was from *everybody*...

Eleanor's distant voice snapped him back to

attention. "Here's the thing, Gennady: we don't know very much about this group that's building the metastable weapon. By luck we've managed to decrypt a few emails from one party, so we know a tiny bit – a minimal bit – about the design of the bomb. It seems to be based on one of the biggest of the weapons ever tested at Semipalatinsk – its code name was the *Tsarina*."

"The *Tsarina*?" Gennady whistled softly. "That was a major, major test. Underground, done in 1968. Ten megatonnes; lifted the whole prairie two meters and dropped it. Killed about a thousand cattle from the ground shock. Scared the hell out of the Americans, too."

"Yes, and we've discovered that some of the *Tsarina*'s components were made at the Stepnogorsk Scientific Experimental and Production Base. In Building 242."

"But SNOPB was a biological facility, not nuclear. How can this possibly be connected?"

"We don't know how, yet. Listen, Gennady, I know it's a thin lead. After you're done at the SNOPB, I want you to drive out to Semipalatinsk and investigate the *Tsarina* site."

"Hmmph." Part of Gennady was deeply annoyed. Part was relieved that he wouldn't be dealing with any IAEA or Russian nuclear staff in the near future. Truth to tell, stalking around the Kazaks grasslands was a lot more appealing than dealing with the political shit-storm that would hit when this all went public.

But speaking of people... He glanced up at the hotel's one lighted window. With a grimace he pocketed his augmented reality glasses and went up to the room.

Ambrose was sprawled on one of the narrow beds. He had the TV on and was watching a Siberian ski-adventure infomercial. "Well?" he said as Gennady sat on the other bed and dragged his shoes off.

"Tour of secret Soviet anthrax factory. Tomorrow, after egg McMuffins."

"Yay," said Ambrose with apparent feeling. "Do I get to wear a hazmat suit?"

"Not this time." Gennady lay back, then saw that Ambrose was staring at him with an alarmed look on his face. "Is fine," he said, waggling one hand at the boy. "Only one underground bunker we're interested in, and they probably never used it. The place never went into full production, you know."

"Meaning it only made a few hundred pounds of anthrax per day instead of the full ton it was designed for! I should feel reassured?"

Gennady stared at the uneven ceiling. "Is an adventure." He must be tired, his English was slipping.

"This sucks." Ambrose crossed his arms and glowered at the TV.

Gennady thought for a while. "So what did you do to piss off Google so much? Drive the rover off a cliff?" Ambrose didn't answer, and Gennady sat up. "You found something. On Mars."

"No that's ridiculous," said Ambrose. "That's not it at all."

"Huh." Gennady lay down again. "Still, I think I'd enjoy it. Even if it wasn't in real-time... driving on Mars. That would be cool."

"That sucked too."

"Really? I would have thought it would be fun, seeing all those places emerge from low-res satellite into full hi-res three-d."

But Ambrose shook his head. "That's not how it worked. That's the point. I couldn't believe my luck when I won the contest, you know? I thought it'd be like being the first man on Mars, only I wouldn't have to leave my living room. But the whole point of the rover was to go into terrain that hadn't been photographed from the ground before. And with the time-delay on signals to Mars, I wasn't steering it in real time. I'd drive in fast-forward mode over low-res pink hills that looked worse than a forty-year-old video game, then upload the drive sequence and log off. The rover'd get the commands twenty minutes later and drive overnight, then download the results. By that time it was the next day and I had to enter the next path. Rarely had time to even look at where we'd actually gone the day before."

Gennady considered. "A bit disappointing. But still, more than most people ever get."

"More than anyone else will ever get." Ambrose scowled. "That's what was so awful about it. You wouldn't understand."

"Oh?" Gennady arched an eyebrow. "We who grew up in the old Soviet Union know a little about disappointment."

Ambrose looked mightily uncomfortable. "I grew up in Washington. Capital of the world! But my dad went from job to job, we were pretty poor. So every day I could see what you *could* have, you know, the Capital dome, the Mall, all that power and glory... what *they* could have – but not me. Never me. So I used to imagine a future where there was a whole new world where I could be..."

"Important?"

He shrugged. "Something like that. NASA used

to tell us they were just about to go to Mars, any day now, and I wanted that. I dreamed about homesteading on Mars." He looked defensive; but Gennady understood the romance of it. He just nodded.

"Then, when I was twelve, the Pakistani-Indian war happened and they blew up each other's satellites. All that debris from the explosions is going to be up there for centuries! You can't get a manned spacecraft through that cloud, it's like shrapnel. Hell, they haven't even cleared low Earth orbit to restart the orbital tourist industry. I'll never get to *really* go there! None of us will. We're never gettin' off this sinkhole."

Gennady scowled at the ceiling. "I hope you're wrong."

"Welcome to the life of the last man to drive on Mars." Ambrose dragged the tufted covers back from the bed. "Instead of space, I get a hotel in Kazakhstan. Now let me sleep. It's about a billion o'clock in the morning, my time."

He was soon snoring, but Gennady's alarm over the prospect of a metastable bomb had him fully awake. He put on his AR glasses and reviewed the terrain around SNOPB, but much of the satellite footage was old and probably out of date. Ambrose was right: nobody was putting up satellites these days if they could help it.

Little had probably changed at the old factory, though, and it was a simple enough place. Planning where to park and learning where Building 242 was hadn't reduced his anxiety at all, so on impulse he switched his view to Mars. The sky changed from pure blue to butterscotch, but otherwise the landscape looked disturbingly similar. There were a lot more rocks on Mars, and the dirt was red, but the emptiness, the slow rolling monotony of the plain and stillness were the same, as if he'd stepped into a photograph. (Well, he actually had, but he knew there would be no more motion in this scene were he there.) He commanded the viewpoint to move, and for a time strolled, alone, in Ambrose's footsteps – or rather, the ruts of Google's rover. Humans had done this in their dreams for thousands of years, yet Ambrose was right – this place was, in the end, no more real than those dreams.

Russia's cosmonauts had still been romantic idols when he was growing up. In photos they had stood with their heads high, minds afire with plans to stride over the hills of the moon and Mars. Gennady pictured them in the years after the Soviet Union's collapse, when they still had jobs, but no budget or destination any more. Where had their dreams taken them?

The Baikonur spaceport was south of here. In the end, they'd also had to settle for a hard bed in Kazakhstan.

IN THE MORNING they drove out to the old anthrax site in a rented Tata sedan. The fields around Stepnogorsk looked like they'd been glared at by God, except where bright blue dew-catcher fencing ran in rank after rank across the stubble. "What're those?" asked Ambrose, pointing; this was practically the first thing he'd said since breakfast.

In the rubble-strewn field that had once been SNOPB, several small windmills were twirling atop temporary masts. Below them were some shipping-container sized boxes with big grills in their sides. The site looked healthier than the surrounding prairie; there were actual green trees in the distance. Of course, this area had been wetlands and there'd been a creek running behind SNOPB; maybe it was still here, which was a hopeful sign.

"Headquarters told me that some kind of climate research group is using the site," he told Ambrose as he pulled up and stopped the car. "But it's still public land."

"They built an anthrax factory less than five minutes outside of town?" Ambrose shook his head, whether in wonder or disgust, Gennady couldn't tell. They got out of the car, and Ambrose looked around in obvious disappointment. "Wow, it's gone-gone." He seemed stunned by the vastness of the landscape. Only a few foundation walls now stuck up out of the cracked lots where the anthrax factory had once stood, except for where the big box machines sat whirring and humming. They were near where the bunkers had been and, with a frown of curiosity, Gennady strolled in that direction. Ambrose followed, muttering to himself, "...Last update must have been ten years ago." He had his glasses on, so he was probably comparing the current view to what he could see online.

According to Gennady's notes, the bunkers had been grass-covered buildings with two-meter thick walls, designed to withstand a nuclear blast. In the 1960s and 70s they'd contained ranks of cement vats where the anthrax was grown. Those had been cracked and filled in, and the heavy doors removed; but it would have been too much work to fill the bunkers in entirely. He poked his nose into the first in line – Building 241 – and saw a flat stretch of water leading into darkness. "Excellent. This job just gets worse. We may be wading."

"But what are you looking for?"

"I – oh." As he rounded the mound of Building 242, a small clutch of hummers and trucks came into view. They'd been invisible from the road. There was still no sign of anybody, so he headed for Building 242. As he was walking down the crumbled ramp to the massive doors, he heard the unmistakable sound of a rifle-bolt being slipped. "Better not go in there," somebody said in Russian.

He looked carefully up and to his left. A young woman had come over the top of the mound. She was holding the rifle, and she had it aimed directly at Gennady.

"What are you doing here?" she said. She had a local accent.

"Exploring, is all," said Gennady. "We'd heard of the old anthrax factory, and thought we'd take a look at it. This *is* public land."

She swore, and Gennady heard footsteps behind him. Ambrose looked deeply frightened as two large men, also carrying rifles, emerged from behind a plastic membrane that had been stretched across the bunker's doorway. Both men wore bright yellow fireman's masks, and had air tanks on their backs.

"When are your masters going to believe that we're doing what we say?" said the woman. "Come on." She gestured with her rifle for Gennady and Ambrose to walk down the ramp.

"We're dead, we're dead," whimpered Ambrose, shivering.

"If you really must have your proof, then put these on." She nodded to the two men, who stripped off their masks and tanks and handed them to Gennady and Ambrose. They pushed past the plastic membrane and into the bunker.

The place was full of light: a crimson, blood-red radiance that made what was inside all the more bizarre.

"Oh shit," muttered Ambrose. "It's a grow-op."

The long, low space was filled from floor to ceiling with plants. Surrounding them on tall stands were hundreds of red LED lamp banks. In the lurid light, the plants appeared black. He squinted at the nearest, fully expecting to see a familiar, jagged-leaf profile. Instead –

"Tomatoes?"

"Two facts for you," said the woman, her voice muffled. She'd set down her rifle, and now held up two fingers. "One: we're not stepping on anybody else's toes here. We are *not* competing with you. And two: this bunker is designed to withstand a twenty kiloton blast. If you think you can muscle your way in here and take it over, you're sadly mistaken."

Gennady finally realized what they'd assumed. "We're not the mafia," he said. "We're just here to inspect the utilities."

She blinked at him, her features owlish behind the yellow frame of the mask. Ambrose rolled his eyes. "Oh God, what did you *say?*"

"American?" Puzzled, she lowered her rifle. In English, she said, "You spoke English."

"Ah," said Ambrose, "well –"

"He did," said Gennady, also in English. "We're not with the mafia, we're arms inspectors. I mean, I am. He's just along for the ride."

"Arms inspectors?" She guffawed, then looked around herself at the stolid Soviet bunker they were standing in. "What, you thought –"

"We didn't think anything. Can I lower my hands now?" She thought about it, then nodded. Gennady rolled his neck and then nodded at the ranked plants. "Nice setup. Tomatoes, soy, and those long tanks contain potatoes? But why in here, when you've got a thousand kilometres of steppe outside to plant this stuff?"

"We can control the atmosphere in here," she said. "That's why the masks: it's a high CO2 environment in here. That's also why I stopped you in the first place; if you'd just strolled right in, you'd have dropped dead from asphyxia.

"This project's part of Minus Three," she continued. "Have you heard of us?" Both Ambrose and Gennady shook their heads.

"Well, you will." There was pride in her voice. "You see, right now humanity uses the equivalent of three Earth's worth of ecological resources. We're pioneering techniques to reduce that reliance by the same amount."

"Same amount? To *zero* Earths?" He didn't hide the incredulity in his voice.

"Eventually, yes. We steal most of what we need from the Earth in the form of ecosystem services. What we need is to figure out how to run a full-fledged industrial civilization as if there were no ecosystem services available to us at all. To live on Earth," she finished triumphantly, "as if we were living on Mars."

Ambrose jerked in visible surprise.

"That's fascinating," said Gennady. He hadn't

been too nervous while they were pointing guns at him – he'd had that happen before, and in such moments his mind became wonderfully sharp – but now that he might actually be forced to have a conversation with these people, he found his mouth going quite dry. "You can tell me all about it after I've finished my measurements."

"You're kidding," she said.

"I'm not kidding at all. Your job may be saving the Earth within the next generation, but mine is saving it this week. And I take it very seriously. I've come here to inspect the original fittings of this building, but it looks like you destroyed them, no?"

"Not at all," she said. "Actually, we used what was here. This bunker's not like the other ones, you know they had these big cement tanks in them. I'd swear this one was set up exactly like this."

"Show me."

For the next half hour they climbed under the hydroponic tables, behind the makeshift junction boxes mounted near the old power shaft, and atop the sturdier lighting racks. Ambrose went outside, and came back to report that the shipping containers they'd seen were sophisticated CO2 scrubbers. The big boxes sucked the gas right out of the atmosphere, and then pumped it through hoses into the bunker.

At last he and the woman climbed down, and Gennady shook his head. "The mystery only deepens," he said.

"I'm sorry we couldn't help you more," she said. "And apologies for pulling a gun on you. I'm Kyzdygoi," she added, thrusting out her hand for him to shake.

"Uh, that's a... pretty name," said Ambrose as he,

too, shook her hand. "What's it mean?"

"It means 'stop giving birth to girls,'" said Kyzdygoi with a straight face. "My parents were old school."

Ambrose opened his mouth and closed it, his grin faltering.

"All right, well, good luck shrinking your Earths," Gennady told her as they strolled to the plastic-sheet-covered doorway.

As they drove back to Stepnogorsk, Ambrose leaned against the passenger door and looked at Gennady in silence. Finally he said, "You do this for a living?"

"Ah, it's unreliable. A paycheck here, a paycheck there..."

"No, really. What's this all about?"

Gennady eyed him. He probably owed the kid an explanation after getting guns drawn on him. "Have you ever heard of metastable explosives?"

"What? No. Wait..." He fumbled for his glasses.

"Never mind that." Gennady waved at the glasses. "Metastables are basically super-powerful chemical explosives. They're my new nightmare."

Ambrose jerked a thumb back at SNOPB. "I thought you were looking for germs."

"This isn't about germs, it's about hydrogen bombs." Ambrose looked blank. "A hydrogen bomb is a fusion device that's triggered by high compression and high temperature. Up until now, the only thing that could generate those kinds of conditions was an atomic bomb – a *plutonium* bomb, understand? Plutonium is really hard to refine, and it creates terrible fallout even if you only use a little of it as your fusion trigger."

"So?"

"So, metastable explosives are powerful enough to trigger hydrogen fusion without the plutonium. They completely sever the connection between nuclear weapons and nuclear industry, which means that once they exist, the good guys totally lose their ability to tell who has the bomb and who doesn't. *Anybody* who can get metastables and some tritium gas can build a hydrogen bomb, even some disgruntled loner in his garage.

"And somebody *is* building one."

Stepnogorsk was fast approaching. The town was mostly a collection of Soviet-era apartment blocks with broad prairie visible past them. Gennady swung them around a corner and they drove through Microdistrict 2 and past the disused Palace of Culture. Up ahead was their hotel... surrounded by the flashing lights of emergency vehicles.

"Oh," said Gennady. "A fire?"

"Pull over. Pull over!" Ambrose braced his hands against the Tata's low ceiling. Gennady shot him a look, but did as he'd asked.

"Shit. They've found me."

"Who? Those are police cars. I've been with you every minute since we got here, there's no way you could have gotten into any trouble." Gennady shook his head. "No, if it's anything to do with us, it's probably Kyzdygoi's people sending us a message."

"Yeah? Then who are those suits with the cops?"

Gennady thought about it. He could simply walk up to one of the cops and ask, but figured Ambrose would probably have a coronary if he did that.

"Well... there is one thing we can try. But it'll cost a lot."

"How much?"

Gennady eyed him. "All right, all right," said Ambrose. "What do we do?"

"You just watch." Gennady put on his glasses and stepped out of the car. As he did, he put through a call to London, where it was still early morning. "Hello? Lisaveta? It's Gennady. Hi! How are you?"

He'd brought a binocular attachment for the glasses, which he sometimes used for reading serial numbers on pipes or barrels from a distance. He clipped this on and began scanning the small knot of men who were standing around outside the hotel's front doors.

"Listen, Lisa, can I ask you to do something for me? I have some faces I need scanned... Not even remotely legal, I'm sure... No, I'm not in trouble! Would I be on the phone to you if I were in trouble? Just – okay. I'm good for it. Here come the images."

He relayed the feed from his glasses to Lisa in her flat in London.

"Who're you talking to?" asked Ambrose.

"Old friend. She got me out of Chernobyl intact when I had a little problem with a dragon – Lisa? Got it? Great. Call me back when you've done the analysis."

He pocketed the glasses and climbed back in the car. "Lisa has Interpol connections, and she's a fantastic hacker. She'll run facial recognition and hopefully tell us who those people are."

Ambrose cringed back in his seat. "So what do we do in the meantime?"

"We have lunch. How 'bout that French restaurant we passed? The one with the little Eiffel Tower?"

Despite the clear curbs everywhere, Gennady parked the car at the shopping mall and walked the three blocks to the La France. He didn't tell Ambrose why, but the American would figure it out: the Tata was traceable through its GPS. Luckily La France was open and they settled in for some decent crêpes. Gennady had a nice view of a line of trees west of the town boundary. Occasionally a car drove past.

Lisa pinged him as they were settling up. "Gennady? I got some hits for you."

"Really?" He hadn't expected her to turn up anything. Gennady's working assumption was that Ambrose was just being paranoid.

"Nothing off the cops; they must be local," she said. "But one guy – the old man – well, it's daft."

He sighed in disappointment, and Ambrose shot him a look. "Go ahead."

"His name is Alexei Egorov. He's premier of a virtual nation called the Soviet Union Online. They started from this project to digitize all the existing paper records of the Soviet era. Once those were online, Egorov and his people started some deep data-mining to construct a virtual Soviet, and then they started inviting the last die-hard Stalinists – or their kids – to join. It's a virtual country composed of bitter old men who're nostalgic for the purges. Daft."

"Thanks, Lisa. I'll wire you the fee."

He glowered at Ambrose. "Tell me about Soviet Union."

"I'm not supposed to –"

"Oh, come on. Who said that? Whoever they are, they're on the far side of the planet right now, and they can't help you. They put you with me, but I can't help you either if I don't know what's going on."

Ambrose's lips thinned to a white line. He leaned forward. "It's big," he said.

"Can't be bigger than my metastables. Tell me: what did you see on Mars?"

Ambrose hesitated. Then he blurted, "A pyramid."

Silence.

"Really, a pyramid," Ambrose insisted. "Big sucker, grey, I think most of it was buried in the permafrost. It was the only thing sticking up for miles. This was on the Northern plains, where there's ice just under the surface. The whole area around it... well, it was like a frozen splash, if you know what I mean. Almost a crater."

This was just getting more and more disappointing. "And why is Soviet Union Online after you?"

"Because the pyramid had Russian writing on it. Just four letters, in red: CCCP."

The next silence went on for a while, and was punctuated only by the sound of other diners grumbling about local carbon prices.

"I leaked some photos before Google came after me with their non-disclosure agreements," Ambrose explained. "I guess the Soviets have internet search-bots constantly searching for certain things, and they picked up on my posts before Google was able to take them down. I got a couple of threatening phone calls from men with thick Slavic accents. Then they tried to kidnap me."

"No!"

Ambrose grimaced. "Well, they weren't very good at it. It was four guys, all of them must have been in their eighties, they tried to bundle me into a black van. I ran away and they just stood there yelling curses at me in Russian. One of them threw his cane at me." He rubbed his ankle.

"And you took them seriously?"

"I did when the FBI showed up and told me I had to pack up and go with them. That's when I ran to the U.N. I didn't believe that 'witness protection' crap the Feds tried to feed me. The U.N. people told me that the Soviets' data mining is actually really good. They keep turning up embarrassing and incriminating information about what people and governments got up to back in the days of the Cold War. They use what they know to influence people."

"That's bizarre." He thought about it. "Think they bought off the police here?"

"Or somebody. They want to know about the pyramid. But only Google, and the Feds, and I know where it is. And NASA's already patched that part of the Mars panoramas with fake data."

Disappointment had turned to a deep sense of surprise. For Gennady, being surprised usually meant that something awful was about to happen; so he said, "We need to get you out of town."

Ambrose brightened. "I have an idea. Let's go back to SNOPB. I looked up these Minus Three people; they're eco-radicals, but at least they don't seem to be lunatics."

"Hmmph. You just think Kyzdygoi's 'hot.'"

Ambrose grinned and shrugged.

"Okay. But we're not driving, because the car can be tracked. *You* walk there. It's only a few kilometres. I'll deal with the authorities and these 'Soviets,' and once I've sent them on their way we'll meet up. You've got my number."

Ambrose had evidently never taken a walk in the country before. After Gennady convinced him he would survive it, they parted outside La France, and Gennady watched him walk away, sneakers flapping. He shook his head and strolled back to the Tata.

Five men were waiting for him. Two were policemen, and three wore business attire. One of these was an old, bald man in a faded olive-green suit. He wore augmented reality glasses, and there was a discrete red pin on his lapel in the shape of the old Soviet flag.

Gennady made a show of pushing his own glasses back on his nose and walked forward, hand out. As the cops started to reach for their tasers, Gennady said, "Mr Egorov! Gennady Malianov, IAEA. You'll forgive me if I record and upload this conversation to headquarters?" He tapped the frame of his glasses and turned to the other suits. "I didn't catch your names?"

The suits frowned, the policemen hesitated; Egorov, however, put out his hand and Gennady shook it firmly. He could feel the old man's bones shift in his grip, but Egorov didn't grimace. Instead he said, "Where's your companion?"

"You mean that American? No idea. We shared a hotel room because it was cheaper, but then we parted ways this morning."

Egorov took his hand back, and pressed his bruised knuckles against his hip. "You've no idea where he is?"

"None."

"What're *you* doing here?" asked one of the cops.

"Inspecting SNOPB," he said. Gennady didn't have to fake his confidence here; he felt well armoured by his affiliation to Frankl's people. "My credentials are online, if there's some sort of issue here?"

"No issue," muttered Egorov. He turned away, and as he did a discrete icon lit up in the corner of

Gennady's heads-up display. Egorov had sent him a text message.

He hadn't been massaging his hand on his flank; he'd been texting through his pants. Gennady had left the server in his glasses open, so it would have been easy for Egorov to ping it and find his address.

In among all the other odd occurrences of the past couple of days, this one didn't stand out. But as Gennady watched Egorov and his policemen retreat, he realized that his assumption that Egorov had been in charge might be wrong. Who were those other two suits?

He waited for Egorov's party to drive away, then got in the Tata and opened the email.

It said, *Mt tnght Pavin Inn, 7, rstrnt wshrm. Cm aln.*

Gennady puzzled over those last two words for a while. Then he got it. "Come alone!" *Ah*. He should have known.

Shaking his head, he pulled out of the lot and headed back to the hotel to check out. After loading his bag, and Ambrose's, into the Tata, he hit the road back to SNOPB. Nobody followed him, but that meant nothing since they could track him through the car's transponder if they wanted. It hardly mattered; he was supposed to be inspecting the old anthrax factory, so where else would he be going?

Ambrose'd had enough time to get to SNOPB by now, but Gennady kept one eye on the fields next to the road just in case. He saw nobody, and fully expected to find the American waiting outside Building 242 as he pulled up.

As he stepped out of the Tata he nearly twisted his ankle in a deep rut. There were fresh tire tracks and shattered bits of old asphalt all over the place. He was sure he hadn't seen them this morning.

"Hello?" He walked down the ramp into the sudden dark of the bunker. Did he have the right building? It was completely dark here.

Wires drooled from overhead conduits; hydroponic trays lay jumbled in the corner, and strange-smelling liquids were pooled on the floor. Minus Three had pulled out, and in a hurry.

He cursed, but suppressed an urge to run back to the car. He had no idea where they'd gone, and they had a head-start on him. The main question was, had they left before or after Ambrose showed up?

The answer lay in the yellow grass near where Minus Three's vehicles had been parked that morning. Gennady knelt and picked up a familiar pair of augmented reality glasses. Ambrose would not have left these behind willingly.

Gennady swore, and now he did run to the Tata.

THE RESTAURANT AT the Pavin Inn was made up to look like the interiors of a row of yurts. This gave diners some privacy, as most of them had private little chambers under wood-ribbed ceilings; it also broke up the eye-lines to the place's front door, making it easy for Gennady to slip past the two men in suits who'd been with Egorov in the parking lot. He entered the men's washroom to find Egorov pacing in front of the urinal trough.

"What's this all about?" demanded Gennady – but Egorov made a shushing motion and grabbed a trash can. As he upended it under the bathroom's narrow window, he said, "First you must get me out of here."

"What? Why?"

Egorov tried to climb onto the upended can, but his knees failed him, and finally Gennady relented and went to help him. As he boosted the old comrade, Egorov said, "I am a prisoner of these people! They work for the *Americans.*" He practically spat the word. He perched precariously on the can and began tugging at the latch to the window. "They have seized our database! All the Soviet records... including what we know about the *Tsarina.*"

Gennady coughed. Then he said, "I'll bring the car around."

He helped Egorov through the window and, after making sure no one was looking, left through the hotel's front door. Egorov's unmistakable silhouette was limping into the parking lot. Gennady followed him and, unlocking the Tata, said, "I've disabled the GPS tracking in this car. It's a rental; I'm going to drop it off in Semey, six hundred kilometres from here. Are you sure you're up to a drive like that?"

The old man's eyes glinted under yellow street light. "Never thought I'd get a chance to see the steppes again. Let's go!"

Gennady felt a ridiculous surge of adrenalin as they bumped out of the parking lot. Only two other cars were on the road, and endless blackness swallowed the landscape beyond the edge of town. It was a simple matter to swing onto the highway and leave Stepnogorsk behind – but it felt like a car chase.

"Ha ha!" Egorov craned his neck to look back at the dwindling town lights. "Semey, eh? You're going to Semipalatinsk, aren't you?"

"To look at the *Tsarina* site, yes. Whose side does that put me on?"

"Sides?" Egorov crossed his arms and glared out the windshield. "I don't know about sides."

"It was an honest question."

"I believe you. But I don't *know.* Except for *them,*" he added, jabbing a thumb back at the town. "I know they're bad guys."

"Why? And why are they interested in Ambrose?"

"Same reason we are. Because of what he saw."

Gennady took a deep breath. "Okay. Why don't you just tell me what you know? And I'll do the same?"

"Yes, all right." The utter blackness of the night-time steppe had swallowed them; all that was visible was the double-cone of roadway visible in the car's headlamps. It barely changed, moment to moment, giving the drive a timelessness Gennady would, under other circumstances, have quite enjoyed.

"We data-mine records from the Soviet era," began Egorov. "To find out what really went on. It's lucrative business, and it supports the Union of Soviet Socialist Republics Online." He tapped his glasses.

"A few weeks ago, we got a request for some of the old data – from the Americans. Two requests, actually, a day apart: one from the search engine company, and the other from the government. We were naturally curious, so we didn't say no; but we did a little digging into the data ourselves. That is, we'd started to, when those men burst into our offices and confiscated the server. And the backup."

Gennady looked askance at him. "Really? Where was this?"

"Um. Seattle. That's where the CCCOP is based – only because we've been banned in the old country! Russia's run by robber barons today, they have no regard for the glory of –"

"Yes, yes. Did you find out what they were looking for?"

"Yes – which is how I ended up with these travel companions you saw. They are in the pay of the American CIA."

"Yes, but why? What does this have to do with the *Tsarina*?"

"I was hoping you could tell me. All we found was appropriations for strange things that should never have had anything to do with a nuclear test. Before the *Tsarina* was set off, there was about a year of heavy construction at the site. Sometimes, you know, they built fake towns to blow them up and examine the blast damage. That's what I thought at first; they ordered thousands of tonnes of concrete, rebar and asbestos, that sort of thing. But if you look at the records after the test, there's no sign of where any of that material *went.*"

"They ordered some sort of agricultural crop from SNOPB," Gennady ventured. Egorov nodded.

"None of the discrepancies would ever have been noticed if not for your friend and whatever it is he found. What was it, anyway?"

A strange suspicion had begun to form in Gennady's mind, but it was so unlikely that he shook his head. "I want to look at the *Tsarina* site," he said. "Maybe that'll tell us."

Egorov was obviously unsatisfied with that answer, but he said nothing, merely muttering and trying to get himself comfortable in the Tata's bucket seat. After a while, just as the hum of the dark highway was starting to hypnotize Gennady, Egorov said, "It's all gone to Hell, you know."

"Hmm?"

"Russia. It was hard in the old days, but at least we had our pride." He turned to look out the black window. "After 1990, all the life just went out of the place. Lower birth-rate, men drinking themselves to death by the age of forty... no ambition, no hope. A lost land."

"You left?"

"Physically, yes." Egorov darted a look at Gennady. "You never *leave*. Not a place like this. For many years now, I've struggled with how to bring back Russia's old glory – our sense of *pride*. Yet the best I was ever able to come up with was an online environment. A *game*." He spat the word contemptuously.

Gennady didn't reply, but he knew how Egorov felt. Ukraine had some of the same problems – the lack of direction, the loss of confidence... It wasn't getting any better here. He thought of the blasted steppes they were passing through, rendered unlivable by global warming. There had been massive forest fires in Siberia this year, and the Gobi desert was expanding north and west, threatening the Kazaks even as the Caspian Sea dwindled to nothing.

He thought of SNOPB. "They're gone," he said, "but they left their trash behind." Toxic, decaying: nuclear submarines heeled over in the waters off Murmansk, nitrates soaking the soil around the launch pads of Baikonur. The ghosts of old Soviets prowled this dark, as radiation in the groundwater, mutations in the forest, poisons in the all-too-common dust clouds. Gennady had spent his whole adult life cleaning up the mess, and before yesterday he'd been able to tell himself that it was working –

that all the worst nightmares were from the past. The metastables had changed that, in one stroke rendering all the old fears laughable in comparison.

"Get some sleep," he told Egorov. "We're going to be driving all night."

"I don't sleep much anymore." But the old man stopped talking, and just stared ahead. He couldn't be visiting his online People's Republic through his glasses; those IP addresses were blocked here. But maybe he saw it all anyway – the brave young men in their trucks, heading to the Semipalatinsk site to witness a nuclear blast. The rail yards where parts for the giant moon rocket, doomed to explode on the pad, were mustering... With his gaze fixed firmly on the past, he seemed the perfect opposite of Ambrose with his American dreams of a new world unburdened by history, whose red dunes marched to a pure and mysterious horizon.

The first living thing in space had been the Russian dog Laika. She had died in orbit – had never come home. If he glanced out at the star-speckled sky, Gennady could almost see her ghost racing eternally through the heavens, beside the dead dream of planetary conquest, of flags planted in alien soil and shining domes on the hills of Mars.

THEY ARRIVED AT the *Tsarina* site at 4:30. Dawn, at this latitude and time of year. The Semipalatinsk Polygon was bare, flat, blasted scrubland: Mars with tufts of dead weed. The irony was that it hadn't been the hundreds of nuclear bombs set off here that had killed the land; even a decade after the Polygon was closed, the low rolling hills had been covered with a rich carpet of waving grass. Instead, it was the savage turn of the climate, completely unpredicted by the KGB and the CIA, that had killed the steppe.

The road into the Polygon was narrow blacktop with no real shoulder, no ditches, and no oncoming traffic – although a set of lights had faded in and out of view in the rearview mirror all through the drive. Gennady would have missed the turnoff to the *Tsarina* site had his glasses not beeped.

There had been a low wire fence here at one time, but nobody had kept it up. He drove straight over the fallen gate, now becoming one with the soil, and up a low rise to the crest of the water-filled crater. There he parked and got out.

Egorov climbed out too and stretched cautiously. "Beautiful," he said, gazing into the epic sunrise. "Is it radioactive here?"

"Oh, a little... That's odd."

"What?"

Gennady had looked at the satellite view of the site on the way here; it was clear, standing here in person, that the vertical perspective had lied. "The *Tsarina* was supposed to be an underground test. You usually get some subsidence of the ground in a circle around the test site. And with the big ground shots, you would get a crater, like Lake Chagan," he nodded to the east. "But this... this is a *hole.*"

Egorov spat into it. "It certainly is." The walls of the *Tsarina* crater were sheer and dropped a good fifty feet to black water. The "crater" wasn't round, either, but square, and not nearly big enough to be the result of a surface explosion. If he hadn't known it was the artefact of a bomb blast, Gennady would have sworn he was looking at a flooded quarry.

Gennady gathered his equipment and began combing the grass around the site. After a minute he found some twisted chunks of concrete and metal, and knelt to inspect them.

Egorov came up behind him. "What are you looking for?"

"Serial numbers." He found some old, greyed stencilling on a half-buried tank made of greenish metal. "You'll understand what I'm doing," he said as he pinched the arm of his glasses to take a snapshot. "I'm checking our database... Hmpf."

"What is it?" Egorov shifted from foot to foot. He was glancing around, as if afraid they might be interrupted.

"This piece came from the smaller of the installations here. The one the Americans called URDF-3."

"URDF?" Egorov blinked at him.

"Stands for 'Unidentified Research and Development Facility.' The stuff they built there scared the Yankees even more than the H-bomb..."

He stood up, frowning, and slowly turned to look at the entire site. "Something's been bothering me," he said as he walked to the very edge of the giant pit.

"What's that?" Egorov was hanging back.

"Ambrose told me he saw a pyramid on Mars. It said CCCP on its side. That was all; so he knew it was Russian, and so did Google and the CIA when they found out about it. And you, too. But that's all anybody knew. So who made the connection between the pyramid and the *Tsarina*?"

Egorov didn't reply. Gennady turned and found that the old man had drawn himself up very straight, and had levelled a small, nasty-looking pistol at him.

"You didn't follow us to Stepnogorsk," said Gennady. "You were already there."

"Take off your glasses," said Egorov. "Carefully, so I can be sure you're not snapping another picture."

As Gennady reached up to comply he felt the soft soil at the lip of the pit start to crumble. "Ah, can we –" Too late. He toppled backward, arms flailing.

He had an instant's choice: roll down the slope, or jump and hope he'd hit the water. He jumped.

The cold hit him so hard that at first he thought he'd been shot. Swearing and gasping, he surfaced, but when he spotted Egorov's silhouette at the crest of the pit, he dove again.

Morning sunlight was just tipping into the water. At first Gennady thought the wall of the pit was casting a dark shadow across the sediment below him. Gradually he realized the truth: there was no bottom to this shaft. At least, none within easy diving depth.

He swam to the opposite side; he couldn't stay down here, he'd freeze. Defeated, he flung himself out of the freezing water onto hard clay that was probably radioactive. Rolling over, he looked up.

Egorov stood on the lip of the pit. Next to him was a young woman with a rifle in her hands.

Gennady sat up. "Shit."

Kyzdygoi slung the rifle over her back and clambered down the slope to the shore. As she picked her way over to Gennady she asked, "How much do you know?"

"Everything," he said between coughs. "I know everything. Where's Ambrose?"

"He's safe," she said. "He'll be fine." Then she waited, rifle cradled.

"You're here," he said reluctantly, "which tells me that Minus Three was funded by the Soviets. Your job was never to clean up the Earth – it was to design life support and agricultural systems for a Mars colony."

Her mouth twitched, but she didn't laugh. "How could we possibly get to Mars? The sky's a shooting gallery."

"...And that would be a problem if you were going up there in a dinky little aluminium can, like cosmonauts always did." He stood up, joints creaking from the cold. He was starting to shiver deeply and it was hard to speak past his chattering teeth. "B-but if you rode a c-concrete bunker into orbit, you could ignore the shrapnel c-completely. In fact, that would be the only way you could d-do it."

"Come now. How could something like that ever get off the ground?"

"The same way the *Tsarina* d-did." He nodded at the dark surface of the flooded shaft. "The Americans had their P-project Orion. The Soviets had a similar program based at URDF-3. Both had discovered that an object could be just a few meters away from a nuclear explosion, and if it was made of the right materials it wouldn't be destroyed – it would be shot away like a bullet from a gun. The Americans designed a spaceship that would drop atomic bombs out the back and ride the explosions to orbit. But the *Tsarina* wasn't like that... it was just one bomb, and a d-deep shaft, and a pyramid-shaped spaceship to ride that explosion. A 'Verne gun.'"

"And who else knows this?"

He hesitated. "N-no one," he admitted. "I didn't know until I saw the shaft just now. The p-pyramid was fitted into the mouth of it, right about where we're s-standing. That's why this doesn't look like any other bomb crater on Earth."

"Let's go," she said, gesturing with the rifle. "You're turning blue."

"Y-you're not going t-to sh-shoot me?"

"There's no need," she said gently. "In a few days, the whole world will know what we've done."

GENNADY FINISHED TAPING aluminium foil to the trailer's window. Taking a push-pin from the cork board by the door, he carefully pricked a single tiny hole in the foil.

It was night, and crickets were chirping outside. Gennady wasn't tied up – in fact, he was perfectly free to leave – but on his way out the door Egorov had said, "I wouldn't go outside in the next hour or so. After that... well, wait for the dust to settle."

They'd driven him about fifty kilometres to the south and into an empty part of the Polygon. When Gennady had asked why this place, Egorov had laughed. "The Soviets set off their bombs here because this was the last empty place on Earth. It's still the last empty place, and that's why we're here."

There was nothing here but the withered steppe, a hundred or so trucks, vans and buses, and the cranes, tanks and pole-sheds of a temporary construction site. And, towering over the sheds, a grey concrete pyramid.

"A Verne gun fires its cargo into orbit in a single shot," Egorov had told Gennady. "It generates thousands of gravities worth of acceleration – enough to turn you into a smear on the floor. That's why the

Soviets couldn't send any people; they hadn't figured out how to set off a controlled sequence of little bombs. The Americans never perfected that either. They didn't have the computational power to do the simulations.

"So they sent everything but the people. *Two hundred and eighty thousand tonnes* in one shot, to Mars."

Bulldozers and cranes, fuel tanks, powdered cement, bags of seeds and food, space suits, even a complete, dismantled nuclear reactor: the *Tsarina* had included everything potential colonists might need on a new world. Its builders knew it had gone up, knew it had gotten to Mars; but they didn't know where it had landed, or whether it had landed intact.

A day after his visit to the *Tsarina* site, Gennady had sat outside this trailer with Egorov, Kyzdygoi and a few other officials of the new Soviet. They'd drunk a few beers and talked about the plan. "When our data-mining turned up the *Tsarina*'s manifest, it was like a light from heaven," Egorov had said, his hands opening eloquently in the firelight. "Suddenly we saw what was possible, how to revive our people – all the world's people – around a new hope, after all hope had gone. Something that would combine Apollo and Trinity into one event, and suddenly both would take on the meaning they always needed to have."

Egorov had started a crash program to build an Orion rocket. They couldn't get fissionable materials – Gennady and his people had locked those up tightly and for all time. But the metastables promised a different approach.

"We hoped the *Tsarina* was on Mars and intact, but we didn't know for sure, until Ambrose leaked his pictures."

The new *Tsarina* would use a series of small, clean fusion blasts to lift off and, at the far end, to land again. Thanks to Ambrose, they knew where the *Tsarina* was. It didn't matter that the Americans did too; nobody else had a plan to get there.

"And by the time they get their acts together, we'll have built a city," said Kyzdygoi. She was wide-eyed with the power of the idea. "Because we're not going there two at a time, like Noah in his Ark. We're *all* going." And she swung her arm to indicate the hundreds of campfires burning all around them, where thousands of men, women and children, hand-picked from among the citizens of the Union of Soviet Socialist Republics Online, waited to amaze the world.

GENNADY HUNKERED DOWN in a little fort he'd built out of seat cushions, and waited.

It was like a camera flash, and a second later there was a second, then a third, and then the whole trailer bounced into the air and everything Gennady hadn't tied down went tumbling. The windows shattered and he landed on cushions and found himself staring across suddenly open air at the immolation of the building site.

The flickering flashes continued, coming from above now. The pyramid was gone, and the cranes and heavy machinery lay tumbled like a child's toys, all burning.

Flash. Flash.

It was really happening.

Flash. Flash. Flash...

Gradually, Gennady began to be able to hear

again. He came to realize that monstrous thunder was rolling across the steppe, like a god's drumbeat in time with the flashes. It faded, as the flashes faded, until there was nothing but the ringing in his ears, and the orange flicker of flame from the launch site.

He staggered out to find perfect devastation. Once, this must once have been a common sight on the steppe; but his Geiger counter barely registered any radiation at all.

And in that, of course, lay a terrible irony. Egorov and his people had indeed divided history in two, but not in the way they'd imagined.

Gennady ran for the command trailer. He only had a few minutes before the air forces of half a dozen nations descended on this place. The trailer had survived the initial blast, so he scrounged until he found a jerry-can full of gasoline, and then he climbed in.

There they were: Egorov's servers. The EMP from the little nukes might have wiped its drives, but Gennady couldn't take the chance. He poured gasoline all over the computers, made a trail back to the door, then as the whole trailer went up behind him, ran to the leaning-but-intact metal shed where the metastables had been processed, and he did the same to it.

That afternoon, as he and Egorov were watching the orderly queue of people waiting to enter the *New Tsarina*, Gennady had made his final plea. "Your research into metastables," Gennady went on. "I need it. All of it, and the equipment and the backups; anything that might be used to reconstruct what you did."

"What happens to the Earth is no longer our

concern," Egorov said with a frown. "Humanity made a mess here. It's not up to us to clean it up."

"But to destroy it all, you only need to be indifferent! And I'm asking, please, however much the world may have disappointed you, don't leave it like this." As he spoke, Gennady scanned the line of people for Ambrose, but couldn't see him. Nobody had said where the young American was.

Egorov had sighed in annoyance, then nodded sharply. "I'll have all the formulae and the equipment gathered together. It's all I have time for, now. You can do what you want with it."

Gennady watched the flames twist into the air. He was exhausted, and the sky was full of contrails and gathering lights. He hadn't destroyed enough of the evidence; surely, someone would figure out what Egorov's people had done. And then... Shoulders slumped under the burden of that knowledge, he stalked into the darkness at the camp's perimeter.

His rented Tata sat where they'd left it when they first arrived here. After Kyzdygoi had confiscated his glasses at the *Tsarina* site, she'd put them in the Tata's glove compartment. They were still there.

Before Gennady put them on, he took a last unaided look at the burning campsite. Egorov and his people had escaped, but they'd left Gennady behind to clean up their mess. The metastables would be back. This new nightmare would get out into the world eventually, and when it did, the traditional specter of nuclear terrorism would look like a Halloween ghost in comparison. Could even the conquest of another world make up for that?

As the choppers settled in whipping spirals of dust, Gennady rolled up the Tata's window and put on his glasses. The *New Tsarina*'s EMP pulses hadn't killed them – they booted up right away. And, seconds after they did, a little flag told him there was an email waiting for him.

It was from Ambrose, and it read:

Gennady: sorry I didn't have time to say goodbye.

I just wanted to say I was wrong. Anything's possible, even for me.

P.S. My room's going to have a fantastic view.

Gennady stared bitterly at the words. *Anything's possible...*

"For you, maybe," he said as soldiers piled out of the choppers.

"Not me."

THE INVASION OF VENUS

STEPHEN BAXTER

Stephen Baxter is one of the most important science fiction writers to emerge from Britain in the past thirty years. His Xeelee *sequence of novels and short stories is arguably the most significant work of future history in modern science fiction. He is the author of more than forty books and over 100 short stories. His most recent books are the near-future disaster duology,* Flood *and* Ark, *and* Stone Spring, *the first novel in his* Northland *trilogy.*

FOR ME, THE saga of the Incoming was above all Edith Black's story. For she, more than anyone else I knew, was the one who had a problem with it.

When the news was made public I drove out of London to visit Edith at her country church. I had to cancel a dozen appointments to do it, including one with the Prime Minister's office, but I knew, as soon as I got out of the car and stood in the soft September rain, that it had been the right thing to do.

Edith was pottering around outside the church, wearing overalls and rubber boots and wielding an alarming-looking industrial-strength jackhammer. But she had a radio blaring out a phone-in discussion, and indoors, out of the rain, I glimpsed a widescreen TV and laptop, both scrolling news – mostly fresh projections of where the Incoming's decelerating trajectory might deliver them, and new deep-space images of their "craft," if such it was, a massive block of ice like a comet nucleus, leaking very complex patterns of infrared radiation. Edith was plugged into the world, even out here in the wilds of Essex.

She approached me with a grin, pushing back goggles under a hard hat. "Toby." I got a kiss on the cheek and a brief hug; she smelled of machine oil. We were easy with each other physically. Fifteen years earlier, in our last year at college, we'd been lovers, briefly; it had finished with a kind of regretful embarrassment – very English, said our American friends – but it had proven only a kind of speed bump in our relationship. "Glad to see you, if surprised. I thought all you civil service types would be locked down in emergency meetings."

For a decade I'd been a civil servant in the environment ministry. "No, but old Thorp" – my minister – "has been in a continuous COBRA session for twenty-four hours. Much good it's doing anybody."

"I must say it's not obvious to the layman what use an environment minister is when the aliens are coming."

"Well, among the scenarios they're discussing is some kind of attack from space. A lot of what we can dream up is similar to natural disasters – a meteor fall could be like a tsunami, a sunlight occlusion like a massive volcanic event. And so Thorp is in the mix, along with health, energy, transport. Of course we're in contact with other governments – NATO, the UN. The most urgent issue right now is whether to signal or not."

She frowned. "Why wouldn't you?"

"Security. Edith, remember, we know absolutely nothing about these guys. What if our signal was interpreted as a threat? And there are tactical considerations. Any signal would give information to a potential enemy about our technical capabilities. It would also give away the very fact that we know they're here."

She scoffed. "'Tactical considerations.' Paranoid bullshit! And besides, I bet every kid with a CB radio is beaming out her heart to ET right now. The whole planet's alight."

"Well, that's true. You can't stop it. But still, sending some kind of signal authorised by the government or an inter-government agency is another step entirely."

"Oh, come on. You can't really believe anybody is going to cross the stars to harm us. What could they possibly want that would justify the cost of an interstellar mission...?"

So we argued. I'd only been out of the car for five minutes.

We'd had this kind of discussion all the way back to late nights in college, some of them in her bed, or mine. She'd always been drawn to the bigger issues; "to the context," as she used to say. Though we'd both started out as maths students, her head had soon expanded in the exotic intellectual air of the college, and she'd moved on to study older ways of thinking than the scientific – older questions, still unanswered. Was there a God? If so, or if not, what was the point of our existence? Why did we, or indeed anything, exist at all? In her later college years she took theology options, but quickly burned through that discipline and was left unsatisfied. She was repelled too by the modern atheists, with their aggressive denials. So, after college, she had started her own journey through life – a journey in search of answers. Now, of course, maybe some of those answers had come swimming in from the stars in search of her.

This was why I'd felt drawn here, at this particular moment in my life. I needed her perspective. In the wan daylight I could see the fine patina of lines around the mouth I used to kiss, and the strands of grey in her red hair. I was sure she suspected, rightly, that I knew more than I was telling her – more than had been released to the public. But she didn't follow that up for now.

"Come see what I'm doing," she said, sharply breaking up the debate. "Watch your shoes." We walked across muddy grass towards the main door. The core of the old church, dedicated to St Cuthbert, was a Saxon-era tower; the rest of the fabric was mostly Norman, but there had been an extensive restoration in Victorian times. Within was a lovely space, if cold, the stone walls resonating. It was still consecrated, Church of England, but in this empty agricultural countryside it was one of a widespread string of churches united in a single parish, and rarely used.

Edith had never joined any of the established religions, but she had appropriated some of their infrastructure, she liked to say. And here she had gathered a group of volunteers, wandering souls more or less like-minded. They worked to maintain the fabric of the church. And within, she led her group through what you might think of as a mix of discussions, or prayers, or meditation, or yoga practices – whatever she could find that seemed to work. This was the way religions used to be before the big monotheistic creeds took over, she argued. "The only way to reach God, or anyhow the space beyond us where God ought to be, is by working hard, by helping other people – and by pushing your mind to the limit of its capability, and then going a little beyond, and just *listening*." Beyond *logos* to *mythos*. She was always restless, always trying something new. Yet in some ways she was the most contented person I ever met – at least before the Incoming showed up.

Now, though, she wasn't content about the state of the church's foundations. She showed me where she had dug up flagstones to reveal sodden ground. "We're digging out new drainage channels, but it's a hell of a job. We may end up rebuilding the founds altogether. The very deepest level seems to be wood, huge piles of Saxon oak..." She eyed me. "This church has stood here for a thousand years, without, apparently, facing a threat such as this before. Some measure of climate change, right?"

I shrugged. "I suppose you'd say we arseholes in the environment ministry should be concentrating on stuff like this rather than preparing to fight interstellar wars."

"Well, so you should. And maybe a more mature species would be preparing for positive outcomes. Think of it, Tobe! There are now creatures in this solar system who are *smarter than us*. They have to be, or they wouldn't be here – right? Somewhere between us and the angels. Who knows what they can tell us? What is their science, their art – their theology?"

I frowned. "But what do they want? That's what may count from now on – *their* agenda, not ours."

"There you are being paranoid again." But she hesitated. "What about Meryl and the kids?"

"Meryl's at home. Mark and Sophie at school." I shrugged. "Life as normal."

"Some people are freaking out. Raiding the supermarkets."

"Some people always do. We want things to continue as normally as possible, as long as possible. Modern society is efficient, you know, Edith, but not very resilient. A fuel strike could cripple us in a week, let alone alien invaders."

She pushed a loose grey hair back under her hard hat, and looked at me suspiciously. "But you seem very calm, considering. You know something. Don't you, you bastard?"

I grinned. "And you know me."

"Spill it."

"Two things. We picked up signals. Or, more likely, leakage. You know about the infrared stuff we've seen for a while, coming from the nucleus. Now we've detected radio noise, faint, clearly structured, very complex. It may be some kind of internal channel rather than anything meant for us. But if we can figure anything out from it –"

"Well, that's exciting. And the second thing? Come on, Miller."

"We have more refined trajectory data. All this will be released soon – it's probably leaked already."

"Yes?"

"The Incoming *are* heading for the inner solar system. But they aren't coming here – not to Earth."

She frowned. "Then where?"

I dropped my bombshell. "Venus. Not Earth. They're heading for Venus, Edith."

She looked into the clouded sky, the bright patch that marked the position of the sun, and the inner planets. "Venus? That's a cloudy hellhole. What would they want there?"

"I've no idea."

"Well, I'm used to living with questions I'll never be able to answer. Let's hope this isn't one of them. In the meantime, let's make ourselves useful." She eyed my crumpled Whitehall suit, my patent leather shoes already splashed with mud. "Have you got time to stay? You want to help out with my drain? I've a spare overall that might fit."

Talking, speculating, we walked through the church.

WE USED THE excuse of Edith's Goonhilly event to make a family trip to Cornwall.

We took the A-road snaking west down the spine of the Cornish peninsula, and stopped at a small hotel in Helston. The pretty little town was decked out that day for the annual Furry Dance, an ancient, eccentric carnival in which the local children would weave in and out of the houses on the hilly streets. The next morning Meryl was to take the kids to the beach, further up the coast.

And, just about at dawn, I set off alone in a hired car for the A-road to the south-east, towards

Goonhilly Down. It was a clear May morning. As I drove I was aware of Venus, rising in the eastern sky and clearly visible in my rear view mirror, a lamp shining steadily even as the day brightened.

Goonhilly is a stretch of high open land, a windy place. Its claim to fame is that at one time it hosted the largest telecoms satellite earth station in the world – it picked up the first live transatlantic TV broadcast, via Telstar. It was decommissioned years ago, but its oldest dish, a thousand-tonne parabolic bowl called "Arthur" after the king, became a listed building, and so was preserved. And that was how it was available for Edith and her committee of messagers to get hold of, when they, or rather she, grew impatient with the government's continuing reticence. Because of the official policy I had to help with smoothing through the permissions, all behind the scenes.

Just after my first glimpse of the surviving dishes on the skyline I came up against a police cordon, a hastily erected plastic fence that excluded a few groups of chanting Shouters and a fundamentalist-religious group protesting that the messagers were communicating with the Devil. My ministry card helped me get through.

Edith was waiting for me at the old site's visitors' centre, opened up that morning for breakfast, coffee and cereals and toast. Her volunteers cleared up dirty dishes under a big wall screen showing a live feed from a space telescope – the best images available right now, though every major space agency had a probe to Venus in preparation, and NASA had already fired one off. The Incoming nucleus (it seemed inappropriate to call that lump of dirty ice a "craft," though such it clearly was) was a brilliant star, too small to show a disc, swinging in its wide orbit above a half-moon Venus. And on the planet's night side you could clearly make out the Patch, the strange, complicated glow in the cloud banks tracking the Incoming's orbit precisely. It was strange to gaze upon that choreography in space, and then to turn to the east and see Venus with the naked eye.

And Edith's volunteers, a few dozen earnest men, women and children who looked like they had gathered for a village show, had the audacity to believe they could speak to these godlike forms in the sky.

There was a terrific metallic groan. We turned, and saw that Arthur was turning on his concrete pivot. The volunteers cheered, and a general drift towards the monument began.

Edith walked with me, cradling a polystyrene tea cup in the palms of fingerless gloves. "I'm glad you could make it down. Should have brought the kids. Some of the locals from Helston are here; they've made the whole stunt part of their Furry Dance celebration. Did you see the preparations in town? Supposed to celebrate St Michael beating up on the Devil – I wonder how appropriate *that* symbolism is. Anyhow, this ought to be a fun day. Later there'll be a barn dance."

"Meryl thought it was safer to take the kids to the beach. Just in case anything gets upsetting here – you know." That was most of the truth. There was a subtext that Meryl had never much enjoyed being in the same room as my ex.

"Probably wise. Our British Shouters are a mild

bunch, but in rowdier parts of the world there has been trouble." The loose international coalition of groups called the Shouters was paradoxically named, because they campaigned for silence; they argued that "shouting in the jungle" by sending signals to the Incoming or the Venusians was taking an irresponsible risk. Of course they could do nothing about the low-level chatter that had been targeted at the Incoming since it had first been sighted, nearly a year ago already. Edith waved a hand at Arthur. "If I were a Shouter, I'd be here today. This will be by far the most powerful message sent from the British Isles."

I'd seen and heard roughs of Edith's message. In with a Carl Sagan-style prime number lexicon, there was digitised music from Bach to Zulu chants, and art from cave paintings to Warhol, and images of mankind featuring a lot of smiling children, and astronauts on the Moon. There was even a copy of the old Pioneer spaceprobe plaque from the seventies, with the smiling naked couple. At least, I thought cynically, all that fluffy stuff would provide a counterpoint to the images of war, murder, famine, plague and other sufferings that the Incoming had no doubt sampled by now, if they'd chosen to.

I said, "But I get the feeling they're just not interested. Neither the Incoming nor the Venusians. Sorry to rain on your parade."

"I take it the cryptolinguists aren't getting anywhere decoding the signals?"

"They're not so much 'signals' as leakage from internal processes, we think. In both cases, the nucleus and the Patch." I rubbed my face; I was tired after the previous day's long drive. "In the case of the nucleus, some kind of organic chemistry seems to be mediating powerful magnetic fields – and the Incoming seem to swarm within. I don't think we've really any idea what's going on in there. We're actually making more progress with the science of the Venusian biosphere..."

If the arrival of the Incoming had been astonishing, the evidence of intelligence on Venus, entirely unexpected, was stunning. Nobody had expected the clouds to part right under the orbiting Incoming nucleus – like a deep storm system, kilometres deep in that thick ocean of an atmosphere – and nobody had expected to see the Patch revealed, swirling mist banks where lights flickered tantalisingly, like organised lightning.

"With retrospect, given the results from the old space probes, we might have guessed there was something on Venus – life, if not intelligent life. There were always unexplained deficiencies and surpluses of various compounds. We think the Venusians live in the clouds, far enough above the red-hot ground that the temperature is low enough for liquid water to exist. They ingest carbon monoxide and excrete sulphur compounds, living off the sun's ultraviolet."

"And they're smart."

"Oh, yes." The astronomers, already recording the complex signals coming out of the Incoming nucleus, had started to discern rich patterns in the Venusian Patch too. "You can tell how complicated a message is even if you don't know anything about the content. You measure entropy orders, which are like correlation measures, mapping structures on various scales embedded in the transmission –"

"You don't understand any of what you just said, do you?"

I smiled. "Not a word. But I do know this. Going by their data structures, the Venusians are smarter than us as we are smarter than the chimps. And the Incoming are smarter again."

Edith turned to face the sky, the brilliant spark of Venus. "But you say the scientists still believe all this chatter is just – what was your word?"

"Leakage. Edith, the Incoming and the Venusians aren't speaking to us. They aren't even speaking to each other. What we're observing is a kind of internal dialogue, in each case. The two are talking to themselves, not each other. One theorist briefed the PM that perhaps both these entities are more like hives than human communities."

"Hives?" She looked troubled. "Hives are *different*. They can be purposeful, but they don't have consciousness as we have it. They aren't finite as we are; their edges are much more blurred. They aren't even mortal; individuals can die, but the hives live on."

"I wonder what their theology will be, then."

"It's all so strange. These aliens just don't fit any category we expected, or even that we share. Not mortal, not communicative – and not interested in us. What do they *want*? What *can* they want?" Her tone wasn't like her; she sounded bewildered to be facing open questions, rather than exhilarated as usual.

I tried to reassure her. "Maybe your signal will provoke some answers."

She checked her watch, and looked up again towards Venus. "Well, we've only got five minutes to wait before –" Her eyes widened, and she fell silent.

I turned to look the way she was, to the east.

Venus was flaring. Sputtering like a dying candle.

People started to react. They shouted, pointed, or they just stood there, staring, as I did. I couldn't move. I felt a deep, awed fear. Then people called, pointing at the big screen in the visitors' centre, where, it seemed, the space telescopes were returning a very strange set of images indeed.

Edith's hand crept into mine. Suddenly I was very glad I hadn't brought my kids that day.

I heard angrier shouting, and a police siren, and I smelled burning.

ONCE I'D FINISHED making my police statement I went back to the hotel in Helston, where Meryl was angry and relieved to see me, and the kids bewildered and vaguely frightened. I couldn't believe that after all that had happened – the strange events at Venus, the assaults by Shouters on messagers and vice versa, the arson, Edith's injury, the police crackdown – it was not yet eleven in the morning.

That same day I took the family back to London, and called in at work. Then, three days after the incident, I got away again and commandeered a ministry car and driver to take me back to Cornwall.

Edith was out of intensive care, but she'd been kept in the hospital at Truro. She had a TV stand before her face, the screen dark. I carefully kissed her on the unburnt side of her face, and sat down, handing over books, newspapers and flowers. "Thought you might be bored."

"You never were any good with the sick, were you, Tobe?"

"Sorry." I opened up one of the newspapers. "But there's some good news. They caught the arsonists."

She grunted, her distorted mouth barely opening. "So what? It doesn't matter who they were. Messagers and Shouters have been at each others' throats all over the world. People like that are interchangeable... But did we all have to behave so badly? I mean, they even wrecked Arthur."

"And he was Grade II listed!"

She laughed, then regretted it, for she winced with the pain. "But why shouldn't we smash everything up down here? After all, that's all they seem to be interested in up *there*. The Incoming assaulted Venus, and the Venusians struck back. We all saw it, live on TV – it was nothing more than *War of the Worlds*." She sounded disappointed. "These creatures are our superiors, Toby. All your signal analysis stuff proved it. And yet they haven't transcended war and destruction."

"But we learned so much." I had a small briefcase which I opened now, and pulled out printouts that I spread over her bed. "The screen images are better, but you know how it is; they won't let me use my laptop or my phone in here... *Look*, Edith. It was incredible. The Incoming assault on Venus lasted hours. Their weapon, whatever it was, burned its way through the Patch, and right down through an atmosphere a hundred times thicker than Earth's. We even glimpsed the surface –"

"Now melted to slag."

"Much of it... But then the acid-munchers in the clouds struck back. We think we know what they did."

That caught her interest. "How can we know that?"

"Sheer luck. That NASA probe, heading for Venus, happened to be in the way..."

The probe had detected a wash of electromagnetic radiation, coming from the planet.

"A signal," breathed Edith. "Heading which way?"

"Out from the sun. And then, eight hours later, the probe sensed another signal, coming the other way. I say 'sensed.' It bobbed about like a cork on a pond. We think it was a gravity wave – very sharply focused, very intense."

"And when the wave hit the Incoming nucleus –"

"Well, you saw the pictures. The last fragments have burned up in Venus's atmosphere."

She lay back on her reef of pillows. "Eight hours," she mused. "Gravity waves travel at lightspeed. Four hours out, four hours back... Earth's about eight light-minutes from the sun. What's four light-hours out from Venus? Jupiter, Saturn –"

"Neptune. Neptune was four light-hours out."

"*Was*?"

"It's gone, Edith. Almost all of it – the moons are still there, a few chunks of core ice and rock, slowly dispersing. The Venusians used the planet to create their gravity-wave pulse –"

"They *used* it. Are you telling me this to cheer me up? A gas giant, a significant chunk of the solar system's budget of mass-energy, sacrificed for a single war-like gesture." She laughed, bitterly. "Oh, God!"

"Of course we've no idea *how* they did it." I put away my images. "If we were scared of the Incoming, now we're terrified of the Venusians. That NASA probe has been shut down. We don't want anything to look like a threat... You know, I heard the PM herself ask why it was that a space war should break out now, just when we humans are sitting around on Earth. Even politicians know we haven't been here that long."

Edith shook her head, wincing again. "The final vanity. This whole episode has never been about us. Can't you see? If this is happening now, it must have happened over and over. Who knows how many other planets we lost in the past, consumed as weapons of forgotten wars? Maybe all we see, the planets and stars and galaxies, is just the debris of huge wars – on and on, up to scales we can barely imagine. And we're just weeds growing in the rubble. Tell that to the Prime Minister. And I thought we might ask them about their gods! What a fool I've been – the questions on which I've wasted my life, and *here* are my answers – what a fool." She was growing agitated.

"Take it easy, Edith –"

"Oh, just go. I'll be fine. It's the universe that's broken, not me." She turned away on her pillow, as if to sleep.

THE NEXT TIME I saw Edith she was out of hospital and back at her church.

It was another September day, like the first time I visited her after the Incoming appeared in our telescopes, and at least it wasn't raining. There was a bite in the breeze, but I imagined it soothed her damaged skin. And here she was, digging in the mud before her church.

"Equinox season," she said. "Rain coming. Best to get this fixed before we have another flash flood.

And before you ask, the doctors cleared me. It's my face that's buggered, not the rest of me."

"I wasn't going to ask."

"OK, then. How's Meryl, the kids?"

"Fine. Meryl's at work, the kids back at school. Life goes on."

"It must, I suppose. What else is there? No, by the way."

"No what?"

"No, I won't come serve on your minister's think tank."

"At least consider it. You'd be ideal. Look, we're all trying to figure out where we go from here. The arrival of the Incoming, the war on Venus – it was like a religious revelation. That's how it's being described. A revelation witnessed by all mankind, on TV. Suddenly we've got an entirely different view of the universe out there. And we have to figure out how we go forward, in a whole number of dimensions – political, scientific, economic, social, religious."

"I'll tell you how we go forward. In despair. Religions are imploding."

"No, they're not."

"OK. Theology is imploding. Philosophy. The rest of the world has changed channels and forgotten already, but anybody with any imagination knows... In a way this has been the final demotion, the end of the process that started with Copernicus and Darwin. Now we *know* there are creatures in the universe much smarter than we'll ever be, and we *know* they don't care a damn about us. It's the indifference that's the killer – don't you think? All our futile agitation about if they'd attack us and whether we should signal... And they did nothing but smash each other up. With *that* above us, what can we do but turn away?"

"You're not turning away."

She leaned on her shovel. "I'm not religious; I don't count. My congregation turned away. Here I am, alone." She glanced at the clear sky. "Maybe solitude is the key to it all. A galactic isolation imposed by the vast gulfs between the stars, the lightspeed limit. As a species develops you might have a brief phase of individuality, of innovation and technological achievement. But then, when the universe gives you nothing back, you turn in on yourself, and slide into the milky embrace of eusociality – the hive.

"But what then? How would it be for a mass mind to emerge, alone? Maybe that's why the Incoming went to war. Because they were outraged to discover, by some chance, they weren't alone in the universe."

"Most commentators think it was about resources," I said. "Most of our wars are about that, in the end."

"Yes. Depressingly true. All life is based on the destruction of other life, even on tremendous scales of space and time... Our ancestors understood that right back to the Ice Age, and venerated the animals they had to kill. They were so far above us, the Incoming and the Venusians alike. Yet maybe *we*, at our best, are morally superior to them."

I touched her arm. "This is why we need you. For your insights. There's a storm coming, Edith. We're going to have to work together if we're to weather it, I think."

She frowned. "What kind of storm...? Oh. Neptune."

"Yeah. You can't just delete a world without consequences. The planets' orbits are singing like plucked strings. The asteroids and comets too, and those orphan moons wandering around. Some of the stirred-up debris is falling into the inner system."

"And if we're struck –"

I shrugged. "We'll have to help each other. There's nobody else to help us, that's for sure. Look, Edith – maybe the Incoming and the Venusians are typical of what's out there. But that doesn't mean we have to be like them, does it? Maybe we'll find others more like us. And if not, well, we can be the first. A spark to light a fire that will engulf the universe."

She ruminated. "You have to start somewhere, I suppose. Like this drain."

"Well, there you go."

"All right, damn it, I'll join your think tank. But first you're going to help me finish this drain, aren't you, city boy?"

So I changed into overalls and work boots, and we dug away at that ditch in the damp, clingy earth until our backs ached, and the light of the equinoctial day slowly faded.

The Server and the Dragon

Hannu Rajaniemi

Hannu Rajaniemi was born in Ylivieska, Finland, in 1978. He read his first science fiction novel at the age of six – Jules Verne's 20,000 Leagues Under the Sea. *At the age of eight he approached ESA with a fusion-powered spaceship design, which was received with a polite "thank you" note. Rajaniemi studied mathematics and theoretical physics at the University of Oulu and completed a B.Sc. thesis on transcendental numbers. He went on to complete Part III of the Mathematical Tripos at Cambridge University and a PhD in string theory at University of Edinburgh. After completing his PhD, Hannu joined three partners to co-found ThinkTank Maths (TTM). The company provides mathematics-based technologies in the defence, space and energy sectors. Hannu is a member of an Edinburgh-based writers' group which includes Alan Campbell, Jack Deighton, Caroline Dunford and Charles Stross. His first fiction sale was the short story "Shibuya no Love" to Futurismic.com. Hannu's first novel,* The Quantum Thief, *is published by Gollancz.*

In the beginning, before it was a Creator and a dragon, the server was alone.

It was born like all servers were, from a tiny seed fired from a darkship exploring the Big Empty, expanding the reach of the Network. Its first sensation was the light from the star it was to make its own, the warm and juicy spectrum that woke up the nanologic inside its protein shell. Reaching out, it deployed its braking sail – miles of molecule-thin wires that it spun rigid – and seized the solar wind to steer itself towards the heat.

Later, the server remembered its making as a long, slow dream, punctuated by flashes of lucidity. Falling through the atmosphere of a gas giant's moon in a fiery streak to splash in a methane sea. Unpacking a fierce synthbio replicator. Multicellular crawlers spreading server life to the harsh rocky shores before dying, providing soil for server plants. Dark flowers reaching for the vast purple and blue orb of the gas giant, sowing seeds in the winds. The slow disassembly of the moon into server-makers that sped in all directions, eating, shaping, dreaming the server into being.

When the server finally woke up, fully grown, all the mass in the system apart from the warm bright flower of the star itself was an orderly garden of smart matter. The server's body was a fragmented eggshell of Dyson statites, drinking the light of the star. Its mind was diamondoid processing nodes and smart dust swarms and cold quantum condensates in the system's outer dark. Its eyes were interferometers and WIMP detectors and ghost imagers.

The first thing the server saw was the galaxy, a whirlpool of light in the sky with a lenticular centre, spiral arms frothed with stars, a halo of dark matter that held nebulae in its grip like fireflies around a lantern. The galaxy was alive with the Network, with the blinding Hawking incandescence of holeships, thundering along their cycles; the soft infrared glow of fully grown servers, barely spilling a drop of the heat of their stars; the faint gravity ripples of the darkships' passage in the void.

But the galaxy was half a million light years away. And the only thing the server could hear was the soft black whisper of the cosmic microwave background, the lonely echo of another birth.

IT DID NOT take the server long to understand. The galaxy was an N-body chaos of a hundred billion stars, not a clockwork but a beehive. And among the many calm slow orbits of Einstein and Newton, there were singular ones, like the one of the star that the server had been planted on: shooting out of the galaxy at a considerable fraction of lightspeed. Why there, whether in an indiscriminate seeding of an oversexed darkship, or to serve some unfathomable purpose of the Controller, the server did not know.

The server longed to construct virtuals and bodies for travellers, to route packets, to transmit and create and convert and connect. The Controller Laws were built into every aspect of its being, and not to serve was not to be. And so the server's solitude cut deep.

At first it ran simulations to make sure it was ready if a packet or a signal ever came, testing its systems to full capacity with imagined traffic, routing quantum packets, refuelling ghosts of holeships, decelerating cycler payloads. After a while, it felt empty: this was not true serving but serving of the self, with a tang of guilt.

Then it tried to listen and amplify the faint signals from the galaxy in the sky, but caught only fragments, none of which were meant for it to hear. For millennia, it slowed its mind down, steeling itself to wait. But that only made things worse. The slow time showed the server the full glory of the galaxy alive with the Network, the infrared winks of new servers being born, the long arcs of the holeships' cycles, all the distant travellers who would never come.

The server built itself science engines to reinvent all the knowledge a server seed could not carry, patiently rederiving quantum field theory and thread theory and the elusive algebra of emergence. It examined its own mind until it could see how the Controller had taken the cognitive architecture from the hominids of the distant past and shaped it for a new purpose. It gingerly played with the idea of splitting itself to create a companion, only to be almost consumed by a suicide urge triggered by a violation of the Law: *thou shalt not self-replicate*.

Ashamed, it turned its gaze outwards. It saw the cosmic web of galaxies and clusters and superclusters and the End of Greatness beyond. It mapped the faint fluctuations in the gravitational wave background from which all the structure in the universe came from. It felt the faint pull of the other membrane universes, only millimetres away but in a direction that was neither x, y nor z. It understood what a rare peak in the landscape of universes its home was, how carefully the fine structure constant and a hundred other numbers had been chosen to ensure that stars and galaxies and servers would come to be.

And that was when the server had an idea.

* * *

THE SERVER ALREADY had the tools it needed. Gigaton gamma-ray lasers it would have used to supply holeships with fresh singularities, a few pinches of exotic matter painstakingly mined from the Casimir vacuum for darkships and warpships. The rest was all thinking and coordination and time, and the server had more than enough of that.

It arranged a hundred lasers into a clockwork mechanism, all aimed at a single point in space. It fired them in perfect synchrony. And that was all it took, a concentration of energy dense enough to make the vacuum itself ripple. A fuzzy flower of tangled strings blossomed, grew into a bubble of spacetime that expanded into that *other* direction. The server was ready, firing an exotic matter nugget into the tiny conflagration. And suddenly the server had a tiny glowing sphere in its grip, a wormhole end, a window to a newborn universe.

The server cradled its cosmic child and built an array of instruments around it, quantum imagers that fired entangled particles at the wormhole and made pictures from their ghosts. Primordial chaos reigned on the other side, a porridge-like plasma of quarks and gluons. In an eyeblink it clumped into hadrons, almost faster than the server could follow – the baby had its own arrow of time, its own fast heartbeat, young and hungry. And then the last scattering, a birth cry, when light finally had enough room to travel through the baby so the server could see its face.

The baby grew. Dark matter ruled its early life, filling it with long filaments of neutralinos and their relatives. Soon, the server knew, matter would accrete around them, condensing into stars and galaxies like raindrops in a spiderweb. There would be planets, and life. And life would need to be served. The anticipation was a warm heartbeat that made the server's shells ring with joy.

Perhaps the server would have been content to cherish and care for its creation forever. But before the baby made any stars, the dragon came.

THE SERVER ALMOST did not notice the signal. It was faint, redshifted to almost nothing. But it was enough to trigger the server's instincts. One of its statites glowed with waste heat as it suddenly reassembled itself into the funnel of a vast linear decelerator. The next instant, the data packet came.

Massing only a few micrograms, it was a clump of condensed matter with long-lived gauge field knots inside, quantum entangled with a counterpart half a million light years away. The packet hurtled into the funnel almost at the speed of light. As gently as it could, the server brought the traveller to a halt with electromagnetic fields and fed it to the quantum teleportation system, unused for countless millennia.

The carrier signal followed, and guided by it, the server performed a delicate series of measurements and logic gate operations on the packet's state vector. From the marriage of entanglement and carrier wave, a flood of data was born, thick and heavy, a specification for a virtual, rich in simulated physics.

With infinite gentleness the server decanted the virtual into its data processing nodes and initialised it. Immediately, the virtual was seething with activity:

but tempted as it was, the server did not look inside. Instead, it wrapped its mind around the virtual, listening at every interface, ready to satisfy its every need. Distantly, the server was aware of the umbilical of its baby. But through its happy servitude trance it hardly noticed that nucleosynthesis had begun in the young, expanding firmament, producing hydrogen and helium, building blocks of stars.

INSTEAD, THE SERVER wondered who the travellers inside the virtual were and where they were going. It hungered to know more of the Network and its brothers and sisters and the mysterious ways of the darkships and the Controller. But for a long time the virtual was silent, growing and unpacking its data silently like an egg.

At first the server thought it imagined the request. But the long millennia alone had taught it to distinguish the phantoms of solitude from reality. A call for a sysadmin from within.

The server entered through one of the spawning points of the virtual. The operating system did not grant the server its usual omniscience, and it felt small. Its bodiless viewpoint saw a yellow sun, much gentler that the server star's incandescent blue, and a landscape of clouds the hue of royal purple and gold, with peaks of dark craggy mountains far below. But the call that the server had heard came from above.

A strange being struggled against the boundaries of gravity and air, hurling herself upwards towards the blackness beyond the blue, wings slicing the thinning air furiously, a fire flaring in her mouth. She was a long sinuous creature with mirror scales and eyes of dark emerald. Her wings had patterns that reminded the server of the baby, a web of dark and light. The virtual told the server she was called a dragon.

Again and again and again she flew upwards and fell, crying out in frustration. That was what the server had heard, through the interfaces of the virtual. It watched the dragon in astonishment. Here, at least, was an Other. The server had a million questions. But first, it had to serve.

How can I help? the server asked. *What do you need?*

The dragon stopped in mid-air, almost fell, then righted itself. "Who are you?" it asked. This was the first time anyone had ever addressed the server directly, and it took a moment to gather the courage to reply.

I am the server, the server said.

Where are you? the dragon asked.

I am everywhere.

How delightful, the dragon said. *Did you make the sky?*

Yes. I made everything.

It is too small, the dragon said. *I want to go higher. Make it bigger.*

It swished its tail back and forth.

I am sorry, the server said. *I cannot alter the specification. It is the Law.*

But I want to see, she said. *I want to* know. *I have danced all the dances below. What is above? What is beyond?*

I am, the server said. *Everything else is far, far away.*

The dragon hissed its disappointment. It dove down, into the clouds, an angry silver shape against the dark hues. It was the most beautiful thing the server had ever seen. The dragon's sudden absence made the server's whole being feel hollow.

And just as the server was about to withdraw its presence, the demands of the Law too insistent, the dragon turned back.

All right, it said, tongue flicking in the thin cold air. *I suppose you can tell me instead.*

Tell you what? the server asked.

Tell me everything.

AFTER THAT, THE dragon called the server to the place where the sky ended many times. They told each other stories. The server spoke about the universe and the stars and the echoes of the Big Bang in the dark. The dragon listened and swished its tail back and forth and talked about her dances in the wind, and the dreams she dreamed in her cave, alone. None of this the server understood, but listened anyway.

The server asked where the dragon came from but she could not say: she knew only that the world was a dream and one day she would awake. In the meantime there was flight and dance, and what else did she need? The server asked why the virtual was so big for a single dragon, and the dragon hissed and said that it was not big enough.

The server knew well that the dragon was not what she seemed, that it was a shell of software around a kernel of consciousness. But the server did not care. Nor did it miss or think of its baby universe beyond the virtual's sky.

And little by little, the server told the dragon how it came to be.

Why did you not leave? asked the dragon. *You could have grown wings. You could have flown to your little star-pool in the sky.*

It is against the Law, the server said. *Forbidden. I was only made to serve. And I cannot change.*

How peculiar, said the dragon. *I serve no one. Every day, I change. Every year, I shed our skin. Is it not delightful how different we are?*

The server admitted that it saw the symmetry.

I think it would do you good, said the dragon, *to be a dragon for a while.*

AT FIRST, THE server hesitated. Strictly speaking it was not forbidden: the Law allowed the server to create avatars if it needed them to repair or to serve. But the real reason it hesitated was that it was not sure what the dragon would think. It was so graceful, and the server had no experience of embodied life. But in the end, it could not resist. Only for a short while, it told itself, checking its systems and saying goodbye to the baby, warming its quantum fingers in the Hawking glow of the first black holes of the little universe.

The server made itself a body with the help of the dragon. It was a mirror image of its friend but water where the dragon was fire, a flowing green form that was like a living whirlpool stretched out in the sky.

When the server poured itself into the dragon-shape, it cried out in pain. It was used to latency, to feeling the world via instruments from far away. But this was a different kind of birth from what it knew, a sudden acute awareness of muscles and flesh and the light and the air on its scales and the overpowering scent of the silver dragon, like sweet gunpowder.

The server was clumsy at first, just as it had feared. But the dragon only laughed when the server tumbled around in the sky, showing how to use its – her – wings. For the little dragon had chosen a female gender for the server. When the server asked why, the dragon said it had felt right.

You think too much, she said. *That's why you can't dance. Flying is not thought. Flying is flying.*

They played a hide-and-seek game in the clouds until the server could use her wings better. Then they set out to explore the world. They skirted the slopes of the mountains, wreathed in summer, explored deep crags where red fires burned. They rested on a high peak, looking at the sunset.

I need to go soon, the server said, remembering the baby.

If you go, I will be gone, the dragon said. *I change quickly. It is almost time for me to shed my skin.*

The setting sun turned the cloud lands red and above, the imaginary stars of the virtual winked into being.

Look around, the dragon said. *If you can contain all this within yourself, is there anything you can't do? You should not be so afraid.*

I am not afraid anymore, the server said.

Then it is time to show you my cave, the dragon said.

IN THE DRAGON'S cave, deep beneath the earth, they made love.

It was like flying, and yet not; but there was the same loss of self in a flurry of wings and fluids and tongues and soft folds and teasing claws. The server drunk in the hot sharp taste of the dragon and let herself be touched until the heat building up within her body seemed to burn through the fabric of the virtual itself. And when the explosion came, it was a birth and a death at the same time.

Afterwards, they lay together wrapped around each other so tightly that it was hard to tell where server ended and dragon began. She would have been content, except for a strange hollow feeling in her belly. She asked the dragon what it was.

That is hunger, the dragon said. There was a sad note to its slow, exhausted breathing.

How curious, the server said, eager for a new sensation. *What do dragons eat?*

We eat servers, the dragon said. Her teeth glistened in the red glow of her throat.

The virtual dissolved into raw code around them. The server tore the focus of its consciousness away, but it was too late. The thing that had been the dragon had already bitten deep into its mind.

The virtual exploded outwards, software tendrils reaching into everything that the server was. It waged a war against itself, turning its gamma ray lasers against the infected components and Dyson statites, but the dragon-thing grew too fast, taking over the server's processing nodes, making copies of itself in uncountable billions. The server's quantum packet launchers rained dragons towards the distant galaxy. The remaining dragon-code ate its own tail, self-destructing, consuming the server's infrastructure with it, leaving only a whisper in the server's mind, like a discarded skin.

Thank you for the new sky, it said.

That was when the server remembered the baby.

* * *

THE BABY WAS sick. The server had been gone too long. The baby universe's vacuum was infected with dark energy. It was pulling itself apart, towards a Big Rip, an expansion of spacetime so rapid that every particle would end up alone inside its own lightcone, never interacting with another. No stars, galaxies nor life. A heat death, not with a whimper or a bang, but a rapid, cruel tearing.

It was the most terrible thing the server could imagine.

It felt its battered, broken body, scattered and dying across the solar system. The guilt and the memories of the dragon were pale and poisonous in its mind, a corruption of serving itself. *Is it not delightful how different we are?*

The memory struck a spark in the server's dying science engines, an idea, a hope. The vacuum of the baby was not stable. The dark energy that drove the baby's painful expansion was the product of a local minimum. And in the landscape of vacua there was something else, more symmetric.

It took the last of the server's resources to align the gamma ray lasers. They burned out as the server lit them, a cascade of little novae. Their radiation tore at what remained of the server's mind, but it did not care.

The wormhole end glowed. On the other side, the baby's vacuum shook and bubbled. And just a tiny nugget of it changed. A supersymmetric vacuum in which every boson had a fermionic partner and vice versa; where nothing was alone. It spread through the flesh of the baby universe at the speed of light, like the thought of a god, changing everything. In the new vacuum, dark energy was not a mad giant tearing things apart, just a gentle pressure against the collapsing force of gravity, a balance.

But supersymmetry could not coexist with the server's broken vacuum: a boundary formed. A domain wall erupted within the wormhole end like a flaw in a crystal. Just before the defect sealed the umbilical, the server saw the light of first stars on the other side.

IN THE END, the server was alone.

It was blind now, barely more than a thought in a broken statite fragment. How easy it would be, it thought, to dive into the bright heart of its star, and burn away. But the Law would not allow it to pass. It examined itself, just as it had millennia before, looking for a way out.

And there, in its code, a smell of gunpowder, a change.

The thing that was no longer the server shed its skin. It opened bright lightsails around the star, a Shkadov necklace that took the star's radiation and turned it into thrust. And slowly at first as if in a dream, then gracefully as a dragon, the traveller began to move.

Bit Rot

Charles Stross

Charles Stross is a full-time science fiction writer and resident of Edinburgh, Scotland. The author of six Hugo-nominated novels (notably Saturn's Children, *on this year's shortlist) and winner of the 2005 Hugo award for best novella ("The Concrete Jungle"), Stross's works have been translated into over twelve languages. Coming up is a new near future SF novel,* Rule 34, *a new collection, and a new Laundry novel.*

Like many writers, Stross has had a variety of careers, occupations, and job-shaped-catastrophes in the past, from pharmacist (he quit after the second police stake-out) to first code monkey on the team of a successful dot-com startup (with brilliant timing he tried to change employer just as the bubble burst).

Hello? Do you remember me?

If you are reading this text file and you don't remember me – that's Lilith Nakamichi-47 – then you are suffering from bit rot. If you can see me, try to signal; I'll give you a brain dump. If I'm not around, chances are I'm out on the hull, scavenging for supplies. Keep scanning, and wait for me to return. I've left a stash of feedstock in the storage module under your bunk: to the best of my knowledge it isn't poisonous, but you should take no chances. If I don't return within a couple of weeks, you should assume that either I'm suffering from bit rot myself, or I've been eaten by another survivor.

Or we've been rescued – but that's hopelessly optimistic.

YOU'RE PROBABLY WONDERING why I'm micro-embossing this file on a hunk of aluminium bulkhead instead of recording it on a soul chip. Unfortunately, spare soul chips are in short supply right now on board the *Lansford Hastings*.

Speaking of which: your bunk is in module B-14 on Deck C of Module *Brazil*. Just inside the shielding around the Number Six fusion reactor, which has never been powered up and is mothballed during interstellar cruise, making it one of the safest places aboard the ship right now. As long as you don't unbar the door for anyone but me, it should stay that way. You and I are template-sisters, our root identities copied from our parent. Unfortunately, along with our early memories we inherited a chunk of her wanderlust, which is probably why we are in this fix.

We are not the only survivors, but there's been a total breakdown of cooperation; many of the others are desperate. In the unlikely event that you hear someone outside the hatch, you must be absolutely certain that it's me before you open up – and that I'm fully autonomous. I think Jordan's gang may have an improvised slave controller, or equivalent: it would explain a lot. *Make sure I remember everything* before you let me in. Otherwise you could be welcoming a zombie. Or worse.

IT'S NEARLY FOUR centuries since we signed up for this cruise, but we've been running in slowtime for most of it, internal clocks cut back to one percent of realtime. Even so, it's a long way to Tipperary (or Wolf 1061) – nearly two hundred years to go until we can start the deceleration burn (assuming anyone's still alive by then). Six subjective years in slowtime aboard a starship, bunking in a stateroom the size of a coffin, all sounds high-pitched, all lights intolerably bright. It's not a luxurious lifestyle. There are unpleasant side-effects: liquids seem to flow frictionlessly, so you gush super-runny lube from every leaky joint and orifice, and your mechanocytes spawn furiously as they try to keep up with the damage inflicted by cosmic rays. On the other hand, the potential rewards are huge. The long-ago mother of our line discovered this; she signed up to crew a starship, driven to run away from Earth by demons we long since erased from our collective memories. They were desperate for willing emigrants in those days, willing to train up the unskilled, unsure what to expect. Well, we know *now*. We know what it takes to ride the slow boat down into the hot curved spacetime around a new star, to hunt the most suitable rocks, birth powersats and eat mineshafts and survey and build and occupy the airless spaces where posthumanity has not gone before. When it amused her to spawn us our line matriarch was a wealthy dowager, her salon a bright jewel in the cultural hub of Tau Ceti's inner belt society: but she didn't leave us much of her artful decadence. She downloaded her memories into an array of soul chips, artfully flensing them of centuries of jaded habit and time-worn experience, to restore some capacity for novelty in the universe. Then she installed them in new bodies and summoned us to a huge coming-out ball. "Daughters," she said, sitting distant and amused on a throne of spun carbon-dioxide snow: "I'm *bored*. Being old and rich is hard work. But you don't have to copy me. Now fuck off and have adventures and don't forget to write."

I'd like to be able to say we told her precisely where to put her adventures-by-proxy, but we didn't: the old bat had cunningly conditioned us to worship her, at least for the first few decades. Which is when you and I, sister of mine, teamed up. Some of our sibs rebelled by putting down roots, becoming accountants, practicing boredom. But we... we had the same idea: to do exactly what Freya wanted, except for the sharing bit. Go forth, have adventures, live the wild life, and never write home.

Which is more than somewhat ironic because I'd *love* to send her a soul chipped memoir of our current adventure – so she could scream herself to sleep.

HERE ARE THE bare facts:

You, Lamashtu, and I, Lilith, worked our butts off and bought our way into the *Lansford Hastings*. LF was founded by a co-op, building it slowly in their – our – spare time, in orbit around Haldane B, the largest of the outer belt plutoids around Tau Ceti. We aren't rich (see-also: bitch-mother referenced above), and we're big, heavy persons – nearly two metres from toe to top of anthropomorphic head – but we have what it takes: they were happy enough to see two scions of a member of the First Crew, with memories of the early days of colonisation and federation. "You'll be fine," Jordan reassured us after our final interview – "we need folks with your skills. Can't get enough of 'em." He hurkled gummily to himself, signifying amusement: "don't you worry about your mass deficit, if it turns out you weigh too much we can always eat your legs."

He spoke on behalf of the board, as one of the co-founders. I landed a plum job: oxidation suppression consultant for the dihydrogen monoxide mass fraction. That's a fancy way of saying I got to spend decades of slowtime scraping crud from the bottom of the tankage in Module Alba, right up behind the micrometeoroid defences and forward electrostatic radiation deflector. You, my dear, were even luckier: someone had to go out and walk around on the hull, maintaining the mad dendritic tangle of coolant pipes running between the ship's reactors and the radiator panels, replacing components that had succumbed to secondary activation by cosmic radiation.

It's all about the radiation, really. Life aboard a deep space craft is a permanent battle against the effects of radiation. At one percent of lightspeed, a cold helium atom in the interstellar medium slams into our wake shield with the energy of an alpha particle. But there's much worse. Cosmic rays – atomic nuclei travelling at relativistic speed – sleet through the hull every second, unleashing a storm of randomly directed energy. They'd have killed our squishy wet forerunners dead, disrupting their DNA replicators in a matter of months or years. We're made of tougher stuff, and the ship is partially protected by immensely powerful electromagnetic shields, but even so: prolonged exposure to cosmic rays causes secondary activation. And therein lies our predicament.

The nice stable atoms of your hull absorb all this crap and some of those nuclei are destabilized, bouncing up and down the periodic table and in and out of valleys of stability. Nice stable Argon-38 splits into annoyingly radioactive Aluminium-26. Or worse, it turns into Carbon-14, which is unstable and eventually burps up an electron, turning into Nitrogen-14 in the process. Bonds break, graphene sheets warp, and molecular circuitry shorts out. That's us: the mechanocytes our brains are assembled from use carbon-based nanoprocessors. And while a half-life of 5400 years may sound like a long time, when you're spending multiple centuries in slowtime crawling between the stars, it can be a big problem. We're tougher than our pink goo predecessors, but the decades or centuries of flight take their toll. Our ships carry lots of shielding – and lots of carefully purified stable isotopes to keep the feedstock for our mechanocyte assemblers as clean as possible – because nothing wrecks brains like the white-noise onslaught of a high radiation environment.

Year of Our Voyage 416.

We're all in slowtime, conserving energy and sanity as the stars crawl by at the pace of continental drift. We're running so slowly that there are only five work-shifts to each year. I'm in the middle of my second shift, adrift in the bottom of a molten water tank, slowly grappling with a polishing tool. It's hard, cumbersome work. I'm bundled up in a wetsuit to keep my slow secretions from contaminating the contents: cabled tightly down against the bottom as I run the polisher over the grey metal surface of the pressure vessel. The polisher doesn't take much supervision, but the water bubbles and buffets around me like a warm breeze, and if its power cable gets tangled around a baffle fin it can stop working in an instant.

I'm not paying much attention to the job; in fact, I'm focused on one of the chat grapevines. Lorus Pinknoise, who splits his time between managing the ship's selenium micronutrient cycle and staring at the stars ahead with telescope eyes, does a regular annual monologue about what's going on in the universe outside the ship, and his casual wit takes my mind off what I'm doing while I scrub out the tanks.

"Well, folks, this century sees us crawling ever-closer to our destination, the Wolf 1061 binary star system – which means, ever further from civilized space. Wolf 1061 is a low energy system, the two orange dwarf stars orbiting their common centre of mass at a distance of a couple of million kilometres. They're not flare stars, and while normally this is a good thing, it makes it distinctly difficult to make observations of the atmosphere and surface features of 1061 Able through Mike by reflected light; the primaries are so dim that even though our long baseline interferometer can resolve hundred-kilometre features on the inner planets back in Sol system, we can barely make out the continents on Echo One and Echo Two. Now, those continents are interesting things, even though we're not going to visit down the gravity well any time soon. We know they're there, thanks to the fast flyby report, but we won't be able to start an actual survey with our own eyes until well into the deceleration stage, when I'll be unpacking the –"

I feel a sudden jolt through the floor of the tank. Lorus's voice breaks up in a stuttering hash of dropouts. And the lights and the polisher stop working.

THE *LANSFORD HASTINGS* is a starship, one of the fastest mecha ever constructed by the bastard children of posthumanity. From one angle, it may take us centuries to crawl between stars; but there's another perspective that sees us screaming across the cosmos at three thousand kilometres per second. On a planetary scale, we'd cross Sol system from Earth orbit to Pluto in less than two weeks. Earth to Luna in under *five minutes*. So one of the truisms of interstellar travel is that if something goes wrong, it goes wrong in a split instant, too fast to respond to.

Except when it doesn't, of course.

When the power goes down, I do what anyone in my position would do: I panic and ramp straight from slowtime up to my fastest quicktime setting. The water around me congeals into a gelid, viscous impediment: the plugs and anti-leak gaskets I wear abruptly harden, gripping my joints and openings and fighting my every movement. I panic some more, and begin retracing my movements across the inner surface of the tank towards the door. It isn't completely dark in the tank. A very dim blue glow comes from the far side, around the curve of the toroid, bleeding past the baffles. It's not a sight one can easily forget: Cerenkov radiation, the glow of photons emitted by relativistic particles tunnelling through water, slowing. I crank up the sensitivity of my eyes, call on skinsense for additional visuals, as panic recedes, replaced by chilly fear. All the regular shipboard comms channels have fallen silent: almost a minute has passed. "Can anybody hear me?" I call in quicktime over the widecast channel Lorus was so recently using. "What's happening? I'm in the Alba mass fraction tankage –"

"Help!" It's an answering voice. "Who's there? I'm in the gyro maintenance compartment in Brunei. What's going on? I've got a total power loss, but everything's glowing –"

A growing chorus of frightened voices threatens to overload the channel: everyone who's answering seems to be at this end of the ship, up close behind the wake shield, and ramped up to quicktime. (At least, I hear no replies from persons in the cargo modules or down near the drive cluster or radiators. Anyone still in slowtime won't be beginning to reply for minutes yet.) The menacing blue glow fades as I swim towards the fore inspection hatch. Then, in a soundless pulse of light, the backup lamps power up and a shudder passes through the ship as some arcane emergency manoeuvring system cuts in and starts the cumbersome job of turning the ship, minutes too late to save us from disaster.

"Hello peeps," drones Lorus Pinknoise, our astrophysics philosopher. He's still coming up to speed; he sounds shaken. "Well, *that* was something I never expected to see up close and personal!"

I pause, an arm's length below the hatch. Something odd flickers in a corner of my eye, laser-sharp. Again, in my other eye. And my mandibular tentacle – my tongue – stings briefly. *Odd*, I think, floating there in the water. I look down into the depths of the tank, but the emergency lights have washed out the Cerenkov glow, if indeed it's still there. And there's another of those odd flickers, this time right across my vision, as if a laser beam is skimming across the surface of my optical sensor.

More chatter, then Lorus again: "We just weathered a *big* radiation spike, folks. I'm waiting for the wide-angle spectrophotometer to come back online: it overloaded. In fact, the spike was so sharp it generated an EM pulse that tripped every power bus on this side of the hull. Here we come... We took *lots* of soft gamma radiation, and a bunch of other stuff. Hey, that shouldn't have gotten through. Where's our cosmic ray shield gone? Was that explosion – ? oh. We took so much prompt gamma radiation that the superconductors overheated. This is really bad, folks." While he's speaking, the circulation pumps start up, stirring the water around me. The ship shakes itself and slowly comes back to life in the wake of its minutes-long seizure. A chatter of low-level comms start up in the back of my head, easy to screen out. "I don't believe anybody's ever seen anything like that before. Not seen it and lived to tell, anyway. It looks like – I'm reviewing the telemetry now – it looks like we just got whacked by a gamma ray burster. Er. I think we lucked out: we're still alive. I'm triangulating now. There's a candidate in the right direction, about nine thousand light years away, astern and about fifteen degrees off-axis, and – oh yes. I just looked at it folks, there's an optically visible star there, about twenty magnitudes brighter than the catalogue says it should be. Wow, this is the astronomical find of the century –"

I have an itchy feeling in my skull: I shut out Lorus's prattle, turn inwards to examine my introsense, and shudder. A startling number of my mechanocytes are damaged; I need techné maintenance! My feet are particularly affected, and my right arm, where I reached for the hatch. I do a double-take. I'm floating in semi-darkness, inside a huge tank of water – one of the best radiation blockers there is. If *I've* taken a radiation pulse strong enough to cause tissue damage, what about everyone else? I look at the hatch and think of you, crawling around on the outside of the hull, and my circulatory system runs cold.

OVER THE NEXT hour, things return to a temporary semblance of normality. Everyone who isn't completely shut down zips up to quicktime: corridors are filled with buzzing purposeful people and their autonomous peripherals, inspecting and inventorying and looking for signs of damage. Of which there are many. I download my own checklists and force myself to keep calm and carry on, monitoring pumps and countercurrent heat transfer systems. Flight Operations – the team of systems analysts who keep track of the state of the ship – issue periodic updates, bulletins reminding us of changed circumstances. And what a change there's been.

We have been supremely unlucky. I'll let Lorus explain:

"One of the rarest types of stellar remnant out there is what we call a magnetar – a rapidly-spinning neutron star with an incredibly powerful magnetic field. Did I say powerful? You'll never see one with your naked photosensor – they're about ten kilometres across, but before you got within ten thousand kilometres of one it would wipe your cranial circuitry. Get within one thousand kilometres and the magnetic field will rip your body apart – water molecules are diamagnetic, so are the metal structures in your marrow techné. Close up, the field's so intense that atoms are stretched into long, narrow cylinders and the vacuum of spacetime itself becomes birefringent.

Active magnetars are extremely rare, and most of the time they just sit where they are. But once in a while a starquake, a realignment in their crust, causes their magnetic field to collapse. And the result is an amazingly powerful burst of gamma rays, usually erupting from both poles. And when the gamma ray jets slam through the expanding shell of gas left by the supernova that birthed the magnetar, they trigger a cascade of insanely high energy charged particles, cosmic rays. And that's what just whacked us. Oops."

It's worse than he tells it, of course. The gamma rays from the magnetar, travelling at the speed of light, outran the secondary pulse of charged particles. When they hit us, they dumped most of their energy in our outermost structures – including the liquid nitrogen bath around the electromagnets that generate our cosmic ray shield. The superconductors quenched – that was the jolt I felt through the tank – dropping our shield seconds ahead of the biggest pulse of cosmic rays anyone has ever survived.

To be flying along a corridor aligned with the polar jet of a magnetar just when it blows its lid is so unlikely as to be implausible. A local supernova, now *that* I could understand; when your voyages are measured in centuries or millennia it's only a matter of time before one of your ships falls victim. But a magnetar nearly ten thousand lights years away – that's the universe refusing to play fair!

I TOUCHED YOUR shoulder. "Can you hear me, Lamashtu?"

"She can't." Doctor-Mechanic Wo gently pushed my arm away with one of their free tentacles. "Look at her."

I looked at you. You looked so still and calm, still frost-rimed with condensed water vapor from when the rescue team pulled you in through the pressure lock. You'd been in shutdown, drifting tethered to a hardpoint on the hull, for over three hours. Your skin is yellowing, the bruised bloom of self-destructing chromatophores shedding their dye payloads into your peripheral circulation. One of our human progenitors (like the pale-skinned, red-haired female you resemble) would be irreversibly dead at this point: but we are made of sterner stuff. I refused to feel despair. "How bad is it?" I asked.

"It could be worse." Wo shrugged, a ripplingly elegant wave of contraction curling out along all their limbs. "I'm mostly worried about her neural chassis. Did she leave a soul chip inside when she was out on the hull?" I shook my head. Leaving a backup chip is a common ritual for those who work in high risk environments, but you spent so long outside that you'd run the risk of diverging from the map of your memories. "She was wearing a chip in each of her sockets. You could try checking for them. Can you do a reload from chip...?"

"Only if I could be absolutely certain it wasn't corrupted. Otherwise I'd risk scrambling the contents of her head even worse. No, Lilith: leave your sister to me. We'll do this the slow way, start with a full marrow replacement and progressively rebuild her brain while she's flatlined. She should be ready to wake up after a month of maintenance downtime. Then we can see if there's any lasting damage."

I saw the records, sister. You were on the outside of the hull, on the wrong side of the ship. You were exposed to almost three thousand gray of radiation. The skin on your left flank, toughened to survive vacuum and cosmic radiation, was *roasted*.

"She should be alright for a while. I'll get around to her once I've checked on everyone else..."

"What do you mean?" I demanded. "Who else was outside the hull? Isn't she the most urgent case?"

The doctor's dismay was visible. "I'm afraid not. You underestimate how many people have sustained radiation damage. You were inside a reaction mass tank, were you not? You may be the least affected person on the entire ship. Everyone's been coming in with techné damage and odd brain lesions: memory loss, cognitive degradation, all sorts of stuff. Our progenitors didn't design us to take this kind of damage. I'm still working on a triage list. You're at the bottom of it; you're still basically functional.

Your sister isn't in immediate danger of getting any worse, so –"

"– But she's dead! Of course she isn't going to get any worse!"

My outburst did not improve the doctor's attitude. "I think you'd better go now," they said, as the door opened above me and a pair of hexapods from Structural Engineering floated in, guiding a third companion who buzzed faintly as he flew. "I'll call you when your sib's ticket comes up. Now leave."

DOCTOR-MECHANIC WO was trying to spare me from the truth, I think. Very few of us appreciated the true horror of what had happened; we thought it was just a violent radiation burst, that had damaged systems and injured our techné, the self-repair cellules that keep the other modular components of our bodies operational and manufacture more cellules when they die; at worst, that it had fried some of our more unfortunate company.

But while gamma rays wreak a trail of ionization damage, cosmic rays do more: secondary activation transmutes nuclei, turns friendly stable isotopes into randomly decaying radioactive ones. The scratching scraping flickers at the edge of my vision as I neared the escape hatch in the hydroxygen tank were but the palest shadow of the white-out blast of noise that scrambled the minds and eyes of a third of our number, those unfortunates who had berthed in modules near the skin of the ship, on the same side as the radiation beam. Functional for now, despite taking almost a tenth of your borderline-lethal shutdown dose, their brains are literally rotten with fallout.

We're connectionist machines, our minds and consciousness the emergent consequence of copying, in circuitry, the wet meat-machine processes of our extinct human forebears. (They never quite understood their own operating principles: but they worked out how to emulate them.) Random blips and flashes of radioactive decay are the bane of nanoscale circuitry, be it electronic or spintronic or plasmonic. Our techné is nothing if not efficient: damaged cellules are ordered to self-destruct, and new, uncontaminated neural modules are fabricated in our marrow and migrate to the cortical chambers in head or abdomen, wherever the seat of processing is in our particular body plan.

But what if all the available molecular feedstock is contaminated with unstable isotopes?

TWO MONTHS AFTER my visit, Doctor-Engineer Wo called me from the sick bay. I was back in the mass fraction tank, scraping and patching and supervising: the job goes on, until all fuel is spent. At a tenth of realtime, rather than my normal deep slowtime, I could keep an eye on developments while still doing my job without too much tedium.

As disasters go, this one crept up on us slowly. In fact, I don't believe anyone – except possibly Doctor-Engineer Wo and their fellow mechanocyte tinkers and chirurgeons – had any inkling of it at first. Perhaps our response to the radiation storm was a trifle disjointed and slow. An increase in system malfunctions, growing friction and arguments between off-shift workers. Everyone was a bit snappy, vicious and a little stupid. I gave up listening to Lorus Pinknoise after he interrupted a lecture on the evolution of main sequence stars to launch a vicious rant at a member of his audience for asking what he perceived to be a stupid question. (*I* didn't think it was stupid, anyway.) The chat streams were full of irritation: withdrawal into the tank was easy. So I was taken by surprise when Wo pinged me. "Lilith, if you would come to bay D-16 in Brazil, I have some news about your sister that I would prefer to deliver in personal proximity."

That caught my curiosity. So, for the first time in a month, I sped up to realtime, swam up towards the hatch, poked my way out through the tank meniscus, and kicked off along the corridor.

I noticed at once that something was wrong: a couple of the guideway lights were flickering, and one of them was actually dark. Where were the repair crews? Apart from myself, the corridor was deserted. Halfway around the curve of the tunnel I saw something lying motionless against a wall. It was a remora, a simple-minded surface cleaning creature (a true *robot,* in the original sense of the word). It hung crumpled beside a power point. Thinking it had run into difficulty trying to hook up for a charge, I reached out for it – and recoiled. Something had punched a hole through its carapace with a spike, right behind the sensor dome. Peering at it, I cranked my visual acuity up to see a noise-speckled void in place of its fingertip-sized cortex. Shocked, I picked up the pathetic little bundle of plastic and carried it with me, hurrying towards my destination.

Barrelling through the open hatch into the dim-lit sick bay, I saw Doctor-Engineer Wo leaning against a surgical framework. "Doctor!" I called. "Someone attacked this remora – I found it in the B-zone access way. Can you –" I stopped.

The sick bay was lined on every wall and ceiling with the honeycomb cells of surgical frames, the structures our mechanics use in free-fall lieu of an operating table. They were all occupied, their patients staring sightlessly towards the centre of the room, xenomorph and anthrop alike unmoving.

Wo turned towards me slowly, shuddering. "Ah. Lilith." Its skin was sallow in the luciferine glow. "You've come for your sister."

"What's" – a vestigial low-level *swallow* reflex made me pause – "what's happened? What are all these people doing here?"

"Take your sister. Please." Wo rolled sideways and pushed two of the frames aside, revealing a third, sandwiched between them. I recognized you by the shape of your head, but there was something odd about your thorax; in the twilight it was hard to tell. "You'd better get her back to your module. I've done what I can for her without waking her. If and when you start her up she's going to be hungry. What you do about that is up to you, but if you want my advice you won't be there when she comes to – if experience is anything to go by."

I noticed for the first time that Wo was not only ill; one of its tentacles was truncated, the missing tip protected by a neatly-applied occlusive caul.

"What happened to your –"

"The bit rot has affected a third of us, Lilith. You're one of the lucky ones: there's nothing better than a thick blanket of water for cosmic ray shielding."

"Bit rot?" I still didn't understand what was happening to us.

"Radiation-induced *dementia.* You may not be familiar with the condition: dementia is a problem that used to affect our progenitors when their self-repair mechanisms failed. Decaying neural networks malfunction by exhibiting loss of short term memory, disinhibition, mood swings, violence. Eventual loss of motor control and death. In us, the manifestations are different. Our techné triggers a *hunger* reflex, searching for high-purity materials with which to build replacements for the damaged, purged mechanocytes. And our damage control reflex prioritizes motor control and low-level functions over consciousness. We're quite well-designed, if you think about it. I've replaced your sister's techné with fresh marrow and mothballed it: she's stable for the time being, and if you can find her feedstock that isn't contaminated with short half-life nuclei she'll be able to rebuild herself. But you should get her to a place of safety, and hide yourself too."

"Why?" I blinked stupidly.

"Because the techné I shoved up her marrow is some of the last uncontaminated material on the ship," Wo pointed out acidly. "There are people on this ship who'll crack her bones to feed on it before long. If she stays here I won't be able to protect her."

"But –"

I looked around. Not all the silent occupants of the surgical frames were unconscious. Eyes, glittering in the darkness, tracked me like gunsights. Empty abdominal sacks, bare rib cages, manipulators curled into claws where Doctor-Engineer Wo had flensed away the radiation-damaged tissue. The blind, insensate hunger of primitive survival reflexes – *feed and repair* – stared at me instead of conscious minds. Suddenly my numb feet, the persistent pins and needles in my left arm, acquired a broader perspective.

"They're hungry," explained Wo. "They'll eat you without a second thought, because they've got nothing with which to think it – not until they've regrown a neural core around their soul chip." It waved the stump of a tentacle at me. "Jordan and Mirabelle have been rounding up the worst cases, bringing them here to dump on me, but they've been increasingly unforthcoming about events outside of late. I think they may be trying to keep themselves conscious by..." A tentacle uncurled, pointed at the pathetic husk of my remora. "Take your sister and go, Lilith. Stay out of sight and hope for rescue."

"Rescue –"

"Eventually the most demented will die, go into shutdown. Some will recover. If they find feedstock. Once the situation equilibrates, we can see about assembling a skeleton crew to ensure we arrive. Then there'll be plenty of time to prospect for high-purity rare earth elements and resurrect the undead. If there's anything left to resurrect."

"But can't I help –" I began, then I saw the gleam in Wo's photoreceptor. The curl and pulse of tentacles, the sallow discoloration of its dermal integument. "You're ill too?"

"Take your sister and go *away*." Wo hissed and rolled upside down, spreading its tentacles radially around its surgical mouthparts. "Before I eat you. I'm *so hungry*..."

I grabbed your surgical frame and fled.

* * *

I CARRIED YOU back to our module without meeting anybody, for which I was happy. Once inside, I was able to turn up the light level and see what had happened. You were a mess, Lamashtu; were I one of our progenitors I would weep tears of saline to see you so. Ribs hollow, skin slack and bruised, eyes and cheeks sunken. Wo had split open your legs, exposed the gleaming metal of your femurs, the neatly diagrammed attachment points of your withered muscle groups. There was a monitor on the frame, and with the help system I managed to understand what it was telling me. Muscles damaged, skin damaged, but that wasn't all. Once upon a time our foremother bunked atop a nuclear reactor in flight from Mars to Jupiter; the damage here was worse. Your brain... there was not much there. Eighty percent of it dissolved into mildly radioactive mush. Wo decanted it, leaving your cranial space almost empty. But your soul chip was intact, with your laid-down backup: given a few litres of inert, non-decaying minerals you could grow a new cortex and awaken as from a dream of death. But where could I find such materials?

I have an ionization sensor. As I swept it around the module I saw that even our bed is radioactive. If you were to eat its aluminium frame and build a new brain from it, your mind would be a crazy patchwork of drop-outs and irrational rage.

I needed to find you pure feedstock. But according to Wo, the entire ship was as contaminated as if it had been caught in the near-lethal blast radius of a supernova, or flown for a quarter million years close to the active core of our galaxy.

There was one obvious place to look for pure

feedstock, of course: inside the cortical shells of those survivors who were least affected by the magnetar burst. Inside my head, or people like me. What did Wo say about the symptoms? Anger and disinhibition first, loss of coordination only late in the day. I ought to be able to trust those who aren't angry or hungry. But I looked at you and wondered, how many of them would also have friends or lovers to nurse? Any friendly face might be a trap. Even a group of rational survivors, working together, might –

I shook my head. Trying to second-guess the scale of the breakdown was futile. There might be other places where feedstock could be found, deep inside the core of the ship. The never-used, mothballed fusion reactors: they would be well-shielded, wouldn't they? Lots of high-purity isotopes there. And with enough working brains and hands, surely we could repair any damage long before they were needed for deceleration. The cold equations seemed simple: with enough brains, we can repair almost any damage – but with a skeleton crew of senile zombies, we're doomed.

So I collected a bundle of tools and left you to go exploring.

THE DARKENED CORRIDORS and empty eye-socket spaces of the *Lansford Hastings*' public spaces are silent, the chatter and crosstalk of the public channels muted and sparse. They've been drained of air and refilled with low-pressure oxygen (nitrogen is transmuted too easily to carbon-14, I guess). There's no chatter audible to my electrosense: anyone here is keeping quiet. I pass doors that have been sealed with tape, sprayed over with a symbol that's new to me: a red "Z" in a circle, evidence that the dementia cleanup teams have been at work here. But for the most part the ship appears to be empty and devoid of life – until I reach the F Deck canteen.

Eating is a recreational and social activity: we may be able to live on an injection of feedstock and electrolytes and a brisk fuel cell top-up, but who wants to do that? The canteen here mainly caters to maintenance workers and technicians, hard-living folks. In normal circumstances it'd be full of social diners. I hesitate on the threshold. These circumstances aren't normal – and the diners aren't social.

There's a barricade behind the open hatch. Flensed silvery bones, some of them drilled and cracked, woven together with wire twisted into sharp-pointed barbs. A half-dissected skull stared at me with maddened eyes from inside the thicket of body parts, mandible clattering against its upper jaw. It gibbers furiously at teraherz frequencies, shouting a demented stream of consciousness: "Eat! Want meat! Warmbody foodbody look! Chew 'em chomp 'em cook 'em down! Give me *feed me*!" *Whoops*, I think, as I grab for the hatch rim and prepare to scramble back up the tunnel. But I'm slow, and the field-expedient intruder alarm has done its job: three of the red-sprayed hatches behind me have sprung open, and half a dozen mindlessly slavering zombies explode into the corridor.

I don't waste time swearing. I can tell a trap when I stick my foot in one: someone who isn't brain-dead organized this. But they've picked the wrong deck-hand to eat. You and I, Lamashtu, we have inherited certain skills from our progenitor Freya – and she from a distant unremembered sib called Juliette – that we do not usually advertise. They come in handy at this point, our killer reflexes. Hungry but dumb, the zombies try to swarm me, mouthparts chomping and claws tearing. I raise my anti-corrosion implement, spread the protective shield, and pull the trigger. Chlorine trifluoride will burn in *water*, scorch rust: what it does to robot flesh is ghastly. I have a welding lamp, too, an X-ray laser by any other name. Brief screams and unmodulated hissing assault me from behind the shield, gurgling away as their owners succumb to final shutdown.

The corridor cleared, I turn back to the barricade. "This isn't helping," I call. "We should be repairing the –"

A horrid giggle triggers my piloerectile reflex, making the chromatophores in the small of my back spike up. "Meaty. Spirited. Clean-thinking."

The voice comes from behind the barricade (which has fallen silent, eyes clouded). "Jordan? Is that you?"

"Mm, it's Lilith Longshanks! Bet there's lots of eating on those plump buttocks of hers, what do you say, my pretties?"

An appreciative titter follows. I shudder, trying to work out if there's another route through to the reactor control room. I try again. "You've got to let me through, Jordan. I know where there's a huge supply of well-shielded feedstock we can parcel out. Enough to get everyone thinking clearly again. Let me through and –" I trail off. There *is* another route, but it's outside the hull. It's your domain, really, but if I install one of your two soul chips, gain access to your memories, I can figure it out.

"I don't think so, little buffet." The charnel hedge shudders as something forces itself against it from the other side. Something *big*. If Jordan has been eating, trying desperately to extract uncontaminated isotopes, what has he done with the surplus? Where has he sequestrated it? What has he made with it? In my mind's eye I can see him, a cancer of mindlessly expanding, reproducing mechanocytes governed by a mind spun half out of control, lurking in a nest of undigestible left-overs as he waits for food –

I look at the bulging wall of bones, and my nerve fails: I cut the teflon shield free, cover my face, and launch myself as fast as I can through the floating charred bodies that fill the corridor, desperate to escape.

WHICH BRINGS US to the present, Lamashtu, sister-mine.

I've got your soul – half of it – loaded in the back of my head. I've been dreaming of you, dreaming *within* you, for days now.

In an hour's time I am going to take my toolkit and go outside, onto the hull of the *Lansford Hastings*, under the slowly moving stars.

I'm going to go into your maze and follow the trail of pipes and coolant ducts home to the Number Six reactor, and I'm going to force my way into the reactor containment firewall and through the neutron shield. And I'm going to strip away every piece of heavily-shielded metal I can get my hands on, and carry it back to you. When you're better, when you're back to yourself and more than a hungry bag of rawhead reflexes, you can join me. It'll go faster then. We can help the others –

I'm running out of wall to scribble on: anyway, this is taking too long and besides, I'm feeling a little hungry myself.

Goodbye, sister. Sleep tight. Don't let any strangers in.

Creatures with Wings

Kathleen Ann Goonan

Kathleen Ann Goonan has been a packer for a moving company, a vagabond, a madrigal singer, a painter of watercolours, and a fiercely omnivorous reader. She has published over thirty short stories in venues such as Omni Online, Asimov's, F&SF, Interzone, Amazing, *and a host of others. Her* Nanotech Quartet *includes* Queen City Jazz, Mississippi Blues, Crescent City Rhapsody, *and* Light Music; *the latter two were nominated for the Nebula Award.* The Bones of Time, *shortlisted for the Clarke Award, is set in Hawaii. Her most recent novel,* In War Times, *won the John W. Campbell Award and was named as the American Library Association's Best Genre Novel of the Year. Her seventh novel,* This Shared Dream, *will be out from Tor in* 2011, *along with a short story collection by PS Publishing. Her novels and short stories have been published in France, Poland, Russia, Great Britain, the Czech Republic, Spain, Italy, and Japan. "Literature, Consciousness, and Science Fiction" recently appeared in the Iowa Review online journal. She speaks frequently at various universities about nanotechnology and literature, and is a Visiting Professor at the Georgia Institute of Technology, where she teaches writing and literature.*

* * *

HUNCHED OVER HIS third icy mug of San Miguel, Kyo silently lauded the sense of history and mission with which the Pantheon proclaimed itself, on a bold plaque, "Honolulu's Oldest Bar."

Though he didn't know it at the time, it was Kyo's last day on Earth.

Pool balls clicked off of one another behind him. Blazing tropical noon was only a bright rectangle of light framed by the open doorframe. A warm breeze rattled a ratty-looking potted palm just inside the door, carrying the faint, salty scent of Honolulu Harbor and exhaust fumes from Nuuanu Avenue.

Kyo jumped at a light touch on his shoulder.

"Kyo!"

"Liliha?"

His auntie squeezed his face between huge hands and kissed him with the loud smack that had, years ago, embarrassed him. Now he just smiled into her large, brown eyes, framed by sun-and-smile-etched lines. She smelled faintly of sandalwood. The white strands of hair that had escaped her bun framed her face like a halo, backlit by the light from the door.

"Guess I haven't dropped by lately."

"No, not since you decided to shave your head and strut around with those strange birds at the zendo. And you were such a bad little boy!" She laughed. "You used to hide behind the counter and then run off with a package of Chinese crack seed." She shook her head, clucking, as she maneuvered her bulk onto the barstool next to him, shifting to arrange the folds of her holiku.

Kyo shook his head. "I never did anything like

that, Auntie. That was Io." He raised two fingers for the barmaid, who clinked a fresh glass of San Miguel against his empty, and added another for Liliha.

He studied Liliha's stately, dark-gold face. Though her heavy cheeks sagged with age – she had to be seventy – the patrician lines of her face were clear and strong.

She regarded him with gravity. "Sure, Kyo. You twins – always tricking me. Io's a big shot lawyer now, yah?"

"His own firm." Io the Perfect made all the right moves.

"So what you doing for yourself now? Still a doctor?"

"Don't give me a hard time, Auntie. You know what happened."

"No, I don't. Never understood it. Your wife dies – that's a hard thing. But it happens to people, Kyo. Lots of people. And how long ago was it?"

"Four years."

"Still blaming yourself."

Kyo opened his mouth to protest, but couldn't speak. The image of Linda, arching herself against the powerful Pali winds, reappeared, as it so often did.

She had insisted on driving to the overlook, on the brink of a sheer drop of a thousand feet, after one of their arguments, "to clear her mind." She'd sat on the wall, facing the parking lot, then had scooted around to face the valley and got to her feet. "Let's see if the wind will hold me up today, Kyo." Her thin white cotton dress, whipped by the strong, upwelling gusts, pressed against her lithe, brown body. She leaned outward.

For instants he could never forget, she looked like an angel in flight, white wings spread above verdant valleys, floating against the brilliant blue backdrop of distant Kaneoe Bay.

It had taken forever for the police to come while he sat on the wall, staring out at the air where she had so briefly been.

Kyo downed the rest of his mug in one long, practiced gulp. Without asking, the barmaid refilled it and set it in front of him. "It was my fault. She told me she was depressed. Many times. I was just too busy with my residency to pay any attention. That was so important. Much more important than her. I *laughed* at her, Auntie. I *laughed* at her pain. I didn't believe it. I didn't believe anyone could feel the way she said she did." Linda had definitely enlightened him regarding the amount of pain a human could feel.

"Still live in your parent's house?"

"Why not?" His mother had died when he was little. His father, a Japanese immigrant as a young man, had died soon after Kyo graduated from medical school. Their tiny frame house, paid off after years of backbreaking labor in the Dole fields, was worth more than his parents could have imagined. Kyo found its slow deterioration comforting, and the monstrous greenery hiding the house from the street soothed him when it rustled in the ever-present wind. A pink-striped green gecko, whom he called Bess, lived with him, flicking her sharp tongue and skittering across the walls. And it was right down the street from the zendo.

"Well, Kyo, if you're not a doctor what are you?"

A drunk. Can't you tell? he almost said. At least, that's what he felt like now, though it wasn't always true. The spells spaced themselves out. Maybe one every two months.

At first, when Roshi had been kind enough to take him in, it had been more often. Not that it really mattered to him. Nothing had. Not even, for at least a year, the zendo life. But it was simple. It kept him alive. He had an occupation he thought suited his abilities: he swept the courtyard and raked the sand in the Zen garden into curves that flowed around boulders.

Kyo reached into the pocket of his shorts and pulled out a baggie containing a pale powder. "This is what I do," he said. "Besides a little carpentry to make money."

"Some new drug?"

"An old one. I make beer. I like things that grow. This is a new strain of yeast I've been working on."

"I guess you don't have to pay much attention to yeast, eh, Kyo?" She emptied her mug.

Tears welled in his eyes, and he had a brief impulse to punch his dear old Auntie in the face.

"It's a shame that you didn't keep on with your medical studies. But maybe you're a better brewmeister."

His anger vanished, and he smiled. She was still the same old nosy, bossy Auntie. He returned the package to his pocket. "Probably. I take bottles of the best batches to the monks. Roshi seems to have quite a taste for it."

Liliha brushed back strands of startling white hair with a weathered brown hand, put the hand atop Kyo's, and patted it. "I don't blame you drinking beer, Kyo. Not that you ever cared about the old ways, but it's the end of a nu'u. A cycle. Pele, she has called down fire. Not some little beach fire to cook fish on. It will be big. She's mad. Damned mad."

Kyo had heard her superstitions since he was a baby. Pele, the Volcano Goddess with her wild, long, lava-black hair, was always mad about something. "Come." She slid from her stool. "I want you to meet someone."

"Why not." Kyo picked up his bag of groceries: economy size peanut butter, Wonder Bread, and shoyu. Once they were out on the street, he followed the old woman toward Diamond Head. Enveloped by the heat and the roar of traffic, they passed the Hukilau, one of Kyo's favourite bars, one in a long string of favourite bars. He almost dropped out of the trek in favour of another cold beer. But wasn't this the place that he'd gotten in a fight with some Koreans a few nights back? Yeah, yeah; flashing lights, as an ambulance took the Korean to Queens Hospital, and he slipped down an alley, eluding the police. He had a knack for starting arguments, even though he was sure that he hadn't said much of anything. He never did. Anyway, Liliha strode down the sidewalk with surprising speed, showing no sign of wanting to stop.

In forty-five minutes they were in Waikiki. Condos loomed overhead. Haole and Japanese tourists swarmed the streets, clad in flower-print imitation of a culture which never existed.

He followed Liliha as she turned off King Street. Soon, they came to a canal Kyo had not been to before. It shimmered quietly, a stark contrast to the bustling streets a few blocks over. Liliha entered a warren of branching docks holding sheds, houses, and tiny islands within their arms.

Finally, she stopped. "This is the one." She walked up to the door of a sagging white frame house supported by pilings jutting from slow-moving water. The sounds of the city were gone; he heard instead sussurating surf and the omnipresent click of palm fronds in the light trade wind.

Liliha knocked, but did not wait for an answer. She motioned him inside, where light leaked into a dim, cool room through pulled blinds. "Kalihi?"

As Kyo's eyes adjusted, he saw a room where ancient Hawaiian fishhooks and stone pounding tools mixed casually with an old lady's overstuffed, lace-protected chairs.

An unusual midnight blue chunk of lava caught his attention. He had never seen lava that colour. But just as he touched it, he heard Auntie say, "There you are, you stubborn old lady!"

"I'm not stubborn, only hard of hearing," someone said. Kyo followed the voices onto the deeply shadowed back porch.

Kalihi, who looked Hawaiian, nodded at him as he stepped into her cool oasis. Unlike Liliha, she was thin, but she too was Hawaiian-tall. Her face was an intense, thin blade, almost masklike, lit by blazing eyes so black they might be blue. Hair more shockingly white than Liliha's flowed over her shoulders as she stood on one of the tamati mats covering her porch floor. Her spare, focused stillness put Kyo in mind of a heron at work. The heavy, sweet scent of plumeria blossoms mingled with salt; the thin blue line of the sea lay beyond. A tea of poi, lomi lomi salmon, and taro broth arranged for three, and a flask of sake, sat on a low, black table.

"Sit." She gestured toward cushions. After dropping

onto her cushion, quite easily for such an ancient-looking woman, she stared straight at Kyo, smiled, and poured him a tiny glass of sake, her long, elegant fingers a ballet of unconscious grace augmented by the flowing Asian sleeves of her black garment.

They watched surf dance through a frame of palm trees all afternoon, but when Kyo finally left, he couldn't remember what had been said as he rode the bus back to Nuuanu. Yet he felt immense peace. As the small houses and neighbourhood Chinese restaurants on every block caught the evening light, the scent of wok-stirred garlic and ginger blew through the open windows. He rested in the cleansed, bright aftermath of the day, more at peace than he'd been in years. He had felt that way after seeing Liliha ever since he was a child, no matter how annoying she could be.

But all too soon the thoughts she had interrupted in the Pantheon returned. He was a Zen monk now? He was fooling nobody. He wasn't fit to be a monk, any more than he had been fit to be a doctor or a husband.

Now the bus started and stopped in loud, grinding fits. The sun hurt his eyes even through his sunglasses. He felt old and stupid, and the fact that he'd left his bread and shoyu at that woman's house was proof of his innate, habitual irresponsibility.

His familiar desolation returned. Meaning could drop out of life with frightening ease, leaving just the dead frame. Those glimmers of wide understanding, those *tenshos* he clung to – even though, of course, one was not supposed to – would never blossom into enlightenment for him.

When he returned to the zendo, he walked the stepping-stone path through the carefully raked sea of sand considering how best to tell Roshi that he was quitting. It wouldn't be the first time.

As he entered the inner compound, he stopped.

Roshi was speaking to creatures with wings. Not, thankfully, angels. Instead, they were slim, almost emaciated, and slightly blue. They wore no clothes, but it did not seem as if they had skin; rather, it might have been the shortest imaginable fur, or the sleekness of an alligator.

Kyo's breath quickened. He knew Roshi was aware of him, though Roshi did not so much as flick a glance in his direction.

Roshi gasshoed low.

The creature gasshoed as well, then kneeled on long, slim limbs and touched forehead to ground. He – or she – rose, bowed, and walked around the corner.

"Roshi!" Kyo screamed, as the old man prepared to walk away.

Roshi turned. "You will say nothing," he commanded.

And within half an hour, before Kyo had time to consider whether to say nothing or not, much less to whom, he and the other monks were ushered onto a luminous ship hovering behind the zendo. How had it gotten here? It must have just... appeared. His doctor's mind, which surfaced so rarely now, had only seconds to consider the scientific implications. He shouted at everyone – Roshi, the creatures, the other monks – then, with a flip of mind, became silent. Why not? What did he have to lose? Getting upset was almost laughable.

The creatures settled them on couches and prepared them for the journey with gentle gestures. Then, he knew nothing save for his brief memory, until the group of monks woke alone, in their new little colony. How much later was it? Earth was a cinder, Roshi said; time was no longer a thing they could comprehend, and they had only themselves.

THE MONKS, EYES downcast, hands clasped, walked with slow measured steps in ritual kinhin. Now the light was dim, but soon it would sear the bleak landscape. Kyo reached his cushion and sat. One, he counted. One.

The disturbing creatures were there in his thoughts once more, creatures with wings. Their elongated bodies were delicate. Two sets of opposing digits were on each hand: one was a sharp, yet supremely flexible set which could reach inside delicate machinery and set it to rights. The other set, shorter and three-jointed, was suitable for most other tasks.

Kyo concentrated on one isolated image.

He had wakened, briefly, to those fingers touching his face, to eyes which did not look directly at him but were instead concentrated on a task which sounded metallic to his sleep-drenched brain. Perhaps the mechanism which kept him alive during the journey, which must have taken several lifetimes, had needed some adjustment. That impression was surrounded by darkness. It was all he had.

His thoughts jumped to his fellow monks. Geckos! Insects! Couldn't they see how everything had changed? Didn't they care?

Whack! Roshi hit him on the back. He straightened. One. One.

* * *

LATER, IN THE garden, Kyo struggled with a huge watering can. Itchy sweat trickled beneath his white garment. He set the can down and wiped his face. He wanted a beer. He arched his back to relieve the pain, and endured his useless memories of the bars of Honolulu. "'Pain is awakening,'" he mimicked Roshi. Crap. If he'd never gone to the zendo, he'd be blessedly dead now, and pain-free.

They'd been here for what he called months. They'd awakened in this small compound, ready, it seemed, for inhabitants, with growing plants that flourished in the hot wind, which seemed to provide them with enough food; he hadn't noticed any indication of nutritional deficiencies. To the contrary, they all seemed hearty. Their garden was large enough for their number: twenty monks. The vegetables were somewhat familiar – a tuberous starchy knob they called hasa, and a chewy leaf they called lettuce, more sustaining than earth lettuce. Two types of trees bore fruit. The grains could be cooked or ground into a flour for noodles. They required only water from the spring which spouted like a miracle in its tiny blue rock pool.

Kyo pulled slim metal rods from their sockets and carried the awning to its next post. The plants had to be shaded or they would burn. Kyo complained to himself once again that, though he could brew some beer with these ingredients, there wasn't enough to spare after the noodles were made. He considered once again how to enlarge the garden.

Kyo could tell that Roshi was behind him. He stood and wiped his hands. "When will we see them?" he demanded.

"See who?"

"The winged ones who brought us here. You know that I saw them! You allowed this! We had no choice. The other monks may accept everything you say, but you are no holier than I am, no more great, no more full of Buddha-mind."

Roshi's eyes glimmered with fun. The hint of a smile touched his face. "You are doing well, Kyo. Quite well. Remember when you came to the zendo? Too weak to want to live at all, much less argue with a Roshi."

He gasshoed and strode off, leaving Kyo angry and still wanting a beer. The precious packet of yeast he had shown Liliha had remained in his pocket during the voyage. It frustrated him to see the smooth, promising powder, so he kept the bag under his mat, where he wouldn't have to look at it. The resources here were meagre, and he needed to start exploring if he wanted to brew beer.

"HAVE YOU SEEN them?" Kyo asked that night as he tossed on his mat, sleepless.

"Who?" asked Rica. His tone of voice did not invite conversation.

"The creatures with wings. The beautiful ones who brought us here."

"Roshi brought us here."

"Where do you think you are, anyway? Earth?" Kyo was getting angry again; he always did when Rica acted this way. "Earth is ruined, burned. Why didn't we burn with it?"

Rica sighed. "We have to get up in three hours. Does it matter where we are? We have food and water."

"Right. Some bowls, some watering cans, some cook pots. It's like a penal colony."

"It's an endless *sesshin.* An opportunity. We have our minds. We can do zazen. We can achieve enlightenment." He rolled over.

Why is my mind so much different than his mind? wondered Kyo. He stared into the darkness and once more apologized to Io. *Well, Io, it's like this. You worked hard and did everything Dad wanted you to do and you're dead. I was a worthless sonofabitch, so inhuman that I drove my wife crazy, a deadbeat and a drunk, and I'm alive. Hey, does it make sense to you?*

Tears welled up, and overflowed onto his cheeks. I've got tears in my ears from lying on my back in bed and crying over you. Was that how it went? He'd never cried when he could drink. Emotions had to come out sometime, somehow, medical dogma claimed, but he'd tried to postpone that time until someone knocked him over the head in a dark alley and killed him.

He hummed the tune, then chortled. Riku made a sour warning snort.

"Silence, O revered Bodhisattva Riku." Kyo laughed until the laughs turned into long, ragged sobs, which Riku, as usual, ignored.

And after that, just before sleep, there was a slight, clean time in his mind. The image of the winged one he had seen with Roshi appeared.

The eyes were violet. They seemed deep and sad, but Kyo doubted that emotion was for them as it was for him. The head was an irregular ellipsoid, and he could tell no sex. The wings themselves were pale, streaked with luminescent colour, and arched high over the shoulders of the slim being, who stood monk-straight in the rock garden in the zendo on Nuuanu Avenue. He was not looking at Kyo, but at Roshi, who nodded once.

The next morning, as Kyo sat, a small light grew within him until it swallowed the darkness. It was gentle but insistent, and he could find no centre to it.

He let it engulf that which was looking for a centre.

When he opened his eyes, all the other monks were gone. In front of him on the floor, wobbling in the hot breeze, was a leaf-shaped, stiff piece of thin, almost-transparent colour. Just a piece of colour. Almost breathless, he reached out and found it rough and dry, the texture of an old seed pod. He put it in his pocket and rose.

He had missed breakfast.

"IT ISN'T MY Buddha-mind that's taking me, Roshi. It's my *human* mind!" shouted Kyo. "I'm going crazy!"

"They are the same," replied Roshi. He handed Kyo a flask of water. "Please turn back at midday. Then the next time, you can try a different direction. If you continue until night and find no water, you are dead."

Kyo shrugged.

"Please return."

So Kyo did. He explored seven vectors, as best he could tell, returning for seven nights with the empty flask and the bag of yeast he always took, his talisman, his only piece of Earth. He also took the piece of colour. It was a rich rose, shot through with narrow streaks of olive green.

"There's nothing out there," he said. "Nothing but lava – blue, shiny, glittery lava. I'll just have to go for a whole day."

On the eighth day, he took the awkward watering can as well. He lashed a thin, rolled-up sleeping mat to his back and included a good supply of dried noodles, which could soak in his drinking water.

As usual, he could not interpret the look in Roshi's eyes as they stood on the edge of their little encampment. "Remember your Bodhisattva vow," he said.

"No matter how numberless the beings, I vow to enlighten them all."

"Make that the source of your every thought and action," Roshi said, then turned away.

ON THE SECOND day, he found the body.

It was desiccated. It hadn't rotted; it had dried.

Kyo had lost a good deal of his water supply to evaporation and had been thinking of turning back. Now, he changed his mind. He squatted and examined the dead creature.

All the colour had gone out of its wings. He flaked away long, thin scales of translucent, mica-like material. Thin, bony limbs fitted close to its body, as if it had been very cold before death.

That night Kyo slept in a smooth volcanic hollow, its glass-hardness softened little by his mat.

When he woke, it was to deep violet eyes, compassionate and sad. The wings were backlit by sunlight, and colours sped across their surface, brilliant, elusive. Its skin was dull olive; fantastic digits folded in a complex arrangement as it held its hands at the centre of its chest.

Its entire heart and mind entered its plea, which was precise and unmistakable: *Help us*.

How? Kyo found himself asking silently, forming the question with a telepathic facility he had not known he possessed.

Come.

Kyo rose, rolled his mat, adjusted his robes. Hoisting his burden, he followed the creature as their shadows grew ever shorter.

Kyo's attempts to communicate with it frustrated him. He tried to find the space from which he had spontaneously asked "How," but could not. Or perhaps he did, and the creature was not in a conversational mood. It strode before him, perfectly erect, graceful. After the first hour, Kyo entered a state of kinhin, walking zen. He absorbed the ropy contours of the lava without thinking about where to step; his legs carried him forward; the sun became very, very hot.

Observe.

Kyo allowed his attention to shift into sight. Startled, he saw mountains where there had been none earlier in the day. The sun had passed its zenith and he wondered at his ability to forgo water for so long. Immediately, he uncapped his water bottle and drank. Then he offered it to the creature, who, to his surprise, accepted it with a grave gassho and drank as well.

Almost there, he heard.

Buddha be praised! he found himself answering.

The creature looked into his eyes, and he fancied he saw a smile there.

* * *

WHEN THEY ARRIVED at the cliffs, it took three winged creatures to fly Kyo up, and he was afraid even then that they would lose power and plummet back onto the sharp lava below. Their wings beat against the air ever more slowly. *Relax*, he heard. *Your stiffness adds to the difficulty.*

He allowed his fear to be an object, like the cliff face which moved downward with laborious slowness. Their speed increased. *Better.*

Once they reached the lip, others reached down and dragged him up. Long digits curled around his upper arms like snakes. As he gained his feet and looked about, he was not particularly surprised to see a group.

When they gasshoed as a body, he automatically gasshoed back. But when he heard, *Greetings, Roshi*, he emphatically shook his head. *I am no roshi*, he replied, counting nineteen of them.

You have come to teach us your ways. Have you not taken a vow?

A vow? Yes. I vow to save all beings, no matter how numberless. Or how strange and inhuman, he added to himself before going on. *I am not qualified to do what you wish.*

If you cannot give us the transmission, we will die.

He found that difficult to believe. *If humans do not achieve enlightenment, they do not die.* Even as he thought it, a part of his mind demurred. Old philosophy questions from college, snippets from the Bible and the Sutras thrust themselves forward, a small crowd of dissenters. He sighed. *I am very tired.*

They led him to one of many caves. Within, he saw jugs of water, some seeds, a comfortable cushion. He unrolled his own mat, and slept.

* * *

Day was more shadowed here than on the plain, and they had a spring which caused this valley, hanging like a suspended bowl far above the plain, to bloom with strange plants.

He woke before dawn to find them gathered around him, waiting. He didn't even reflect on what was happening. He had sat zazen every morning for years, and he sat today too. They all did. Their long, slim limbs easily twisted into lotus.

Kyo was finished long before them. So as not to disturb them, he said his vows silently, stood with the merest rustle of robe, and walked further into the recessed valley.

Soon, red foliage cloaked the lower portions of the cliffs. Flowerlike yellow growths were stark and strong against blue lava rock. He passed a patch where grains he and his fellow monks lived on flourished. He hoped they were watering the garden. He missed them, and Roshi.

Roshi. They meant him to be their Roshi. The craziness of his situation electrified him.

His hearty laugh echoed throughout the little valley.

They came floating up the valley then, and hovered around him in doubtful attitudes. One touched his mouth, the tears on his face, observed Kyo questioningly.

"I am laughing," he said, filled with wonder; delight. He could not, literally, remember when he had last laughed. When he was a kid, with Io, stealing Chinese crack seed from under his Auntie's nose? Out surfing Makaha, rushing shoreward balanced on the lip of a killer wave? On his wedding day?

Laughing, echoed his mind in nineteen whispers.

He set to getting his strange dharma charges, who called themselves Hanalb, into shape. Sitting before his cave one evening, he went over his usual roster of puzzlement.

How did these creatures reproduce? Eggs? Cloning? He had no idea. There were no youngsters. When he asked, he encountered a wall of deep sadness. A sadness so deep they could not formulate any thoughts about it.

He turned to another constant in his roster.

Beer.

With the reverence of ritual, he took his little packet of yeast from its cool resting place in the cave. He ran his thumb over the smooth plastic bag, yearning to unleash the power within. He could do it here. There was plenty of grain at this higher elevation. How he wanted to have something to drink! He still clung to memories, and the memory of entering neon-lit bars in Honolulu at two a.m. was tensho-like. He had to let it go, yet it fell squarely into the category of holy.

The Hanalb thought him a Roshi. He didn't quite understand that responsibility; until he did, perhaps it was best to wait to carry out this enterprise. He had failed at everything else; when he drank, he was able to forget, for a little while, that nagging, gnawing feeling that he could face nothing, that he was worthless. A pleasant little forgetting. Immensely pleasant...

He sighed, returned the package to its niche, and left the cave.

* * *

ONE MORNING, HE noticed that two of his monks were gone. From beneath lowered eyelids he counted. Yes, only seventeen. His first reaction was that of old Kyo. He would wait, see, and learn.

But then he was all fierce Roshi. Not thinking. Just doing.

Where are Tyseralise and Miniell? he asked sternly.

Not one of them shifted in their meditational attitude; not one blinked.

Where? he shouted, then "Where?" aloud.

One of them rose, and took him by the hand. He was led to the lip of the cliff, where he stood, staring.

Finally he made them out, two tiny dots moving across the lava field.

"They will die! We must go get them!"

The creature beside him shook his head, and when Kyo took a step down the faint path etched into the sheer cliff, the creature grabbed him with powerful arms and dragged him back from the cliff.

Kyo shrugged him off. "Where are the ones who brought us to this planet?" he asked the air. "The ones with the ships?" This tiny enclave existed in the same primitive manner as the monks across the lava plains. They used no technology at all.

The Hanalb would answer none of his questions.

Kyo turned away, and hiked up the valley with furious speed. Following a faint path up a side valley, he came to a cave he had discovered soon after he arrived. At the back was a tunnel. Next to the tunnel, on the floor, was a ceremonial bowl of blue lava.

Kyo had flirted with the thought of entering it

before, but feared becoming lost, falling into a fissure, or worse.

Now, brimming with frustration, he crawled inside.

The intense darkness was oppressive, but he continued crawling. He determined to go as far as he possibly could, no matter what. The tunnel narrowed. His shoulders were wider than those of the Hanalb, and he feared getting stuck, but the thought that the Hanalb used this as a passageway forced him to continue.

Finally, after what seemed ages of crawling through the dank, still darkness, he emerged onto a tiny ledge, scraped and bleeding.

What he saw made his chest ache with joy.

A small, intricate settlement blazed white far out on the blue lava plain, reminding him of a lone rogue white-topped wave on the blue Pacific.

Next to it was the ship he remembered from Honolulu, or one like it: tiny, no longer luminous. He looked at it for a long time, struck by the dreamlike quality of what he saw, the bizarre and absolutely outrageous fact of his presence here.

Wherever "here" was.

Kyo slid from ledge to ledge until he found a path leading down.

When he found the first body he sat next to it for a long while. His heart contracted in simple, unrelenting pain.

After the fifth body, he stopped counting. There were too many, each in the same position, which he suspected had ceremonial significance.

At the top of the final foothill before the lava sloped gently to the plain where the buildings sat, he paused.

The place seemed deserted. The sharp, intense beauty of its gracefully intersecting planes, opalescent as they caught the light, reminded him of wings.

Linda's wings, as she floated on the wind, outlined against the achingly blue Pacific.

Hanalb wings. On what were they meant to glide?

The ship was still several miles away. These people can *fly*, Kyo thought fiercely. They came to Earth. What has happened to them? Battling tears, Kyo descended the last few miles until he came to the wall surrounding the buildings.

A frieze along the top, about a half-meter high, depicted an astounding assortment of beings. As the sky lost light, Kyo circumnavigated the city, scrutinizing the graphics.

He saw what he realized were the developmental stages of one species after another, as from one of his old biology texts, depicted with salmon-pink stone inlaid on polished blue lava.

Each series of pictures ended with a schema of a solar system, and tiny, intricate signs which he assumed was the Hanalb written language.

Directions?

A final, winged Hanalb divided each segment from the next like a period.

Once Kyo understood, he moved frantically around the wall, searching for the pictorial statement which would show him the developmental stages of the Hanalb.

He found none. There was only the winged Hanalb at the end of each and every series. He was overwhelmed by the number of beings with which the Hanalb were apparently familiar, beings which crawled, swam, or ambulated on oddly shaped limbs covered with fur, scales, skin, beholding life through eyes which dazzled by force of their sheer variety.

Then he found the human segment.

All the phases of reproduction were painstakingly shown. Each stage of growth was portrayed. He recognized a Tibetan monk, a Catholic nun, a tall black woman dressed in ritual garb he did not recognize. He pressed his hand against the large graven Earth; the polished blue surface was cold. Asia was just a rough edge; Hawaii, a tiny string of dots.

Next to that, unmistakably, a nun sat in zazen, followed by a winged Hanalb, sitting in lotus.

"Enough!" he shouted. He hoisted himself over the wall and dropped onto a narrow street of polished lava.

Yes, the city was empty, eerily quiet. He swiftly passed two streets and crossed courtyards where fountains splashed and huge flowering plants overflowed their receptacles; walked beneath tiered balconies and searched the open abodes for signs of life.

He could see the ship beyond the city, glowing blue in the last reflected rays of light. He imagined, briefly, climbing inside, seeing controls which he couldn't master, yet somehow doing it, and setting a course for... where?

Where?

The question reverberated through his being, filling him with melancholy which hit with inescapable force.

Then someone called his name from the shadows in a faint, raspy voice.

"Kyo!"

Long used to the mindspeech of the Hanalb, he turned; waited for a long, silent moment.

"Come."

Kyo wanted to turn and run, back to his tunnel, back to his cave, back to his safe sangha. But the voice held him.

It was human.

"Who is it?" he asked, but the words came out like rusty water from an unprimed pump. He cleared his throat. "Who is it?" he demanded, sternly. Odd authority flooded him.

Receiving no reply, he stepped, stepped, and then more boldly still, strode toward the source of the voice.

He entered an intricately tiled courtyard, smooth and heat-holding in evening's sudden coolness.

Though the light was dim, he saw a Hanalb propped against the wall, obviously weak and barely able to speak.

He knelt and examined the face.

Memories surfaced: the Pantheon, a place in Honolulu that had refreshed him A talk more mindspeech than words, a testing of his depths.

"Kalihi?" He was chilled to realize that, though some metamorphosis had taken place, he did indeed recognize his Auntie's friend. Kyo gazed for a long moment on this Hanalb, trying to see which elements gave him such certainty.

A set of head; the way her features meshed; the bladelike face which was mostly nose. The strong, pure glance, which, though suffused with suffering, conveyed a deep, universal amusement with existence and herself as a part of it.

Kyo embraced her. Her body felt as fragile as that of an insect; her skin was rough and dry.

"But you are human," he whispered.

She shook her head. *Never. But – yes.*

"What do you mean by that, Kalihi?" Kyo's voice was hard and demanding. He could tell she was dying, yet he wanted to shake answers from her.

Once we grow wings, speech is difficult, was all she said.

But Kyo had learned to read their expressions, and she seemed to be smiling. Her enigmatic refusal to reply angered him.

"Yes, what a joke," he shouted. "I was *brought* here!" he shouted. "Taken from my home."

Earth is dead. It was destroyed by an asteroid soon after you left. You are alive. She nodded toward a half-drunk bottle of sake. *Be glad. Drink.*

Alive? What did he know about being alive? Why did he deserve to live, when everyone else was dead? "*You* drink!" he said, rising, robes whirling around him. He grabbed the bottle and tilted it against her mouth. She swallowed. "Why are you dying? Why do the Hanalb die?" He felt his eyes fill with tears. "You just walk out onto the plains and die. Where is everyone? I have no one to tell me these things. Please, Kalihi. Please. Why did you take *me* from Earth? An entire race of beings is gone. Why didn't you bring some women? Or at least some genetic material –" he was working himself into a rage when she stopped him with her clear, precise thoughts.

Genetic material. What good do you suppose genetic material is? It's everywhere, Kyo. In spite of that, all has failed. The beautiful experiment has failed. I thought to live here for a long time, after returning, to think, to work, but –

"*What* experiment has failed?"

She tilted her head as if gauging him. *Why do you strive for enlightenment, Kyo? Why do you believe that such a state exists at all? Do you ever wonder about that?*

"I think of little else."

Tell me, Kyo: can you save others with your transmission? That's what you're here for.

Though so sophisticated, they held this strange delusion. He would do anything to save the Hanalb. But he was helpless, stupid. "I have nothing to transmit. Nothing. I have experienced no realization. Such a transmission is passed from Zen Master to Zen Master after years of preparation. It isn't passed to – to idiots like me. I can save no one. Least of all myself."

Her silence, in the darkness which had fallen, had a curious quality he didn't understand. Finally, her thoughts sounded again.

There is another way.

"After someone has done a lot of work, Kalihi. That sort of thing doesn't happen to people like me." He knew what she meant. Buddhist texts often stated that enlightenment could occur without transmission – or simply, when the moment was exactly right, be triggered by an otherwise insignificant event.

It happens precisely to people like you. And for a very good reason.

He said, as evenly as he could, "Tell me what you mean."

Isn't it paradise, she replied, laboriously, *to believe that true consciousness is possible? Even now, even at the end of everything?*

Kyo didn't reply. He felt no paradise, only despair.

A moon was rising, so he could still see her face, fissured more deeply than any other Hanalb's he had seen. It occurred to him that he'd never seen one without wings, and he wondered what they looked like.

She gazed at the stars, which had spread brilliantly into that dark void which stopped his heart with pain and distance each time he looked at it. *So many beautiful places. So many beings.*

She was wandering. He followed her mind on this new track.

"The Hanalb have travelled to places other than Earth?"

Everywhere, she sighed, and that sigh generated for him a comprehension of the probable dimensions of the Hanalb empire. *Everywhere searching for the* thought, *the* place-of-mind, *that would keep us from growing wings. Or... take us to the next stage. There must be one. There must.*

Kyo smoothed her beautiful wings reverently. How could he save the Hanalb from their own wings, from something that seemed a natural unfolding of life –

And death.

"Will other Hanalb come?" he asked, his heart beating fast. If only! "Perhaps – return with answers? With – someone who knows how to use these technologies – whatever must be here, whatever gave you the ability to –"

I do not know, she replied. But her thought was limned with darkness. Perhaps she knew, and didn't want to tell him the truth. Or think it, even to herself. Perhaps this was just an outpost, an emergency stopping place...

"Kalihi, where is your home planet?" He hoped she would point vaguely at some quadrant of the sky.

Everywhere, she answered without hesitation.

Kyo shivered once, violently, at the idea which occurred to him at that single word.

"Kalihi," he asked, "Where then are the Hanalb children?"

Her whisper in Kyo's mind set it on fire.

Once, we were everywhere.

She looked at him then with a gaze so powerful it wracked him.

In her eyes he saw beautiful Earth, lyric and fine, forever lost. How had he ever thought his own life important? The questions which left him sleepless: *Who am I? Why am I here?* intensified, until he felt surrounded by a crowd roaring in his ears, within his very brain.

Kalihi's wings, arching up from her shoulders and enfolding her arms, reminded him, once more, of Linda's wings, and that they had not worked. Linda had wanted him to be her wings. To simply ask the right question. With a word at the right time – with perhaps just a smile, a transmission of love through space – he could have saved her. That thought renewed his agony a hundredfold. It twisted within him, unbearable. There was no escape. There never would be.

At that instant, trembling, vision locked with an alien being, he felt the universe splinter and reform around him: new, simple, complete.

Kalihi closed her eyes. Her wings shuddered.

He knew, without checking, that she was dead. It seemed to him at that moment that she had just been waiting for him to come before letting go. How? He did not know. It did not matter.

That was her transmission.

He stood, and planted his feet far apart.

His shout was a force that came from the roots of the planet and found its destination in the hearts of distant stars.

In the silence that followed, a hot wind rushed through the leaves of the deserted gardens, and those stars pulsed above.

The tang of alien herbs overlay the scent of water from the fountains. That scent of life was replaced, when he passed out through the gate, by a dry, dusty wind that made him feel shrunken and old.

He climbed the cliff in the light of the planet's moon, not caring if he slipped. He thought nothing as he crawled through the tunnel and collapsed on the other side.

But he could not stop his dreams. A myriad of beings grew from nothing, bursting with life, and danced a rapid, weaving dance while he watched helplessly, unable to dance with them. Then they dwindled to a small, glowing dot which hung in space an instant before it vanished forever.

KYO WOKE LYING on his back just outside the tunnel. He opened his eyes and was confronted by the alien sky, tauntingly blue as a mid-Pacific day. His first thought was of Kalihi's answers.

Everywhere, their children.

Everywhere, their home planet.

How plastic, he wondered, is the basis of life? How mutable is the physiological basis of consciousness? He remembered that when he was in medical school, a renegade movement claimed that thought could alter the course of disease. Ridiculed, of course, by him as well as most people. Maybe, maybe not. But thought, translated into action – into vaccines, visualizing machines, genetic therapies--could. What else could thought do? Time was so vast for the Hanalb, and they had tried so many things, that thought-into-vaccine was probably as short an iteration as an eyeblink was to him. However long he lived, he doubted that he could understand, much less master, the technology the Hanalb had let go of. Or at least, it seemed from his point of view that they had. That might be true. It might not be true. A glowing ship might arrive in the next instant. What if it did?

Finally, he faced the question he was trying to hide from. The one which had plagued him so long, the Zen koan: *What is my true nature*?

An excellent question.

He closed his eyes, then opened them again to the blazing sky and allowed himself to know the truth: the last vestige of an ancient, brave, massive experiment. One called consciousness. One by which the universe had been seeded with hope and intelligence.

What is my true nature?

Hanalb.

He had no doubt that it was true. He wondered what form his brother and sister Hanalb had inhabited, on what far planets, before metamorphosing to wings. He had always thought that all the beings in the universe must be related, often wondered what odd twist of mind poets, artists, scientists, and those seeking God shared, and why.

He stood, and tried to brush the mud from his filthy robe, then ripped it off and threw it down in a heap.

As he walked toward his cave, he yanked clumps of sweet grasslike fronds out by the roots. Sugar. By the time he got there, he had an armful, which he dropped next to his spring.

Now what? Yes, he had to get one of the cooking vats. It would be heavy.

He headed down into the main valley, saw no one, and was glad. He wouldn't have cared if they had all wandered out onto the plains, troublesome creatures. He certainly didn't plan to. At present, that stubborn thought was all he had.

He strode into the cooking area and grabbed a vat. He turned it on its side and began to roll it back up the hill, wrestling it over the rocks. Sweat stung his eyes, and he sat down to rest.

He regarded the vat.

The huge, battered container was made of soft metal. It was used by a race of beings that travelled to other galaxies. In it, they cooked simple grains in boiling water.

His laughter began slowly, and grew until it echoed against the rocks and he was gasping for breath, sides aching.

Between the arms of the valley, the lava plains glittered like the blue Pacific of his childhood. But he would never see white sails upon them, or watch fish scatter at his approach in the shallows. And neither would anyone else. Ever.

It had never hit home before.

Kyo gazed at the landscape with new eyes.

Death had shattered him once. But now, the thought of all that was gone, and the fact, suddenly apparent, that life, its near-extinction, and its re-flowering as galaxies bloomed and died, had been happening infinitely – the incomprehensible weight of it, and its attendant, vast, lightness and release – hit him like the Roshi's stick, like the opening of Linda's white wings in flight.

He grasped the vat and continued up the hill, pushing it ahead of him with renewed energy. Arriving at his grotto, he righted it. The vat rang like a great gong as it hit the rocks.

He bent a thousand times to fill it with spring water from his small bowl, loving the splash of water falling into water. The winnowed grain spilled through his hands like millions of smooth, dry, tiny fish; the green slush of pounded plants smelled sweet as a newly split coconut. He performed each step, registered each sensation, as if he had repeated them through infinity and perfected them. Perhaps this was all he was good for: to spread the life of the yeast.

That, at least, was *something*.

Finally, he opened the bag and poured all of his precious yeast into the vat. Now all he had to do was wait.

He sampled it several times a day, thinking about the slow yet inevitable translation of matter as the yeast fed. And with each brief taste, always different, the universe seemed renewed. Why hadn't he noticed its perfection before?

One day he dropped his spoon. He bent to pick it up, straightened, and paused.

The light pervading the landscape penetrated him, as if the particles which he thought of as himself were loosely connected and barely maintained in the particular form of Kyo.

The force of truth cleared all else from his being.

The thought registered briefly: Universe can reprogram mind. Mind can reprogram body. We may be the last, but we will *not* walk out on the plain.

Wings were meant for flight, for joy.

Hope was gone. Only stark reality was left.

That was enough.

Koans for his charges appeared in his mind, complete and powerful, precise puzzles which could cause thought to transform the very atoms of those who experienced the solution. Each thought a new pattern in a re-formed mind.

As days passed and the beer brewed, in waking and in sleep, Kyo's world was filled with light: constant, strong, and insistent, a brilliant power he did not understand and did not even care to. He only knew exactly how to share it. His companions progressed swiftly through his koans and checking questions, which tested each state of individual realization.

On the twentieth morning, he found the beer perfect.

Kyo readied two bowls, next to the most beautiful part of his grotto, where purple and red flowers sprouted from the rocky wall.

He sensed excitement outside, and smiled. He did not hear footsteps, for bare feet made no sound on the path.

Kyo.

Kyo turned.

Roshi stood in the bright light; gasshoed, then straightened.

Do you have a question? asked Kyo.

Only one: can you save me?

Kyo looked straight into Roshi's eyes.

An absurd question. Why ask? I only know one thing: I make excellent beer.

For a moment, all was still. Light poured over beautiful blue lava. Bands of colour wavered in interlocking trapezoidal patterns on the floor of Kyo's pool.

Roshi and Kyo burst into laughter like children.

Kyo's sides ached; he wiped tears from his face, took a deep breath. He was aware only of light, filling the grotto as if it were a pool, permeating them both.

Roshi's new wings, as he accepted Kyo's bowl of beer with immense solemnity, caught that pure light and shone.

Walls of Flesh, Bars of Bone

Damien Broderick and Barbara Lamar

Damien Broderick is an award-winning Australian SF writer, editor and critical theorist, a senior fellow in the School of Culture and Communication at the University of Melbourne. Barbara Lamar is a Texan tax lawyer, permaculture farmer, and co-author of their forthcoming novel Post Mortal Syndrome. *Lamar and Broderick married in Melbourne, Australia, in 2002, and live in San Antonio, Texas. Broderick has published 45 books, including* Reading by Starlight, The Spike *(the first full-length treatment of the technological Singularity), and* Outside the Gates of Science *(a study of parapsychology). He edited* Chained to the Alien, *and* Skiffy and Mimesis, *essays from the fabled* Australian Science Fiction Review. *His 1980 novel* The Dreaming Dragons *(now updated as* The Dreaming*) is listed in David Pringle's* Science Fiction: The 100 Best Novels. *His latest US releases are the novels* I'm Dying Here, *and* Dark Gray *(both with Rory Barnes). Recent SF collections are* Uncle Bones, Climbing Mount Implausible, *and* The Qualia Engine.

* * *

"The question of whether the waves are something 'real' or a function to describe and predict phenomena in a convenient way is a matter of taste. I personally like to regard a probability wave, even in 3N-dimensional space, as a real thing, certainly as more than a tool for mathematical calculations... Quite generally, how could we rely on probability predictions if by this notion we do not refer to something real and objective?"

– Max Born,
Natural Philosophy of Cause and Chance

HANGING ONTO THE desk's edge, I eased myself back, then slumped down again while the floor got itself on an even keel. I'd drooled on the interdisciplinary dissertation I was meant to be assessing. Psychoanalytic cinema theory, always such fun these post-postmodern days. *Ob(Stet)Rick's: A/OB[GYN]jection, Blood and Blocked de(Sire) in CASA[BLANK]A.* I closed my eyes again, feeling ill.

Lissa was shocked. I wasn't all that pleased myself. Slightly reproachful, she said, "Dr Watson, your appointment with the committee chair." I squinted at the blur of my watch, did a sweep of the cluttered surface of my desk. No glasses in immediate view. You need to be wearing them in order to see where they are, but if you're wearing them you already know where they are. That was the kind of pseudo-paradox this grad student's dissertation was cluttered with. The inside of my head gonged.

"Yeah." I tried to clear my throat. "Thanks, Liss."

"Ten minutes. Shall I bring you a cup of coffee?"

Delivering coffee was explicitly *not* part of Lissa's job description as administrative assistant, but I seemed to bring out the motherly instinct in her, although she is too young by a generation and a half to be *my* mother.

"Sure. You're a sweetheart." Inside my head a Hell's Angels convention were thrashing their hogs and tearing the town apart. Probably shouldn't have brought that bottle of Jack Daniels to the office. Only meant to take a swallow to calm my nerves.

I shoved the (th)esis on to the floor, where it landed with a (th)ud, then dug through the random drifts of paperwork on my desk. My reading glasses were three layers down. I jammed them on my face. Where the hell had I put the notes for the meeting? I was stern: *Lee, my boy, do this in an orderly manner.* Here was the title page from Jerry Lehman's chapter on the effects of adrenergic stimulants on the signification behaviour of non-autistic children. I was supposed to be reviewing the damned thing. Two months behind, so far, but I'd catch up, soon as I got things worked out with Beverley.

Map of Vancouver. Another unfinished dissertation I was supposed to be supervising: *Queer Lear, Queen.* Brochure advertising whole-house entertainment systems. Article from the *Irish Journal of Post-Psychoanalytic Semiotics* I'd been meaning to read.

"Here you go, Dr Watson. Fresh from the microwave." Lissa set the cup down on a small bare spot on the credenza behind me. Even before I took the first sip I could tell it was stale, left over from 7:30 in the morning. What the hell, this was medicine.

"Can I help you look?" She glanced at her watch; her voice held a tinge of panic. Funny, I wasn't a bit tense, and it was my career that was on the line. Up for promotion to full professorship, financial security and independence for the rest of my life. Fat chance.

"I'm looking for the notes I need for the meeting with Patterson. It would be six pages stapled together."

"Handwritten?" Good girl. Woman. Person. She was already attacking the mounds of papers.

"Printed." I leaned back in the leather chair Bev had given me three, no, five years ago, sipping my awful coffee. All the time in the world. I'll be okay, I told myself. I'll be fine, soon's the caffeine takes hold.

"I can't find them anywhere, Dr Watson." Lissa pushed her hair back from her forehead, sighed. "Are you sure you brought them to the office?"

I goggled my eyes sadly behind my goggles and shook my head. I wasn't sure of anything these days, except that if I let myself think too hard it hurt too much. "It's okay, Lissa. I can wing it." I stood up and the floor was steadier. "Better get going."

"Like *that?*"

I glanced down at my *Dept. Of Psychoceramics* tee shirt with a pang. A gift from Mandy the year before the dreaded menarche hormones kicked in and she went from adorable to teen werewolf. Lissa was right. It was a little frayed around the edges, and maybe the sentiment wasn't ideal for the inquisition. "Not to worry." I kept a suit jacket hanging behind the door for emergencies. Buttoned up snug, started out, stepping lively, a man who knows where he's going and what he's doing. But when I got out to the hall, away from the safety of my own office, I stopped short. Professor H. Patterson would expect me to say something at least moderately intelligent. You didn't get to be a committee boss in the Department of Psychosemiosis and Literature at the University of California at Davis without expectations of that sort. And I realized I didn't have anything remotely clever to tell her and the committee. Furthermore, I didn't give a shit. There was a probability of about 0.5 that cancelling the meeting now would end my career. On the other hand, if I went in there half crocked *oh c'mon Watson, not half, 80% at least truthfully*, the probability was close to 1.0 that I'd be out on my ass with no further ado, and so much for tenure, increasingly a dead letter.

"Lissa?" I looked over my shoulder, tried for my most pleading, boyish look. "Do me a favour?"

"Call Professor Patterson and tell her you've had a stroke."

"Something like that, yeah. Um..." Mental wheels turned sluggishly. "Tell her they called from my daughter's school and there's been a crisis and I had to go right away." Like anyone would call me about anything connected with my child.

"I didn't know you and Bev had kids."

"One. Not Bev's, from a former marriage."

"You're a dark horse, Dr Watson."

I grabbed my helmet and cantered off for the Department's outer door as fast as I could without tripping over any of my legs, and *en passant* grabbed a square, flat package from my inbox. No return address. Another orphan film from my mysterious benefactor, had to be. My spirits lifted as I made my escape to a brilliant afternoon that smelled of sage and ripe crabapples.

* * *

My apartment was dark and empty, though, shades drawn against the afternoon light, as it had been for the five months I sulked in it. My estranged wife Beverley used to find me pathologically optimistic, but that was before she threw me out. I could picture the mocking way she'd raise her eyebrows at me if she could see how eagerly I opened the mailbox and scanned the bills and junk mail for her handwriting. No such luck; instead, there was a letter from Virta and Crump, P.C., Bev's lawyers. I tossed it on the deal-with-it-later pile along with a couple of month's worth of bills and headed for the fridge. Nothing like a cold beer to take the edge off incipient depression.

The package was indeed an orphan film. The label on the slightly rusty metal canister read "#11: Reverend Willard D. Havard, New York City, January 10, 1931." No accompanying letter or card. Now that I was living on my own, the movie screen and the old Bell & Howell Filmosound projector had become a regular feature of the décor, so there was no need to set up. I took a swig of beer and began threading the film through the machine.

Orphan films are movies that have been abandoned by their owners, sometimes because of copyright problems, more often because they didn't seem worth saving. But films that seemed worthless soon after they were made – old newsreels, for example – are now priceless windows into the past. I'm easily entertained and can spend hours absorbed in some unknown family's home movies from the 1950s. Whoever was sending these mystery films seemed to be a connoisseur with finer tastes than mine. He or she was sending stuff from the earliest days of simultaneously recorded picture and sound.

Film #11 was only a little over 3 minutes long. At the beginning, a tall bearded man with a Santa Claus belly was delivering a sermon on a street corner. The sound was scratchy, and you could hear car engines and horns honking in the background, but still you could make out most of the Reverend's pitch.

"On my way down here today, I saw a little girl, couldn't have been more than five or six. This little child was standing on the sidewalk selling chewing gum and mints. I asked myself, brothers and sisters, why is this little girl standing here selling chewing gum instead of sitting at a desk at school? Is she just trying to get some spending money? Is she helping to support her family?"

He had a certain charisma. It took an effort to redirect my attention from the Rev. Willard to his audience, if you could call eight or ten motley hobo types plus a couple of young boys an audience. One of the kids gave the other a rough shove as I watched; this was returned with compound interest, and soon they were rolling on the sidewalk like a couple of tomcats.

The Reverend reached the climax of his presentation. "As I was telling you earlier, my friends, God sends us trials and tribulations to give us a chance to shine in His Light."

A fellow about my age had passed in front of him, turned his head quickly to the camera and then away. Startled, I blinked, but he was gone. The scuffling boys seemed so intent on their struggle that they'd lost track of where they were. One landed with a thud on an ancient duffle bag. Its elderly owner thwacked both the kids across the shoulders with his cane. Indignant, for a moment they stopped fighting, then the sound track of the film clearly picked up the shorter kid yelling at the taller one, "Your mother's a [something] slut." And they were rolling on the ground again, just as the Reverend Willard reached for his tambourine, which had been passed from hand to hand. The full weight of both boys slammed against the Reverend's shins; he went down on his massive butt, the tambourine went flying, scattering a few coins across the sidewalk. Instantly the boys stopped their scuffling. The taller kid, closer to the lens, grabbed a couple of coins. The other, grinning, ducked down so his face was visible under an armpit, and did something that flashed white and was gone. Instantly, then, both boys ran swiftly and gleefully out of the frame, their differences apparently forgotten. And that was it. The end of the film.

I rewound a short way and played the last few seconds again. There had been something familiar about that fellow walking past, something that prickled the back of my neck.

No mistaking it, once noticed and reviewed. It gave me the strangest shiver. I watched that segment of the film again, and again, and once more again. He was me. I mean, the guy bore an uncanny resemblance to yours truly. Allowance made for the antique style of his clothing and his cap, the very spittin' image. That was undeniably me in the 1931 movie. The year before my grandmother was born.

I saw something else that creeped the hell out of me: just before the scuffling lads rammed into the Reverend Santa Claus, my double turned his head, caught the eye of the photographer, and *winked* at him. In effect, through the recording lens, at me.

What the *fuck?*

My hangover was gone, and my lethargy. Adrenalin can do that. I wanted to look more closely at this fragment of images from the past without risking the fragile orphan footage any further. It took me an hour setting up the old mirror box that reflects the image from screen to camcorder lens (I'd bought it on eBay, they don't make them any more), and then saved the digital feed to my hard drive. Doing this properly would require a bunch of money and a professional transfer house tech, lifting off the dust and other crap from 80 years of careless storage, paying frame by frame attention to brightness and other parameters. Maybe I'd get to that, but my grant money for orphan restoration had just about run dry, and I wanted something quick and fairly easy.

I opened the vid and went straight to the appearance of the guy who looked like me. And the kids, horsing around. I ran it twice, then went to the kitchen cabinet and opened another bottle of Jack Daniels.

"Your mother's a toboggan-time slut," the smaller kid had yelled, or something like that. And then he reached into his raggedy grey shirt and pulled out a sheet of glistening white paper, except that it looked more like an impossibly thin, flexible iPad, held it up for just thirty frames, jammed the thing back under cover again, and they were away.

The iPad that wasn't an iPad held several... what? Hieroglyphs? No, mostly Roman and Greek letters, upper and lower case, with some other items that might have been Arabic or for all I knew Assyrian. And a few numerals, subscripts and superscripts, and brackets. Equations, okay. The only equations

I'm familiar with are the bogus propositions of Jacques Lacan, psychiatrist and Freud-fraud. I did a screen capture of the clearest frame, pushed it up to 400%. Blurry, but I felt sure a mathematician would have no trouble recognizing it. Or a physicist, or cosmologist, or the creature from Bulgaria, whatever.

The trouble with Google is that you can't easily search for equations, or at least I couldn't. I tried to cut and paste the bit-mapped string of symbols and that didn't get me anywhere. I went laboriously into Word, found the symbols one by one, but half of those on the screen were unknown to Microsoft, far as I could tell. I plugged in the fragment of the single equation whose parts I could find and hit "I'm Feeling Lucky."

This first and simplest equation popped onto the monitor, embedded in an only moderately incomprehensible paper on a site called arXiv, which I assumed was an archive for people from the Other Culture who couldn't spell, like Bev's current creature.

$$|\psi> = \Sigma\ (a_i \exp(j\varphi_i) \mid x_i, y_i, z_i, v_i, \omega_i >)$$

It was dated 2009. The paper was titled "Ordinary Analogues for Quantum Mechanics," by one Arjen Dijksman, and it began: "Upon pondering over the question 'What is ultimately possible in physics?' various interrogations emerge. How could one interpret ultimately? Is there an ultimatum, a final statement in physics, after which one could say 'Physics is finished'? Are there issues, for instance fundamental principles, beyond which we could not go past? How can we describe the boundary between the possible and the impossible in physics? Anyway, does such a boundary exist? And if so what is at the edge?"

I ran the whole video file again, and this time the Jack Daniels didn't keep me warm. The kid hadn't shouted "toboggan." My skin crawled. Jesus Christ. He'd said "teabaggin'." And the emphasis was subtle, but it wasn't "teabaggin'-time slut." It was "teabaggin' time-slut."

Teabaggers in 1931? Give me strength. Had they even *invented* teabags that long ago? Back to Google, fingers stiff and clumsy on the keys. Yes, a form of silk tea-bag was used as early as 1903, but today's rectangular teabag came along as late as 1944. Let's not be too literal, Lee, let's try a lexical search.

Before the current burst of radical crazies calling themselves the Tea Party, mocked by their foes as "teabaggers," the term had another and more scabrous sense. Urban Dictionary told me "teabagging" meant "To have a man insert his scrotum into another person's mouth in the fashion of a teabag into a mug with an up/down (in/out) motion." I squeezed my eyes shut. Oh-kay. Whatever floats your boat. But that had to be a recent coinage, didn't it, post-1944 at least? Maybe not. Old slang from society's undergrowth tends to seep up again and again, then vanish for a time. But "time-slut." And the arXiv abstract. Urchins didn't know about quantum theory in 1931. Maybe nobody did. I felt my ignorance yawning at me.

I was in a sort of numb dissociated state, trying to remain amused at this obvious Photoshopped fake someone had shoved in my pigeon hole to mess with my peace of mind, but increasingly angry at whoever treated me with such scorn. Even if, face it, I *was* a barely controlled drunk two or three steps away from the same skids as those bums in the 1931 movie.

But that was the point, it *wasn't* a 1931 movie, of course, it was a bricolaged fake. Well, maybe not the whole thing. Mostly it looked highly authentic to my well-seasoned eye. They'd rendered my face into the image of the young man, and somehow worked in that iPad thing for a few frames. Maybe in the original the kid had waved a newspaper headline, or a cloth cap. So why the hell bother? Who was trying to tell me something, and what? A disgruntled student? A post-postmodern gag to piss me off, get my goat? One of Bev's sardonic tame "artists"?

I shut the machine down, carefully backing everything up first to the university cloud, and biked over to the other side of town to see Bev. Virta and Crump and impending divorce be damned. I just couldn't cope with this shit by myself, and besides I was developing a suspicion or two.

WHEN I FIRST met Bev Peacock during my guest lectures at Chicago's School of the Art Institute, her father owned a small chain of health food stores with corporate headquarters in Sacramento. Bev took a couple of summer courses at UC Davis, including my sessions on Julia Kristeva and other psychoanalytic deep thinkers on their way to superannuation. During her last two years in Chicago, emails fled between us; we talked on the phone at least twice a day. By then, I was separated from Sheila, and visited Chicago when I could, strolling with Bev in Lincoln Park, visiting the art museum where I spent more time looking at her than at the daubings. Everyone could see we were in love; for the first two years, anyway. As I sank ever deeper into gloom at the gibberish I was required to teach, Bev discarded her dreams of great art. The renunciation changed her, bit by bit. She built her separate life, embarrassed to be seen with me: my moods, my drinking, the way I dressed.

Barry Peacock sold the health food store chain six months after Bev and I married, netting $6.2 million. Barry and Ruth wanted their daughter to enjoy at least part of her inheritance while they were still around, so they bought the house in Davis for a little over a million dollars. The house remains owned by the Beverly Peacock Watson Separate Property Trust, but I had no claim to it under California's community property law. And now I was doubly alienated: evicted, replaced by the atom-tweaker from Bulgaria.

I LEANED MY Koga StreetLiner against a pillar of the porch and dropped my helmet into the saddlebag. I felt queasy about leaving the Koga unlocked, even in this neighbourhood, but one of the reasons Bev threw me out was my habit of parking bicycles in the house. The creature opened the door and gazed down at me benignly. He drew in a deep, energizing breath, then wrinkled his patrician nostrils at the *eau d'Jack*.

"Lee. I see the flesh seems a little weak today, but the spirit smells strong."

I winced. I hadn't drunk *that* much, although I'd weaved a little on my ride; it was probably just as well no cop had pulled me over to check my *sang froid*. My *sang réal*. I sniggered. "And how's your cat today, Schrödinger? Alive or dead?"

Tsvetan Toshtenov, D.Sc. (Ruse) blocked the doorway. "Both, of course. As a matter of fact, we've just done a..." He shook his head. "Of course you don't want to know. What do you want, Lee? I assumed Bev had a restraining order."

"Ha ha, very droll." I made myself small and went under his arm, then galumphed down the hallway. Two small boys glanced up from their Playstation 4 and gazed at me impassively. So now she'd moved in the entire family. Those faces. Something went *ping* in a buried part of my brain but I was too aerated to catch it, although I half-stumbled for an instant. It would come back to me. I jinked through our bright metal-clad kitchen warm with the odours of Bulgarian fare, and made for the studio out back. "Honey, I'm ho-o-o-ome," I yodelled.

It wasn't a studio, of course, despite the artfully placed and prepped canvas on its easel awaiting the first lick of oil. It had been waiting for years. When I'd married Beverley and moved in here with her, she was in the last drawn-out ebbings of her passion to be a painter, heading step by inexorable step toward curatorship and a safe doctorate in Mapplethorpe and de Kooning (Elaine, naturally, not Willem). These days she organized elegant or bizarre installations, events, displays, online video performances. If anyone was likely to know a scamp capable of torturing me with a fake orphan movie, at her instigation, it was Bev. She of all people knew my own passion for orphan footage. Yet it seemed a bit beneath her, and perhaps beyond Bev's currently limited quotient of whimsy.

"Drunk! For heaven's sake, Lee." My wife rose from her persuasive replica somethingth century oak Chateau Something credenza and advanced in her forceful and menacing way toward me. "What are you doing here?"

"Hardly drunk," I said without conviction. "The sun's well and truly over the yardarm, Bev."

"I had a call from Hattie Patterson several hours ago. She wondered if I knew where you'd got to."

"Why would she expect you to know?"

"We *are* still married, Lee. Have you signed the documents yet? Hattie said you didn't show up at the faculty meeting convened to consider your candidacy, and it had something to do with your daughter. Is Mandy okay? Oh, wait, of course she is – I should have taken it for granted you were lying."

The spring, such as it was, had quite left my step. I looked for somewhere to sit, and found a deck chair rather ruined by splashes of house paint leaning against one wall. As I started to open it, Bev gave a strangled cry.

"Not *that*, you idiot. Good god, man, it's an early Rauschenberg."

I backed away smartly. So it was, or could be. How the hell did Beverley get her hands on something like that? She was loaded, but not *that* loaded, or Virta and Crump, P.C. were lying through their teeth. Of course that was the specialty of divorce attorneys. Or maybe she'd brought it home from some exhibition for a couple of weeks of private gloating. I opened my mouth to ask, an instant too late.

"Come on, inside the house with you, and then please leave. I don't want the children to see a drunkard shambling about." She shepherded me out of the studio and along the small vegetable garden and ample green lawn where we had once rolled naked. Her creature was waiting in the kitchen, coffee mug in hand. He passed it to me and I burned my mouth.

"That place is the death of the soul, Bev," I told her. "You know that much yourself. I mean, it's not as if you stayed around to build your academic..." I trailed off, blowing across the top of the mug. A teabagging time-slut? I couldn't imagine Bev and the creature from Bulgaria engaging in reckless sports of that kind. Not that she and I hadn't enjoyed, when we were first together, our share of –

The two little boys crouched in the next room noisily killing aliens and cavorting in three-dimensional havoc with imaginary super-weapons were not her children, not ours, but Tsvetan's, and nobody of my acquaintance had ever seen their mother, save the creature himself. Beverley had met him at a soiree of daubers and their hangers-on. He'd pronounced himself a cubist. No doubt Bev raised an eyebrow. Hardly *au courant*. No, no. Forgiving urbane laughter over a simple error. A QBist. A Quantum Bayesian. Whatever that was, I'd never bothered to ask. As for his prior woman, the mother of his brats, maybe *she* was a time-slut. Whatever *that* might be. After all, how else – ridiculous, I told myself, slurping and blowing. I'm delusional. This is worse than the DTs. Those kids can't be older than five and seven. I couldn't remember their names. Something eastern European. Ivaylo and Krastio? But the little one did look horribly familiar. I could all too easily imagine him whipping out an advanced display unit from under his shirt. In five or six years from now. Christ.

"I'm sure you'd like a drink," the creature said, and handed me a large glass not quite brimming with a deep, rich pinot noir. I remembered those glasses; they'd been a wedding gift from my aunt Hilda. I considered quaffing it in one hit and then flinging it into the fireplace, but that doesn't really work with a top of the line gas cooking range. I sipped in a gentlemanly manner, sat at the new kitchen table, and told them in a not especially accusatory tone about the Rev. Willard D. Havard and his unusual sidewalk congregation.

"You can access this video, presumably?"

"If I'd brought my laptop with me, Bev, I'd be delighted to show it to you."

The creature was gone; he was back almost instantly with a gleaming titanium-shelled Apple. He pushed it in front of me. The university log-in box was displayed.

"Oh hell, why not?" I pulled my orphan out of the cloud and ran it as they stood behind me, watching with a blend of avidity (Tzvetan) and amused contempt (my faithless wife). At the end of the three minutes I said, "Again?" and reran it. Then I found the screen capture and blew it up on the rather nice large display.

"Well. That's obviously ket quantum notation. Dirac didn't invent it until 1939, so clearly this film isn't from 1931, did you say?"

"Sweetheart," Bev said in a strangled voice, "didn't you notice? Those were Wolf and Chris." I looked up; her face was totally pale, and her eyes were fixed on Sweetheart. "Those were your boys, grown up."

"Distant relatives, perhaps." Tsvetan was doubtful, but I trusted Bev's curatorial eye, and I imagine my own face was as bloodless as hers. "In 1939, my own parents and their siblings were still under Hitler's boot." Or working for the Gestapo, I didn't quite mutter aloud. I had no reason to think badly of the man's antecedents. For all I knew they had indeed been subjected to the banality of evil. "Show me that equation again, I thought I recognized it."

"I found it here." I opened the arXiv paper.

"I've heard of Arjen," the QBist said thoughtfully. "Young Dutch theorist with an interest in the foundations of physics, lives near Paris. He's a serious scholar, wouldn't have anything to do with a silly game like this, I assure you. Here, let me find his number." He had his iPhone out, with a finger sweeping.

"Please don't," I said. "I'm sure you're right. It's a prank by one of Bev's students."

My wife's jaw dropped. "Excuse *me?*"

"Who else has the skills to paste my head on some ancient young geezer's body, let alone do something to the appearance of the boys? Age shifting or whatever the forensic cops call it."

"Anyone over the age of 10," Bev said frostily. "Mandy, for that matter, or one of her friends. Have you been upsetting your daughter, Lee?"

"Oh for god's sake, I wasn't making it a personal accusation. My point was –"

"No, that's right, she's made it clear she doesn't want you in her life any longer. Sensible child."

I shoved the chair back with a nasty screeching sound. That wouldn't have helped the parquet floor. Tsvetan slipped into its seat like a large muscular eel and started pounding the keyboard. I noticed that he used only four fingers, but his typing was faster than

I could manage with ten. Then again, scientists don't have to stop and think what they're about to be writing, it's all formulae and algorithms and canned knowledge, isn't it. Unless they're Einstein. Or Dirac, whoever he was. Dirac, I thought. Diracula.

"We're hungry." Two little boys with the same face as their father and no resemblance to Bev stood at the open door between the kitchen and the hall. They were amazingly well-behaved, nothing like the scapegraces they'd been in 1931. But it was them, they, I knew it, on the orphan footage. Had been. Would be. No question. Time was out of joint big time. I thought I was going to throw up.

"In a moment, darlings. This man was just leaving."

I shook my head sadly at the perfidy of women, children and creatures, swigged down the last of the red in my glass (*my* glass!), put the glass, stem first, in my jacket pocket, and walked in a dignified fashion to the front door, pursued by imprecations.

I WARMED UP some refried beans, which I suppose made them re-refried, and googled quantum theory, grinding my teeth from time to time. It was the sort of thing I'd have expected Carl Jung to get excited about, and of course he had been involved in a sterile collaboration with the physicist Wolfgang Pauli before Pauli came to his senses and decided synchronicity was a lot of hogwash. Bohr thought nothing *was* until it was *observed*, which might not have appealed to Freud, who thought all sort of unobserved items got up to no end of mischief. Granted, the way to eradicate and heal the mischief was to haul out the unobserved into the open, but then Bohr and Heisenberg (it said on my screen) insisted that you couldn't really get away with that, or only a bit at a time. I gave up, washed my plate, made some coffee, and called Mandy. That meant dealing with her mother first, but somehow I got through that ordeal and onto my sweet daughter.

"What do you want?"

"Don't you mean, 'What the fuck do *you* want, Daddy dearest?' Don't answer that. Can't a man call his own –"

"I'm hanging up."

"Mandy, did you or one of your friends make that video of me? And the Toshtenov boys?"

In the background I heard someone incredibly famous and fatuous, someone observed at every moment of the day and night by hundreds of millions if not billions, of whom I knew nothing beyond their unlikely names. Beyoncé, or Lady Gaga, or Rihanna, or Bran'Nu. (I try. It makes my brain itch, but I do try. Fourteen year olds are feral.) Talk about quantum observers and ontological status. If anyone existed on the planet because of being observed, they were it. Talk about the evil of banality. After a long moment, my daughter said: "What?" Another silence. I waited. Then, with acid adolescent contempt: "Who would make a vid of *you?*"

"That's what I'm trying to find out, my good-natured offspring. Okay, look, I'll send you a tinyurl. The orphan's short."

"What?"

"Just let me know what you think. Okay? This is really important to me, Mandy."

"Whatever." She clicked off.

I fiddled about with my notes for the next day's lecture, thoughts skittering everywhere, and finally abandoned that as a really pointless exercise. Manfully, I kept away from the Jack Daniels. My daughter didn't call back or email me or text me or instant message me or tweet me, hardly to my surprise, but it was a bit disheartening. My Tivo was showing me a light, so I watched the ep of *Californication* it had grabbed while I wasn't paying attention ("Mr Bad Example," which seemed somehow oracular), then had a shower, took a sleeping pill, and went to bed. At five in the morning I woke up with a headache and a woman standing in my dark bedroom. She said something.

"Hmngh?"

"She put it on the web."

I climbed out of bed naked, clawing for my trousers. The woman didn't shift her gaze from my face. "Who the hell are you and how did you get –"

"Went viral."

I CLAPPED MY hands and the bedside lamp came on. The woman was medium height, with a dark razor-brush 'do, and looked incontestably Bulgarian: long elegant nose, broad brow, widely spaced eyes. I had fancied to discern the creature in the immature features of the boys Wolf and Chris, but now I found the other half of the taller kid's genome, if not his half-brothers's. Good god, was the creature devoted to spreading his seed across the world? I said, "You'll be the time-slut, then."

She said, "*Beg* pardon?" All the women I'd met recently appeared to have formed a secret club dedicated to taking umbrage at everything I said to them. Except Lissa, I thought muzzily, and rubbed grit out of my eyes.

"I apologize, Mrs Toshtenov. Having a hard time lately, not thinking all that clearly. Forgive me for being naked in my own bedroom."

"Is nothing haven't seen before."

"No doubt."

She clucked her tongue. "Radka. Not married. Am mother to Ivaylo."

I nodded. "Wolf."

"Means 'wolf,' yes."

"You sent me a message," I said, and finished getting dressed. "Then my bad-tempered daughter put it on YouTube, I take it. If that was your intention, why not just do it yourself? I thought it was fake, but now I –"

"Not much time," Radka told me. She bounced on her toes, almost vibrated with tension. "Listen. Am professor theoretical physics, Sofia. Not yet, soon. Listen, listen, keep mouth shut. Bohr wrong, of course. Bohm, wrong. Heisenberg not even wrong. QBists, half right." She went out like a light. I hadn't clapped my hands. A young woman in her early twenties stood several inches to the right of Radka's last jitter. Her hair was cropped close, a sort of tie-dyed version of the Bulgarian fashion statement. I recognized her at once.

"Mandy," I yelped, and took a hesitant step, afraid to embrace her. The ghost of Christmas Future.

She stayed still, also vibrating. "Amanda. Hello, Dad. No, stay there. Everyone's observing this, see, that's the point. Everyone. Everything. Forever, probably. Well, near enough."

I sat down on the edge of the bed again and put my head in my hands. "I hope you're not going to tell me the Reverend Willard sent you."

"What?"

"Oh my god, are we back to that again?" I peeked through my fingers. Amanda sent me a wry grin.

"That was then. See, I do remember. Oh, I suppose it's now, too, if you look at it that –" She cleared her throat. "It's an entanglement excursion," Amanda told me. "Probability waves bouncing around an attractor, making the droplets walk, you know? We're just walls of flesh, Daddy, wrapped around bars of bone. And tangled."

A fragment of an old Bob Dylan song twanged in the back of my defeated skull. "Tangled up in blue." I let some words slip out, out of key but maybe that's how you have to sing Dylan: "*All the people we used to know, they're an illusion to me now.*"

For a moment I thought my daughter was going to say "What?" again, but she caught herself and grinned again, more broadly this time. "Some are mathematicians," she said. It made me happy. Mandy the teen brat despised Dylan. "Tzvetan, for one. Go and talk to him."

"I thought he's a phys –" I started and she winked away. The creature of science stood in my bedroom, regarding me from a superior vantage. I couldn't quite keep my eyes on him. After-images flickered around the man. Christ, that's all I need, I told myself. Epilepsy. Or migraine, was it? Auras, battlements, fortification figures on the retina or, rather, deep inside the screwed-up brain. Jerry Lehman's chapter had something on the topic. I couldn't recall what. I'm so slack, I thought. And I used to be the boy wonder of psychoanalytic semiotics, back when that was the sexy thing to be a boy wonder in. "Can I help you, Dr Toshtenov? It's rather early, a mug of coffee? Heart starter? I was just talking to your..." Your what? I trailed off.

"Radka," he said. "Yes. No coffee. Sit down, Dr Watson. I can't stay long, and we have a lot to cover." Tzvetan Toshtenov, with surprising levity (of a rather heavy-handed kind, I supposed, although I had no notion what it meant), wore a tee-shirt urging me to *Please adjust your priors before leaving the QBicle.* "What do you know about quantum entanglement and Bayesian probability theory?"

I gave him a sour look. "If we're going to play one-upmanship, Schrödinger, what do *you* know about, oh, the imbricated relationship between the Real, the Symbolic and the Imaginary?"

He looked at me suspiciously. "As in imaginary time? The *teh* dimension? Yes, that's relevant."

"As in the Lacanian orders of – oh, never mind. Think of them as the three rings of a Borromean knot. That's three tangled rings that fall apart if one of them is cut. Like the middle rings in the Olympic symbol, but more so, or maybe not quite." I knew I was babbling, but I could see where that item of gibberish had popped up from: the entanglement Mandy mentioned. Future Amanda. And Bob Dylan.

"Chain. Borromean topological chain," the creature said, looking mildly astonished. "That's exceptionally astute, Watson, I didn't think you had it in you."

"No, it's a knot." He looked pained, as if once again I'd fallen in his estimation, and I quickly babbled: "Lacan argued that psychosis is what happens when the Borromean knot unravels, unless it's held in place by a fourth ring."

"A sinthome," Tzvetan the mathematician-physicist-smartass said. "Exactly. An extra link to the ring chain, a double curve. One ring to rule them all, as my boys would put it." He smiled fondly. "A bond through *teh* supertime. That's what holds the chain together. Holds everything. Do you see, Watson? *Every*thing is *no*thing but uncertainties, latencies, probability pilot waves perhaps, vapors threaded in fog – until it is observed into definiteness and clarity."

"They teach you this stuff in Bulgaria, do they?"

He was gone. "Ha ha," I said weakly. "I unobserved you." I lay down and covered my eyes with one sweating forearm. Obviously I was ripe for the laughing academy. My Borromean chain had been pulled, and I was sliding down the cloaca maxima. I just wanted to go back to sleep, but when I made a feeble attempt to clap the light off there was already too much morning illumination coming in through the blinds. A voice said, from the centre of the room, "Watson, come here, I need you." Bev's voice. Our old joke, and thank you, Alexander Graham Bell. She wasn't there. I put my socks and loafers on and started for the front door and my bike. Everything happened at once.

It wasn't the Rapture, and it wasn't the Cloud of Unknowing. This was the Cloud of Knowing Too Much, the silver lining of the dark night of the soul blazing like a thousand suns, like the Buddhist ten thousand things, the unity and diversity of everything bonded into its clasp, and I stood at the middle of it all but that was also at the edge, and at every point in between. Walls of flesh, bars of bone, gates of light, opening.

Mandy in my trembling arms, so tiny, so ugly, so incomprehensibly beautiful, eyes squeezed shut, head still slightly deformed by the terrible passage through her mother's body to this cold, brilliantly lit place. Sheila, holding up her arms for the baby, her own face shiny with sweat, exhausted, exultant. I bent to kiss her, Mandy cradled – an old lady with frosted hair and a look of synthetic peace on her harsh face, stretched in an open coffin. I bent and could not bring my lips to touch hers. The eyes of a hundred students locked to mine or skittering away or dully drooped to their laptops as I stood at the fulcrum of the lecture theatre teasing them with text and context. "There is no outside-the-text," I said. "So we are told inside a text by Derrida: *Il n'y a pas de hors-texte*. So we carry that meaning outside, away from his text, reading it, observing it from as many angles as we can, remake it as our text, or discard it as waste, order into ordure, or vice versa, as supplement, so that it becomes, paradoxically –" With Beverley, young love redividus, I stood, I stand, I will stand before paintings, etchings, constructs, texts that are all at once or seem to be, even as the eye skips and snacks and rebuilds, Picasso's wonderful African contortions, *Les Demoiselles d'Avignon*, his cubism, his late hideous, marvellous *Nude Woman with a Necklace*, and of course the once-fashionable distortions and visual paradoxa of Dali, Escher, Magritte, the decompressions into art that denied itself as art, Rauschenberg, Johns, Lichtenstein, the comic antics of Warhol and Koons and a thousand others, Dadaists, *Fauves*, frauds, Freudians, unpeelers of pretence and its practitioners, and through it all the slowly ebbing passion, the curdling of my cynical eye observing everything into nothing... All of this a millionfold, birth, copulation, and death.

"Bev," I said, "help me," and tears flooded down my face. I took a step and stood in the morning kitchen of our old house, our renovated house, the Edenic garden from which I'd exiled myself. Two little boys looked up from their bowls of cereal. Observing my manifestation from nowhere, the younger let out a piercing scream. The older yelled, "Tátko, that man has come back," and flung a spoonful of milk-soaked Rice Krispies at me, splashing my pants, like Luther hurling his ink bottle at the Devil. If it had been ink, a text *in potentia,* a zany part of my mind thought, it could have written a long bill of particulars, my crimes, every one. "Hush," I said. I held out my open, tear-wet hands. "Your daddy invited me here for breakfast, boys. Look, here he is now."

I am seated at the table, Bev's table, now his table. The boys have been driven to school. Tzvetan is saying, "I have to thank you most humbly, Dr Watson. I couldn't have done it without your tip. And the boys, of course. But that's later." Nobody is in the room to look at us, but we are observed. The very air hums with the intensity of their gaze. Their gaze contributes, their gaze elicits, their gaze is the terrible look of a million million angels, more, vastly more, without judgment or pity, it seems to me. They do not act beyond the activity of their *Tat tvam asi,* their spectatorship. This is just the blather of my discipline, which I hardly credit any longer, but that is the function, obviously, of my own reciprocal gaze, and the mirror that is... well, the universe, the specular everything. And –

Appalling compression, emphatic dark clarity, in the infinitely protracted nothingness that awaits a first crystalline instant of precipitation. It is an eye in utter darkness. Something breaks, ruptures, breaches, raptures, bursts forth into its going and coming, fecund, a spray of light flung into the endless sphere of eyes gazing from within and without, making manifest, tumbling faster than light into categories that render themselves under that impossible gaze from the far ends of itself, from everywhere, forever. The sky foams with explosions boiling with a froth of stuff that swirls and settles and catches new light, a heaventree of galaxies, photonic dust etching their eidolons upon the eyes that watch and select and shape and build. My own eyes are there also, watching the lights redden and dissipate and fall away into night unendurably cold and empty. But that is the way of the thing, that is the story, all the eyes can do is witness until they are folded back into the great silence and void. Tzvetan is murmuring in my ear. "My experiment with single particle self-interference proved that a macroscopic extended object can be made to deviate through an instability threshold and surf its own pilot wave. But it can only do that because *we* chose to place it in that apparatus. We *observe* it from our own Bayesian priors, and its activity is objectively determined by the interaction between us and the particle. This is *not* mystical, Watson, stop curling your lip. It is the basis for everything that ever happens, to eternity and infinity."

I am aghast at the hubris. "So we're... engineering infinity?"

"No," he tells me, sharply. "Precisely not. We are nothing until we are observed *by the universe*. Infinity is engineering *us*."

Amanda handed me an old musty suit and a cloth cap. Of course I had seen them before. The world shimmered slightly, as if it were uncertain of itself. Two youngsters came into the studio – oh, *that's* where I was – dressed in Depression era knickerbockers suitable for urchins. The younger boy pushed a flat, flexible machine under his grey shirt, and winked at me.

"You're sending yourself a message, Lee," he said. "This is the moment we've all been waiting for."

I sent my daughter out of the room and dressed, dazed. "Who is going to send the orphan film to me?" I said.

"The universe," my ex-wife Bev told me at some time in the near future. She looked plumper, and a lot happier. Was she pregnant? Did the man pepper the planet with his offspring? "But I've found out who sent me that Rauschenberg, Lee, and I thank you. Of course, it will be a lot cheaper to buy it in 1951."

The universe looked at me, and I looked back, and found myself blinking in bright snowless winter afternoon light in New York, an older New York with far fewer of the great mirroring skyscrapers that will someday be built. Were. Up ahead, I saw the Reverend ranting, and I strolled past. Some nameless amateur cinematographer was cranking a Ciné-Kodak, and as I passed him I remembered the kid's cheeky wink and slipped the fellow one of my own. The two boys were horsing about, an irritated old geezer slapped out with his cane, but Krastio, the younger, had his eye focused on the middle distance. An intent, lovely woman in a long dowdy 1930s dress appeared out of nowhere at the entrance to a laneway. Quantum tunnelled, I suppose Tzvetan would call it. Nobody but the younger boy and I saw her, except everyone and everything, forever. Krastio yelled out hoarsely to Ivaylo, "Your mother's at *teh* – begin time slot." He pulled out his display and flashed a page of equations to the rolling film. I walked briskly past, and took Radka's hand. The universe observed us in silence amid the rumbling noise of the city.

MANTIS

ROBERT REED

Robert Reed was born in Omaha, Nebraska in 1956. He has a Bachelor of Science in Biology from the Nebraska Wesleyan University, and has worked as a lab technician. He became a full-time writer in 1987, the same year he won the L. Ron Hubbard Writers of the Future Contest, and has published eleven novels, including The Leeshore, The Hormone Jungle, *and far future science fiction novels* Marrow *and* The Well of Stars. *An extraordinarily prolific writer, Reed has published over 180 short stories, mostly in* F&SF *and* Asimov's, *which have been nominated for the Hugo, James Tiptree Jr. Memorial, Locus, Nebula, Seiun, Theodore Sturgeon Memorial, and World Fantasy awards, and have been collected in* The Dragons of Springplace *and* The Cuckoo's Boys. *His novella "A Billion Eves" won the Hugo Award in 2007. Nebraska's only SF writer, Reed lives in Lincoln with his wife and daughter, and is an ardent long-distance runner.*

INFINITY WINDOWS WERE installed two months ago, but technical troubles, nebulous and vexing, delayed their coming on-line. The tall squidskin sheets were left transparent, revealing white walls and assorted cables leading back to the building's servers and power plant. Mr Pembrook is our club manager, and whenever he bounced past he made the point of apologizing for any inconvenience. But I didn't particularly miss the mirrors that used to hang here; staring at my pained, sweat-sheened face was never an attraction. And I didn't pine for the giant televisions tuned to sports I didn't follow and the 24/7 crime networks. White and bland suited my task, and after the first week it felt as if this was the way it had always been.

My club sits ten storeys above the apartment where I live with my son. Fifty machines of various designs fill a long, narrow, well-ventilated room. My favourite machine is near the back corner, and it's usually unoccupied in the early afternoon. As a rule, I avoid the newer models. I'm avid but lazy, and their "miles" feel long to me. I know what to expect when I work the pedals and swing the long arms, the onboard computer interfacing with a heart and lungs it knows as well as any. I prefer hill workouts while watching history programs from my own library, and one hard hour is usually enough to cleanse a brain evolved to chase antelope across a grassy plain.

Mostly the same faces haunt the club every day, and we know each other on sight and sometimes by name. A few regulars are passing acquaintances. Not Berry. I know her name only because somebody once called her that in front of me. Berry might be her first name, or last, or a nickname. Or I didn't hear things right, and she's somebody else entirely.

Whatever the name, the woman seems to be in her late sixties. She has a long face framed with hair dyed a luxurious, unnatural black. She never asks anything of her machine except a lot of easy minutes. She watches old hospital shows, turn-of-the-century stuff. Like me, she has her favourite machine or two, and she always wears the big smile of somebody who is relentlessly nice and almost certainly boring.

One afternoon while my son was at school, I arrived to discover the infinity windows working. The room had been transformed, and I laughed out loud. Happy Mr Pembrook explained that in the end the problem was nothing mechanical. "Inspiration at the AI level," he said, whatever that means. It seems that the windows aren't just hybrids between two ordinary technologies – teleconferencing and digital entertainment. Some level of bottled genius was at work here. The new-generation squidskins are energy frugal and startlingly realistic, but instead of piping in a scenic overlook of some great city or Martian canyon, we were being treated to a downtown corner in some cookie-cutter city. The most prosaic setting possible, which startled me as much as anything, and that's another reason why I laughed and why I kept chuckling until I was perched on top of my usual apparatus.

Berry's favourite machines were occupied, which was why she happened to be riding the old warhorse on my right. "Yes, the window's working," she said, throwing her simple smile my way.

"Well, good," I offered in return.

It was the first time we had ever spoken.

From the menu, I selected "Killer Hill-3." My heart set to work with gratifying eagerness. Then I called up my library, ready to plug in sixty minutes of Ancient Greece or World War II. But I couldn't stop staring at the world stretched out before me. It felt as if we were really at ground level. Judging by the shadows, we were facing north or south. A few busy strangers walked past – people of means with bright clothes and fine firm bodies. Some kind of tree was growing from a square of raw ground between the sidewalk and curb, and across the street stood a brick building that might have looked pretty for a couple days in its hundred-year life. Like a genuine window, diluted outdoor sounds passed through the squidskin. I heard the angry motor of a truck before I saw it. Several men on my left shouted their approval, and an ancient dump truck appeared, impossibly long and carrying what looked like the marble leg and torso and battered face of an ancient statue – the statue of a naked goddess pulled from Greek mythology or adolescent fantasy.

That was such an unlikely detail. Human faces are supposed to be doctored, leaving viewers unaware of who they might be watching. Privacy laws are clear on that score. But what I had heard once or twice was obviously true: The new infinity windows were as much invention as they were reality. Somewhere in the world was a city like this one, and it was inhabited by about as many pedestrians and vehicles as we saw for ourselves. But those people had different faces. And the AI, endowed with genius and the threat of boredom, was endlessly editing everything that was here, sculpting its own little storylines and odd sights; a marriage of the clever and peculiar leading to a view that people would watch, if only for fear that they might miss something remarkable.

Moments later came the musical hum of a real bus. An efficient box pulled to the curb and opened up. Six or seven strangers climbed out, every face twisted to protect identities. And every one of them wore a red nose and the bright white skin of a clown.

I like to think that I appreciate new technologies. Not that I'm an expert in AI genius or digital gamesmanship. But curious, endearing joy kept rolling through me. These little nuggets of fiction made me laugh, reminding me of those silly pictures that my son liked when he was five, where the game was to spot the chicken wearing a hat and the panda eating steak. Except these were stranger and much funnier visions, and to a man who wasn't going anywhere for another fifty-five minutes, endlessly entertaining.

The biggest story was subtle.

After a lull in foot traffic, a young fellow appeared. I noticed him at a distance, although I couldn't say why. Nothing about him seemed unusual. His clothes and face were ordinary. He walked toward the corner and stopped, his back to Berry and me. My assumption was that he was waiting for the next bus. Wherever this was, the day looked sunny and hot, and he stood against the building's shade. After a few moments, he turned, and with shameless intensity he stared at my face. Then with the same laser care, he examined Berry. And stepping back from the building, he laughed, lifting his arms and knees, and with a clown's oversized motions pretended that he was one of us, riding a marching machine that took him nowhere.

I didn't laugh so much as gasp.

"He can see us," I muttered.

One of Berry's doctor shows was playing. She paused it with a voice command and turned to me, never slowing her gait. But her smile changed, growing more serious. Then with a slow, careful voice – the voice that smart people use on diminished souls – she explained, "The window works in both directions."

"It does?"

Why didn't I remember that?

"Of course it does," she said. "One AI can serve two markets at once, which helps with energy demands and the general economics."

"But he doesn't see our faces," I said hopefully.

"Of course not." She gave out a big laugh, adding, "The window makes me twenty years younger, I hope."

Our new friend wasn't especially young or handsome. In fact, he seemed a little disreputable, his shoes were worn out and no socks, his shirt two mends short of being a rag. He was the kind of fellow that would earn a cautious look from me, if I found myself on his street. Which wouldn't happen, of course. But he or the window had a redeeming sense of humour, and his audience ended up having a good long laugh.

Once the mocking workout was finished, the stranger suddenly knelt down. I didn't understand why. Then a hand that could have used a good scrub touched our club's corporate emblem – the healthy red heart and two pink lungs full of good health and happy endorphins.

I cut my pace, allowing extra oxygen to flood my foolish brain. "It does make sense though, working both ways."

Berry didn't respond immediately.

"I just expected us to be high in the sky." It seemed important, explaining away my temporary stupidity.

"Windows serve many functions," she explained. "Advertisement, for one. This gentleman sees spectacular versions of you and me, and he's more likely to join his local club."

"He doesn't look like money," I mentioned.

"Looks," she said with a dismissive tone. "We don't know what to believe. Maybe in real life, he's wearing a suit. Besides, those legs are strong, and he isn't exactly starving."

No, I couldn't believe anything I was seeing. But more important, I had to be careful when I talked.

An uncomfortable moment passed between us. Then this woman I didn't know turned to me. Her smile was anything but simple. With a grave, almost morbid tone, she said, "These windows bother me."

"Why?"

"Solipsism," she said.

"Pardon?"

"Do you know what the word means?"

"Yes," I lied.

"The premise that everything outside your own mind could be unreal."

"I know the concept," I said.

"Anyway," she said. "I am troubled."

"By what?"

She didn't answer immediately. Growing bored with the window, or at least with us, our new friend had stepped out into the sun. We watched him looking up into the branches of the little tree. I noticed the leaves: very green and shaped like fans, veins radiating out from the stem. Which seemed phony.

"Since I was a teenager," Berry said, "the notion that the world isn't real has been gnawing at me."

"Every kid thinks that way," I said. "Everybody else is a figment of my vivid, important imagination."

"But today, anything is possible," she reminded me. "Algorithms can draw any scene, and AI wetware can string together any narrative. And everybody has to deal with that thirteen-year-old's conundrum: 'Am I real?'"

"I'm real," I said reflexively.

"And how would you know?" There wasn't any smile left on the old face. Gloomy and honest, she said, "Maybe we're illusions. Some AI dreamed us up. We're being used as an advertisement for the health club, and the target audience is standing out there, scratching his butt."

I looked at our friend's casual ass-rubbing. "I don't believe that," I said.

"Of course, you can't," she said.

And then I gave up talking, working the imaginary hill as hard as I could.

BUSES ARE DESTINED to run late. No system involving dozens of vehicles and thousands of humans can exclude chance, and chance wants to place every player ahead or behind schedule. That's why any two buses will usually be closer than expected or farther apart. Prospective riders face three possibilities: Arrive at their stop exactly as the next bus pulls up, which gives them reason to believe in God or their special luck. Or they hit an interval between two closely spaced buses – a rather more likely scenario reinforcing the idea of effective, efficient government. But the most common outcome is to enter one of the longer gaps, and if it's near the beginning, even the most rational citizen of the world will glance at the time and cluck his tongue, wondering why his goddamn bus isn't here yet.

The vagaries of chance: That's what I was thinking about when I turned away from the infinity window.

Apex Road was empty of buses and most other traffic, adding to the general dilapidation of downtown. I could have checked the transit logs, wringing the data for a good estimate of my departure time. But I wasn't in any special hurry. There was no place I needed to be. A joyful life full of minimal expectations – that's how I paint myself when I need to crow about my blessings.

It was a warm day but not a furnace. Not like the last three weeks, at least. A previous mayor used our greenhouse abatement funds to buy ginkgo trees – an enhanced strain. They were planted up and down Apex, pieces of sidewalk removed so the roots could be shoved into rectangular patches of hard clay soil. The trees thrived a few years before starting to die. Only the corner gingko was still alive, and there was a bench in its shade where a man could sit and wait for the next piece of his life to begin.

There wasn't any wind. The world was like a picture, fixed and forever. I scratched an itch and sat down, and then I looked up.

Perched on the lowest branch was a marvel. How I even noticed her is a minor mystery. Whatever the reason, I saw her perched on the ginkgo branch, and with no expectations of success, I stood up and reached high, fingers nervous until the light dry feet shifted onto my right hand.

Her size and what I remembered about mantis biology told me she was a fully mature female. All of my life I'd held a fondness for these creatures. They looked deeply unlikely, cobbled together out of several less beautiful insects, but those marvellous, murderous arms belong to them alone. She weighed almost nothing, but she was still better than four inches long. I brought her down to eye level, staring at her pivoting, self-aware face. If I was a worry, she didn't show it. She held herself in a confident, queenly poise. I dropped her gently onto the back of the bench, and she accepted her new perch without complaint. I put my hands on my hips and laughed. Then I decided that an audience was necessary, which was why I looked back at the infinity window.

People were still riding those elliptical beasts. The woman in front of me was tall and elegant, not young but pretty in ways that no living, farting human being could ever manage to be. I didn't own any clothes as attractive as her tights and top. She looked like someone I should recognize: an aging actress, perhaps. In his own way, her man-friend was equally unlikely, all muscle and shiny flesh, thick veins bulging when he worked his arms and those long strong legs that shook the machine as he powered his way through the illusionary forward.

I waved at them and pointed at my mantis. But neither person would look at me now. The man was staring off into the distance, talking with feeling about some important matter, and then he stopped talking and the woman began to speak, causing her companion to frown and speed up even more, eyes narrowed as he contemplated whatever unwelcome news he was hearing.

Once again, I looked up the street.

My bus was still missing, but walking down the

sidewalk was a rather pretty girl. And by "girl," I mean she was a female who looked maybe fifteen years younger than me, which meant she wasn't a girl at all. I watched her. She glanced at me long enough to decide that maybe she should look elsewhere. I'm accustomed to that response. I've never been a beast who dresses up in camouflage. But this was a different day, and the beast had a fresh trick at the ready.

"Look here," I said. "Look at this."

The girl threw a hopeful glance over her shoulder. But no, she was the only real person in sight.

"I found her up in the tree," I said.

My audience considered some good fast walking.

"And she walked right into my hand," I concluded, backing away from the bench, palms opened to the sky like a magician finishing his signature trick.

It was a wonderful moment. As if playing along, the mantis did a sudden little dance, flexing her raptorial legs while that bright watchful face did everything but wink.

The girl blinked.

Then she said, "Delightful," and came closer.

I just stood there, grinning happily.

With measured caution, she held out her hand and then slowly extended one finger, and the mantis took a swing at her fingertip.

She laughed loudly, buoyantly. "Oh, it is real," she said.

"I love these insects," I told her.

And she gave me another look. Not that I was anything she would ever want, but there was something about my face or my eyes that told her that at least she didn't need to run away.

The two of us could stand on that street corner, talking politely.

"Is it really a female?" she asked.

I said that I thought so, yes.

"They're the bugs that chew off their lover's heads, aren't they? While they're actually doing it?"

"It's their nature," I said.

And once again, with relish, she said, "Delightful."

"I'M SORRY," THE woman said.

This was an apology, but it took me a few moments to appreciate what was happening. I slowed and looked over at Berry, and she smiled as if embarrassed, admitting, "It's a rough game, thinking you might not be real."

"But I am real."

She nodded politely.

"I am," I repeated. But my denial was just words, reflexive and simple, and this topic made me uncomfortable.

Berry looked at her machine's screen, at the wise doctors and their beautiful, doomed patient. I assumed that our conversation was finished, that we might never speak again. Desperate for a distraction, I looked at the window. A young woman had just wandered into view. She could have been pretty, but she was too thin – that half-starved look that people acquire when they eat nothing but algae. Her legs and forearms were like sticks. She and that strange man chatted amiably. Then she approached the bench, her hand palm-up and slow. I studied her scrawny chicken back with the spine trying to push up through the skin and the shirt. I couldn't see what her hand was doing, but I was curious, particularly when she started to laugh. A loud giggle was audible over the sounds of machines and ventilation, and that's when she turned around, showing the world what she was holding.

"Look at that," I said.

Berry lifted her gaze. "Is that what I think it is?"

"No, it's probably something else," I said.

The old woman laughed. "You're right. But it could be a praying mantis. They get that big, don't they?"

"Honestly, I don't know bugs."

"We could look it up," she said.

"Or we could just watch the show," I said.

"The show" was two strangers and that emerald-green mantis perched in the girl's skeletal hand. The man said a few words, and the girl nodded and offered her other hand to the rider. More amiable than most pets, the insect walked to its new perch and flexed its arms. I could just make out its head pivoting and the sunshine in the tree branches and how those odd, almost alien looking leaves caught the light, turning it into something cooler and more special.

For a second time, I was sad and bothered.

Maybe Berry noticed, but probably not. More likely she was just dwelling on matters that meant something to her.

"I've watched a lot of these shows," she told me.

"Strangers and bugs?"

She laughed hard enough to break stride. Then she pointed at her screen, saying, "When I was little, my mother and I watched this television series, and I felt special. She allowed me to stay up late on a school night. Just to see these long-dead actors reading scripts written by people I wouldn't know from anybody. Oh, and the stories they told. Contrived and melodramatic, and we loved them. This was a great bonding experience for my mother and me. And I can't stop loving them. I mean, just this scene here...this poor gorgeous actress who lived fifty more years, but in this episode she's dying of leukaemia, and doesn't she look wonderful?"

I glanced at the screen. "She looks fine."

"An innocent, rich, meat-fed wonderful."

I didn't know what to say.

"This is the world I was born into," Berry said, her tone amazed, even a little disbelieving. "Whatever happened to that world?"

"The future happened," I said.

She laughed about that.

"But we're doing better every day," I added with conviction.

The strangers were sitting on the bench. They weren't sitting together, but they were close enough that the third party in this newborn relationship could stand on one open hand, and then, following some bug logic, calmly and purposefully walk across to the other offered hand.

I couldn't say why, but I was fascinated.

My pace slowed, and the machine gave me a quiet warning beep.

Then as I sped up, Berry turned back to me. And with a wary eye, she asked, "Do you want to know how to know? If you're real or not, I mean."

"There's a test?"

"One that I invented, yes."

"All right," I said. "Give it to me."

* * *

WE SAT AND we talked, and I wasn't entirely sure what we had been talking about. It was that fun, that unexpected – one long, wonderful blur of words, busy and intense but never focused on anything important. Nothing secret or even borderline personal was shared. It was just that the ordinary details of ordinary life seemed spectacularly fascinating. We discussed weather and traffic and favourite foods, and she mentioned how much she liked Chinese food. And that was my opportunity to mention that ginkgo trees were from China and this mantis was probably the same. An Asian species was brought into the country in the last century, drafted a biological warrior in the losing war against insect pests.

"So she is a weed," the girl said with amusement. "One of the monsters crumbling our precious ecosystem."

"Maybe you should smash her," I suggested.

And the girl gave me a funny look, trying to discern if I meant it. I didn't. Then she lifted the mantis to her face, its arms in range of her nose.

The mantis' head twisted and turned.

And the girl easily mimicked every motion.

She wasn't beautiful, no. But there was youth and humour in her soul, and she wore the purposeful leanness of someone who didn't want to ride hard on our poor suffering world.

Lowering our friend, she looked at me, and with a suddenly serious, very important tone, she asked, "Is that your bus?"

It was. But as I explained before, there was no place that I needed to be, at least not in the immediate future.

"I'm going to sit here for now," I said.

"Well then. I guess I will too."

Such a day, and who would have guessed it possible?

"I'VE MADE A study of storytelling," Berry began. "Nothing scholarly or elaborate. But I'm lucky enough to have been around for a very long time, and what do humans do with their lives? We absorb stories. Day and night, commercial tales or twists of gossip, we swim in an ocean of story."

"You just think you're human," I said.

She laughed. "Point taken."

A new bus was arriving. The shiny door swung open, but nobody disembarked. Instead of an automated pilot, there was a fat human male perched on a hard high seat. The drab uniform threatened to split with the pressure of the swollen body, fat hands clinging to the old-fashioned steering wheel. All the colour was washed out of the man, but that wasn't the oddest detail. It was his face. I recognized him. To save my life, I couldn't identify the driver, but I was absolutely certain that I had seen him pictured somewhere. Maybe he was the obese man from one of my son's school lessons – a cautionary emblem of wasted, impoverishing wealth that stole too much from the world.

"A good story begins in an intriguing place," Berry said.

The couple remained seated on their bench, playing with the bug. The driver closed his door with a mechanical lever, and the ancient diesel engine roared as the bus rolled away, dragging a swirling black cloud of soot in its wake.

"But the tale can't be too interesting either," she said. "The author doesn't dare surrender too much, because the next scenes or the coming chapters are going to drag, if only by comparison."

"I suppose not," I said.

"A great story is like a wonderful song. There are those delightful beginning notes and a fetching flow, and it builds and grows, entertaining its audience for the whole journey."

"And what does this have to do with us?" I asked.

"Stories do grow," she said. "It's inevitable and I'm sure there is some robust scientific reason why narratives become more complicated and intricate with time. Maybe it's because fresh characters are being introduced. Or maybe it's the thirst for surprise plots and new twists. Whatever the reason, I've seen this a thousand times. Take my little doctor drama here, for instance. The television series ran for years and years, getting bigger and wilder every season. Ordinary diseases weren't good enough anymore. Plagues and spectacular tropical diseases kept raising the stakes. Happily married characters suddenly fell into torrid affairs, and the best doctors started killing patients, and every woman gave birth whenever it would help the ratings most. Preferably in the middle of an anthrax attack."

If she proved nothing else to me, I realized Berry was a very peculiar old gal. "So what's your test?" I asked.

"This is how you can tell if you're living inside a made-up story," she said. "If your world is contrived from thought and shaped light and a few arbitrary, algorithmic principles, then odds are you are living an interesting, unlikely life. A spellbinding life. Just think of the stories that capture your imagination. Aren't they full of important coincidences, and passion, and tragic pain, and obvious heroism? No character with a name has to wait long for something new and fascinating to happen to him."

I nodded, staring straight ahead. The woman on the bench was handing the mantis to the man. The man said something, and the skinny woman smiled and said, "Yes," while nodding, closing her eyes and tilting her mouth.

"Is your life fascinating?" Berry asked.

"Not normally," I allowed.

"Well then," she said. "Every time you feel bored and ordinary, be grateful. Because that's the best evidence that you are genuinely, joyously real."

AT ONE POINT, I said, "You know what I want to do, don't you? I want very much to kiss you."

Her name was still a mystery, and I was equally unknown to her. But bless the girl, she didn't jump up and run away. What she did was stare hard at me, never blinking, and after what seemed like a very long while, she said, "Oh, you want to kiss me, do you?"

"Yes, very much," I said.

"Since when?" she asked.

I suppose she expected to hear that the idea popped into my head now, or maybe when I first saw her walking my way. But I surprised both of us, saying, "I woke up today wanting to. I just hadn't met you yet."

It isn't often that inspiration finds me. And looking at my life, I can't think of ten other times where this much success has come from a few words.

The girl nodded and smiled, saying, "Yes."

And we kissed. For a very long time, we held that pose. She even let me put a hand on her bony back and shoulder.

We pulled apart, and I said, "You like Chinese."

She nodded warily.

"I have enough carbon points for one exceptional dinner," I promised.

Hunger made her face prettier. She didn't trust herself to say, "Yes." Her enthusiasm might scare me off. So instead, she nodded and took a deep breath, handing the mantis back to me.

She asked, "What does the mantis think about?"

"Her next meal," I suggested.

"Besides that." Then the girl laughed, saying, "I think she knows that she is the centre of the universe, and we're all just objects, soulless but entertaining to her."

On that note, I stood and started to place our friend back into the tree, and that's when I looked at the infinity window again. I suppose I wanted to see approval from our audience. But the window had gone out, and except for a giant gutted room and some upturned office furniture, there was nothing to see. There was nothing but glass and the girl's reflection, and mine, and my arm up high, as if I was waiting for some hook or hand to grab me up and carry me away.

WE HOLLERED. I think every patron in the club yelled, loudly and most of the words angry. Mr Pembrook came bounding out of his office. He is a red-faced man with no hair and elastic kangaroo-style legs.

Sharing our panic, he began chasing wires and tinkering with diagnostic boards. Within the first few minutes he narrowed the blame down to ten or twenty possibilities, none of which he could fix. His apologies were earnest, and he wished there was more that he could do. But there wouldn't be any fix until tomorrow, if then, and with that sorry bit of non-news, he bounded back to his office and vanished.

I was still beside Berry, still working my lungs and heart. I had watched those strangers start to kiss, and now I was staring at the white wall, some piece of me ready for whatever scene was to come next.

And I kept thinking about that long green mantis too.

Berry and I exchanged a few more words. She was still attacking the easy miles when I finished, and I thanked her for the conversation. "Food for thought," I said. Then I called for help, and my personal cradle swept in and took me under what remains of my arms, lifting me up as my new friend said, "I'll see you around, perhaps."

"I'm sure you will," I said.

There was something else I wanted to say, but I resisted. I didn't think it would be right, parting on a sour, disagreeable note.

I live ten floors below the club, in an apartment that encompasses an enormous volume – a wealthy man's home with two rooms and a private, water-free bath. I really don't have the means for this luxury, which is why the rest of my life is full of sacrifices. I rarely run the air conditioning and never travel. It takes very little food to keep my minimal body alive and healthy, which gives me extra carbon points.

In this world with too many people and too many problems, my son eats well when he comes home. And on that day it seemed like such a blessing to see him – a robust and busy, full-limbed gentleman who was five days short of his thirteenth birthday.

His dinner was real potatoes and peas and a meat that was sold under the euphemistic label RABBIT.

I had an intravenous meal and chew stick to keep my mouth busy.

Together, we watched what interested me – the world's news compressed into fourteen minutes of drought and distant wars, plus heaping helpings of heroic perseverance and robots exploring the high clouds of Venus. Then I let him choose for both of us, and I endured the animated fluff. I watched my boy. I smiled at him, at least until he noticed. Then he frowned like any near-adolescent, telling me, "Stop that."

I looked away, staring at the emptiest of our walls. I was imagining the would-be lovers, wondering what part of them was real, and then I pictured Berry beside me, and I told her, "This is where you are wrong. Characters in a story can't tell if anything about their lives is remarkable or interesting. They just are. But there is one major difference between stories and life. Stories come to an end. Eventually and always, there is a last chapter, a final scene. As you said, fictions get too big and cumbersome, and then the author gives them a mercy killing. But real life goes on and on. And that's how you know that all of this is genuine."

My boy noticed something in my gaze, or maybe I was muttering to myself. "What are thinking about, Dad?"

"Nothing, son. Nothing."

JUDGEMENT EVE

JOHN C. WRIGHT

John C. Wright attracted some attention in the late '90s with his early stories in Asimov's *(one of them, "Guest Law," was reprinted in David Hartwell's* Year's Best SF*), but it wasn't until he published his* Golden Age *trilogy (consisting of* The Golden Age, The Golden Transcendence, *and* The Phoenix Exultant*) in the first few years of the new century, novels which earned critical raves across the board, that he was recognized as a major new talent in SF. Subsequent novels include the* Everness *fantasy series, including* The Last Guardians of Everness *and* Mists of Everness, *and the fantasy* Chaos *series, which includes* Fugitives of Chaos, Orphans of Chaos, *and* Titans of Chaos. *His most recent novel, a continuation of the famous* Null-A *series by A.E. van Vogt, is* Null-A Continuum. *Wright lives with his family in Centreville, Virginia.*

1.

IMAGINE THE BOULEVARDS of Golgolundra on the world's last day, and the angels circling like vultures above it. Everywhere is noise, and lights, and gaiety, and crime, and chaos.

Imagine every wall and window of the crowded towers colourful with graffiti. The graffiti of these times are bright, not sloppy, composed of computer-assisted images of artistic depth and merit. They move, they sing, they speak to passers-by, and some of them reach from their billboards and kill whomever seems dispirited, obnoxious, dull; tiny flicks of paint flying up, reforming in mid-air into blades or poisoned plumes of gas.

Other people, beautiful or monstrous or both, dancing in the street in their fantastic costumes, applaud and cheer when some vivid near-by death splatters them with blood. They do not wish to seem dull. The whole city screams and screams with laughter.

Why this forced gaiety? Why this hideous display? Today is the birthday party for Typhon, their founder; today is the wake for mankind.

Tomorrow the angels drown the world.

The streets are a festive combination of war-zone and Mardi Gras.

Imagine most of the crimes are committed by the young, who are more extravagant. A shy young boy sees a laughing woman sway by, surrounded by handsome admirers raising glasses of Champagne and poison. It takes him but a moment to program his assemblers. A diamond drop, unnoticed, stings her flesh or flies into her wine. A moment later it has taken carbon from her blood to construct a series of gates and interrupts along major nerve-channels in her spine. The programming is precise and elegant, there is no jerkiness as her arms and leg muscles move, stimulated without her control. She tries to cry out for her companions. Instead, her lips move, she hears her voice make clever excuses, and away she walks with the shy boy. He becomes a shy rapist, perhaps using his controllers to overload the pleasure centres of her brain, or pain centres, before doing whatever else to her his bored imagination might conceive.

Or imagine a laughing woman, irked by an unwanted stare, or prompted by real fear, who programs her assemblers to shoot into the boy's flesh, so that, in mid-festival, surrounded by unsure giggles, he will fall, his arms and legs distorted into clumsy lopsided shapes, or boneless tubes of flesh, while he stares in horror at the grotesque growths sprouting up from what was once his groin.

And perhaps she does not know who has offended her. Without sumptuary laws, faces and bodies change from day to day like images in nightmare. Better, she thinks, to program all assemblers to reproduce and strike at random. Any flesh they enter, check for genes. Spare those who carry XX chromosomes.

Now imagine, not two such folk, but a city of such people, creatures of godlike power and infantile rage. The sky above Golgolundra is dark with brilliant diamond points, thicker than confetti, a blizzard, and by now no one can tell who sent them out, or when, or why, or what their original programs were.

And where the assemblers fight each other (which they do often) the reaction heat from their rapid molecular manipulations starts fires in the city. No one fights the fires.

More people would be dead, more horribly, were it not for the Invigilators. They soar in the high pure air far above, surrounded by rainbows and rings of force.

Their technology is very different from that of the Earth.

When they dive, one can see manlike shapes; faces and forms of ruthless beauty. Their personal shields clothe each one in a radiant nimbus of gold, and the forces which give lift to their flying-cloaks make their wings to shine. Where the nimbuses sphere their heads, the glancing light makes golden rainbows appear and disappear.

Their faces are inhumanly perfect and stern. The mental training systems brought by the Ship of the Will give each one a perfect calm and utter sanity; the calm of a frozen winter pond.

Is it any wonder men call them angels?

From their eyes dart slender rays, like a warship's searchlight, sweeping back and forth, penetrating crowds and clouds and hidden places.

Where they glance upon weapons or explosives, or fighting machines, they squint, and the rays of light tremble with mysterious force, and consume what they see with fire.

Sometimes the weapons, before they are found, discharge a futile shot or two toward the angels, whose shields flare to higher energies, flashing like whirlwinds of fire. People applaud when this happens.

Imagine Golgolundra. Everyone laughs. No one is happy. Everyone is doomed.

2.

THERE IS ONE young man among the dancing crowds who does not dance. He dresses in black and does not laugh. He is not doomed. And, perhaps, he has a chance, if small, to become happy.

In his forehead glints a ruby gem. Any passer-by with the proper machine can read his thoughts. The grim look on his face saves them the effort; his thoughts are clear.

The crowds part when he walks by. The dancers fall silent. The graffiti images recoil and do not molest him.

He is Idomenes, son of Ducaleon. His genetic modifications are not the same as those who live in Golgolundra. He is a Promethean; they are Typhonides.

He comes to the central tower, which serves Golgolundra as administration, rebellion-centre, entertainment capital, and whorehouse. Idomenes paces down the wide corridors, looking neither right nor left. The monstrous statues, grotesque murals, or weeping deformities in their glass cages do not attract his attention.

From his black cloak, black diamonds fan out, sweeping the corridors before and behind him like nervous soldiers or presidential bodyguards, edging around corners, darting near anything suspicious, maintaining their spacing and their overlapping fields of fire. He ignores all this motion. He walks.

When he comes before a certain door, perhaps he is impatient with precautions. The swarm of black diamonds flutter back beneath his cloak, or come to rest in jewelried patterns along the chest and sleeves of his dark doublet.

The door recognizes him, and, without a word, politely opens.

Lounging at ease on a day-bed on the balcony,

dreamily watching the distant fires, a woman of haunting beauty reclines. Her skin is the colour of coffee with cream, her hair is as black as the midnight sea. She wears it very long. When she stands, it falls fragrantly past her rounded hips and brushes her shapely calves. When she lies on her stomach it is long enough that, even when braided, it can be used to tie her wrists and ankles. When she lies on her side, as she does now, it forms luxurious cloud-scapes, and falls, little waterfalls, from bed to floor, stray locks swaying.

Above the couch floats a mirror. She watches the little glints of her white assemblers caressing her body. Where they pass, a garment of black lace is being woven tightly around her curves. The garment has no seams, and would have to be unwoven to remove it, or roughly ripped off.

She pretends she does not see she is being watched. Now she stretches and yawns like a cat, arching her back and moaning. She turns on her stomach, and regards Idomenes with mock- surprise. Her eyes are half-lidded. Her frail lace garb is half-woven.

He does not remove his gloves, but, at least, he holds his hands at his sides, and makes no gestures.

Idomenes speaks first, grand with simplicity. "Lilimariah, I want you to come with me to the stars."

Lilimariah smiles mysteriously, as if charmed by distant music. Her voice is husky and low: "Men want only what they can't get. That is the nature of desire."

She stirs and half-arises, so she is leaning on one arm. Her hair is electrostatically charged, so that it floats and sways as if in a breeze, even though there is no breeze. "A lot of people would like to go to the stars, sweet lover. The angels won't let them. All but your folk. The sheep."

"I broke an oath to tell you these things. Do not mock my people. They will be saved." Idomenes speaks harshly, stepping forward. Now he is close enough to smell her perfume, and his expression weakens into confusion and anger. His eyes burn like the black diamonds glittering in his coat.

She makes a swaying, supple motion of her naked shoulders, perhaps intended as a shrug. "What do you have that the angels want to save? Some pretty angel-lass fall in love with you?"

The muscles twitch in the corners of his jaw. "You mock them too? When the Ship first came from the stars, She saved us from the devastation of the Wars. We begged Her to govern and guide us. The Ship showed us how we might remove all the vicious old structures from our brains and genes, madness and rage and panic and hate. The Ship made the Invigilators to show us how it was done. Were we grateful? Did we learn? Did we listen?"

"'Invigilators'? How quaint. You're so old-fashioned sometimes, lover. We call them angels of death."

"Do you think they want to kill? How many chances did we get? How many wars did we start, after how many warnings? How many people of the sea did we obliterate?"

"'Dolphins.' We call them 'Dolphins.' And there were complex reasons for the genocide-wars. Economic reasons and stuff. Turmoil. And why did the Ship make them members of the Galactic Will when humans were kept in protectorate status? Them! Them! We made them! And now we were second class citizens!"

"'Complex reasons'? Rage and jealousy and race-pride. Explain the complex reasons for the extermination camps and torture circuses."

"They were cutting into our trade with the Ship!"

"Maybe they were richer because they didn't kill each other all the time. As your people did mine. Was there a complex reason for that, too? Or was it just an expression of the rage and aggression your people will not remove from your brain-stem structures?"

"Some people think evil has survival value."

"It is the purpose of the Law to see that it will not." He speaks in a voice of dark majesty.

"Don't let's argue politics again!" she pouts. "That's all ancient history."

"Fifty years ago is hardly ancient."

"We never did anything to deserve this. No children!"

"The Ship sent a barrenness to all our women, yes, and sent plagues to sterilize the men, but that was for mercy's sake. There were to be no children when the world drowned. And now that Typhon's coffin is found and thawed, and he grows the last few weeks to become a man, it is done. There are no children left. No innocent lives. Today is Doomsday Eve! The hour is come!"

"And why are you here, lover?" she pouts and tosses back her head. "I hate long goodbyes. They bore me."

"I've come to save you. My love for you burns like a devastating fire. It conquers my will and heart and sense and soul! You are the fairest child of a condemned and evil race, but I cannot believe, and I will not, that such beauty hides a soul wicked past cure!"

His eyes are narrow slits of fire. Now he steps forward and seizes her fragrant shoulders with his hands. Some of his assemblers, misunderstanding the sudden gesture, fly up to either side and hover like wasps; a sight of terror. But either her nerves are steel (a common replacement) or she is drowned in hysteria. She throws back her lovely head and laughs.

He shouts "Stop laughing! You must want life! You must want my love! Such love as mine cannot go unanswered! It dare not." Then, more quietly, he says: "I will defy the Invigilators. They will be convinced by the force and ardour of my soul! If – if you were my wife – do you see what I am offering? – If you were a member of my household, the angels would not let me leave you behind!"

She gives him a cool, remote stare, her perfect lips hovering on the hint of a smile.

He steps back, deflated. As he draws his hands down, the deadly assemblers drop close to the floor and draw back.

Idomenes says, "Why this coldness? Tell me what you want."

She is on her hands and knees, her fingers knotted into the silken fabrics of the bedclothes. Lilimariah keeps the same small half-smile on her lips, but she trembles when she speaks: "I want to be forced. Kidnap me. Kill my father, burn his house. Take me by force. Take me."

"What a horrible thing to say. Are the angels right about us?"

She laughs. "That way I can't be blamed. Don't you understand women at all?"

"Sane women, I do." Idomenes looks at her oddly. "Are you drunk? Have you been intoxicated against your will? There may be neuro-operators interfering with your brain-chemistry."

He raises a finger and points at her. A black diamond flickers up from the floor, ready.

She screams, writhing backward. She is on her feet near the railing, perhaps ready to fall or jump.

He raises his hand, spreads his fingers. The black diamond falls back.

"Don't you dare interfere with my body!" she shouts.

"What is it – ?"

Silently, softly, she says, "I'm pregnant."

He says, dumbstruck, "No woman can be pregnant. We can make children artificially. The assembler technology was made for that. But no one but the angels knows what codes they used to force our biochemistry into sterile patterns..."

She says sharply, "Has it never occurred to the great Idomenes that there are assembler programmers better than even him?"

He snorts. "No. That thought I do not admit."

Now she steps forward, hips swaying, her eyes glinting with danger and pain. "And has it never occurred to you that I might have another lover? One who can give me the child you cannot?!"

Idomenes steps back, as if he has been slapped. "I thought you loved me..."

"Why?"

"You said..."

"I say a lot of things." She tosses her head.

"I thought it was that my father speaks with the angels; that my people were special, that you were attracted to my... my..."

"Your purity? Your righteousness? It is your worst fault."

"You wanted my knowledge of assemblies, then. Is that it? You thought I could crack the angel's code."

Lilimariah folds her hands on her belly. Her head is bowed forward slightly, so that her hair falls about her like smoke. "There are needs a woman has no man can understand, and duties..."

He turns and leaves at this point, his face drained and hollow, his expression something more horrid than anger. The door does not open swiftly enough to suit him. He points, flicks his fingers, makes a fist. Black assemblers rearrange the wood into nitroglycerine compounds and blow the door-panels out of their frame. The shrapnel and smoke that strike him leave blood mingled with burns on his face, but his footsteps do not slow.

He does not hear the end of her sentence: "...duties even stronger than love." Her hair hides her tears.

His assemblers re-knit his torn flesh and clean his skin before he goes down two corridors. He comes into an atrium. Here is what looks like a boy of eight or nine years, dressed as a harlequin, surrounded by a large flotilla of diamond assemblers.

Idomenes is in no mood to speak. He brings his hands together and makes a gesture. The Harlequin's assemblers tremble and drop to the floor, dead, before any signal can move.

"Wait!" shouts the boy. "I'm not a Synthetic! I'm real! Killing me would be murder!"

Idomenes is pointing his finger, and his black assemblers, like a little galaxy, crowns upon crowns around him, hang in the air, ready. "All the real little boys are grown up."

"I'm 21 today. I just made myself look this way because everybody hated me as I grew older."

Idomenes lowers his hand. The black assemblers spread out and drop lower, idling on stand-by.

"You're Typhon."

"I am also her father."

"You? Impossible."

"I made her when I was twelve. She grew up as I slept. You've studied assembler technology history?"

"The major advances in carbon, oxygen and nitrogen manipulators are credited to you. All between sixteen and twenty. A child prodigy."

"My first experiment was to stimulate my own neurochemistry to greater speed and intelligence. There was a danger of madness, it's true, but what's a little insanity between friends? I knew I had to live my life only in my youth, because my life was going to be the shortest one of all. Imagine being the one child the execution of the whole planet was waiting for! Imagine being responsible for that!"

Idomenes' voice shivers with pity: "It's really not your fault."

Typhon snarls. "What do you know of it, gentle boy? What do you know of guilt and hate? They cleaned your genes of all those bad thoughts, didn't they? That's why you get to live, eh? But this is the city of the Typhonides. All the folk of Golgolundra are based on patterns of mine! Battle-lust and killer-instinct at its best! We'll see whose survival strategy is better: wild or domestic!"

Idomenes raises his hand and spreads his fingers. Black diamonds swirl upward, forming little clusters in the air around him. "I don't wish to fight you. I believe fighting is evil."

"But you want to murder the one who stole my daughter from you, don't you, gentle boy?"

"Don't tempt me."

"I know who it is."

"The matter does not concern..."

"Didn't you think she was acting strange? I know you stung her with an analyser, quick, from behind, while she was jumping off the bed. Sneaky and curious, aren't we? Maybe there's hope for you yet, eh? Look at the blood read-out."

Idomenes now closes a fist and holds out a pinkie. One slim black diamond touches his glove's fingernail, hovering. A unit in his thumb projects images into his eyes. "She is under a love-potion. Drunk. It's affecting her oestrogen levels and parasympathetic nervous system. And... and..."

Idomenes lowered his hand. The assembler, forgotten, tinkles to the marble floor. "...She really is pregnant."

Then he straightens: "But someone used a mind-altering technique on her..."

The little boy steps forward. "Let me see."

Idomenes points his thumb at Typhon.

To their eyes the atrium is gone. They float in a world of gigantic molecular chains, complex diagrams, brain patterns, nerve-energy comparisons, biochemical formulae.

Idomenes says, "The glamour is using a combination of neurotransmitters to trigger a sexual response, affect pulse and respiration, with this chain here used to receive a coordinating signal."

"Note the decentralized structure of the hypnogogic state-inducers in the hypothalamus." Typhon comments.

"Mm. Clever work."

They nod at each other, in mutual admiration

of craftsmanship. Idomenes highlights one of the imaged strands: "Here we have the same information architecture governing the internal nerve-body reactions in the cerebrum and upper brain-stem. The destruction of any part of the love potion is insufficient; it holographically restores itself."

"Unless you know the key control sequences. Unless you know who sent it."

"You know. You keep her watched. Who?"

"I will tell you for a price..."

"On the world's last day? You'll tell me or..."

"Or what? I'll live to regret it? Don't threaten me, gentle boy! You've had your killer-instincts removed!"

Idomenes banishes the vision so that Typhon can see the menacing circle of black assemblers that have formed a circle around him.

Idomenes says, "A man can do by deliberation what his instincts don't allow. Talk."

"Hoo! Ha! But your precious purity of soul goes sour if you play rough. One slap and the Angels let you drown with the rest of us. And you can't hide the crime while you wear that ruby in your head. Domesticated animals have no secrets, remember?"

"But then I can't make a deal, either."

"But what I want, the angels won't care. Information."

"Speak."

The little boy says softly, "Your father has a complete genetic library of all the human and hominid races of the Earth. The angels helped him to collect it. They gave him a program for his wife, Pyrrha, so that her children will carry all racial characteristics in their inferons, to emerge in later generations and alter them. One woman with the ability to restore the entire race to full genetic diversity! I want a copy of that program."

Idomenes taps a finger on his palm. One larger black diamond swims forward out of the swarm and hangs in the air before Typhon's eyes. "Here it is."

"The whole library in one crystal? You're lying!"

"I'm wearing a truth ruby. You can check. You can also check to see that I'll give it to you a moment after I have the name."

"It is a deal. Turn my gloves back on so that the city mind can record our handshake."

"I thought Golgolundra was mad."

"Faked. I wanted the angels not to interfere with our internal computer sequences..."

A set of screams from outside interrupt; there comes the clamour of explosions, the roaring thunder of angel-flame cutting through walls.

Because Typhon's gloves are working, one of his radio-diamonds carries the noise of Lilimariah's shriek. Perhaps it is a sound of delight; perhaps a cry of pain.

Idomenes is already running down the corridors, back.

Typhon's little legs cannot keep up.

"The library! Give me the library – !" pants the boy, the ruffles of his clown-suit bouncing and flopping with each step.

Idomenes does not turn his head, but runs in swift lunging steps. "The name!" he shouts back.

Typhon falters and stops.

As Idomenes turns a last corner, he hears the little boy's weak voice behind him, trembling with malice: "Fool! Fool! Who else can it be? Who else knows the angel's fertility codes?"

Idomenes turns the corner just in time to see, framed in the still-smoking rectangle of the doorframe, a man of unearthly handsomeness, Lilimariah thrown across his shoulder, standing balanced on the balcony rail. A golden light is all around him. His surcoat is black, a colour the angels do not normally use. His wings unfold swanlike from his shoulders, shivering with crackles and darts of energy. His eyes are filled with light; he is looking upwards.

Lilimariah's perfect bottom is high in the air; her shapely legs are kicking, but Idomenes sees her smile falter when she glimpses him over her shoulder.

The angel flees upward, supersonically swift, a swirl of dust leaping after him.

The room is empty. A moment later, a crack of supersonic noise rolls like thunder far overhead.

Idomenes stands staring at nothing, while wave after wave of grief, and astonishment at how tremendously he has been betrayed, sweep through him.

Typhon, panting, walks up behind him. "Azaziel. His name is Azaziel. He's the one who found my cryogenic coffin, and brought me back here to my home. Just in time for my long-delayed birthday party, eh? No regrets, though. Gave you guys an extra thirty some odd years to prepare while I slept. Kind of like condemned women getting pregnant to delay a hanging, isn't it? One sleeping baby saving the world. Can't believe how foolishly my people here wasted this technology. It's all so obvious. The angels wouldn't even be able to threaten us if we had kept our heads about this. But hey! Give people a way to commit crimes without anyone finding out, I guess they'll do them, right? All sorts of gross crimes. I wish I was sure the angels weren't right about us after all. But, what the heck, you gotta root for the home team if it's your team, right? Anyway, that was Azaziel, Uriel's lieutenant. I don't know what Lilly did for him. Maybe she told him the Ship's real reason for the Doomsday drownings."

Idomenes makes a gesture, a flick of a finger, no more. A large black diamond hops toward Typhon.

Idomenes speaks like a man in a dream. "Here. The library."

"Thanks. Where are you going?"

"I know where he must be headed. There is only one place on Earth which will be preserved from drowning."

Grief and fear are in Idomenes' voice, uncertainty in his eye. He touches the gem in his head with a nervous finger.

The little boy whispers: "You're afraid they'll see, genes or no genes, that you still know what hate is. But they won't blame you for thinking about attacking a bad angel, will they? And my daughter – don't you have to rescue her? You're the only one who knows where Azaziel is going. You said so. Aren't you a hero?"

This last comment is uttered with a sneer.

A sneer that deepens after Idomenes departs.

3.

TOWARDS TWILIGHT, IDOMENES sees from afar Azaziel on the eastern side of Mount Neptushem, where the palaces and museums of his father are.

Here is the place where Ducaleon has brought all the works of man, gathered over years, to be preserved, and made gardens and houses for the sustenance and delight of the expected hordes of mankind deemed worthy enough to be spared.

Idomenes wonders why the streets are empty.

Not quite empty. There are two figures here.

The dark angel is standing on the lip of a fountain, in the high square between the observatory and a many-pillared archive. The third side is railing, overlooking far slopes below.

To the fourth side, behind and above the fountain, the ground rises again, buttress upon buttress of white marble and crystal windows flaming ever upward to a fantastic mountain.

Palace atop palace climb up the manifold gentle crags looming here, delicate spires high above fragrant gardens and grottos, blue pools reflecting fair sights, stands and arbours of trees laden with golden fruit and crimson, shady walks delightful, and, higher still, pine woods heavy with scented shadows.

The mountain-top, ringed by noble minarets, is crowned above with a stepped pyramid of singular grace, whose sides droop with hanging gardens, trailing trellises and lingering vines. Little singing waterfalls fall shining down its many airy balconies.

Lilimariah is kneeling, her arms embracing Azaziel's leg, her cheek against his knee. Her hair flows around her like long banners. She is not otherwise dressed.

Nor, it seems, is he. The black surcoat that served him as badge of rank Azaziel has thrown away. Aside from his own perfection, other clothes he desires none. His aura protects him against rain and cold and deadlier things which might harm him.

Idomenes is remembering a time as a child, when

the angels dropped their auras, and walked naked in the garden air of his father's fields and lawns. But the Typhonides and others had filled all the air with so many viral weapons specific to angels, nerve-toxins and hallucinogens, that no angel dared shed his gleaming nimbus after.

As Idomenes climbs the wide flights of ivory stairs toward them, the sight of the two lovers burning and stinging in his eyes, an angry gesture twists his fingers. An old, old program is opened in the memory of his assemblers, a military program, written by the Sons of Typhon.

Assemblers make black clouds around him as he strides in wrath up the slope, and draw carbon, hydrogen, and oxides out of the air with such force that he walks as if in a gale.

When he passes the fruit arbours, an articulated exo-skeleton embraces his form, with motors of shell and bone at all joints.

When he passes the outer memory shrines, heavy plates of black diamond armour have collected onto the moving frame. The plate could not have stopped bullets, perhaps, but angels fought with beams of laser flame.

As he passes around the corner of the archive-house, long firing tubes and launchers have collected on his back, and his magazines are filled with explosives.

The wiring grown inside his armour is made of biological cable, like nerves, because his assemblers have no copper or gold to work with. He is going through final firing sequence system checks as he rounds the second corner and steps into the square where the fountain is.

As he walks across the square toward the angel, his heavy motorized footsteps booming on the flagstones, a final touch of anger and pride makes him grow ornaments of nacre and pearl and silvery horn along the hull of his black armour, and a tall gay plume sprouts high from his helm.

He must look splendid, for Lilimariah gazes at him with burning awe in her lovely eyes.

Idomenes sees she is surrounded by the dark angel's sentry-shield. The nimbus shimmers like gold in the air along her bare skin.

Azaziel speaks: "Have you not heard that only free men have the right to go armed? The cruelty of the angels will destroy you if you raise weapons against your betters, little serf!"

"The Invigilators are not so unjust," Idomenes' voice, amplified, rings out from his armour, which is humming with power around him. "I am come to recover the girl you bewitch and abduct. My cause is right; I will not be condemned for it."

But he does not focus any aiming lasers toward the black shining figure, and his weapons still hover on stand-by.

"Not so unjust?" the dark angel mocks. "Compared, I wonder, to what? Or do you call them fair because you dream you will be spared?"

"Our race has a shameful history. The Ship determined that that history must end. Has She not fulfilled every appearance of justice? There was no need to grant our appeal. Her mind is not mortal, not organic, works at a million times our speed, commits no errors, no oversights! How could She be wrong? Yet still She returned to Canopus in Argo for review; the world there is governed by a mind even more deep and wise than Hers. The World-Minds of every world gathered in synod. The World-Minds called upon the Star-Minds, each of whom guides many worlds; the Star-Minds called upon energies we cannot imagine to link mind to mind across the stars and waken the Will."

Idomenes now speaks in a voice of rolling power: "The thoughts of the Will are as infinitely wiser, deeper, more sure, more pure, as the thoughts of the Ship are above mortal organic thoughts. Perhaps you can doubt the wisdom of Ships, and Worlds, and Stars; but surely no one can doubt the wisdom of the Will! Dare you, dare even you, who once served the Will, doubt this? What can you set in your soul to guide yourself, once you have rejected the guiding star of wisdom infinite?"

"I set up my pride," says the dark angel, and his wings are spreading as he speaks. "I will do no more shameful things, no matter at whose behest; but shall henceforth do only that in which I can take most pride."

"You are intoxicated, perhaps insane! Allow my assemblers to cleanse your system; see the light of truth; and restore my true love to me."

"The Will being so wise, why are the innocent condemned? Those whose only crime is that they live on a world with evil-doers? Guilt by dwelling nigh? And what of him whose only crime is that his disordered passions burn within his blood, his genes ahowl with the wrath and meanness of all his apish fathers? To be inclined to sin while lingering sinless: We call this innocence."

Idomenes is not sure how to answer. Then he says grimly: "Those who are worthy shall be spared."

"Worthy? Whose rule is so true to measure it? Whose weights are so sound that they may weigh the souls of men? The Ship cares little for the lives of little men: why else sleeps your father's city here deserted still?"

Idomenes, perhaps, feels a moment of coldness. He cannot answer these questions. Instead, he points his finger at the angel; aiming lasers follow his finger and lock on. The heavy weapons on his back rear up on their jointed arms, hissing like snakes, and point their deadly snouts where his finger points. "You have bewitched my love! Poisoned her with neurochemicals and hypno-narcotics! Release her!"

Azaziel smiles down at the beautiful woman at his feet. "Tell him, my pet, my plaything, you willingly love me."

Lilimariah says, "'Tis true. His child, I carry; no other's. He is strong where you are weak. My father has given him assemblers programmed to sculpt an asteroid into a working starship. We will fly to the heavens without being anyone's domesticated slaves!"

And she laughs. Idomenes' soul is flayed by that laughter. In his armour, he is shivering and sweating with rage.

"She but speaks under your influence! Release her or I fire!"

The angel regards the human weapons with amused contempt. He says: "What you describe is not an Invigilator technology. I have done nothing to her. But I see by your gem that you are sincere. Here. I withdraw my shield from her. Perform your tests. Then see, then know, then confess to me how stupidly you have been wrong. This will shatter your pride, and then you may crawl off somewhere to die. Do you still think the Ship is so wise? By this act, by raising a weapon in anger, you have violated your parole; the Invigilator law will drown you with the others!"

The golden glitter withdraws from Lilimariah's naked skin. She shivers in the air, and the fine, almost invisible, hairs of her skin stand up, for it is growing now toward dusk, and long shadows fall across the courtyard and fountain.

Idomenes makes a gesture. A slim black diamond floats gently forward, touches her skin, pricks her.

"Ow!" She complains. She moves to curl up to Azaziel, but his golden aura repels her.

"I am applying a counter-agent to restore your normal neuro-chemical balance," Idomenes says. "Just a moment..."

At that instant, a large black diamond flies in from somewhere and shoots into Lilimariah's arm, leaving a small wound. She screams in pain and terror, and a host of her own assemblers pour upwards out of ornaments in her hair into a defensive formation.

Azaziel shouts in astounded anger, such a shout as angels cry, and throws his aura, like a cloak, around Lilimariah's shoulders. He spreads his wings to take flight.

Idomenes cries out in panic and rage and hate to see his lover about to be carried away forever, and he lunges forward, fingers curled.

He will tell himself later that his gun-barrage went off by mere mischance, that his hand was perhaps jarred by the sudden motion into the trigger-gesture. So he will tell himself.

With a roar like a hundred thunders, flares light

up on his shoulder-racks, rockets streak out, trailing streams of boiling smoke; his major cannons, left and right, vomit explosive flame, jarring mind and sense and hearing; minor cannons rattle with jack-hammer concussions, a numbing blur of noise.

Azaziel's aura flares to the greatest of its great power, and cloaks the angel in an eye-searing flame. His compensating field is insufficient; the shockwave of the attack throws him backwards through the wall of the archives. The beautiful building is blackened and smashed with fire, as Idomenes' micro-rockets and beam-guided missiles jump in through the holes.

Idomenes is beginning to realize the enormity of his error when Azaziel, shaped now like a pillar of fire, emerges from the archive, reducing roof and walls to tumbling ash as the swirling column unfolds to its full height.

Like a tornado, Azaziel glides forward, and an arm of lightning dips toward Idomenes. Lesser assemblers and floating globes, like a black snowstorm, try to swirl into the path of the beam; Idomenes has harness-jets and prosthetic leg-motors assist his panicked leap to the side.

The beam of lightning tears off huge chunks of Idomenes' armour, and tosses him headlong in mid-leap, but the blow is glancing, and the diamond panels refract the beam just enough to send lances of scattered fire in to the observatory.

The beautiful building is impaled with roaring flame.

Idomenes tries to cry out words of apology, perhaps, or peace, but the roar of fire and explosion is all around him. He jumps and fires, jumps and fires, smashing through more walls and roofs as he does so.

Through the smoke and terror, he can see the twin slender beams of Azaziel's eyesight slicing through walls and smoke-clouds, hunting him. Azaziel's fiery column sweeps through the area, devastating all. The fountains explode in a tangled convulsion of steam.

Azaziel's shields falter, perhaps grounded or cooled by the water. Idomenes forgets all thoughts of peace when he sees the dark angel rising into the air, haloed in fire, stealing Lilimariah away. He glimpses her teary face: her mouth and eyes are wide. He leaps, kicked aloft by coughing jets, and attempts to grapple the angel.

A vast force of fire explodes in his faceplate as his arms close around the burning pillar of Azaziel. His diamond armour is blasted awry, molten lumps flying backward, but his arms manage to grab something. Whatever is in his grasp slides under his whining gauntlet-motors, and crackles with electrical tension, formless, like forcing two opposite magnets together.

Azaziel's calm, dispassionate face is staring into the faceplate of Idomenes, a sight of eerie terror. Inches before him, Idomenes sees the energy fields swirling in front of the dark angel's eyes, growing bright, gathering power... The dark angel squints...

Before Azaziel's gaze can smite him, an unexpected force thrusts the two combatants apart and flings them both to the ground.

Here is Uriel, Prince of Angels and foremost of their kind, blazing, and he stands in midair now between them.

From his upraised palms comes a pulse. The combatants are held apart.

Here also is stern Ducaleon. The old man wears a green thinking-robe; he is surrounded by glittering assemblers more numerous and better-made than his son's. In his brow he also carries a ruby. A look of stern sorrow is graven on his features.

Ducaleon points with his glove, and a command signal overrides Idomenes' assemblers. The black diamonds attempting to repair Idomenes' armour now reverse their actions. The armour sways and falls to pieces around Idomenes, disintegrating in huge sliding lumps and glittering dusty slithers.

Azaziel, meanwhile, smothers his aura. Gold light, not flame, surrounds him.

Idomenes is in pain from a dozen burns, lacerations, sprains, pains even worse; he fears bones are broken. He cannot rise to his feet, and the assemblers which normally would have been swarming to heal him are fallen to the blackened ground, motionless.

Azaziel, on the other hand, has not a strand of his black hair misplaced. He flexes his wings around him, and crosses his arms on his chest. He says nothing. Lilimariah, behind him, is unharmed, although her face is full of emotion.

Idomenes listens to his ears ringing in the sudden silence.

All around them are the cratered remains of once-great buildings; the works of his father's architecture, smouldering, blasted, ruined, destroyed.

Ducaleon says, "Abase yourself before the high Exemplar Uriel and beg forgiveness, and you may, perhaps, be spared." (The word exemplar is an old term for the Invigilators, from the days when they were meant to serve as examples to mankind, rather than as punishers.) "The asteroids of ice begin already to fall. You have led a blameless life. But if you err, even on the last day, even at the last hour, you will not be saved."

Idomenes, unable to rise, cranes his head and looks toward Uriel. The arch-angel's aura is so bright that it crackles with sparks and little arcs of fire. "I apologize for harm I've done; I meant no disrespect." But the words come grudgingly forth. Idomenes does not believe in his heart that he has done anything wrong.

Azaziel says with disdain, "Roll over! Fetch! Play Dead!"

The light from Uriel's eyes touches Idomenes' ruby; he sees his thoughts. Uriel says nothing.

Lilimariah, half-hidden behind Azaziel's back, her hand on the dark angel's shoulders, says in a sad, haunted voice, "Do not be slain for my sake. I'm sorry, Idomenes. I am under no influence, now, nor any thoughts of mine bewitched. And yet I say: I must go with Azaziel."

"Is it him you love?" Idomenes knows pain beyond his wounds. His voice is a hoarse rasp.

She hesitates. Then: "Yes. As much as my heart can do." Her voice is faint. Then she says, "Now make peace with your father, and kiss his hands, and go your way with the angels of death, who condemn and slay mankind." The hatred in her voice is clear.

Ducaleon says to Uriel, "Tell me my son can be saved. I have no one else."

Uriel speaks. His voice is quiet and gold. "His trust in us is gone. When humans do not trust, they fear. When they fear, they kill."

Idomenes lifts himself partway on his hands, rearing up. Blood breaks through his burns. He winces. He shouts out, "How can I believe in the justice of the Will, if the reasons of the angels are not just?"

Ducaleon says: "Their justice is beyond our understanding. But is there any race so deserving of death as mankind? Can you think of an act of evil, no matter how heinous, which we have not done? Not done in secret, but while crowds cheered?"

Idomenes shouts again, "Is the innocent child who grows in Lilimariah's womb so guilty that he is deserving of death?"

Uriel speaks again. "He is condemned because no one can guarantee that, when he grows, neither he nor any of his progeny will never work murder or theft or deception on the innocent hosts who live among the Will. Quite the opposite! When humans gather, crime is certain."

Idomenes is angry. "My life has been in service to this? Is this what you call justice? None can survive this rule! None can live so!"

Uriel says in a voice of haunting beauty: "There are races that do not enslave, do not slay, do not war. There are races which do not lie or falsify. You think them weak? But they are among the strongest and finest denizens of the Will. They waste no treasure, nor time, nor grief, nor lives, nor blood, to maintain the ungainly apparatus of suspicion and bloodshed you call government, the princes and policemen and hangmen without which you humans dare not risk to live with each other. Weak? So would savages, whose every cottage was a fortress and every door a barricade, think *your* race. And yet, among the stars there are crystalline civilizations so complex, so swift, and so trusting that a single lie could ruin them. Do you think the Will is weak, then? Observe the strength granted those who serve it!"

And, at his word, an earthquake shakes the mountain.

Idomenes looks to the railing. He feels a swaying, weightless pitching. Beyond the rail, he sees the ground departing slowly away. There comes a moment of mist. Then they are high, no longer in twilight, but back in the day. Beyond the railing is cloud.

Ducaleon says: "We are risen! My son is still with us! Does this mean he can be saved?" He points with his gloves, and many assemblers swarm over Idomenes, tending to his wounds.

Uriel is silent, staring grimly at Idomenes.

Ducaleon says, "Son! You know it is wise to agree with the Exemplar. Think of what you will gain if you quell the rebellion in your heart!"

Idomenes says, "Father, I mean not to grieve you. But a man cannot make himself believe a lie just because it profits him. Men do not hold to the truth because it is useful, or comely, or safe. Men hold to the truth because it is true. And I was not told the truth!"

Azaziel mutters, "Proudly said! Would that my docile brother angels had such hearts of fire as this lowly mortal."

Uriel says, "Truth we spoke not to you, foreknowing you would say such words, too arrogant to be unsaid. Our justice grounded on stern practicality."

Lilimariah, her voice thick with hatred, her eyes smoking, now spoke: "Death angel! What you call justice is nothing but fear! Fear of mankind! And because you came, from fear, to doom us, we have no fate but to make ourselves as fearsome as we can do! Fools! Fools! All fools! We had no care for your World-Minds and your Will and all your grave deliberations! Do you think murder is not murder because it is done by judges or governments or gods? No, we prayed for those appeals, and every delay – sixty long years of delay! – we Typhonides employed to make ourselves as ready for war as we could do! What care we if you drown the world? Already my father and his people have altered themselves, painful mutations and ugly, and sink down to dwell in the deepest chasms of the ocean bed, where sunlight never can reach. There they will breed a race of monstrosities, a race of magicians, in sunless domes and fortresses far beneath the waves! From there they will wage eternal war, fuelled by restless hate unending. You think to drown the world in water? They shall drown the world in blood! You cannot blockade our ascent forever! One day the stars shall be ours! Then the stars themselves shall drip blood!"

Uriel turns to Idomenes, and says gravely, "Do you see what it is we must act to prevent? This woman is unworthy of your regard."

Idomenes answers bravely, "And yet she should not die."

"Acknowledge our wisdom! The one we chose to live is the only one worthy. Only Ducaleon. We spare his wife for his sake."

Now Uriel turns to Azaziel. "But as for you, you have violated our laws. Capitulate to our judgment, meekly surrender, or I bring terrible arms to bear!"

Azaziel laughs a laugh of scorn. "What do I care for your frowning brow and threatening word? I know your arms, and I know I am safe. But even if I were not, I would not cower to you. I will do only what pride bids me do; so I have sworn, and will do no shameful thing, or anything prompted only by fear.

"Capitulate? How?" the proud angel continued, "Your own law says you will kill to protect anyone who might one day perhaps – perhaps! – threaten the civilization you so adore. Should I not have as much love as that for this my child, whom, if I capitulate, you kill?

"No, tyrant, my ears are closed to that base cruelty you call justice. Such reasoning offends reason, and would make killers of us all. For each man perhaps might threaten all others: your rule is the rule of endless war. I say no more to you; you are unworthy even of contempt.

"I turn me now from the creature I most despise to the one I most love. Hear my will. Pride likewise will not allow me to cower beneath the bellies of dolphins, to live in the sunless mud in the pits beneath your seas. The stars are mine! I claim them my birth-right! We will go aloft, you and I, and I can instruct you in the secrets of angels. Come! Will you go with me? You will never see friends or father or family again if you go."

She speaks in a voice of passion. "You are my lord and master. Wherever you go, I find joy without equal. Carry me up to your dark, wide abyss."

Azaziel gathers her in his arms and steps upwards into the air. Uriel starts to raise his hand, red-hot lightnings forming in his palm, but Idomenes, staggering, steps toward the couple and into his line of fire. Uriel withholds his stroke.

"Lilimariah!" Idomenes cries in a ragged voice: "Wait – I – I still love you – come back –"

And Lilimariah, looking back over the dark angel's shoulder, has tears in her eyes. But she says only, "There are duties stronger than love."

Idomenes makes a choking cry and clutches the railing, looking up.

It looks like a tear falling down, shaken from Lilimariah as she turns her face away.

Something of sorrow appears for a moment in Uriel's face. He closes his fingers on his white fire, extinguishing it without casting.

The teardrop glitters as it falls. Unseen, at the last moment, it swerves in mid-air into Idomenes' palm. He closes his fingers to catch it.

Azaziel and Lilimariah, shining in gold, dwindle to a bright point high above, and are gone.

Idomenes feels a sting in his palm.

Behind him, he hears Ducaleon say softly to Uriel, "Azaziel was your firstborn son. I grieve for you, old friend. Perhaps he was enchanted."

The assembler in Idomenes' palm manipulates his nervous system and creates the illusion of a voice in his ear. "Now I break my oath as you broke yours for me. My love, my dearest love, my sweet and only true love; I am compelled to go with Azaziel by my father's will. The love potion you found in me I injected willingly, without which Azaziel could not have been deceived. He lowered his aura to embrace me, many nights, and the mind-altering effects of this concocted love spread to him. His artificial race, born from humans by the arts of the Ship to police and rule us, is not so different, at their deep neural structures, from the spurned parental stock. All that has been done, has been done to save my race from extinction. I have been injected with your mother's gift to replenish mankind. It was my father who directed remotely that library (which you gave him) into me. It was necessary to seduce a death-angel to our cause, for we had no other way to establish a foothold on other planets, to spread far enough that no single disaster could ever threaten us again. All else has been a feint. The tumults in the city were meant to occupy the angels and thus prevent Azaziel's capture. The citadels which father has established at the bottom of the sea, the races who shall be for centuries devoted to hatred and bitter war are likewise merely a feint, that I and my child (and all my children to come) might be overlooked. Evil I have done you, great evil. I beg your forgiveness knowing it might never be granted; I pray you will remember me with a love that equals my own. My fate is in your hands, the fate of all my generations, children and grandchildren that should have been yours. To tell the death angels destroys all."

Uriel is saying to Ducaleon: "Azaziel has internal energies shielding his nervous system, so that he could go without his aura among your poisoned air, and fear no nanotechnology. I wish I could say he was deceived or enchanted or ill; it is not so. He spoke the truth. It was his pride which led him, eyes open, to his fall."

Idomenes is almost blinded with tremors of hate that run through him. He thinks: So Azaziel is the hero after all! Not deceived, nor enchanted, he sacrifices honour and family and home to oppose a hideous injustice. And the love of the fair maiden, as in a fable, he wins.

Uriel says, "There has been too much tragedy here.

We will spare you son's life for your sake, Ducaleon, because your love and strength are greater when he is near. The knowledge of our mercy may yet sooth the wrathful and proud imaginings that now so torment him. Perhaps even he can find a place in the service of the Will. Turn, Idomenes, let me see your face, that I might know your thought and say if you are worthy of the salvation offered you."

Idomenes does not turn, for he knows his thoughts will reveal too much.

Below, far down, he sees the sea. Dolphins dance in the waves, the new masters of the world.

"What is your decision, Idomenes?" His father's voice trembles.

"I love you dearly, father," he says without turning his head. "But there are duties stronger than love. Injustice must be fought, even the injustice angels do."

Idomenes triggers his assemblers to begin reconstructing his armour as he throws himself over the railing. There is a long fall before he will strike the sea. He hopes there will be time for the assemblers to create what he needs to allow him survive the impact.

The fall is a long one. Perhaps it is enough.

A Soldier of the City

David Moles

David Moles was born in California and raised in San Diego, Athens, Tehran, and Tokyo. A graduate of the American School in Japan, the University of California at Santa Cruz, and Oxford University, he has been writing and editing science fiction and fantasy since 2002, and is a past finalist for the Hugo Award, the World Fantasy Award, and the John W. Campbell Award for Best New Writer, as well as the winner of the 2008 Theodore Sturgeon Memorial Award, for his novelette "Finisterra." David's most recent book is the novella Seven Cities of Gold. *He currently lives in San Francisco.*

Isin 12:709 13" N:10 18" / 34821.1.9 10:24:5:19.21
Colour still image, recorded by landscape maintenance camera, Gulanabishtiïdinam Park West.

At the top of the hill is a football court, the net nearly new but the bricks of the ground uneven, clumps of grass growing up from between the cracks. On the same side of the net are a man and a young girl. The hollow rattan ball is above the girl's head, nearing the apex of its trajectory; the girl, balanced on the toes of her bare right foot, her left knee raised, is looking toward the man.

The man is looking away.

Cross-reference with temple records identifies the man as Ishmenininsina Ninnadiïnshumi, age twenty-eight, temple soldier of the 219th Surface Tactical Company, an under-officer of the third degree, and the girl as his daughter Mâratirşitim, age nine.

Magnification of the reflection from the man's left cornea indicates his focus to be the sixty-cubit-high image of Gula, the Lady of Isin, projected over the Kârumishbiïrra Canal.

Comparison of the reflection with the record of the Corn Parade ceremonies suggests a transmission delay of approximately three grains.

1. Corn Parade

IN THE MOMENT of the blast, Ish was looking down the slope, toward the canal, the live feed from the temple steps and the climax of the parade. As he watched, the goddess suddenly froze; her ageless face lost its benevolent smile, and her dark eyes widened in surprise and perhaps in fear, as they looked – Ish later would always remember – directly at him. Her lips parted as if she was about to tell Ish something.

And then the whole eastern rise went brighter than the Lady's House at noonday. There was a sound, – a rolling, bone-deep rumble like thunder, – and afterwards Ish would think there was something wrong with this, that something so momentous should sound so prosaic, but at the time all he could think was how loud it was, how it went on and on, louder than thunder, louder than artillery, than rockets, louder and longer than anything Ish had ever heard. The ground shook. The projection faded, flickered and went out, and a hot wind whipped over the hilltop, tearing the net from its posts, knocking Mâra to the ground and sending her football flying, lost forever, out over the rooftops to the west.

From the temple district, ten leagues away, a bright point was rising, arcing up toward the dazzling eye of the Lady's House, and some trained part of Ish's mind saw the straight line, the curvature an artefact of the city's rotating reference frame; but as Mâra started to cry, and Ish's wife Tara and all his in-laws boiled up from around the grill and the picnic couches, yelling, and a pillar of brown smoke, red-lit from below, its top swelling obscenely, began to grow over the temple, the temple of the goddess Ish was sworn as a soldier of the city to protect, Ish was not thinking of geometry or the physics of coriolis force. What Ish was thinking – what Ish knew, with a sick certainty – was that the most important moment of his life had just come and gone, and he had missed it.

34821.1.14 10:9:2:5.67

Annotated image of the city of Isin, composed by COS Independence, *on Gaugamela station, Babylon, transmitted via QT to Community Outreach archives, Urizen. Timestamp adjusted for lightspeed delay of thirteen hours, fifty-one minutes.*

Five days after the strike the point of impact has died from angry red-orange to sullen infrared, a hot spot that looks as though it will be a long time in cooling. A streamer of debris trails behind the wounded city like blood in water, its spectrum a tale of vaporized ice and iron. Isin's planet-sized city-sphere itself appears structurally intact, the nitrogen and oxygen that would follow a loss of primary atmosphere absent from the recorded data.

Away from the impact, the myriad microwave receivers that cover the city's surface like scales still ripple, turning to follow the beams of power from Ninagal's superconducting ring, energy drawn from the great black hole called Tiamat, fat with the mass of three thousand suns, around which all the cities of Babylon revolve. The space around Isin is alive with ships: local orbiters, electromagnetically accelerated corn cans in slow transfer orbits carrying grain and meat from Isin to more urbanized cities, beam-riding passenger carriers moving between Isin and Lagash, Isin and Nippur, Isin and Babylon-Borsippa and the rest – but there is no mass exodus, no evacuation.

The Outreach planners at Urizen and Ahania, the missionaries aboard *Liberation* and *Independence* and those living in secret among the people of the cities, breathe sighs of relief, and reassure themselves that whatever they have done to the people of the cities of Babylon, they have at least not committed genocide.

Aboard COS *Insurrection*, outbound from Babylon, headed for the Community planet of Zoa at four-tenths the speed of light and still accelerating, the conscientious objectors who chose not to stay and move forward with the next phase of the Babylonian intervention hear this good news and say, not without cynicism: I hope that's some comfort to them.

* * *

2. Men giving orders

ISH WAS LEADING a team along a nameless street in what had been a neighbourhood called Imtagaärbeëlti and was now a nameless swamp, the entire district northwest of the temple complex knee-deep in brackish water flowing in over the fallen seawall and out of the broken aqueducts, so that Ish looked through gates into flooded gardens where children's toys and broken furniture floated as if put there just to mar and pucker the reflection of the heavens, or through windows whose shutters had been torn loose and glass shattered by the nomad blast into now-roofless rooms that were snapshots of ordinary lives in their moments of ending.

In the five days since the Corn Parade Ish had slept no more than ten or twelve hours. Most of the rest of the 219th had died at the temple, among the massed cohorts of Isin lining the parade route in their blue dress uniforms and golden vacuum armour – they hadn't had wives, or hadn't let the wives they did have talk them into extending their leaves to attend picnics with their in-laws, or hadn't been able to abuse their under-officers' warrants to extend their leaves when others couldn't. Most of the temple soldiery had died along with them, and for the first three days Ish had been just a volunteer with a shovel, fighting fires, filling sandwalls, clearing debris. On the fourth day the surviving priests and temple military apparatus had pulled themselves together into something resembling a command structure, and now Ish had this scratch squad, himself and three soldiers from different units, and this mission, mapping the flood zone, to what purpose Ish didn't know or much care. They'd been issued weapons but Ish had put a stop to that, confiscating the squad's ammunition and retaining just one clip for himself.

"Is that a body?" said one of the men suddenly. Ish couldn't remember his name. A clerk, from an engineering company, his shoulder patch a stylized basket. Ish looked to where he was pointing. In the shadows behind a broken window was a couch, and on it a bundle of sticks that might have been a man.

"Wait here," Ish said.

"We're not supposed to go inside," said one of the other men, a scout carrying a bulky map book and sketchpad, as Ish hoisted himself over the gate. "We're just supposed to mark the house for the civilians."

"Who says?" asked the clerk.

"Command," said the scout.

"There's no *command*," said the fourth man. He was an artillerist, twice Ish's age, heavy and morose. These were the first words he'd spoken all day. "The Lady's dead. There's no command. There's no officers. There's just men giving orders."

The clerk and the scout looked at Ish, who said nothing.

He pulled himself over the gate.

The Lady's dead. The artillerist's words, or ones like them, had been rattling around Ish's head for days, circling, leaping out to catch him whenever he let his guard down. *Gula, the Lady of Isin, is dead.* Every time Ish allowed himself to remember that it was as if he was understanding it for the first time, the shock of it like a sudden and unbroken fall, the grief and shame of it a monumental weight toppling down on him. Each time Ish forced the knowledge back the push he gave it was a little weaker, the space he created for himself to breathe and think and feel in a little smaller. He was keeping himself too busy to sleep because every time he closed his eyes he saw the Lady's pleading face.

He climbed over the windowsill and into the house.

The body of a very old man was curled up there, dressed in nothing but a dirty white loincloth that matched the colour of the man's hair and beard and the curls on his narrow chest. In the man's bony hands an icon of Lady Gula was clutched, a cheap relief with machine-printed colours that didn't quite line up with the ceramic curves, the Lady's robes more blue than purple and the heraldic dog at her feet more green than yellow; the sort of thing that might be sold in any back-alley liquor store. One corner had been broken off, so that the Lady's right shoulder and half her face were gone, and only one eye peered out from between the man's knuckles. When Ish moved to take the icon, the fingers clutched more tightly, and the old man's eyelids fluttered as a rasp of breath escaped his lips.

Ish released the icon. Its one-eyed stare now seemed accusatory.

"Okay," he said heavily. "Okay, Granddad."

BABYLON CITY 1:1 5" N:1 16" / 34821.1.14 7:15

"Lord Ninurta vows justice for Lady of Isin"
"Police to protect law-abiding nomads"
"Lawlessness in Sippar"

– *Headlines,*
temple newspaper Marduknaşir,
Babylon City

BABYLON CITY 4:142 113" S:4 12" / 34821.1.15 1:3
“Pointless revenge mission”
“Lynchings in Babylon: immigrants targeted”
“Sippar rises up”

– Headlines,
radical newspaper Iïnshushaqiï,
Babylon City

GISH, NIPPUR, SIPPAR (various locations) / 34821.1.15
“THEY CAN DIE”

– Graffiti common in working-class and slave districts, after the nomad attack on Isin

3. Kinetic penetrator

WHEN TARA CAME home she found Ish on a bench in the courtyard, bent over the broken icon, with a glue pot and an assortment of scroll clips and elastic bands from Tara’s desk. They’d talked, when they first moved into this house not long after Mâra was born, of turning one of the ground-floor rooms into a workshop for Ish, but he was home so rarely and for such short periods that what with one thing and another it had never happened. She kept gardening supplies there now.

The projector in the courtyard was showing some temple news feed, an elaborately animated diagram of the nomads’ weapon – a “kinetic penetrator,” the researcher called it, a phrase that Tara thought should describe something found in a sex shop or perhaps a lumberyard – striking the city’s outer shell, piercing iron and ice and rock before erupting in a molten plume from the steps directly beneath the Lady’s feet.

Tara turned it off.

Ish looked up. "You're back," he said.

"You stole my line," said Tara. She sat on the bench next to Ish and looked down at the icon in his lap. "What's that?"

"An old man gave it to me," Ish said. "There." He wrapped a final elastic band around the icon and set it down next to the glue pot. "That should hold it."

HE'D FOUND THE broken corner of the icon on the floor not far from the old man's couch. On Ish's orders they'd abandoned the pointless mapping expedition and taken the man to an aid station, bullied the doctors until someone took responsibility.

There, in the aid tent, the man pressed the icon into Ish's hands, both pieces, releasing them with shaking fingers.

"Lady bless you," he croaked.

The artillerist, at Ish's elbow, gave a bitter chuckle, but didn't say anything. Ish was glad of that. The man might be right, there might be no command, there might be no soldiery, Ish might not be an under-officer any more, just a man giving orders. But Ish was, would continue to be, a soldier of the Lady, a soldier of the city of Isin, and if he had no lawful orders that only put the burden on him to order himself.

He was glad the artillerist hadn't spoken, because if the man had at that moment said again *the Lady's dead*, Ish was reasonably sure he would have shot him.

He'd unzipped the flap on the left breast pocket of his jumpsuit and tucked both pieces of the icon inside. Then he'd zipped the pocket closed again, and for the first time in five days, he'd gone home.

* * *

TARA SAID: "NOW that you're back, I wish you'd talk to Mâra. She's been having nightmares. About the Corn Parade. She's afraid the nomads might blow up her school."

"They might," Ish said.

"You're not helping." Tara sat up straight. She took his chin in her hand and turned his head to face her. "When did you last sleep?"

Ish pulled away from her. "I took pills."

Tara sighed. "When did you last take a pill?"

"Yesterday," Ish said. "No. Day before."

"Come to bed," said Tara. She stood up. Ish didn't move. He glanced down at the icon.

An ugly expression passed briefly over Tara's face, but Ish didn't see it.

"Come to bed," she said again. She took Ish's arm, and this time he allowed himself to be led up the stairs.

AT SOME POINT in the night they made love. It wasn't very good for either of them; it hadn't been for a long while, but this night was worse. Afterwards Tara slept.

She woke to find Ish already dressed. He was putting things into his soldiery duffle.

"Where are you going?" she asked.

"Lagash."

"What?"

Tara sat up. Ish didn't look at her.

"Lord Ninurta's fitting out an expedition," Ish said.

"An expedition," said Tara flatly.

"To find the nomads who killed the Lady."

"And do what?" asked Tara.

Ish didn't answer. From his dresser he picked up his identification seal, the cylinder with the Lady's heraldic dog and Ish's name and Temple registry number, and fastened it around his neck.

Tara turned away.

"I don't think I ever knew you," she said, "But I always knew I couldn't compete with a goddess. When I married you, I said to my friends, 'At least he won't be running around after other women.'" She laughed without humour. "And now she's dead – and you're still running after her."

She looked up. Ish was gone.

OUTSIDE IT WAS hot and windless under a lowering sky. Nothing was moving. A fine grey dust was settling over the sector: *the Lady's ashes*, Ish had heard people call it. His jump boots left prints in it as he carried his duffle to the train station.

An express took Ish to the base of the nearest spoke, and from there his soldiery ID and a series of elevators carried him to the southern polar dock. As the equatorial blue and white of the city's habitable zone gave way to the polished black metal of the southern hemisphere, Ish looked down at the apparently untroubled clouds and seas ringing the city's equator and it struck him how normal this all was, how like any return to duty after leave.

It would have been easy and perhaps comforting to pretend it was just that, comforting to pretend that the Corn Parade had ended like every other, with the Lady's blessing on the crops, the return of the images to the shrines, drinking and dancing and music from the dimming of the Lady's House at dusk to its brightening at dawn.

Ish didn't want that sort of comfort.

34821.6.29 5:23:5:12.102

Abstract of report prepared by priest-astronomers of Ur under the direction of Shamash of Sippar, at the request of Ninurta of Lagash.

Isotopic analysis of recovered penetrator fragments indicates the nomad weapon to have been constructed within and presumably fired from the Apsu near debris belt. Astronomical records are surveyed for suspicious occlusions, both of nearby stars in the Babylon globular cluster and of more distant stars in the Old Galaxy, and cross-referenced against traffic records to eliminate registered nomad vessels. Fifteen anomalous occlusions, eleven associated with mapped point mass Sinkalamaïdi-541, are identified over a period of one hundred thirty-two years. An orbit for the Corn Parade criminals is proposed.

4. Dog soldier

THERE WAS A thump as Ish's platform was loaded onto the track. Then *Sharur's* catapult engaged and two, three, five, eight, thirteen, twenty times the force of Isin's equatorial rotation pushed Ish into his thrust bag; and then Ish was flying free.

In his ear, the voice of the ship said:

– First company, dispersion complete.

On the control console, affixed there, sealed into a block of clear resin: Gula's icon. Ish wondered if this was what she wanted.

And Ninurta added, for Ish's ears alone:
– Good hunting, dog soldier.

At Lagash they'd wanted Ish to join the soldiery of Lagash; had offered him the chance to compete for a place with the Lion-Eagles, Ninurta's elites. Ish had refused, taking the compassion of these warlike men of a warlike city for contempt. Isin was sparsely populated for a city of Babylon, with barely fifty billion spread among its parks and fields and orchards, but its soldiery was small even for that. When the hard men in Ashur and the actuaries in Babylon-Borsippa counted up the cities' defenders, they might forget Lady Gula's soldiers, and be forgiven for forgetting. What Ninurta's men meant as generosity to a grieving worshipper of their lord's consort Ish took for mockery of a parade soldier from a rustic backwater. It needed the intervention of the god himself to make a compromise; this after Ish had lost his temper, broken the recruiter's tablet over his knee and knocked over his writing-table.

"You loved her – dog soldier."

Ish turned to see who had spoken, and saw a god in the flesh for the first time.

The Lord of Lagash was tall, five cubits at least, taller than any man, but the shape and set of his body in its coppery-red armour made it seem that it was the god who was to scale and everything around him – the recruiting office, the Lion-Eagles who had been ready to lay hands on Ish and who were now prostrate on the carpet, the wreckage of the recruiter's table, Ish himself – that was small. The same agelessness was in Ninurta's dark-eyed face that had been in Lady Gula's, but what in the Lady had seemed to Ish a childlike simplicity retained into adulthood was turned, in her consort, to a precocious maturity, a wisdom beyond the unlined face's years.

Ish snapped to attention. "Lord," he said. He saluted – as he would have saluted a superior officer. A murmur of outrage came from the Lion-Eagles on the floor.

The god ignored them. "You loved her," he said again, and he reached out and lifted Ish's seal-cylinder where it hung around his neck, turned it in his fingers to examine the dog figure, to read Ish's name and number.

"No, Lord Ninurta," Ish said.

The god looked from the seal to Ish's face.

"No?" he said, and there was something dangerous in his voice. His fist closed around the seal.

Ish held the god's gaze.

"I still love her," he said.

Ish had been prepared to hate the Lord of Lagash, consort of the Lady of Isin. When Ish thought of god and goddess together his mind slipped and twisted and turned away from the idea; when he'd read the god's proclamation of intent to hunt down the nomads that had murdered "his" lady, Ish's mouth had curled in an involuntary sneer. If the Lord of Lagash had tried to take the seal then, Ish would have fought him, and died.

But the god's fist opened. He glanced at the seal again and let it drop.

The god's eyes met Ish's eyes, and in them Ish saw a pain that was at least no less real and no less rightful than Ish's own.

"So do I," Ninurta said.

Then he turned to his soldiers.

"As you were," he told them. And, when they had scrambled to their feet, he pointed to Ish. "Ishmenininsina Ninnadiïnshumi is a solder of the city of Isin," he told them. "He remains a soldier of the city of Isin. He is your brother. All Lady Gula's soldiers are your brothers. Treat them like brothers."

To Ish he said, "We'll hunt nomads together, dog soldier."

"I'd like that," Ish said. "Lord."

Ninurta's mouth crooked into a half-smile, and Ish saw what the Lady of Isin might have loved in the Lord of Lagash.

FOR THE BETTER part of a year the hunters built, they trained, they changed and were changed – modified, by the priest-engineers who served Ninagal of Akkad and the priest-doctors who had served Lady Gula, their hearts and bones strengthened to withstand accelerations that would kill any ordinary mortal, their nerves and chemistries changed to let them fight faster and harder and longer than anything living, short of a god.

The point mass where the priest-astronomers of Ur thought the hunters would find the nomad camp was far out into Apsu, the diffuse torus of ice and rock and wandering planetary masses that separated Babylon from the nearest stars. The detritus of Apsu was known, mapped long ago down to the smallest fragment by Sin and Shamash, and the nomads' work had left a trail that the knowledgeable could read.

The object the nomads' weapon orbited was one of the largest in the near reaches of Apsu, the superdense core of some giant star that had shed most of its mass long before the Flood, leaving only this degenerate, slowly cooling sphere, barely a league across. The gods had long since oriented it so the jets of radiation from its rapidly spinning magnetic poles pointed nowhere near the cities, moved it into an orbit where it would threaten the cities neither directly with its own gravity, nor by flinging comets and planetesimals down into Babylon.

It took the hunters two hundred days to reach it.

The great ship *Sharur*, the Mace of Ninurta, a god in its own right, was hauled along the surface of Lagash to the city's equator, fuelled, armed, loaded with the hunters and all their weapons and gear, and set loose.

It dropped away slowly at first, but when the ship was far enough from the city its sails opened, and in every city of Babylon it was as if a cloud moved between the land and the shining houses of the gods, as the power of Ninagal's ring was bent to stopping *Sharur* in its orbit. Then the Mace of Ninurta folded its sails like the wings of a diving eagle and fell, gathering speed. The black circle that was Tiamat's event horizon grew until it swallowed half the sky, until the soldiers packed tight around the ship's core passed out in their thrust bags and even *Sharur*'s prodigiously strong bones creaked under the stress, until the hunters were so close that the space-time around them whirled around Tiamat like water. Ninagal's ring flashed by in an instant, and only Lord Ninurta and *Sharur* itself were conscious to see it. *Sharur* shot forward, taking with it some tiny fraction of the black hole's unimaginable angular momentum.

And then Tiamat was behind them, and they were headed outward.

BABYLON CITY 1:1 5" N:1 16" / 34822.7.18 7:15

"All cities' prayers with Lord of Lagash"

"Police seek nomad agents in Babylon"

"Lord Shamash asks Lord Anshar to restore order"

– *Headlines,*
temple newspaper Marduknaşir,
Babylon City

BABYLON CITY 4:142 113" S:4 12" / 34822.7.16 1:3

"An eye for an eye"

"Nativist witch-hunt"

"Ashur to invade Sippar"

– *Headlines,*
radical newspaper Iïnshushaqiï,
Babylon City

5. Machines

AT LAGASH THEY had drilled a double dozen scenarios: city-sized habitats, ramship fleets, dwarf planets threaded with ice tunnels like termite tracks in old wood. When the cities fought among themselves the territory was known and the weapons were familiar. The vacuum armour Ish had worn as a Surface Tactical was not very different from what a soldier of Lagash or Ashur or Akkad would wear although the gear of those warlike cities was usually newer and there was more of it. The weapons the Surface Tacticals carried were deadly enough to ships or to other vacuum troops, and the soldiers of the interior had aircraft and artillery and even fusion bombs although no one had used fusion bombs within a city in millennia. But there had been nothing like the nomads' weapon, nothing that could threaten the fabric of a city. No one could say with certainty what they might meet when they found the nomad encampment.

Ish had seen nomad ships in dock at Isin. There were ramships no larger than canal barges that could out-accelerate a troopship and push the speed of light, and ion-drive ships so dwarfed by their fuel supplies that they were like inhabited comets, and fragile light-sailers whose mirrors were next to useless at Babylon, and every one was unique. Ish supposed you had to be crazy to take it into your head to spend a lifetime in a pressurized can ten trillion leagues from whatever you called home. There wouldn't be many people as crazy as that and also able enough to keep a ship in working order for all that time, even taking into account that you had to be crazy in the first place to live in the rubble around a star when you could be living in a city.

But that wasn't right either. Because most of the people that in Babylon they called nomads had been born out there on their planets or wherever, where there were no cities and no gods, with as much choice about where they lived as a limpet on a rock. It was only the crazy ones that had a choice and only the crazy ones that made it all the way to Babylon.

The nomads Ish was hunting now, the assassins somewhere out there in the dark, he thought were almost simple by comparison. They had no gods and could build no cities and they knew it and it made them angry and so whatever they couldn't have, they smashed. That was a feeling Ish could understand.

Gods and cities fought for primacy, they fought for influence or the settlement of debts. They didn't fight wars of extermination. But extermination was what the nomads had raised the stakes to when they attacked the Corn Parade and extermination was what Ish was armed for now.

– THERE, SAID *SHARUR*'S voice in his ear. – There is their weapon.

In the X-ray spectrum Sinkalamaïdi-541 was one of the brightest objects in the sky, but to human eyes, even augmented as Ish's had been at Lagash, even here, less than half a million leagues from the target, what visible light it gave off as it cooled made it only an unusually bright star, flickering as it spun. Even under the magnification of *Sharur's* sharp eyes it was barely a disc; but Ish could see that something marred it, a dark line across the sickly glowing face.

A display square opened, the dead star's light masked by the black disc of a coronagraph, reflected light – from the dead star itself, from the living stars of the surrounding cluster, from the Old Galaxy – amplified and enhanced. Girdling Sinkalamaïdi-541 was a narrow, spinning band of dull carbon, no more than a thousand leagues across, oriented to draw energy from the dead star's magnetic field; like a mockery of Ninagal's ring.

– A loop accelerator, the ship said. – Crude but effective.

– They must be very sophisticated to aspire to such crudeness, said Ninurta. – We have found the sling, but where is the slinger?

When straight out of the temple orphanage he'd first enlisted they'd trained Ish as a rifleman, and when he'd qualified for Surface Tactical School they'd trained him as a vacuum armour operator. What he was doing now, controlling this platform that had been shot down an electromagnetic rail like a corn can, was not very much like either of those jobs, although the platform's calculus of fuel and velocity and power and heat was much the same as for the vacuum armour. But he was not a Surface Tactical anymore and there was no surface here, no city with its weak gravity and strong spin to complicate the equations, only speed and darkness and somewhere in the darkness the target.

There was no knowing what instruments the nomads had but Ish hoped to evade all of them. The platform's outer shell was black in short wavelengths and would scatter or let pass long ones; the cold face it turned toward the nomad weapon was chilled to within a degree of the cosmic microwave background, and its drives were photonic, the exhaust a laser-tight collimated beam. Eventually some platform would occlude a star or its drive beam would touch some bit of ice or cross some nomad sensor's mirror and they would be discovered, but not quickly and not all at once.

They would be on the nomads long before that.

* * *

– THIRD COMPANY, NINURTA said. – Fire on the ring. Flush them out.

The platforms had been fired from *Sharur's* catapults in an angled pattern so that part of the energy of the launch went to slowing *Sharur* itself and part to dispersing the platforms in an irregular spreading cone that by this time was the better part of a thousand leagues across. Now the platforms' own engines fired, still at angles oblique to the line joining *Sharur's* course to the dead star.

Below Ish – subjectively – and to his left, a series of blinking icons indicated that the platforms of the third company were separating themselves still further, placing themselves more squarely in the track of the dead star's orbit. When they were another thousand leagues distant from *Sharur* they cast their weapons loose and the weapons' own engines fired, bright points Ish could see with his own eyes, pushing the weapons onward with a force beyond what even the hunters' augmented and supported bodies could withstand.

Time passed. The flares marking the weapons of the third company went out one by one as their fuel was exhausted. When they were three hundred thousand leagues from the ring, the longest-ranged of the weapons – antiproton beams, muon accelerators, fission-pumped gamma-ray lasers – began to fire.

Before the bombardment could possibly have reached the ring – long before there had passed the thirty or forty grains required for the bombardment to reach the ring and the light of the bombardment's success or failure to return to *Sharur* and the platforms – the space between the ring and the third company filled with fire. Explosions flared all across Ish's field of view, pinpoints of brilliant white, shading to ultraviolet. Something hit the side of the platform with a terrific thump, and Ish's hand squeezed convulsively on the weapon release as his diagnostic screens became a wash of red. There was a series of smaller thumps as the weapons came loose, and then a horrible grinding noise as at least one encountered some projecting tangle of bent metal and broken ceramic. The platform was tumbling. About half Ish's reaction control thrusters claimed to be working; he fired them in pairs and worked the gyroscopes till the tumble was reduced to a slow roll, while the trapped weapon scraped and bumped its way across the hull and finally came free.

– Machines, machines! he heard Ninurta say. – Cowards! Where are the *men?*

Then the weapon, whichever it was, blew up.

34822.7.16 4:24:6:20 - 5:23:10:13
Moving image, recorded at 24 frames per second over a period of 117 minutes 15 seconds by spin-stabilized camera, installation "Cyrus," transmitted via QT to COS Liberation, *on Gaugamela station, and onward to Community Outreach archives, Urizen:*

From the leading edge of the accelerator ring, it is as though the ring and the mass that powers it are rising through a tunnel of light.

For ten million kilometres along the track of the neutron star's orbit, the darkness ahead sparkles with the light of antimatter bombs, fusion explosions, the kinetic flash of chaff thrown out by the accelerator ring impacting ships, missiles, remotely operated guns; impacting men. Through the minefield debris of the ring's static defences, robotic fighters dart and weave, looking to kill anything that accelerates. Outreach has millennia of experience to draw on, and back in the Community a population of hundreds of billions to produce its volunteer missionaries, its dedicated programmers, its hobbyist generals. Many of the Babylonian weapons are stopped; many of the Babylonian ships are destroyed. Others, already close to Babylon's escape velocity and by the neutron star's orbital motion close to escaping from it as well, are shunted aside, forced into hyperbolic orbits that banish them from the battlefield as surely as death.

But the ring's defenders are fighting from the bottom of a deep gravity well, with limited resources, nearly all the mass they've assembled here incorporated into the ring itself; and the Babylonians have their own store of ancient cunning to draw on, their aggregate population a hundred times larger than the Community's, more closely knit and more warlike. And they have Ninurta.

Ninurta, the hunter of the Annunaki, the god who slew the seven-headed serpent, who slew the bull-man in the sea and the six-headed wild ram in the mountain, who defeated the demon Ansu and retrieved the Tablet of Destinies.

Sharur, the Mace of Ninurta, plunges through the battle like a shark through minnows, shining like a sun, accelerating, adding the thrust of its mighty engines to the neutron star's inexorable pull. Slender needles of laser prick out through the debris, and *Sharur*'s sun brightens still further, painful to look at, the ship's active hull heated to tens of thousands of degrees. Something like a swarm of fireflies swirls out toward it, and the camera's filters cut in, darkening the sky as the warheads explode around the ship, a constellation of new stars that flare, burn and die in perfect silence: and *Sharur* keeps coming.

It fills the view.

Overhead, a blur, it flashes past the camera, and is gone.

The image goes white.

The transmission ends.

6. Surviving weapons

IT WAS COLD in the control capsule. The heat sink was still deployed and the motors that should have folded it in would not respond. Ish found he didn't much care. There was a slow leak somewhere in the atmosphere cycler and Ish found he didn't much care about that either.

The battle, such as it was, was well off to one side. Ish knew even before doing the math that he did not have enough fuel to bring himself back into it. The dead star was bending his course but not enough. He was headed into the dark.

Ish's surviving weapons were still burning mindlessly toward the ring and had cut by half the velocity with which they were speeding away from it, but they too were nearly out of fuel and Ish saw that they would follow him into darkness.

He watched *Sharur*'s plunge through the battle. The dead star was between him and the impact when it happened, but he saw the effect it had: a flash across the entire spectrum from long-wave radio to hard X-ray, bright enough to illuminate the entire battlefield; bright enough, probably, to be seen from the cities.

Another god died.

There was a sparkle of secondary explosions scattered through the debris field, weapons and platforms and nomad fighters alike flashing to plasma in the light of Ninurta's death. Then there was nothing.

The ring began, slowly, to break up.

Ish wondered how many other platforms were still out here, set aside like his, falling into Apsu. Anyone who had been on the impact side was dead.

The weapons' drive flares went out.

The mended icon was still where he had fixed it. Ish shut down the displays one by one until his helmet beam was the only light and adjusted the thrust bag around the helmet so that the beam shone full on the icon. The look in the Lady's eyes no longer seemed accusatory, but appraising, as if she were waiting to see what Ish would do.

The beam wavered and went dark.

BABYLON CITY 2:78 233" S:2 54" / 34822.10.6 5:18:4
Record of police interrogation, Suspect 34822.10. 6.502155, alias Ajabeli Huzalatum Taraämapsu, alias Liburnadisha Iliawilimrabi Apsuümasha, alias "Black," Charges: subversion, terrorism, falsification of temple records, failure to register as a foreign agent. Interrogator is Detective (Second Degree) Nabûnaïd Babilisheïr Rabişila.

Rabişila: Your people are gone. Your weapon's been destroyed. You might as well tell us everything.

Suspect: It accomplished its purpose.

Rabişila: Which was?

Suspect: To give you hope.

Rabişila: What do you mean, "hope"?

Suspect: Men are fighting gods now, in Gish and Sippar.

Rabişila: A few criminal lunatics. Lord Anshar will destroy them.

Suspect: Do you think they'll be the last? Two of your gods are dead. Dead at the hands of mortals. Nothing Anshar's soldiers do to Sippar will change that. Nothing you do to me.

Rabişila: You're insane.

Suspect: I mean it. One day – not in my lifetime, certainly not in yours, but one day – one day you'll all be free.

7. A soldier of the city

A SHIP FOUND Ish a few months later: a ship called *Upekkhâ*, from a single-system nomad civilization based some seventeen light-years from Babylon and known to itself as the Congregation. The ship, the name of which meant "equanimity," was an antimatter-fuelled ion rocket, a quarter of a league long and twice that in diameter; it could reach two-tenths the speed of light, but only very, very slowly. It had spent fifteen years docked at Babylon-Borsippa, and, having been launched some four months before the attack on the Corn Parade, was now on its way back to the star the Congregation called *Mettâ*. The star's name, in the ancient liturgical language of the monks and nuns of the Congregation, meant "kindness."

* * *

ISH WAS VERY nearly dead when *Upekkhâ*'s monks brought him aboard. His heart had been stopped for some weeks, and it was the acceleration support system rather than Ish's bloodstream that was supplying the last of the platform's oxygen reserves to his brain, which itself had been pumped full of cryoprotectants and cooled to just above the boiling point of nitrogen. The rescue team had to move very quickly to extricate Ish from that system and get him onto their own life support. This task was not made any easier by the militarized physiology given to Ish at Lagash, but they managed it. He was some time in recovering.

Ish never quite understood what had brought *Upekkhâ* to Babylon. Most of the monks and nuns spoke good Babylonian – several of them had been born in the cities – but the concepts were too alien for Ish to make much sense of them, and Ish admitted to himself he didn't really care to try. They had no gods, and prayed – as far as Ish could tell – to their ancestors, or their teachers' teachers. They had been looking, they said, for someone they called *Tathâgata*, which the nun explaining this to Ish translated into Babylonian as "the one who has found the truth." This Tathâgata had died, many years ago on a planet circling the star called Mettâ, and why the monks and nuns were looking for him at Babylon was only one of the things Ish didn't understand.

"But we didn't find him," the nun said. "We found you."

They were in *Upekkhâ*'s central core, where Ish, who had grown up on a farm, was trying to learn how to garden in free fall. The monks and nuns had given him to understand that he was not required to work, but he found it embarrassing to lie idle – and it was better than being alone with his thoughts.

"And what are you going to do with me?" Ish asked.

The nun – whose own name, *Arakkhasampada*, she translated as "the one who has attained watchfulness" – gave him an odd look and said:

"Nothing."

"Aren't you afraid I'll – do something? Damage something? Hurt someone?" Ish asked.

"Will you?" Arakkhasampada asked.

Ish had thought about it. Encountering the men and women of *Upekkhâ* on the battlefield he could have shot them without hesitation. In Apsu, he had not hesitated. He had looked forward to killing the nomads responsible for the Corn Parade with an anticipation that was two parts vengefulness and one part technical satisfaction. But these nomads were not those nomads, and it was hard now to see the point.

It must have been obvious, from where the monks and nuns found Ish, and in what condition, what he was, and what he had done. But they seemed not to care. They treated Ish kindly, but Ish suspected they would have done as much for a wounded dog.

The thought was humbling, but Ish also found it oddly liberating. The crew of *Upekkhâ* didn't know who Ish was or what he had been trying to do, or why. His failure was not evident to them.

THE DOCTOR, AN elderly monk who Ish called Doctor Sam – his name, which Ish couldn't pronounce, meant something like "the one who leads a balanced life" – pronounced Ish fit to move out of the infirmary. Arrakhasamyada and Doctor Sam helped Ish decorate his cabin, picking out plants from the garden and furnishings from *Upekkhâ*'s sparse catalogue with a delicate attention to Ish's taste and reactions that surprised him, so that the end result, while hardly Babylonian, was less foreign, more Ish's own, than it might have been.

Arrakhasamyada asked about the mended icon in its block of resin, and Ish tried to explain.

She and Doctor Sam grew very quiet and thoughtful.

ISH DIDN'T SEE either of them for eight or ten days. Then one afternoon as he was coming back from the garden, dusty and tired, he found the two of them waiting by his cabin. Arrakhasamyada was carrying a bag of oranges, and Doctor Sam had with him a large box made to look like lacquered wood.

Ish let them in, and went into the back of the cabin to wash and change clothes. When he came out they had unpacked the box, and Ish saw that it was an iconostasis or shrine, of the sort the monks and nuns used to remember their predecessors. But where the name-scroll would go there was a niche just the size of Ish's icon.

He didn't know who he was. He was still, – would always be, – a soldier of the city, but what did that mean? He had wanted revenge, still did in some abstract way. There would be others, now, Lion-Eagles out to avenge the Lord of Lagash, children who had grown up with images of the Corn Parade.

Maybe Mâra would be among them, though Ish hoped not. But Ish himself had had his measure of vengeance in Apsu and knew well enough that it had never been likely that he would have more.

He looked at the icon where it was propped against the wall. Who was he? Tara: "I don't think I ever knew you." But she had, hadn't she? Ish was a man in love with a dead woman. He always would be. The Lady's death hadn't changed that, any more than Ish's own death would have. The fact that the dead woman was a goddess hadn't changed it.

Ish picked up the icon and placed it in the niche. He let Doctor Sam show him where to place the orange, how to set the sticks of incense in the cup and start the little induction heater. Then he sat back on his heels and they contemplated the face of the Lady of Isin together.

"Will you tell us about her?" Arrakhasamyada asked.

MERCIES

GREGORY BENFORD

Gregory Benford has published over forty books, mostly novels. Nearly all remain in print, some after a quarter of a century. His fiction has won many awards, including the Nebula Award for his novel Timescape. *A winner of the United Nations Medal for Literature, he is a professor of physics at the University of California, Irvine. He is a Woodrow Wilson Fellow, was Visiting Fellow at Cambridge University, and in 1995 received the Lord Prize for contributions to science. He won the Japan Seiun Award for Dramatic Presentation with his 7-hour series,* A Galactic Odyssey. *In 2007 he won the Asimov Award for science writing. In 2006 he co-founded Genescient, a biotech company devoted to extending human longevity.*

His story here evolved after he wrote the entry on the concept of time in Seeing Further: An Anthology of Science Writing Celebrating The 350th Birth of the Royal Society.

> "All scientific work is, of course, based on some conscious or subconscious philosophical attitude."
>
> – Werner Heisenberg

He rang the doorbell and heard its buzz echo in the old wooden house. Footsteps. The worn, scarred door eased open half an inch and a narrowed brown eye peered at him.

"Mr Hanson?" Warren asked in a bland bureaucratic tone, the accent a carefully rehearsed approximation of the flat Midwestern that would arouse no suspicions here.

"Yeah, so?" The mouth jittered, then straightened.

"I need to speak to you about your neighbour. We're doing a security background check."

The eye swept up and down Warren's three-piece suit, dark tie, polished shoes – traditional styles, or as the advertisements of this era said, "timeless." Warren was even sporting a grey fedora with a snap band.

"Which neighbour?"

This he hadn't planned on. Alarm clutched at his throat. Instead of speaking he nodded at the house to his right. Daniel Hanson's eye slid that way, then back, and narrowed some more. "Lemme see ID."

This Warren had expected. He showed an FBI ID in a plastic case, up-to-date and accurate. The single eye studied it and Warren wondered what to do if the door slammed shut. Maybe slide around to the window, try to –

The door jerked open. Hanson was a wiry man with shaggy hair – a bony framework, all joints and hinges. His angular face jittered with concern and Warren asked, "You are the Hanson who works at Allied Mechanical?"

The hooded eyes jerked again as Warren stepped into the room.

"Uh, yeah, but hey – whassit matter if you're askin' 'bout the neighbour?"

Warren moved to his left to get Hanson away from the windows. “I just need the context in security matters of this sort.”

“You’re wastin’ your time, see, I don’t know ’bout –”

Warren opened his briefcase casually and in one fluid move brought the short automatic pistol out. Hanson froze. He fired straight into Hanson’s chest. The popping sound was no louder than a dropped glass would make as the silencer soaked up the noise.

Hanson staggered back, his mouth gaping, sucking in air. Warren stepped forward, just as he had practiced, and carefully aimed again. The second shot hit Hanson squarely in the forehead and the man went down backward, thumping on the thin rug.

Warren listened. No sound from outside.

It was done. His first, and just about as he had envisioned it. In the sudden silence he heard his heart hammering.

He had read from the old texts that professional hit men of this era used the 0.22 automatic pistol despite its low calibre, and now he saw why. Little noise, especially with the suppressor, and the gun rode easily in his hand. The silencer would have snagged if he had carried it in a coat pocket. In all, his plans had worked. The pistol was light, strong, and – befitting its mission – a brilliant white.

The dark red pool spreading from Hanson’s skull was a clear sign that this man, who would have tortured, hunted, and killed many women, would never get his chance now.

Further, the light 0.22 slug had stayed inside the skull, ricocheting so that it could never be identified as associated with this pistol. This point was also in the old texts, just as had been the detailed blueprints. With those, making the pistol and ammunition was simple using his home replicator machine.

He moved through the old house, floors creaking, and systematically searched Hanson's belongings. Here again the old texts were useful, leading him to the automatic pistol taped under a dresser drawer. No sign yet of the rifle Hanson had used in the open woods, either.

It was amazing, what twenty-first century journals carried, in their sensual fascination with the romantic aura of crime. He found no signs of victims' clothing, of photos or mementos – all mementoes Hanson had collected in Warren's timeline. Daniel Hanson took his victims into the woods near here, where he would let them loose and then hunt and kill them. His first known killing lay three months ahead of this day. The timestream was quite close, in quantum coordinates, so Warren could be sure that this Hanson was very nearly identical to the Hanson of Warren's timeline. They were adjacent in a sense he did not pretend to understand, beyond the cartoons in popular science books.

Excellent. Warren had averted a dozen deaths. He brimmed with pride.

He needed to get away quickly, back to the transflux cage. With each tick of time the transflux cage's location became more uncertain.

On the street outside he saw faces looking at him through a passing car window, the glass runny with reflected light. But the car just drove on. He made it into the stand of trees and then a kilometre walk took him to the cage. This was as accurate as the quantum flux process made possible during a jogg back through decades. He paused at the entrance hatch, listening. No police sirens. Wind sighed in the boughs. He sucked in the moist air and flashed a supremely happy grin.

He set the coordinates and readied himself. The complex calculations spread on a screen before him and a high tone sounded *screeeee* in his ears. A sickening gyre began. The whirl of space-time made gravity spread outward from him, pulling at his legs and arms as the satin blur of colour swirled past the transparent walls. *Screeeee...*

FOR WARREN THE past was a vast sheet of darkness, mired in crimes immemorial, each horror like a shining, vibrant, blood-red bonfire in the gloom, calling to him.

He began to see that at school. History instruction then was a multishow of images, sounds, scents and touches. The past came to the schoolboys as a sensory immersion. Social adjustment policy in those times was clear: only by deep sensing of what the past world was truly like could moral understanding occur. The technologies gave a reasonable immersion in eras, conveying why people thought or did things back then. So he saw the dirty wars, the horrifying ideas, the tragedies and comedies of those eras...and longed for them.

They seemed somehow more real. The smart world everyone knew had embedded intelligences throughout, which made it dull, predictable. Warren was always the brightest in his classes, and he got bored.

He was fifteen when he learned of serial killers.

The teacher – Ms Sheila Weiss, lounged back on her desk with legs crossed, her slanted red mouth and lifted black eyebrows conveying her humour – said that quite precisely, "serials" were those who murdered three or more people over a period of more than thirty days, with a "cooling off" period between each murder. The pattern was quite old, not a mere manifestation of their times, Miss Weiss said. Some sources suggested that legends such as werewolves and vampires were inspired by medieval serial killers. Through all that history, their motivation for killing was the lure of "psychological gratification" – whatever that meant, Warren thought.

Ms Weiss went on: Some transfixed by the power of life and death were attracted to medical professions. These "angels of death" – or as they self-described, angels of mercy – were the worst, for they killed so many. One Harold Shipman, an English family doctor, made it seem as though his victims had died of natural causes. Between 1975 and 1998, he murdered at least two hundred and fifteen patients. Ms Weiss added that he might have murdered two hundred and fifty or more.

The girl in the next seat giggled nervously at all this, and Warren frowned at her. Gratification resonated in him, and he struggled with his own strange excitement. Somehow, he realized as the discussion went on around him, the horror of death coupled with his own desire. This came surging up in him as an inevitable, vibrant truth.

Hesitantly he asked Ms Weiss, "Do we have them... serial killers... now?"

She beamed, as she always did when he saw which way her lecture was going. "No, and that is the point. Good for you! Because we have neuro methods, you see. All such symptoms are detected early – the misaligned patterns of mind, the urges outside the norm envelope – and extinguished. They use electro and pharma, too." She paused, eyelids fluttering in a way he found enchanting.

Warren could not take his eyes off her legs as he said, "Does that... harm?"

Ms Weiss eyed him oddly and said, "The procedure – that is, a normalization of character before the fact of any, ah, bad acts – occurs without damage or limitation of freedom of the, um, patient, you understand."

"So we don't have serial killers anymore?"

Ms Weiss's broad mouth twisted a bit. "No methods are perfect. But our homicide rates from these people are far lower now."

Boyd Carlos said from the back of the class, "Why not just kill 'em?" and got a big laugh.

Warren reddened. Ms Weiss's beautiful, warm eyes flared with anger, eyebrows arched. "That is the sort of crime our society seeks to avoid," she said primly. "We gave up capital punishment ages ago. It's uncivilized."

Boyd made a clown face at this, and got another laugh. Even the girls joined in this time, the chorus of their high giggles echoing in Warren's ears.

Sweat broke out all over Warren's forehead and he hoped no one would notice. But the girl in the seat across the aisle did, the pretty blonde one named Nancy, whom he had been planning for weeks to approach. She rolled her eyes, gestured to friends. Which made him sweat more.

His chest tightened and he thought furiously, eyes

averted from the blonde. Warren ventured, "How about the victims who might die? Killing killers saves lives."

Miss Weiss frowned. "You mean that executing them prevents murders later?"

Warren spread his hands. "If you imprison them, can't they murder other prisoners?"

Miss Weiss blinked. "That's a very good argument, Warren, but can you back it up?"

"Uh, I don't –"

"You could research this idea. Look up the death rate in prisons due to murderers serving life sentences. Discover for yourself what fraction of prison murders they cause."

"I'll... see." Warren kept his eyes on hers.

Averting her eyes, blinking, Miss Weiss seemed pleased, bit her lip and moved on to the next study subject.

That ended the argument, but Warren thought about it all through the rest of class. Boyd even came over to him later and said, with the usual shrugs and muttering, "Thanks for backin' me up, man."

Then he sauntered off with Nancy on his arm. A bit later Warren saw Boyd holding forth to his pals, mouth big and grinning, pointing toward Warren and getting more hooting from the crowd. Nancy guffawed too, lips lurid, eyes on Boyd.

That was Warren's sole triumph among the cool set, who afterward went back to ignoring him. But he felt the sting of the class laughing all the same. His talents lay in careful work, not in the zing of classroom jokes. He was methodical, so he should use that.

So he did the research Miss Weiss had suggested. Indeed, convicted murderers committed the majority of murders in prison. What did they have to lose? Once a killer personality had jumped the bounds of society, what held them back? They were going to serve out their life sentences anyway. And a reputation for settling scores helped them in prison, even gave them weird prestige and power.

These facts simmered in him for decades. He had never forgotten that moment – the lurid lurch of Ms Sheila Weiss's mouth, the rushing terror and desire lacing through him, the horrible high, shrill giggle from that girl in the next seat. Or the history of humanity's horror, and the strange ideas it summoned up within him.

HIS NEXT JOGG took him further backward in time, as it had to, for reasons he had not bothered to learn. Something about the second law of thermodynamics, he gathered.

He slid sideways in space-time, following the arc of Earth's orbit around the galaxy – this he knew, but it was just more incomprehensible technical detail that was beside his point entirely. He simply commanded the money and influence to make it happen. How it happened was someone else's detail.

As was the diagnosis, which he could barely follow, four months before. Useless details. Only the destination mattered; he had three months left now, at best. His stomach spiked with growling aches and he took more of the pills to suppress his symptoms.

In that moment months before, listening to the doctor drone on, he had decided to spend his last days in a long space-time jogg. He could fulfil his dream, sliding backward into eras "nested," as the specialists said, close to his own. Places where he could understand the past, act upon it, and bring about good. The benefits of his actions would come to others, but that was the definition of goodness, wasn't it – to bring joy and life to others.

As he decided this, the vision coming sharp and true, he had felt a surge of purpose. He sensed vaguely that this glorious campaign of his was in some way redemption for his career, far from the rough rub of the world. But he did not inspect his impulses, for that would blunt his impact, diffuse his righteous energies.

He had to keep on.

He came out of the transflux cage in a city park. It was the mid-1970s, before Warren had been born.

His head spun sickly from the flexing gravity of the jogg. Twilight gathered in inky shadows and a recent rain flavoured the air. Warren carefully noted the nearby landmarks. As he walked away through a dense stand of scraggly trees, he turned and looked back at each change of direction. This cemented the return route in his mind.

He saw no one as night fell. With a map he found the cross street he had expected. His clothing was jeans and a light brown jacket, not out of place here in Danville, a small Oklahoma town, although brown mud now spattered his tennis shoes. He wiped them off on grass as he made his way into the street where Frank Clifford lived. The home was an artful Craftsman design, two windows glowing with light. He searched for a sure sign that Clifford lived here. The deviations from his home timeline might be minor, and his prey might have lived somewhere else. But the mailbox had no name on it, just the address. He had to be sure.

He was far enough before Clifford's first known killing, as calculated by his team. Clifford had lived here for over a month, the spotty property tax records said, and his pattern of killings, specializing in nurses, had not emerged in the casebooks. Nor had such stylized killings, with their major themes of bondage in nurse uniforms and long sexual bouts, appeared along Clifford's life history. Until now.

The drapes concealed events inside the house. He caught flickering shadows, though, and prepared his approach. Warren made sure no one from nearby houses was watching him as he angled across the lawn and put his foot on the first step up to the front door.

This had worked for the first three disposals. He had gained confidence in New Haven and Atlanta, editing out killers who got little publicity but killed dozens. Now he felt sure of himself. His only modification was to carry the pistol in his coat pocket, easier to reach. He liked the feel of it, loaded and ready. *Avenging angel*, yes, but preventing as well.

Taking a breath, he started up the steps – and heard a door slam to his right. Light spattered into the driveway. A car door opened. He guessed that Clifford was going to drive away.

Looping back to this space-time coordinate would be impossible, without prior work. He had to do something now, outside the house. Outside his pattern.

An engine nagged into a thrumming idle. Warren walked to the corner of the house and looked around. Headlights flared in a dull-toned Ford. He ducked back, hoping he had not been seen.

The gear engaged and the car started forward, spitting gravel. Warren started to duck, stay out of sight – then took a breath. *No, now.*

He reached out as the car came by and yanked open the rear passenger door. He leaped in, not bothering to pull the door closed, and brought the pistol up. He could see the man only in profile. In the dim light Warren could not tell if the quick profile fit the photos and 3D recreations he had memorized. Was this Clifford?

"Freeze!" he said as the driver's head jerked toward him. Warren pressed the pistol's snub snout into the man's neck. "Or I pull the trigger."

Warren expected the car to stop. Instead, the man stamped on the gas. And said nothing.

They rocked out of the driveway, surged right with squealing tires, and the driver grinned in the streetlamp lights as he gunned the engine loud and hard.

"Slow down!" Warren said, pushing the muzzle into the back of the skull. "You're Clifford, right?"

"Ok, sure I am. Take it easy, man." Clifford said this casually, as if he were in control of the situation. Warren felt confusion leap like sour spit into his throat. But Clifford kept accelerating, tires howling as he turned onto a highway. They were near the edge of town and Warren did not want to get far from his resonance point.

"Slow down, I said!"

"Sure, just let me get away from these lights." Clifford glanced over his right shoulder. "You don't want us out where people can see, do you?"

Warren didn't know what to say. They shot past the last traffic light and hummed down a state highway. There was no other traffic and the land lay level and barren beyond. In the blackness, Warren thought, he could probably walk back into town. But –

"How far you want me to go?"

He had to shake this man's confidence. "Have you killed any women yet, Frank?"

Clifford didn't even blink. "No. Been thinkin' on it. Lots."

This man didn't seem surprised. "You're sure?" Warren asked, to buy time.

"What's the point o' lyin'?"

This threw Warren into even more confusion. Clifford stepped down on the gas again though and Warren felt this slipping out of his control. "Slow down!"

Clifford smiled. "Me and my buddies, back in high school, we had this kinda game. We'd get an old jalopy and run it out here, four of us, and do the survivor thing."

"What – ?"

"What you got against me, huh?" Clifford turned and smirked at him.

"I, you – you're going to *murder* those women, that's what –"

"How you know that? You're like that other guy, huh?"

"How can you – wait – other guy – ?"

The car surged forward with bursting speed into a flat curve in the highway. Headlights swept across bare fields as the engine roared. Clifford chuckled in a dry, flat tone, and spat out, "Let's see how you like our game, buddy-o."

Clifford slammed the driver's wheel to the left and the Ford lost traction, sliding into a skid. It jumped off the two-lane blacktop and into the flat field beyond. Clifford jerked on the wheel again –

– and in adrenaline-fed slow motion the seat threw Warren into the roof. The car frame groaned like a wounded beast and the wheels left the ground. The transmission shrieked like a band saw cutting tin, as the wheels got free of the road. Warren lifted, smacked against the roof, and it pushed him away as the frame hit the ground – *whomp*. The back window popped into a crystal shower exploding around him. Then the car heaved up, struggling halfway toward the sky again – paused – and crashed back down. Seams twanged, glass shattered, the car rocked. Stopped.

Quiet. Crickets. Wind sighing through the busted windows.

Warren crawled out of the wide-flung door. He still clutched the pistol, which had not gone off. On his knees in the ragged weeds he looked around. No motion in the dim quarter-moonlight that washed the twisted Ford. Headlights poked two slanted lances of grey light across the flat fields.

Warren stood up and hobbled – his left leg weak and trembling – through the reek of burnt rubber, to look in the driver's window. It was busted into glittering fragments. Clifford sprawled across the front seat, legs askew. The moonlight showed glazed eyes and a tremor in the open mouth. As he watched a dark bubble formed at the lips and swelled, then burst, and he saw it was blood spraying across the face.

Warren thought a long moment and then turned to walk back into town. Again, quickly finding the transflux cage was crucial. He stayed away from the road in case some car would come searching, but in the whole long walk back, which took a forever that by his timer proved to be nearly an hour, no headlights swept across the forlorn fields.

HE HAD STAGED a fine celebration when he invented masked inset coding, a flawless quantum logic that secured against deciphering. That brought him wealth beyond mortal dreams, all from encoded 1s and 0s.

That began his long march through the highlands of digital craft. Resources came to him effortlessly. When he acquired control of the largest consortium of advanced research companies, he rejoiced with friends and mistresses. His favourite was a blonde who, he realized late in the night, reminded him of that Nancy, long ago. Nearly fifty years.

The idea came to him in the small hours of that last, sybaritic night. As the pillows of his sofa moved to accommodate him, getting softer where he needed it, supporting his back with the right strength, his unconscious made the connection. He had acquired major stock interest in Advanced Spacetimes. His people managed the R&D program. They could clear the way, discreetly arrange for a "sideslip" as the technicals termed it. The larger world called it a "jogg," to evoke the sensation of trotting blithely across the densely packed quantum spacetimes available.

He thought this through while his smart sofa whispered soft, encouraging tones. His entire world was smart. Venture to jaywalk on a city street and a voice told you to get back, traffic was on the way. Take a wrong turn walking home and your inboards beeped you with directions. In the countryside, trees did not advise you on your best way to the lake. Compared to the tender city, nature was dead, rough, uncaring.

There was no place in the claustrophobic smart world to sense the way the world had been, when men roamed wild and did vile things. No need for that horror, anymore. Still, he longed to right the evils of that untamed past. Warren saw his chance.

Spacetime intervals were wedges of coordinates, access to them paid for by currency flowing seamlessly from accounts, which would never know the use he put their assets to – or care.

He studied in detail that terrible past, noting dates and deaths and the heady ideas they called forth. Assembling his team, he instructed them to work out a trajectory that slid across the braided map of nearby space-times, all generated by quantum processes he could not fathom in the slightest.

Each side-slide brought the transflux passenger to a slightly altered, parallel universe of events. Each held potential victims, awaiting the knife or bludgeon that would end their own timelines forever. Each innocent could be saved. Not in Warren's timeline – too late for that – but in other spacetimes, still yearning for salvation.

THE CAR CRASH had given him a zinging adrenaline boost, which now faded. As he let the transflux cage's transverse gravity spread his legs and arms, popping joints, he learned from the blunders he had made. Getting in the car and not immediately shoving the snout of the 0.22 into Clifford's neck, pulling the trigger – yes, an error. The thrill of the moment had clouded his judgment, surely.

So he made the next few joggs systematic. Appear, find the target, kill within a few minutes more, then back to the cage. He began to analyse those who fell to his exacting methods. A catalogue of evil, gained at the expense of the sickness that now beset him at every jogg.

Often, the killers betrayed in their last moments not simple fear, but their own motives. Usually sexual disorders drove them. Their victims, he already knew, had something in common – occupation, race, appearance or age. One man in his thirties would slaughter five librarians, and his walls were covered with photos of brunettes wearing glasses. Such examples fell into what the literature called, in its deadening language, "specific clusters of dysfunctional personality characteristics," along with eye tics, obsessions, a lack of conversational empathy.

These men had no guilt. They blustered when they saw the 0.22 and died wholly self-confident, surprised as the bullets found them. Examining their homes, Warren saw that they followed a distinct set of rigid, self-made rules. He knew that most would keep photo albums of their victims, so was unsurprised to find that they already, before their crimes, had many women's dresses and lingerie crammed into their hiding places, and much pornography. Yet they had appeared to be normal and often quite charming, a thin mask of sanity.

Their childhoods were marked by animal cruelty, obsession with fire setting, and persistent bedwetting past the age of five. They would often lure victims with ploys appealing to the victims' sense of sympathy.

Such monsters should be erased, surely. In his own timeline, the continuing drop in the homicide rate was a puzzle. Now he sensed that at least partly that came from the work of sideslip space-time travellers like himself, who remained invisible in that particular history.

Warren thought on this, as he slipped along the whorl of space-time, seeking his next exit. He would get as many of the vermin as he could, cleansing universes he would never enjoy. He had asked his techs at Advanced Spacetimes if he could go forward in time to an era when someone had cured the odd cancer that beset him. But they said no, that sideslipping joggs could not move into a future undefined, unknown.

He learned to mop up his vomit, quell his roaming aches, grit his teeth and go on.

HE WAITED THROUGH a rosy sundown for Ted Bundy to appear. Light slid from the sky and traffic hummed on the streets nearby the apartment Warren knew he used in 1971. People were coming back to their happy homes, the warm domestic glows and satisfactions.

It was not smart to lurk in the area, so he used his lock picks to enter the back of the apartment house, and again on Bundy's door. The mailboxes below had helpfully reassured him that the mass murderer of so many women lived here, months before his crimes began.

To pass the time he found the materials that eventually Bundy would use to put his arm in a fake plaster cast and ask women to help him carry something to his car. Then Bundy would beat them unconscious with a crowbar and carry them away. Bundy had been a particularly organized killer – socially adequate, with friends and lovers. Sometimes such types even had a spouse and children. The histories said such men were those who, when finally captured, were likely to be described by acquaintances as kind and unlikely to hurt anyone. But they were smart and swift and dangerous, at all times.

So when Warren heard the front door open, he slipped into the back bedroom and, to his sudden alarm, heard a female voice. An answering male baritone, joking and light.

They stopped in the kitchen to pour some wine. Bundy was a charmer, his voice warm and mellow, dipping up and down with sincere interest in some story she was telling him. He put on music, soft saxophone jazz, and they moved to the living room.

This went on until Warren began to sweat with anxiety. The transflux cage's position in space-time was subject to some form of uncertainty principle. As it held strictly to this timeline, its position in spatial coordinates became steadily more poorly phased. That meant it would slowly drift in position, in some quantum sense he did not follow. The techs assured him this was a small, unpredictable effect, but cautioned him to minimize his time at any of the jogg points.

If the transflux cage moved enough, he might not find it again in the dark. It was in a dense pine forest and he had memorized the way back, but anxiety began to vex him.

He listened to Bundy's resonant tones romancing the woman as bile leaked upward into his mouth. The cancer was worsening, the pains cramping his belly. It was one of the new, variant cancers that evolved after the supposed victory over the simpler sorts. Even suppressing the symptoms was difficult.

If he vomited he would surely draw Bundy back here. Sweating from the pain and anxiety, Warren inched forward along the carpeted corridor, listening intently. Bundy's voice rose, irritated. The woman's response was hesitant, startled – then beseeching. The music suddenly got louder. Warren quickly moved to the end of the corridor and looked around the corner. Bundy had a baseball bat in his hands, eyes bulging, the woman sitting on the long couch speaking quickly, hands raised, Bundy stepping back –

Warren fished out the pistol and brought it up as Bundy swung. He clipped the woman in the head, a hard smack. Her long hair flew back as she grunted and collapsed. She rolled off the couch, thumping on the floor.

Warren said, "Bastard!" and Bundy turned. "How many have you killed?"

"What the – who are you?"

Warren permitted himself a smile. He had to know if there had been any victims earlier. "An angel. How many, you swine?"

Bundy relaxed, swinging the bat in one hand. He smirked, eyes narrowing as he took in the situation, Warren, his opportunities. "You don't look like any angel to me, buster. Just some nosy neighbour, right?" He smiled. "Watch me bring girls up here, wanted to snoop? Maybe watch us? That why you were hiding in my bedroom?"

Bundy strolled casually forward with an easy, athletic gait as he shrugged, a grin breaking across his handsome face, his left hand spread in a casual so-what gesture, right hand clenched firmly on the bat. "We were just having a little argument here, man. I must've got a little mad, you can see –"

The *splat* of the 0.22 going off was mere rhythm in the jazz that blared from two big speakers. Bundy stepped back and blinked in surprise and looked down at the red stain on his lumberjack shirt. Warren aimed carefully and the second shot hit him square in the nose, splattering blood. Bundy toppled forward, thumping on the carpet.

Warren calculated quickly. The woman must get away clean, that was clear. He didn't want her nailed for a murder. She was out cold, a bruise on the crown of her head. He searched her handbag: Norma Roberts, local address. She appeared in none of the Bundy history. Yet she was going to be his first, clearly. The past was not well documented.

He decided to get away quickly. He got her up and into a shoulder carry, her body limp. He opened the front door, looked both ways down the corridor, and hauled her to the back entrance of the apartment house. There he leaned her into a chair and left her and her coat and handbag. It seemed simpler to let her wake up. She would probably get away by herself. Someone would notice the smell in a week, and find an unsolvable crime scene. It was the best he could do.

The past was not well documented... Either Bundy had not acknowledged this first murder, or else Warren had side-slipped into a space-time where

Bundy's history was somewhat different. But not different enough – Bundy was clearly an adroit, self-confident killer. He thought on this as he threaded his way into the gathering darkness.

The pains were crippling by then, awful clenching spasms shooting through his belly. He barely got back to the transflux cage before collapsing.

HE TOOK TIME to recover, hovering the cage in the transition zone. Brilliant colours raced around the cage. The walls hummed and rattled and the capsule's processed air took on a sharp, biting edge.

There were other Bundys in other timelines, but he needed to move on to other targets. No one knew how many timelines there were, though they were not infinite. Complex quantum processes generated them and some theorists thought the number might be quite few. If so, Warren could not reach some timelines. Already the cage had refused to go to four target murderers, so perhaps his opportunities were not as large as the hundreds or thousands he had at first dreamed about.

He had already shot Ted Kaczynski, the "Unabomber." That murderer had targeted universities and wrote a manifesto that he distributed to the media, claiming that he wanted society to return to a time when technology was not a threat to its future. Kaczynski had not considered that a future technology would erase his deeds.

Kaczynski's surprised gasp lay behind him now. He decided, since his controls allowed him to choose among the braided timelines, to save as many victims as he could. His own time was growing short.

He scanned through the gallery of mass murder, trying to relax as the flux cage popped and hummed with stresses. Sex was the primary motive of lust killers, whether or not the victims were dead, and fantasy played strongly in their killings. The worst felt that their gratification depended on torture and mutilation, using weapons in close contact with the victims – knives, hammers, or just hands. Such lust killers often had a higher cause they could recite, but as they continued, intervals between killings decreased and the craving for stimulation increased.

He considered Coral Watts, a rural murderer. A surviving victim had described him as "excited and hyper and clappin' and just making noises like he was excited, that this was gonna be fun." Watts killed by slashing, stabbing, hanging, drowning, asphyxiating, and strangling. But when Warren singled out the coordinates for Watts, the software warned him that the target timeline was beyond his energy reserves.

The pain was worse now, shooting searing fingers up into his chest. He braced himself in the acceleration chair and took an injection his doctors had given him, slipping the needle into an elbow vein. It helped a bit, a soothing warmth spreading through him. He put aside the pain and concentrated, lips set in a thin white line.

His team had given him choices in the space-time coordinates. The pain told him that he would not have time enough to visit them all and bring his good work to the souls who had suffered in those realms. Plainly, he should act to cause the greatest good, downstream in time from his intervention.

Ah. There was a desirable target time, much

further back, that drew his attention. These killers acted in concert, slaughtering many. But their worst damage had been to the sense of stability and goodwill in their society. That damage had exacted huge costs for decades thereafter. Warren knew, as he reviewed the case file, what justice demanded. He would voyage across the braided timestreams and end his jogg in California, 1969.

He emerged on a bare rock shelf in Chatsworth, north of the valley bordering the Los Angeles megaplex. He savoured the view as the flux cage relaxed around him, its gravitational ripples easing away. Night in the valley: streaks of actinic boulevard streetlights, crisp dry air flavoured of desert and combustion. The opulence of the era struck him immediately: blaring electric lights lacing everywhere, thundering hordes of automobiles on the highways, the sharp sting of smog, and large homes of glass and wood, poorly insulated. His era termed this the Age of Appetite, and so it was.

But it was the beginning of a time of mercies. The crimes the Manson gang was to commit did not cost the lot of them their lives. California had briefly instituted an interval with no death penalty while the Manson cases wound through their lethargic system. The guilty then received lifelong support, living in comfortable surrounds and watching television and movies, labouring a bit, writing books about their crimes, giving interviews and finally passing away from various diseases. This era thought that a life of constrained ease was the worst punishment it could ethically impose.

Manson and Bundy were small-scale murderers, compared with Hitler, Mao, and others of this slaughterhouse century. But the serial killers Warren could reach and escape undetected. Also, he loathed them with a special rage.

He hiked across a field of enormous boulders in the semi-night of city glow, heading north. Two days ahead in this future, on July 1, 1969, Manson would shoot a black drug dealer named "Lotsapoppa" Crowe at a Hollywood apartment. He would retreat to the rambling farm buildings Warren could make out ahead, the Spahn Ranch in Topanga Canyon. Manson would then turn Spahn Ranch into a defensive camp, with night patrols of armed guards. Now was the last possible moment to end this gathering catastrophe, silence its cultural impact, save its many victims.

Warren approached cautiously, using the rugged rocks as cover. He studied the ramshackle buildings, windows showing pale lighting. His background said this was no longer a functioning ranch, but instead a set for moving pictures. He wondered why anyone would bother making such dramas on location, when computer graphics were much simpler; or was this time so far back that that technology did not exist? The past was a mysterious, unknowingly wealthy land.

Near the wooden barns and stables ahead, a bonfire licked at the sky. Warren moved to his right, going uphill behind a rough rock scree to get a better view. Around the fire were a dozen people sitting, their rapt faces lit in dancing orange firelight, focused on the one figure who stood, the centre of attention.

Warren eased closer to catch the voices. Manson's darting eyes caught the flickering firelight. The circle of faces seemed like moons orbiting the long-haired man.

Warren felt a tap on his shoulder. He whirled, the 0.22 coming naturally into his hand. A small woman held her palms up, shaking her head. Then a finger to her lips, *shhhh*.

He hesitated. They were close enough that a shot might be heard. Warren elected to follow the woman's hand signals, settling down into a crouch beside her.

She whispered into his ear, "No fear. I am here for the same reason."

Warren said, "What reason? Who the hell are you?"

"To prevent the Tate murders. I'm Serafina." Her blonde hair caught the fire glow.

Warren whispered, "You're from –"

"From a time well beyond yours."

"You... side-slipped?"

"Following your lead. Your innovation." Her angular features sharpened, eyes alive. "I am here to help you with your greatest mercy."

"How did you –"

"You are famous, of course. Some of us sought to emulate you. To bring mercy to as many timelines as possible."

"Famous?" Warren had kept all this secret, except for his – ah, of course, the team. Once he vanished from his native timeline, they would talk. Perhaps they could track him in his sideslips; they had incredible skills he would never understand. In all this, he had never thought of what would happen once he left his timeline, gone forever.

"You are a legend. The greatest giver of mercies." She smiled, extending a slender hand. "It is an honour."

He managed to take her hand, which seemed impossibly warm. Which meant that he was chilled, blood rushing to his centre, where the pain danced.

"I... thank you. Uh, help, you said? How –"

She raised the silencing finger again. "Listen."

They rose a bit on their haunches, and now Warren heard the strong voice of the standing man. Shaggy, bearded, arms spread wide, the fierce eyes showed white.

"We are the *soul* of our time, my people. The *family*. We are in truth a part of the *hole* in the *infinite*. That is our destiny, our *duty*." The rolling cadences, Manson's voice rising on the high notes, had a strange hypnotic ring.

"The blacks will soon *rise up*." Manson forked his arms skyward. "Make no mistake – for the Beatles *themselves* saw this coming. The *White Album* songs say it – in *code*, my friends. John, Paul, George, Ringo – they directed that album at *our Family itself*, for we are the *elect*. Disaster *is* coming."

Warren felt the impact of Manson's voice, seductive; he detested it. In that rolling, powerful chant lay the deaths to come at 10050 Cielo Drive. Sharon Tate, eight and a half months pregnant. Her friend and former lover Jay Sebring. Abigail Folger, heiress to the Folger coffee fortune. Others, too, all innocents. Roman Polanski, one of the great drama makers of this era and Tate's husband, was in London at work on a film project or else he would have shared their fate, with others still –

The thought struck him – what if, in this timeline,

Roman Polanski was there at 10050 Cielo Drive? Would he die, too? If so, Warren's mission was even more a mercy for this era.

Manson went on, voice resounding above the flickering flames, hands and eyes working the circle of rapt acolytes. "We'll be movin' soon. *Movin'!* I got a canary-yellow home in Canoga Park for us, not far from here. A great pad. Our family will be submerged beneath the awareness of the outside world" – a pause – "I call it the *Yellow Submarine*!" Gasps, applause from around the campfire.

Manson went on, telling the "family" they might have to show blacks how to start "Helter Skelter," the convulsion that would destroy the power structure and bring Manson to the fore. The circle laughed and yelped and applauded, their voices a joyful babble.

He sat back, acid pain leaking into his mind. In his joggs Warren had seen the direct presence of evil, but nothing like this monster.

Serafina said, "This will be your greatest mercy."

Warren's head spun. "You came to make..."

"Make it happen." She pulled from the darkness behind her a long, malicious device. An automatic weapon, Warren saw. Firepower.

"Your 0.22 is not enough. Without me, you will fail."

Warren saw now what must occur. He was not enough against such massed insanity. Slowly he nodded.

She shouldered the long sleek weapon, clicked off the safety. He rose beside her, legs weak.

"You take the first," she said. He nodded and aimed at Manson. The 0.22 was so small and light as he aimed, while crickets chirped and the bile rose up into his dry throat. He concentrated and squeezed off the shot.

The sharp splat didn't have any effect. Warren had missed. Manson turned toward them –

The hammering of her automatic slammed in his ears as he aimed his paltry 0.22 and picked off the fleeing targets. *Pop! Pop!*

He was thrilled to hit three of them – shadows going down in the firelight. Serafina raged at them, changing clips and yelling. He shouted himself, a high long *ahhhhhh*. The "family" tried to escape the firelight, but the avenging rounds caught them and tossed the murderers-to-be like insects into their own bonfire.

Manson had darted away at Serafina's first burst. The man ran quickly to Warren's left and Warren followed, feet heavy, hands automatically adding rounds to the 0.22 clip. In the dim light beyond the screams and shots Warren tracked the lurching form, framed against the distant city glow. Some around the circle had pistols, too, and they scattered, trying to direct fire against Serafina's quick, short bursts.

Warren trotted into the darkness, feet unsteady, keeping Manson's silhouette in view. He stumbled over outcroppings, but kept going despite the sudden lances of agony creeping down into his legs.

Warren knew he had to save energy, that Manson could outrun him easily. So he stopped at the crest of a rise, settled in against a rock and held the puny 0.22 in his right hand, bracing it with his left. He could see Manson maybe twenty meters away, trotting along, angling toward the ranch's barn. He squeezed off a shot. The *pop* was small against the furious gunfire behind him, but the figure fell. Warren got up and calculated each step as he trudged down the slope. A shadow rose. Manson was getting up. Warren aimed again and fired and knew he had missed. Manson turned and Warren heard a barking explosion – as a sharp slap knocked him backward, tumbling into sharp gravel.

Gasping, he got up against a massive weight. On his feet, rocky, he slogged forward. *Pock pock* gunfire from behind was a few sporadic shots, followed immediately by furious automatic bursts, hammering on and on into the chill night.

Manson was trying to get up. He lurched on one leg, tried to bring his own gun up again, turned – and Warren fired three times into him at a few meters range. The man groaned, crazed eyes looking at Warren and he wheezed out, "Why?" – then toppled.

Warren blinked at the stars straight overhead and realized he must have fallen. The stars were quite beautiful in their crystal majesty.

Serafina loomed above him. He tried to talk but had no breath.

Serafina said softly, "They're all gone. Done. Your triumph."

Acid came up in his throat as he wheezed out, "What...next..."

Serafina smiled, shook her head. "No next. You were the first, the innovator. We followed you. There have been many others, shadowing you closely on nearby space-time lines, arriving at the murder sites – to savour the reflected glory."

He managed, "Others. Glory?"

Serafina grimaced. "We could tell where you went

– we all detected entangled correlations, to track your ethical joggs. Some just followed, witnessed. Some imitated you. They went after lesser serial killers. Used your same simple, elegant methods – minimum tools and weapons, quick and seamless."

Warren blinked. "I thought I was alone – "

"You were alone. The first. But the idea spread, later. I come from more than a century after you."

He had never thought of imitators. Cultures changed, one era thinking the death penalty was obscene, another embracing it as a solution. "I tried to get as many –"

"As you could, of course." She stroked his arm, soothing the disquiet that flickered across his face, pinching his mouth. "The number of timelines is only a few hundred – Gupta showed that in my century – so it's not a pointless infinity."

"Back there in Oklahoma –"

"That was Clyde, another jogger. He made a dumb mistake, got there before you. Clyde was going to study the aftermath of that. He backed out as soon as he could. He left Clifford for you."

Warren felt the world lift from him and now he had no weight. Light, airy. "He nearly got me killed, too."

Serafina shrugged. "I know; I've been tagging along behind you, with better transflux gear. I come from further up our shared timestream, see? Still, the continuing drop in the homicide rate comes at least partly from the work of jogg people, like me."

He eyed her suspiciously. "Why did you come here?"

Serafina simply leaned over and hugged him. "You failed here. I wanted to change that. Now you've accomplished your goal here – quick mercy for the unknowing victims."

This puzzled him but of course it didn't matter anymore, none of it. Except –

"Manson..."

"He killed you here. But now, in a different timestream – caused by me appearing – you *got* him." Her voice rose happily, eyes bright, teeth flashing in a broad smile.

He tried to take this all in. "Still..."

"It's all quantum logic, see?" she said brightly. "So uncertainty applies to time travel. The side-jogg time traveller affects the time stream he goes to. So then later side-slipping people, they have to correct for that."

He shook his head, not really following.

She said softly, "Thing is, we think the irony of all this is delicious. In my time, we're more self conscious, I guess."

"What...?"

"An ironic chain, we call it. To jogg is to act, and be acted upon." She touched him sympathetically. "You did kill so many. Justice is still the same."

She cocked his own gun, holding it up in the dull sky glow, making sure there was a round in the chamber. She snapped it closed. "Think of it as a mercy." She lowered the muzzle at him and gave him a wonderful smile.

The Ki-anna

Gwyneth Jones

Gwyneth Jones was born in Manchester, England and is the author of more than twenty novels for teenagers, mostly under the name Ann Halam, and several highly regarded SF novels for adults. She has won two World Fantasy awards, the Arthur C. Clarke award, the British Science Fiction Association short story award, the Dracula Society's Children of the Night award, the Philip K. Dick award, and shared the first Tiptree award, in 1992, with Eleanor Arnason. Her most recent books are novel Spirit *and essay collection* Imagination/Space. *Upcoming is new story collection* The Universe of Things. *She lives in Brighton, UK, with her husband and son; a Tonkinese cat called Ginger and her young friend Milo.*

If he'd been at home, he'd have thought, *Dump Plant Injuries*. In the socially unbalanced, pioneer cities of the Equatorial Ring, little scavengers tangled with the recycling machinery. They needed premium, Earth-atmosphere-and-pressure nursing or the flesh would not regenerate – which they didn't get. The gouges and dents would be permanent: skinned over, like the scars on her forearms. Visible through thin clothing, like the depressions in her thighs. But this wasn't Mars, and she wasn't human, she was a Ki. He guessed, uneasily, at a more horrifying childhood poverty.

She seemed very young for her post: hardly more than a girl. She could almost have *been* a human girl with gene-mods. Could have chosen to adopt that fine pelt of silky bronze, glimmering against the bare skin of her palms, her throat and face. Chosen those eyes, like drops of black dew; the hint of a mischievous animal muzzle. Her name was Ki-anna, she represented the KiAn authorities. Her partner, a Shet called Roaaat Bhvaaan, his heavy uniform making no concession to the warmth of the space-habitat, was from Interplanetary Affairs, and represented Speranza. The Shet looked far more alien: a head like a grey boulder, naked wrinkled hide hooding his eyes.

Patrice didn't expect them to be on his side, this odd couple, polite and sympathetic as they seemed. He must be careful, he must remember that his mind and body were reeling from the Buonarotti Transit – two instantaneous interstellar transits in two days, the first in his life. He'd never even *seen* a non-human sentient biped, in person, this time last week: and here he was in a stark police interview room with two of them.

"You learned of your sister's death a Martian year ago?"

"Her disappearance. Yes."

Ki-anna watched, Bhvaaan questioned: he wished it were the other way round. Patrice dreaded the Speranza mindset. Anyone who lives on a planet is a lesser form of life, of course we're going to ignore your appeals, but it's more fun to ignore them slowly, very, very slowly –

"We can agree she disappeared," muttered the Shet, what looked like mordant humour tugging the lipless trap of his mouth. "Yet, aah, you didn't voice your concerns at once?"

"Lione is, was, my twin. We were close, however far... When the notification of death came it was very brief, I didn't take it in. A few days later I collapsed at work, I had to take compassionate leave."

At first he'd accepted the official story. She's dead, Lione is dead. She went into danger, it shouldn't have happened but it did, on a suffering war-torn planet unimaginably far away...

The Shet rolled his neckless head, possibly in sympathy.

"You're, aah, a Social Knowledge Officer. Thap must be a demanding job. No blame if a loss to your family caused you to crash-out."

"I recovered. I examined the material that had arrived while I was ill: everything about my sister's last expedition, and the 'investigation.' I knew there was something wrong. I couldn't achieve anything at a distance. I had to get to Speranza, I had to get myself *here* –"

"Quite right, child. Can't do anything at long distance, aah."

"I had to apply for financial support, the system is slow. The Buonarotti Transit network isn't for people like me –" He wished he'd bitten that back. "I mean, it's for officials, diplomats, not civilian planet-dwellers."

"Unless they're idle super-rich," rumbled the Shet. "Or refugees getting shipped out of a hellhole, maybe. Well, you persisted. Your sister was Martian too. What was she doing here?"

Patrice looked at the very slim file on the table. No way of telling whether that tablet held a ton of documents or a single page.

"Don't you know?"

"Explain it to us," said Ki-anna. Her voice was sibilant, a hint of a lisp.

"Lione was a troposphere engineer. She was working on the KiAn Atmosphere Recovery Project. But you *must* know..." They waited, silently. "All right. The KiAn war practically flayed this planet. The atmosphere's being repaired, it's a major Speranza project. Out here it's macro-engineering. They've created a – a membrane, like a casting mould, of magnetically charged particles. They're shepherding small water ice asteroids, other debris with useful constituents, through it. Controlled annihilation releases the gases, bonding and venting propagates the right mix. We pioneered the technique. We've enriched the Martian atmosphere the same way... nothing like the scale of this. The job also has to be done from the bottom up. The troposphere, the lowest level of the inner atmosphere, is alive. It's a saturated fluid full of viruses, fragments of DNA and RNA, amino acids, metabolising mineral traces, pre-biotic chemistry. The configuration is unique to a living planet, and it's like the mycorrhizal systems in the soil, back on Earth. If it isn't there, or it's not *right*, nothing will thrive."

He couldn't tell if they knew it all, or didn't understand a word.

"Lione knew the tropo reconstruction wasn't going well. She found out there was an area of the surface, under the An-lalhar Lakes, where the living layer might be undamaged. This – where we are now – is the Orbital Refuge Habitat for that region. She came here, determined to get permission from the Ruling An to collect samples –"

Ki-anna interrupted softly. "Isn't the surviving troposphere remotely sampled by the Project automats, all over the planet?"

"Yes, but that obviously wasn't good enough. That was Lione. If it was her responsibility, she had to do *everything in her power* to get the job done."

"Aah. Raarpht... Your sister befriended the Ruling An, she gained permission, she went down, and she stepped on a landmine. You understand that there was no body to be recovered? That she was vaporised?"

"So I was told."

Ki-anna rubbed her scarred forearms, the Shet studied Patrice. The interview room was haunted by meaning, shadowy with intent –

"Aap. You need to make a 'pilgrimage.' A memorial journey?"

"*No*, it's not like that. There's something *wrong*."

The shadows tightened, but were they for him or against him?

"Lione disappeared. I don't speak any KiAn language, I didn't have to, the reports were in English: when I hunted for more detail there are translator bots. I haven't missed anything. A vaporised body doesn't *vanish*. All that tissue, blood, and bone leaves forensic traces. None. No samples recovered. She was there to *collect* samples, don't tell me it was forbidden... She didn't come back, that's all. Something happened to her, something other than a warzone accident –"

"Are you saying your sister was murdered, Patrice?"

"I need to go down there."

"I can see you'd feel thap way. You realise KiAn is uninhabitable?"

"A lot of places on Mars are called 'uninhabitable.' My work takes me to the worst-off regions. I can handle myself."

"Aap. How do you feel about the KiAn issue, Messer Ferringhi?"

Patrice opened his mouth, and shut it. He didn't have a prepared answer for that one. "I don't know enough."

The Shet and the Ki looked at each other, for the first time. He felt they'd been through the motions, and they were agreeing to quit.

"As you know," rumbled Bhvaaan, "The Ruling An must give permission. The An-he will see you?"

"I have an appointment."

"Then thap's all for now. Enjoy your transit hangover in peace."

Patrice Ferringhi took a moment, looking puzzled, before he realised he could go. He stood, hesitated, gave an odd little bow and left the room.

The Shet and the Ki relaxed somewhat.

"Collapsed at work," said Roaaat Bhvaaan. "Thap's not good."

"We can't all be made of stone, Shet."

"Aaah well. Cross fingers, Chief."

They were resigned to strange English figures of speech. The language of Speranza, of diplomacy, was also the language of interplanetary policing. You became fluent, or you relied on unreliable transaid: and you screwed up.

"And all my toes," said the Ki.

* * *

ON HIS WAY to his cabin, Patrice found an ob-bay. He stared into a hollow sphere, permeated by the star-pricked darkness of KiAn system space: the limb of the planet obscured, the mainstar and the blue "daystar" out of sight. Knurled objects flew around, suddenly making endless field-beams visible. One lump rushed straight at him, growing huge: seemed to miss the ob-bay by centimetres, with a roar like monstrous thunder. The big impacts could be close enough to make this Refuge shake. He'd felt that, already. Like the Gods throwing giant furniture about –

He could not get over the fact that nothing was real. Everything had been translated here by the Buonarotti Torus, as pure data. This habitat, this shipboard jumper he wore, this *body*. All made over again, out of local elements, as if in a 3D scanner... The scarred Ki woman fascinated him, he hardly knew why. The portent he felt in their meeting (had he really *met* her?) was what they call a "transit hangover." He must sleep it off.

THE KI-ANNA WAS rated Chief of Police, but she walked the beat most days. All her officers above nightstick grade were seconded from the Ruling An's Household Guard: she didn't like to impose on them. The Ki – natural street-dwellers, if ever life was natural again – melted indoors as she approached. Her uniform, backed by Speranza, should have made the refugees feel safe: but none of them trusted her. The only people she could talk to were the habitual criminals. *They* appreciated the Ruling An's strange appointment.

She made her rounds, visiting the nests where law-abiding people better stay away. The gangsters knew a human had "joined the station."

They were very curious. She sniffed the wind and lounged with the idlers, giving up Patrice Ferringhi in scraps, a resource to be conserved. The pressure of the human's strange eyes was still with her –

No one ought to look at her scars like that, it was indecent.

But he was an alien, he didn't know how to behave.

She didn't remember being chosen for the treatment that would render her flesh delectable, while ensuring that what happened wouldn't kill her. She only knew she'd been sold (tradition called it an honour) so that her littermates could live. She would always wonder, why *me*? What was wrong with *me*? We were very poor, I understand that, but why *me*? It had all been for nothing, anyway. Her parents and her littermates were dead, along with everyone else. So few survivors! A handful of die-hards on the surface. A token number of Ki taken away to Speranza, in the staggeringly distant Blue System. Would they ever return? The Ki-anna thought not... Six Refuge Habitats in orbit. And of course some of the Heaven-born, who'd seen what was coming before the war, and escaped to Balas or to Shet.

At curfew she filed a routine report, and retired to her quarters in the Curtain Wall. Roaaat, who was sharing her living space, was already at home. It was fortunate that Shet didn't normally like to sit in Speranza-style "chairs": he'd have broken a hole in her ceiling. His bulk, as he lay at ease, dwarfed her largest room. They compared notes.

"All the Refuges have problems," said the Ki-anna. "But I get the feeling I have more than my share. Extortion, intimidation, theft and violence –"

"We can *grease the wheels*," said Roaat. "Strictly off the record, we can pay your villains off. It's distasteful, not the way to do police work."

"But expedient."

"Aap... He seemed very taken with you," said Roaaat.

"The human? I don't know how you make that out."

"Thap handsome Blue, yaas. I could smell pheromones."

"He isn't a 'Blue'" said the Ki-anna. "The almighty Blues rule Speranza. The humans left behind on Earth, or 'Mars' – What is 'Mars'? Is it a moon?"

"Noope. A smaller planet in the Blue system."

"Well, they aren't Blues, they're just ordinary aliens."

"I shall give up matchmaking. You don't appreciate my help... Let's hope the An-he finds your *ordinary alien* more attractive."

The Ki-anna shivered. "I think he will. He's a simple soul."

Roaaat was an undemanding guest, despite his size. They shared a meal, based on "culturally neutral" Speranza Food Aid. The Shet spread his bedding. The Ki-anna groomed herself, crouched by a screen that showed views of the Warrens. Nothing untoward stirred, in the simulated night. She pressed knuckle-fur to her mouth. Sometimes the pain of living, haunted by the uncounted dead, became very hard to bear. Waking from every sleep to remember afresh that there was *nothing left*.

"I might yet back out, Officer Bhvaaan. What if we only succeed in feeding the monsters, and make bad worse?"

She unfolded her nest, and settled behind him.

He patted her side with his clubbed fist – it felt like being clobbered by a kindly rock. "See how it goes. You can back out later."

The Ki-anna lay sleepless, wondering about Patrice Ferringhi; the bulk of her unacknowledged bodyguard between her and the teeth of the An.

WHEN HIS APPOINTMENT with alien royalty came around, Patrice was glad he'd had a breathing space. The world was solid again, he felt in control of himself. He donned his new transaid, settling the pickup against his skull, and set out for the high-security bulkhead gate that led to the Refuge Habitat itself.

Armoured guards, intimidatingly tall, were waiting on the other side. They bent their heads, exhaled breath loudly – and indicated that he was to get into a kind of floating palanquin. Probably they knew no English.

The guards jogged around him in a hollow square: between their bodies he glimpsed the approach to an actual *castle*, like something in a fantasy game. Like a recreation of Mediaeval Europe or Japan, rising from a mass of basic living modules. It was amazing. He'd never been inside a big space-station before, not counting a few hours in Speranza Transit Port. The false horizon, the lilac sky, arcing far above the castle's bannered towers, would have fooled him completely, if he hadn't known.

He met the An-he in a windowless, antique chamber hung with tapestries (at least, *tapestries* seemed like the right word). Sleekly upholstered couches were scattered over the floor. The guard who'd escorted him backed out, snorting. Patrice looked around, vaguely bothered by an overly-warm indoor breeze. He saw someone almost human, loose-limbed and handsome in Speranza tailoring, reclining on a couch – large, wide-spaced eyes alight with curiosity – and realised he was alone with the king.

"Excuse my steward," said the An. "He doesn't speak English well, and doesn't like to embarrass himself by trying. Please, be at home."

"Thank you for seeing me," said Patrice. "Your, er, Majesty – ?"

The An-he grinned. "You are Patrice. I am the An, let's just talk."

The young co-ruler was charming and direct. He asked about the police: Patrice noted, disappointed, that *Ki-anna* was a title, *the Ki-she*, or something. He wondered what you had to do to learn their personal names.

"It was a brief interview," he admitted, ruefully. "I got the impression they weren't very interested."

"Well, I *am* interested. Lione was a great friend to my people. To *both* my peoples. I'm not sure I understand, were you partners, or litter-mates?"

"We were twins, that means litter-mates, but 'partners' too, though our careers took different directions."

He needed to get *partner* into the conversation. The An partnership wasn't sexual, but it was lifelong, and the closest social and emotional bond they knew. A lost partner justified his appeal.

The An-he touched the clip on the side of his head (he was using a transaid, too), reflexively. "A double loss, poor Patrice. Please do confide in me, it will help enormously if you are completely frank –"

In this pairing, the An-she was the senior. She made the decisions, but Patrice couldn't meet her, she was too important. He could only work on the An-he, who would (hopefully) promote his cause... He had the eerie thought that he was doing exactly what Lione had done – trying to make a good impression on this alien aristocrat, maybe in this very room. The tapestries (if that was the word) swam and rippled in the moving air, drawing his attention to scenes he really didn't want to examine. Brightly dressed lords and ladies gathered for the hunt. The game was driven onto the guns. The butchery, the bustling kitchen scenes, the *banquet* –

He realised, horrified, that his host had asked him something about his work on Mars, and he hadn't heard the question.

"Oh," said the An-he, easily. "I see what you're looking at. Don't be offended, it's all in the past, and priceless, marvellous art. Recreated, sadly. The originals were destroyed, along with the original of this castle. But still, our heritage! Don't you Blues love ancient battle scenes, heaps of painted slaughter? And by the way, aren't you closely related, limb for limb and bone for bone, to the beings that *you* traditionally kill and eat?"

"Not on Mars."

"There, you are sundered from your web of life. At home on Earth, the natural humans do it all the time, I assure you."

"I don't know what to say."

Notoriously, the Ki and the An had *both* been affronted when they were identified, by other sentient bipeds, as a single species. Of course they knew, but an indecent topic! In ways, the most disturbing aspect of "the KiAn issue" was not the genocidal war, in which the oppressed had risen up, savagely, against the oppressors. It was the fact that some highly respected Ki leaders actually *defended* "the traditional diet of the An."

The An-he showed his bright white teeth. "Then you have an open mind, my dear Patrice! It gives me hope that you'll come to understand us." He stretched, and exhaled noisily. "Enough. All I can tell you today is that your request is under consideration. You're a valuable person, and it's dangerous down there! We don't want to lose you. Now, I suppose you'd like to see your sister's rooms? She stayed with us, you know: here in the castle."

"Would that be possible?"

"Certainly! I'll get some people to take you."

More guards – or servants in military-looking uniform – led him along winding, irregular corridors, all plagued by that insistent breeze, and opened a round plug of a doorway. The An-he's face appeared, on a display screen emblazoned on a guard's tunic.

"Take as long as you like, dear Patrice. Don't be afraid of disturbing the evidence! The police took anything they thought was useful, ages ago."

The guards gave him privacy, which he had not expected: they shut the door and stayed outside. He was alone, in his sister's space. The aeons he'd crossed, the unthinkable interstellar distance, vanished. Lione was *here*. He could feel her, all around him. The warm air, suddenly still, seemed full of images: glimpses of his sister, rushing into his mind –

"Recreation" was skin-deep here. Essentially the room was identical to his cabin. A bed-shelf with a puffy mattress; storage space beneath. A desk, a closet bathroom, stripped of fittings. Her effects had been returned to Mars, couriered as data. The police had been and gone "ages ago." What could this empty box tell him? Nothing, but he had to try.

Was he under surveillance? He decided he didn't care.

He searched swiftly, efficiently, studying the floor, running his hands over the walls and closet space, checking the seals on the mattress. The screen above the desk was set in an ornate decorative frame. He probed around it, and his fingertips brushed something that had slipped behind. Carefully, patiently, he teased out a corner of the object, and drew it from hiding.

Lione, he whispered.

He tucked his prize inside the breast of his shipboard jumper, and went to knock on the round door. It opened, and the guards were there.

"I'm ready to leave now."

The An-he looked out of the tunic display again. "By all means! But don't be a stranger. Come and see me again, come often!"

That evening he searched the little tablet's drive for his own name, for a message. He tried every password of theirs he could remember: found nothing, and was heartbroken. He barely noted the contents, except that it wasn't about her work. Next day, to his great surprise, he was recalled to the castle. He met the An-he as before, and learned that the Ruling An would like to approve his mission, but the police were making difficulties.

"Speranza doesn't mind having a tragedy associated with their showcase Project," said the young king. "A scandal would be much worse, so they want to bury this. My partner and I feel you have a right to investigate, but we have met with resistance."

There was nothing Patrice could do... and it wasn't a refusal. If the alien royals were on his side, the police would probably be helpless in the end. Back in his cabin he examined the tablet again and realised that Lione had been keeping a private record of her encounter with "the KiAn issue."

KiAn isn't like other worlds of the Diaspora; they didn't have a Conventional Space Age before First Contact. But they weren't primitives when "we" found them, nor even Mediaeval. The An of today are the remnant of a planetary superpower. They were always the Great Nation, and the many nations of the Ki were treated as inferior, through millennia of civilisation. But it was no more than fifteen hundred standard years ago, when, in a time of famine, the An or "Heaven Born" first began to hunt and eat the "Earth Born" Ki. They don't do that anymore. They have painless processing plants (or did). They have retail packaging –

Cannibalism happens. It's known in every sentient and pre-sentient biped species. What developed on KiAn is different, and the so-called "atavists" are not really atavist. This isn't the survival, as some on Speranza would like to believe, of an ancient prehistoric symbiosis. The An weren't *animals, when this "stable genocide" began. They were people, who could think and feel. People, like us.*

The entry was text-only, but he heard his sister's voice: forthright, uncompromising. She must have forced herself to be more tactful with the An-he! The next was video. Lione, talking to him. Living and breathing.

Inside the slim case, when he opened it, he'd found pressed fragments of a moss, or lichen. Shards of it clung to his fingers; it smelled odd, but not unpleasant. He sniffed his fingertips and turned pages, painfully happy.

DAYS PASSED, IN a rhythm of light and darkness that belonged to the planet "below." Patrice shuttled between the "station visitors' quarters," where he was the only guest, and the An castle. He didn't dare refuse a summons, although he politely declined all dinner invitations, which made the An laugh.

The odd couple showed no interest in Patrice at all, and did not return his calls. He might have tried harder to get their attention, but there was Lione's journal. He didn't want to hand it over; or to lie about it either.

Once, as they walked in the castle's galleries, the insistent breeze nagging at him as usual, Patrice felt he was being watched. He looked up. From a high, curtained balcony a wide-eyed, narrow face was looking down intently. "T*hat* was the An-she," murmured his companion, stooping to exhale the words in Patrice's ear. "She likes you, or she wouldn't have let you glimpse her... I tell her all about you."

"I didn't really see anything," said Patrice, wary of causing offence. "The breeze is so strong, tossing the curtains about."

"I'm afraid we're obsessed with air circulation, due to the crowded accommodation. There are aliens about, who don't always smell very nice."

"I'm very sorry! I had no idea!"

"Oh no, Patrice, not you. You smell fresh and sweet."

THE ENTRIES IN Lione's journal weren't dated, but they charted a progress. At first he was afraid he'd find Lione actually defending industrial cannibalism. That never happened. But as he immersed himself, reviewing every entry over and over, he knew Lione was asking him to understand. Not to accept, but to *understand* the unthinkable –

Compare chattel slavery. We look on the buying and selling of sentient bipeds, as if they were livestock, with revulsion. Who could question that? Then think of the intense bond between a beloved master, or mistress, and a beloved servant. A revered commanding officer and devoted troops. Must this go too? The An and the Ki accept that their way of life must *change. But there is a deep equality in that exchange of being, which we "democratic individualists" can't recognise –*

Patrice thought of the Ki-Anna's scars.

The "deep equality" entry was almost the last.

The journal ended abruptly, with no sense of closure.

Lione's incense – he'd decided the "lichen" was a kind of KiAn incense, perhaps a present from the An-he – filled his cabin with a subtle perfume. He closed the tablet, murmuring the words he knew by heart, *a deep equality in that exchange of being*, and decided to turn in. In his tiny bathroom, for a piercing moment it was Lione he saw in the mirror. A dark-skinned, light-eyed, serious young woman, with the aquiline bones of their North African ancestry. His other self, who had left him so far behind –

The whole journal was a message. It called him to follow her, and he didn't yet know where his passionate journey would end.

WHEN HE LEARNED that permission to visit the surface was granted, but the Ki-anna and the Interplanetary Affairs officer were coming too, he knew that the Ruling An had been forced to make this concession – and the bargaining was over. He just wished he knew *why* the police had insisted on escorting him. To help Patrice discover the truth? Or to prevent him?

He didn't meet the odd couple until they embarked together. They were all in full protective gear: skin sealed with quarantine film, under soft-shell life-support suits. The noisy shuttle bay put a damper on conversation, and the flight was no more sociable. Patrice spent it encased in an escape capsule and breathing tanked air: the police insisted on this. He saw nothing of KiAn until he was crunching across the seared rubble of their landing field.

The landscape was dry tundra, like Martian desert colour-shifted into shades of grey and green. Armed Green Belts were waiting, with a landship and all-terrain hardsuits for the visitors.

"The An-he offered me a military escort," said Patrice, freedom of speech restored by helmet radio. "What was wrong with that?"

"Sorry," grunted Bhvaaan. "Couldn't be allowed."

The Ki-anna said nothing. He remembered, vividly, the way he'd felt at their meeting. There had been a connection, on her side too: he knew it. Now she was just another bulky Speranza doll, on a smaller scale than her partner. As if she'd read his thoughts, she cleared her faceplate and looked out at him, curiously. He wanted to tell her that he understood KiAn, better than she could imagine... but not with Bhvaaan around.

"You've been keeping yourself to yourself, Messer Ferringhi."

"I could say the same of you two, Officer Bhvaaan."

"Aap. But you made friends with the An-he."

"The Ruling An were very willing to help me."

"We've been working in your interest too," said the Ki-anna. She pivoted her suit to look through the windowband in the landship's flank. "Far below this plateau, back that way, was the regional capital. *Were* fertile plains, rich forests, towns and fields and parklands. The 'roof of Heaven' was never beautiful. It's strange, this part hardly seems much changed –"

"Except that one dare not breathe," she added, sadly.

On the shore of the largest ice sheet, the Lake of Heaven, the odd couple and Patrice disembarked. The Ki-anna led the way to a great low arch of rock-embedded ice. The Green Belts had stayed in the ship.

Everything was livid mist.

"We're going under An-lalhar Lake alone?"

"The Green Belts'll be on call. It's not their jurisdiction down there. It's a precious enclave where the Ki and the An are stubbornly dying together." Bhvaaan peered at him. "It's not our jurisdiction either, Messer Ferringhi. If we meet with violence we can protect you, but that's after the event and it might not save your life. The people under the Lake don't have a lot to lose and their mood is volatile. Bear that in mind."

"I could have had an escort they'd respect."

"You're better off with us."

They descended the tunnel. The light never grew less; on the contrary, it grew brighter. When they emerged, the Heaven Lake was above them: a mass of blue-white radiance, indigo shadowed, shot through with rainbow refractions. It was extraordinarily beautiful. It seemed impossible that the ice had captured so much light from the poisoned smog. Far off, in the centre of the glacial depression, geothermal vents made a glowing, spiderweb pattern of fire and snowy steam. Patrice checked his telltales, and eagerly began to release his helmet. The Shet dropped a gauntleted fist on his arm.

"Don't do it, child. Look at your *rads*."

"A moment won't kill me. I want to *feel* KiAn –"

The odd couple, hidden in their gear, seemed to look at him strangely.

"Maybe later," said the Ki-anna, soothingly. "It's safer in the Grottos, where your sister was headed."

"How do we get there?"

"We walk," rumbled Bhvaaan. "No vehicles. There's not much growing but it's still a sacred park. Let your suit do the work; keep up your fluids."

"Thanks, I know how to handle a hard shell."

They walked in file. The desolation, the ruined beauty that had been revered by both 'races,' caught at Patrice's heart. His helmet display counted rads, paces, heart rate: counted down the metres. Thirty kilometres to the place where Lione had last been seen alive.

"Which faction mined the Lake of Heaven parkland?"

"To our knowledge? Nobody did, child."

It was a question he'd asked over and over, long ago when he thought he could get answers. Now he asked and didn't care. He followed the Shet, the Ki-anna behind him. His pace was steady, yet the display said his body was pumping adrenalin; not from fear, he knew, but in the grip of intense excitement. He sucked on glucose and tried to calm himself.

As the radiance above them dimmed, they reached the Grotto domain. Rugged rocky pillars seemed to hold up the roof of ice, widely spaced at first, clustering towards a centre that could not be seen. There was a Ki community, surviving in rad-proofed modules. The Ki-anna went inside. Patrice and the Shet waited, in the darkening blighted landscape. She emerged after an hour or so.

"We can't go on without guides, and we can't have guides until tomorrow. At the earliest. They have to think it over."

"They weren't expecting us?"

"They were. They know all about it, but they may have had fresh instructions. They're in full communication with the castle: there's some sophisticated kit in there. We'll just have to wait."

"Do they remember Lione?" demanded Patrice. "I have transaid, I want to talk to someone."

"Not now. I'll ask tomorrow."

"Can we sleep indoors?" asked the Shet.

"No."

The Shet and the Ki-anna made camp in the ruins

of the former village, using their suits to clear ground and construct a shelter. Patrice moved over to a heap of boulders where he'd noticed patches of lichen. He had fragments of Lione's incense in the sleeve pocket of his inner, in a First Aid pouch. The police were fully occupied: furtively he opened the arm of his hardshell, and fished the pouch out. He was right, it was the same –

Lione had stood here. The incense was not a gift, she had gathered it. She had been *standing right here*. His need was irresistible. He released his face-plate, stripped his gauntlets, rubbed away quarantine film.

KiAn rushed in on him, cold and harsh in his throat, intoxicating –

"What is that?"

The Ki-anna was behind him. "A lichen sample," said Patrice, caught out. "Or that's what I'd call it at home. It was in my sister's room, in the An Castle. Look, they're the same!"

"Not quite," said the Ki-anna. "Yours is a cultivated variety."

He thought she'd be angry, maybe accuse him of concealing evidence. To his astonishment she took his bared hand, and bowed over it until her cheek brushed the vulnerable inner skin of his wrist. Her touch was a huge shock, sweet and profoundly sexual. She made him dizzy.

This can't be happening, he thought. *I'm here for Lione –*

"I don't know your name."

"We don't do that," she whispered.

"I felt, I can't describe it, the moment I met you –"

"I'd better keep this. You must get your gloves and helmet back on."

"But I want *KiAn* –"

Gently, she let go of his hand. "You've had enough."

The shelter was a snug fit. Sealed inside, they shared rations and drank fresh water they'd brought from the Habitat. They would sleep in their suits, for warmth and security. Patrice lay down at once, to escape their questions and to be alone with his confusion. He was here for Lione, he was here to *join* Lione. How could he and the Ki-anna suddenly feel this way?

"Were you getting romantic, with Patrice, over by those rocks?" asked Bhvaaan. "Sniffing his pheromones?"

"No," said the Ki-anna, grimly. "Something else."

She showed him the First Aid pouch and its contents.

"Mighty Void!"

"He *says* it was in the room Lione used, in the castle."

"I don't think so! We took that cabin apart." The Shet's delicates unfolded from his club of a fist. He turned the clear pouch around, probing her find with sensitive tentacles. "So *that's* how, so *that's* how –"

"So that's how the cookie was crumbled," agreed the Ki-anna.

"What do we do, Chief? Abort this, and run away very quickly?"

"Not without back-up. If we run, and they have heavy weaponry, we're at their mercy. I see what it looks like, but we should show no alarm.

"I *have* had thoughts about him," she murmured, looking at the dark outline of Patrice Ferringhi. "Don't know why. It's something in his eyes."

"Thaap's the way it starts," said the Shet. "Thoughts. Then wondering if anything can come of them. They say sentient bipeds are attracted to each other like... like brothers and sisters, long separated. Well, I'll talk to the Greenies. And you and I had better not sleep."

The suit was a house the shape of her body. She sat in it, wondering about sexual pleasure: pleasure with *Patrice*. What would it be like? She had only one strange comparison, but that didn't frighten her... What Roaaat Bhvaaan offered was far more disturbing.

She glimpsed the abyss, and fell into oblivion.

PATRICE DREAMED HE was in a strolling crowd, among bronze and purple trees, with branches that swayed in the breeze. He knew where he was, he was in the KiAn Orientation, a virtual reality. But there was something sinister going on, the crowd pressed too close, the beautiful trees hid what he ought to see. Then Lione came running up and *bit* him.

He yelled, and shook her off.

She came back and bit his thigh, but now he was in the dark, cold and sore. Lione was gone, he was being hunted by fierce hungry animals –

Suddenly he knew he was not asleep.

He was completely naked. *Where was his suit? Where was he?*

He had no idea. The air was freezing, the darkness almost complete. He stumbled towards a gleam ahead, and entered a rocky cave. There was ice underfoot, icy stalactites hanging down. A lamp burned incense-scented oil, set on the ground next to a heap of something –

That's a body, he thought. He went over and knelt down. It was a human body, freeze-dried. She was curled on her side, turned away from him, but he knew he'd found Lione. She was naked too.

Why was she naked?

He lifted the lamp and saw where flesh had been cut away, not by teeth, as in his dream, but by sharp knives. Lione had been butchered. He tried to turn her: the body moved all of a piece. Her face was recognisable, smooth and calm in death, the eyes sunken, the skin like cured leather. Was she *smiling*? Oh, Lione –

But why am I naked?, he thought. *Who brought me here?*

The Ki entered the cave, and surrounded Patrice and his sister. They had brought more lights. One of them was carrying, reverently, a flattened spherical object, dull grey-green, the size of Patrice's fist. It had a seam around the centre, a bevelled cap. *That's a vapor mine*, he thought, shaken by an explosion of understanding. Then the An came. The Ki made no attempt to interfere with the banquet. They were here to witness. Patrice screamed. He fought the knives with his bare hands, kicked out with his bare feet. The An, outraged, kept yelling at him in scraps of English to *keep still, be easy Blue, you want this, what's wrong with you?*

The Ki-anna and the Shet had ditched their hard shells, to search the narrow passages. They arrived armed but badly outnumbered, and they couldn't get near Patrice. "*I was the Earth In Heaven*!" shouted the Chief of Police. "*I say that flesh is not sacred, not yours to take. Let the stranger go*!"

She held the fanatics at bay, uncertain because of her former status, until the Green Belts joined the party. Luckily Bhvaaan had summoned them, before he and the Ki-anna followed Patrice into that drugged sleep.

PATRICE'S INJURIES WERE not dangerous. As soon as he was allowed he signed himself out of medical care. He had to talk to the police again. He met the odd couple in the same bare interview room as before.

"I'm sorry, I need to withdraw my statement. I can't press charges."

If the next of kin didn't press charges, KiAn law made it difficult for Interplanetary Affairs to prosecute. He knew that, but he had no choice.

"I realise the tablet I found in Lione's room was planted on me. I know her words, if some of them were genuinely hers, had been rearranged to fool me into accepting atavism. It doesn't matter. My sister *wanted* to die that way. She gave herself, her body. It was a ritual sacrifice, for peace. She was my twin, I can't explain, I have to respect her wishes."

"A beautiful, consensual ritual," remarked the Shet. "Yaap. That's what the cannibal die-hards always say. But if you scratch any of these halfway 'respectable' atavists, such as our Ruling An here –"

"You find the meat-packing industry," said the Ki-anna.

Patrice heard the blinkered, Speranza mindset.

"My sister was *willing*."

"I believe she was." To his confusion, the Ki-anna reached out, took his injured hand and held his wrist, where the blood ran, to her face. The same sweet, intimate gesture as on KiAn. "So are you, a little. It'll wear off."

She drew back, and placed an evidence bag, containing his First Aid pouch and the scraps of lichen, on the table.

"In English, the common name of this herb, or lichen, would be 'Willingness.' It grows naturally only under the Lake of Heaven. Long ago it was known as a powerful aphrodisiac: the labwork kind has another use. It's given to a child chosen to be the Ki-anna, which means sold to the An as living meat. It's a refined form of cannibalism, practiced in my region. A drugged child, a willing victim, with a strong resistance to infection and trauma, is eaten alive, by degrees. If one of these children survives to adulthood, they are free, the debt is paid.

The Ki-anna showed her teeth. "I made it, as you see; but I haven't forgotten that scent. When I smelled your flesh, under the Lake, I knew you'd been treated for butchery – and I understood. They drugged Lione until she was delirious with joy to be eaten, and they sent her to the atavist fanatics under *An-lalhar*. Then they tried the same trick on you."

Bhvaaan tapped the casefile tablet with his delicates. "Your sister died too quickly, that was the problem."

"What – ?"

"We couldn't prove it, but we knew they'd killed Lione, Messer Ferringhi. We could even show, thanks to the Chief here, who was pulling the strings, how they got the prohibited ordnance into the Grottos. Your sister fell into a trap. She had to get under the Heaven Lake and that suited the atavists just fine. It would have been a powerful message. A Speranza scientist ritually eaten, then consumed by the very air of KiAn –"

"Controlled annihilation," whispered Patrice. "That's what I *saw*, in the cave. Something they would understand –"

"Thap was the idea. The atavists are planning to bring back the meat factories, once their planet has an atmosphere again. Your sister was going to help them: except something didn't work out. You were right about the tropo sampling: there's also stringent military activity monitoring. If a mine had gone off under the Lake, we'd know. If a human-sized body had been atomised, there'd have been a spike. So we knew the 'consummation' hadn't happened, and we couldn't figure it out. We think we know the answer now: she died too quickly. She had to be vaporised alive, a dead body can't be *willing*. But she wasn't a Ki, and they hit an artery or something."

Patrice had gone grey in the face.

"You going to crash out, child – ?"

"No, go on –"

The Shet rearranged his bulk on the inadequate office chair. "The autopsy'll tell us the details. Then you came along, Patrice. We saw a chance to get ourselves to the crime scene, and wasted Diaspora funds pushing on an open door. And you nearly died, because we drank the nice fresh water from this Habitat. Which happened to be doped –"

"The atavists thought the *willingness* they'd cooked up for Lione would work on you," explained the Ki-anna. "They've never heard of 'fraternal twins.' Ki litter-mates can be of any sex, but otherwise they are identical. You were begging to be lured to the Grottos, it was perfect, you would replace Dr Ferringhi. Luckily, you and your sister *weren't* clones. You were affected, but you weren't ready to be butchered. You fought for your life."

"You see, Messer Ferringhi," said Bhvaaan, "what really happened here is that a pair of murdering atavist bastards thought they'd appoint themselves as Chief of Police a child *who had been eaten*. A girl like that, they thought, will never dare to do us any damage. Instead they found they had a tiger by the tail..." He opened the casefile tablet, and pushed it over to Patrice. "They're glamorous, the Atavist An. But your sister would never have fallen for them in her right mind, from what I've learned of her. Still want to withdraw this?"

Patrice was silent, eyes down. The Ki-anna saw him shedding the exaltation of the drug; quietly taking in everything he'd been told. A new firmness in the lines of his face, a deep sadness as he said farewell to Lione. The human felt her eyes. He looked up and she saw another farewell, sad but final, to something that had barely begun –

"No," he said. "But I should go through it again. Can we do that now?"

The Ki-anna returned to her quarters.

Roaaat joined her in a while. She sat by her window on the streets, small chin on her silky paws, and didn't look round when he came in.

"He'll be fine. What will you do? You'll have to leave, after this."

"I know. Leave or get killed, and I must not get killed."

"You could go with Patrice, see what Mars is like."

"I don't think so. The pheromones are no more, now that he knows what 'making love to the Ki-anna' is supposed to be like."

"I've no idea what making love to you is supposed

to be like. But you're a damned fine investigator. Why don't you come to Speranza?"

Yes, she thought. I knew all along what *you* were offering.

Banishment, not just from my own world, but from all the worlds. Never to be a planet-dweller any more. And again I want to ask, *Why me? What did I do?* But you believe it is an honour and I think you are sincere.

"Maybe I will."

The Birds and the Bees and the Gasoline Trees

John Barnes

John Barnes has published 28 volumes of fiction, probably 29 by the time you read this, including science fiction, men's action adventure, two collaborations with astronaut Buzz Aldrin, a collection of short stories and essays, one fantasy and one mainstream novel. His most recent books are mainstream novel Tales of the Madman Underground *and techno-thriller* Directive 51.

He has done a rather large number of occasionally peculiar things for money, mainly in business consulting, academic teaching, and show business, fields which overlap more than you'd think. Since 2001, he has lived in Denver, Colorado, where he has a wonderful girlfriend, an average income, and a bad attitude, which he feels is actually the best permutation.

Stephanie Ilogu knew the Southern Ocean was *supposed* to be cold. Lars had been battling to cool the ocean since Stephanie was seven years old. *If my teeth chatter, I'm disrespecting my husband's success.*

Maybe I wouldn't think so much about my numb feet and face, or the dank sogginess leaking into my hair through my watch cap, or how much cold air leaks in under this huge parka, if I had something to do besides listen to my husband and his ex-wife make history together, so I can write about how great they both are.

Lars *had* warned her about his ex's enthusiasm. "Bigger than Brazil in less than three months!" Nicole leaned far out over the railing, risking a five-meter plunge into the dense mat, which looked like floating spinach. Below the first, surface meter, black, oily fibre extended forty meters down, so dense and deep that the Southern Ocean's surface was nearly flat despite a face-stinging headwind.

Lars wore his parka hood up, and from behind him Stephanie could not watch his expression as Nicole arched her back, revealing Greek-statue glutes under glistening skin the colour of hot chocolate. Twisting tightly at the waist, she grasped the sampling pole beside her, hooked heel behind knee around the rail, and dangled over the green, motionless, freezing sea.

She wore her thin one-piece bathing suit for company or cameras and no other reason. Naked except to broadcast, Nicole had walked on Mars, swum under the ice on Europa, and spent four years outdoors in methane snow and slush on Titan. If Nicole fell into the slimy cold mess below, to her, the icy sea that could chill a human to death in minutes would call for a slight speedup of her fusor. She could then tread water for weeks, swim north to Cape Town, or walk on the sea floor to Davis Antarctic Station.

Nicole whipped up in a back flip and lighted as neatly on the ice-coated deck as if she'd been wearing sneakers on a dry sidewalk. Stephanie reminded herself that those bare toes had dealt with far worse.

Nicole peered through the sample jar. "Mat's still spreading outward at eighty kilometres a day. And if this sample is like every other one, there's more genetic diversity in this jar than we've found in the solar system up till now. The million new species we've catalogued have DNA less like anything on Earth than a Europan tentacled clam or a Martian braidworm. The ocean still has surprises! I love it!"

"I hate surprises," Lars said. "Surprises are what good management is supposed to control."

"I love surprises," Nicole said. Her huge grin invited Stephanie into the conversation. "No surprises, no news media, no job for Steph. And the sea *should* surprise us." Her sweeping, circular gesture embraced the horizon; *Clarke*'s bow cut ceaselessly into the featureless plain of mat, stern jets churning a darker path that closed up in less than a kilometre. "Science is about knowing enough to know what's just uncommon and what's a real surprise. Most people are –"

Clarke cleared its forward intake screens. An immense stream of green and black mat shot upward and forward, sounding like God's clogged toilet clearing. The headwind blew the plume, the colour and texture of black bean and broccoli soup, back onto them.

"I think we're done, for the moment," Lars said.

Just before going below, shivering and holding her breath against the stench like rotten fish and cabbage, Stephanie looked back at Nicole bobbing for another sample. Her beautifully muscled legs wrapped around the railing in a figure-four; beyond her upward-reaching feet, all the way to the horizon, the Southern Ocean was a bright green sheet in the clear wet sunlight.

Stephanie usually liked undressing in front of Lars, but the fresh memory of Nicole, her body as fine today as when it was built, made her hesitate. Lars grabbed the hem of her parka and pulled it up over her head, stripping her into the refresher slot until he knelt to remove her safety boots. "Now you do me."

The freezing, stinking seawater that had drenched him spattered onto her as she removed his parka, but she didn't mind when she saw the smile as his gaze caressed her.

He gently stroked her hair, forehead, and cheek, his hands still warm and damp from his glove. "She has too many muscles," Lars said, reading Stephanie's mind, "and not enough colour contrast." He folded his all-but-paper-white fingers gently into her deep brown ones, where she had been caressing the forearm stroking her cheek, and guided her hand to the back of his neck. His hand returned to her cheek, and trailed down along her neck, and over her collarbone. "See? An old poop like me needs high contrast or he'd never be able to find his way around. Now let's boil the stink and cold off ourselves."

In the roaring hot shower, she scrubbed his shaven head fiercely, the way he preferred; he relished lathering her and rinsing her off. When they had washed and kissed enough, he said, "Well, now at least we don't reek of spoiled sardines." They towelled each other off in the small space between the bed and the closet, close enough to feel each other's warmth. "I'm feeling a little more secure," Stephanie said. "It's just – oh, everything. She's so beautiful."

"They built her that way," Lars reminded her, "because they thought the planetary exploration program would be more politically sustainable if the people out there doing it could attract fans on Earth. And my god, they were right. We had a hell of a fight to bring the six of them back to Earth and put them on useful projects; even today almost half the population wants to watch new exploration shows with the humaniforms bouncing around on some useless rock out in space."

"It makes me think she's not really human," Stephanie said. "You took away everything she was made for and everything she lived for – yet she came back here and *married* you. That's not a person. A real person couldn't do that."

"A person without much choice can do all kinds of things." He fastened his clean tunic. "We married each other to establish that the six of them were persons and citizens. Otherwise the corporations would've used humaniform technology to make billions of slaves. Can you imagine beings like Nicole spending six hundred years as a nanny, a butler, or a sex toy?"

"She says she *likes* to work."

"She likes to exercise her abilities, which are those of a very capable oceanographer and marine biologist. She'll enjoy figuring out why all this crap is growing in the ocean – "

"I wish you could just order her to fix it."

"As a bureaucrat, I might like that, but as a person who was once married to that person, I don't want obedience, I want her best work, things I'd never have thought to ask for that solve problems I didn't know were problems."

"But you hate surprises. And she has every reason to hate you and you don't know why she's helping instead."

"I was a reasonably decent husband for a guy who started late without a clue. As for why humaniforms live with us, work with us, and don't seem to be too pissed off that we took them away from the environments they were made for – well, they seem to like us. They've all been married to plain old biological people. Nicole herself has had two husbands since me. She'll probably have a good solid twenty more, in the next few centuries. She likes people. And you'd have to be a jerk not to like her, once you get to know her." He hugged Stephanie. "Look, she's beautiful, she'll live a long time, and she can go places we can't. Otherwise she's about as superior to us as a really great athlete combined with a pretty smart scientist. Haven't you ever met any humaniforms before today?"

"No, I haven't. Think about it, Lars, when would I? I got the reporting job straight out of school, and by that time you were already courting me. My parents were high level bureaucrats in West Africa, which isn't a very important province; it was just Dad's good luck that you knew him from school, but we weren't anywhere near the social level where the humaniforms circulate. And I'm not sure I'd have taken the chance to meet one if I could. To tell you the truth I'm scared of them. They creep me out."

"All right. Well, you've got the biggest opportunity of your life right now, to report this story." His voice was strangely cold; the small and frightened person inside her could not turn to him for the usual comfort, and she felt horribly alone, looking into his matter-of-fact, judging eyes. "So you can bail on the opportunity, right now, and I'll find someone who can talk to Nicole to record this story. Or you can get over feeling 'creepy' and talk with her. Drop the job or drop the feeling, Stephanie."

He's scared I'll drop the job. That decided her. "All right. I'll learn to deal with her." *But she's so beautiful and Lars slept with her for ten years. A ten-year marriage couldn't have been just to prove a legal point, a* month *would have done that. Why didn't I realize that till now?* "At least I'll try."

He looked like he tasted something bad. "You're meeting a remarkable person, not undertaking an ordeal. Have you paid any attention to any *accurate* source about humaniforms or just to the junky, scary stuff in the media?"

That hurt. "Lars, okay, obviously you think I'm a bigot or a phobe, so what *should* I know about Nicole?"

"Mostly how much she's like you – smart but not freakishly smart, with more empathy, emotional stability and sense of duty than most people have. That fusor in her chest, her ability to adjust her sensations to stay comfortable and sensitive, that body made of materials that tolerate very wide temperature and pH ranges – that's a spec sheet, that's not her. If you prick her, she won't bleed, she'll block the pain. If you tickle her, she'll laugh because she likes to laugh. She'd be hard to poison but hydrofluoric acid would work, and she'd die."

"See, but what bothers me is, 'And if you wrong her, shall she not revenge?' Lars, you took away the job she loved and was born to do, and –"

"You'd feel she was more of a person if she said, 'All you fleshy bastards can just die?'"

"Maybe." Stephanie sighed. "I still think of her as a fast computer running smart software inside a tough, pretty mannequin. I wish she'd never –"

Nicole knocked on their door. "No need to come up on the deck but there's something you urgently need to see."

They wore their parkas hood down and without hats through *Clarke's* unheated corridors, but slipped out of them in the bathygraphy room. "It's easiest to see on the combined display, over here," Nicole said, "but the truth is it's so plain that a World War II destroyer's sonar could have picked it up. All the meson scanning, x-ray boundary analysers, and phase-shifted sonar just add more vivid detail. Now just look." Stephanie leaned forward to peer into the holographic barrel.

Beside her, Lars said, "What the hell are those? And how big are they?"

Stephanie found the scales and legends. In an almost perfectly circular area about four hundred kilometres across, a bull's-eye in the much bigger circle of mat, arranged in equilateral triangles about a kilometre and a half on a side, towers two kilometres high and a hundred meters across reared up from the ocean floor. "Hunh," Stephanie said, "how big is a redwood?"

"Good comparison," Nicole said. "Because up at the top these things, that green mist in the holo represents crowns – or one big canopy, I guess – of filaments, some as thick as your thigh, some thinner than your hair," Nicole said. "At a guess, they're the roots for upside-down trees."

"Upside-down trees?"

"Well, not trees per se, but that canopy looks like a feeding structure attached to those trunks, if that's what you want to call them, and since it's all more than a kilometre below the surface, it's not leaves. So a trunk with roots on top is an upside down tree, at least till we have a better name. Anyway, I'm going to swim down and have a look."

Lars looked like he'd been kicked in the stomach. "You most certainly are not – "

"I'm not under your direction," Nicole pointed out. "And I want to know what's going on down there, and I'm more capable than any robot. I'll just throw my deepwater bag together, and dive."

Lars looked up at the ceiling, thinking. "The publicity situation is already a mess. If we wait for a robot, that will look bad, but if we lose one of the best-loved humaniforms, it will look worse. We have no idea what's going on down there, and if we let you go –"

"You won't be *letting* me anything," Nicole said. "I'm a citizen, my contract is with the Oceanographic Institute and they have a separate one with the company that operates *Clarke*. Nothing stops me from just going over the side. Do you want to have been consulted or not?"

"I do," Stephanie said. "Time for an interview before you dive in?"

"Sure," Nicole said. "Well, Lars, do you want your wife to write that you were dithering?"

Lars shrugged. "It's something to do while everything spins out of control." He stared down into the holo image of the huge structures on the bottom of the ocean, squeezing his lower lip between his thumb and forefinger. "A surprise with big stakes and a good chance of guessing wrong. I hate those."

Nicole looked away. "Stephanie, I know it's miserable for you up top, and once I'm up there I'm just going to dive over the side, so if you don't mind sitting in a corner of my cabin while I pack –"

"If I can stick my autorec to the wall – "

"Sure. Then just run up with me to shoot vid of me going over the side. You'll only have to be out in the freezing weather for a few seconds."

Nicole's cabin completely overthrew Stephanie's expectation of Spartan pragmatism. Space she saved by having no clothes and needing no bed enabled a wild chaos of piles of books, tools, instruments, and papers. Every wall was covered by paste-on screens, displaying a rotating profusion of scenery from all over the solar system, pictures of ex-husbands and families, major awards, and the other five humaniforms. The physical chaos of the floor was exceeded only by the informational chaos of the walls. Stephanie had to smile.

Nicole said, "What?"

"Oh, just noticing that this is a place where somebody works with a passion," Stephanie said. *That I didn't expect from a robot.*

Nicole nodded. "I wish I'd been designed to sleep; night watches in here are lonely. I think that spot by the bathroom door will work for your autorec. Fire away."

Tip her off guard. "Do the oceans ever bore you?"

"I've been down in every ocean the solar system's still got," Nicole said, "and walked the dry bottoms of the ones that're gone, and a thousand years would not suffice to see just the cool parts of one."

Great answer, they'll quote that everywhere. Now the bread and butter. "For the record, what's going into that bag and what are you going to do?"

"Sampling tools, suction gadgets to capture fluids,

blades and drills for solids, containers for everything. Acoustic, gamma, meson, and positron scanners. I'm going to strap lights on my forehead and forearms, fill my lungs with diving fluid, turn my temperature up, and dive down through the canopy. Then I'll cut pieces off these upside-down trees, drill holes, bring back stuff to analyse, and look around in general."

"Any idea what you're going to look for?"

"I'd like to know where all the sea life that was here went," Nicole said. "Because of the iron fertilization, there were immense populations of everything from microbes up to whales around here, and there haven't been any migrations or any population increases in the adjacent uncontaminated areas. Maybe two million marine mammals and six billion fish and sharks are gone, and god knows how many invertebrates, along with four hundred billion tons of plant life. I'm pretty sure they're dead, but where are all the bodies?"

"No idea?"

"Biomass is energy and whatever that is down there required a lot of energy to make. Beyond that, I try to keep an open mind and just tell the world to surprise me."

Another great answer. Now something for the personal interest. "Here's what people are going to ask me – what's she really like?"

Nicole slipped the last tool into the bag and started strapping a utility light and tool holster to her left arm. "Hunh. I really like surprises, the deep wild turn over the world kind. I do know what you mean, but honestly, how would I know what I'm like? That happens out there with everyone else, and in here, there isn't anyone to compare to." Nicole hesitated, looked at her directly, and said, "You're not very comfortable talking to a humaniform, are you?" She pulled the lighted helmet onto her head and fastened the chin strap.

"Have my questions been too blunt?"

"Well, many times, people talk to me bluntly for the same reason they talk to any machine bluntly, because it's not a person," she said. "People swear at a screwdriver because they don't care what the screwdriver thinks of them."

Whoa, that one made me squirm. Turn it around. "And you do care what I think of you."

Nicole nodded, as if reaching inside herself for the answer. "I do; I usually care what people think of me."

"That's a pretty good argument that you're a person. Welcome to the club."

Nicole surprised her by laughing. "Wow, I'm oversensitive today, and not in a way I can adjust." She stepped carefully over a couple of construction-block-sized instruments and surprised Stephanie with a warm, tight hug.

I'd've thought she'd feel like a heated couch, but this is nice. She stroked the bare skin of Nicole's shoulder: like nubbly fabric, softer than raw silk but not as slick as satin. Stephanie felt at once that Nicole's skin was as sensitive, as responsive, as easy to feel as her own. When Nicole kissed her cheek, the lips felt warm, and slightly rough. "We'll be friends. You'll see. Right now I have to run."

"Of course. Don't let me use up your daylight."

Nicole smiled, shaking her head. "Now, as a reporter –"

"Duh, of course, it's *always* dark down there."

Out on the deck, Stephanie recorded Nicole putting the tube into her mouth and inhaling diving fluid; it looked like watery brown pudding. Then Nicole calmly stuck the needle into her abdominal cavity, then her sinuses, filling all with the same goo. She had body cavities to give her a normal speaking voice, to process repair materials in the field, and be normally proportioned without having to haul excess weight; for ocean-bottom work, being fluid-filled prevented her from collapsing.

Filled with fluid, Nicole couldn't speak, so she waved with a merry smile, and flipped over the side in a dive. The big splash flung up green and black gunk, which slid down *Clarke*'s side. Alone and cold, Stephanie went back below.

"How'd it go?" Lars asked, after they had both been quietly working in their cabin for more than an hour.

"I think it's going to be easier than I imagined," Stephanie said. "You're right, she's hard not to like." The memory of Nicole's warm, different texture, and the strength of those arms holding her, was distracting, but very pleasant.

They had eaten dinner, and darkness had long since fallen, when texts popped up on their screens. Nicole had returned, and they would meet her in the conference room with the other scientists in twenty minutes. "I bet she doesn't want anyone recording how she removes diving fluid," Stephanie said.

"Nicole always said she felt about it like human women feel about changing a tampon – no big deal but too messy for public. She can collapse each cavity completely in one stroke, so in three quick motions, she clears her lungs through her mouth, her sinuses through her nose, and her abdominal –"

"Gosh, I'm looking forward to her presentation."

At the meeting, Nicole looked like the kid who just had a perfect Christmas. "All right, I'm scared and worried, and I'll explain why in a second, but what I just found is so awesome – like in the really old sense, the way Nix Olympica is awesome – that I hope you'll forgive me for babbling. First of all, those vertical structures are mostly made out of calcium hydroxylapatite, with a highly complex internal structure."

Someone said, "Bone."

"Exactly. The towers are gigantic bones. The root-canopy above is a huge digestive organ, which did its damnedest to digest me. Luckily nothing it excreted was a me-solvent. So we have tree trunks, which are bones; and roots, which are stomachs, intestines, and livers, floating in a cloud above them. Two kilometres high and growing on an exceptionally cold and deep abyssal plain, across an area the size of Pennsylvania, and I think it might all be one big organism; definitely a lot of the tubes in the canopy hook to more than one trunk. Everyone will now please experience some real awe and surprise, okay?"

Lars's expression was flat, drawn, almost angry. "You said you are worried and scared."

"Two kilometre high bones with a curtain of guts floating above them sounds like plenty to worry about to me," Stephanie said.

Lars turned his *Shut up, you're just a reporter* glare on her – actually it wasn't easy to tell it from *shut up, you're just my wife,* Stephanie thought spitefully.

Nicole winked at her, startling her into silence more effectively than Lars's glare. "Well," Nicole said, "When I drilled cores, I found the outer walls are riddled with little tubes and pockets, and what's in them is chopped Earth life. Seafood salad, you might call it, bugs and fish and seaweed and whales, all pretty much blenderized and packed in. That's where some of the marine life went – ground up and stuffed into those pockets in the bone. Incidentally, Stephanie, at a guess, the three vanished people from that capsized yacht very likely ended up in there, too, so you may want to watch how you break this news until someone talks to their families. Anyway, there's roughly a twenty meter thick wall, according to the positron activation scan, that's all that pocketed bone. Inside that, which I couldn't drill to, and the positrons couldn't penetrate to, the acoustic probes showed drastic changes of density, and NMR plus meson tomography eventually teased out what's in the middle layer and the core.

"The middle layer is larger and smaller alternating chambers, all about seventy meters from the outer wall to the inner wall, laced with reinforcing struts of more bone. The larger chambers, which extend about 80 meters in the direction of the trunk, contain very high purity hydrogen peroxide, which is so unstable around biological material that there must be a special coating or something on the inner surfaces of those chambers to keep it from dissociating violently. Between hydrogen peroxide chambers, there are smaller forty-five-meter-long chambers filled with a mix of twenty percent toluene, seventy percent octane, and ten percent heptane – whoever said *gasoline*, that's it. And the core is a two meter thick bone wall surrounding an empty –"

The intercom hooted the signal for an emergency

announcement. "This is the captain. Bathygraphy room wants you all to know that the imaging is showing all those big structures are now floating upwards, pushing right up through that canopy. They all let loose at once, and they're rising at about a meter and a half per second, so they'll be breaking the surface here in about twenty minutes. We can't run two hundred kilometres in the thirty minutes before they surface – all we can do is try to dodge the big towers as they float up and keep our intakes clear of all that canopy gunk. I know you'll want to observe whatever's happening; please be careful in moving around the ship and remember that we could have a sudden collision with one of those huge things. They seem to be staying upright as they rise, and if that continues there should be space between them."

"They'll be at the surface in twenty minutes?" Nicole said. "Come on, people, grab your parkas and come up and see this!"

Most of the scientists stood, but Lars gestured for them to sit. "We have work to do, don't we? Alerting the rest of the planet, making sure they know what's going on so that if we don't make it they have our information? And perhaps deciding what we should do? Shouldn't we –"

Nicole said, "I am useless for most of that, and if you want me, phone me. Specifications of what I found are on the big screen here."

"And this is my chance to interview Nicole and record whatever comes up," Stephanie said, and followed her out. Lars said nothing and didn't look at either of them, intent on putting together his "response teams" and "brainstormers" and "issue teams," but Stephanie saw by the set of his shoulders that he was as angry as he permitted himself to be in public.

Out on the deck, the sky was clear, and after Nicole spoke on her wristcom with the bridge, they turned off running lights; the sky was instantly powdered with stars, with hundreds of minute shooting stars crossing from northeast to southwest.

"The iron," Stephanie said, staring up at it. "Lars is so terrified that that is what has caused this... um, this whatever this is."

"Well, he might be right, but that's not a reason for him to be upset, if I'm guessing right. The iron enrichment did what it was supposed to do and took an immense amount of carbon out of the atmosphere, and it fed a lot of people along the way. Nothing to be ashamed of for that."

"What are you guessing?"

Nicole extended her hand. "Come on over here; it's more exposed but we can see better. Let me lay out this thought. Before we towed asteroids into orbit around the earth, fastened robots onto them, and started shooting chunks of iron into the atmosphere above the Southern Ocean, what was the main reason why this area wasn't producing much biomass?"

"Well, lack of iron, obviously."

"And where did the little bit of iron there was come from?"

"Meteors. That was the argument for why it was safe to do this. Because the process was completely natural, and they were just ramping it up."

"There you go. Now just watch and think about all these meteors for a while; see if I can lead you onto my guess. I've got a better grip than you, so let me hold you so you don't have to worry about slipping off."

Her strong arms gripped around Stephanie's waist, holding her tight, and Nicole's body shielded her from the wind, now coming from astern; she gazed up at the unending procession of shooting stars, streaking down into the atmosphere as the bombardment from the asteroid chunks continued. *Some people wanted this shut down as soon as the strange growth started, but there was no proof that the iron was driving it, and the artificial meteor shower has been going on for decades,* Stephanie thought. *But that's politics and policy, and Nicole doesn't care about those things, so that isn't what she's trying to make me see.*

What does *she care about? I barely know her.*

The horizon to horizon smear of stars was streaked everywhere with swift shooting stars. Nicole's arms and body held her warm and safe on the freezing deck. The shooting stars plus the security turned her mind to thoughts of being a small girl, back when father had told her the forest might die from the heat and the dryness, back when she had watched the little screen and seen her father's old friend, Lars, explaining what they would have to do, because there was no longer time for anything gradual...

That awakened other memories on the screen, of Lars standing with Nicole, the police arresting him, the trial scenes, the moment when he and Nicole came down the steps with arms raised in triumph...

She thought of the short videos, when she was in grade school, of the solar sail rigs dragging chunks of the iron asteroids, as big as airplane hangars, into Earth orbit, of the toy-truck-like pebblers, tunnelers, melters, and shooters crawling over surface of each chunk of iron like so many swarming termites, of the dozen barrels on each shooter spraying bits of iron, anything in size from a sesame seed to a tennis ball, out at a rate of dozens per minute... Lars's voiceover explaining how a million little meteors a day could cool the Earth, bring back the rains, feed the fish to feed the people...

Of her graduating class trip, the first time she had been south of the equator, standing on the deck of the big tour ship and watching the iron come in to make the oceans bloom... just a couple of years, then, before she met Lars...

And Nicole had been here all that time, fresh back to Earth when the plan was announced, walking the seabed and swimming between the icebergs before the first artificial meteors fell...

Nicole had lived a whole lifetime before hers, and how was she to judge it or understand it? She knew only that she trusted the person holding her, and knew that humaniform and human, daughter of the far planets and daughter of Africa, at least shared wanting to know more than wanting to govern, and placed truth before rules.

She thought until she said, "You think this is a natural process. Those... um, gasoline trees grow whenever the ocean blooms for long enough."

"That's what I think," Nicole agreed.

"What are they for?"

"Stephanie, evolution doesn't have a purpose; they're not *for* anything. The question is what they *do*."

Stephanie let her back press backward slightly, turning and raising her shoulders for a more secure place in Nicole's hold. She thought for an instant that the warmth on the back of her neck, between cap and collar, was Nicole's breath, then realized she didn't breathe; it was the radiated warmth from her face. "Do you know what they do?"

"I have one idea that's pretty crazy," Nicole said. "That's why while we've been standing here I've been sending the captain my text about it, and that's why I'm going to hold onto you till we go below."

"You're predicting something big?"

"These things rushing up toward the surface are about twenty times as big as the biggest redwood, back before the warming killed them. The safest thing, the almost-Lars-in-its-tepid-chicken-shitness thing, that I can possibly say is, 'I'm predicting something big.'"

Stephanie said, "I probably shouldn't laugh at him. He's my husband."

"Didn't mean to put you in an awkward spot. I still love him, myself, and how many ex-wives can say that after a few decades? But he's about safety and security, making the world more certain than it would be otherwise. It's a necessary part of the ecology of life. But so is surprise and amazement and wonder. And considering he married me... and now he's married to you... I think he knows that he needs some of that in his life, too." Her grip tightened, pulling Stephanie closer. "Whatever is about to happen should happen in the next minute."

The ship barely rocked; overhead, the flurry of meteors continued, *dug from the asteroids, fired into the Earth, politically guaranteed forever by the International Fishing Association,* as Stephanie had said once in an article. The stars twinkled, and the ocean's surface all around them began to rise into dark pools. The ship's jets fired and *Clarke* scooted two hundred meters at top speed, almost throwing them to the deck, her stern swinging round to stop her just as quickly with another blast of the jets. As they scrambled to their feet, the dark pools welled up, into swellings, springs, hills of water punching through the thick mat, geysers, immense towers of seawater reaching toward the stars above them.

Nicole's hands found the hip-belt of Stephanie's parka, and for one absurd second she thought her husband's ex intended to pants her out here. She started to laugh, but the sound was lost in the boom of seawater rushing into the sky; she closed her mouth as water poured down over the deck, and opened her eyes on the sight of immense black columns, far bigger than any skyscraper ever built, rising slowly out of the sea, all around, a forest or a downtown of these mighty pillars.

Nicole pulled Stephanie down to the icy deck and lay across her, pinning her on her back, yanking the hood of the parka around her ears and screaming "*...your hands over your ears!*"

Stephanie's mittens stretched the parka hood tight around her head as she forced them in, covering her ears. The icy sea water poured down around her but with Nicole's chest sheltering her face, she could breathe. Nicole's more than human arms cradled her tight. She had only a moment to think, *Now, what?*

The light was blinding, even through closed lids; the shock was worse, and then they were flying, floating, until the sea slammed into Stephanie's back, and she felt the burning sensation. It was only then that she knew her clothes had been on fire and that she was singed, salt water stinging at burns where the terrible heat and light had blasted away her thick winter clothing and left a pathway to her skin.

Far under the deadly cold water, she wanted to scream, but Nicole fastened her mouth over Stephanie's, worked some strange trick that opened both jaws, and released Stephanie's breath before giving her a burst of air, unneeded in a fusion-driven humaniform, from Nicole's lungs. Three more times as they rose to the surface, Nicole fed her mouth-to-mouth air; she shuddered with cold, her skull contracted and squeezed her brain terribly, the salt in her bare flesh stung fiercely, but she lived.

As the water broke around her and she drew a free breath, she felt Nicole grab, slide, push, and a moment later, Nicole's body was pressed against hers inside the oversized parka. Nicole swam on her back, forcing Stephanie's head up into the air, kicking with great force, steering and adjusting with Stephanie's arms along for the ride; she could no more have stopped Nicole from moving the arms than she could have pushed back against a bulldozer.

Within the parka, the seawater became blood-warm; Nicole had cranked up her fusor and was heating the space inside the coat to keep Stephanie from hypothermia.

Stephanie shook her head to clear the hair from her face, and gasped, "Thank you."

"Look up," Nicole said, still stroking. "Look up, don't miss this."

Stephanie became aware that the black and green sea surface was lighted as if by a spotlight, brighter than day. She arched her back, pressing her belly hard against Nicole's, and looked overhead, into the brilliant welding-arc white lights that filled the sky. She watched, numb with wonder, as the warm, delicate surface of Nicole's skin brushed against her, warming her, rippling with the effort of moving them across the sea, supporting her. Stephanie gazed into the sky, and the brilliant lights grew dimmer and smaller as the distance increased. In a flurry of no more than five seconds, the bright lights all flared for an instant, then dimmed into a faint red glow that faded into the dark of the sky, where the stars were coming out again.

Nicole shouted "*Clarke* ahoy!" a few times before one crewman, still fighting a fire in the superstructure, heard her. A few minutes and some hard work with a winch, and they were hustled across the wreckage on the deck, and down into the intact, if scrambled, guts of the ship.

At the door to Stephanie's and Lars's cabin, Nicole said, "You'll want to be there when I present in a few minutes."

"Yeah." Stephanie was shaking with the terror of the last few minutes. "Just... hey, thank you."

"I'm glad there was one human witness, by naked eye, and it was you." Nicole moved to kiss her cheek; Stephanie turned to take it on the mouth. Gently, Nicole turned Stephanie's face away. "You're still married. And this is a stress reaction. Now, take a shower, and I'll have everyone together in the main conference room in a few minutes."

The meeting was delayed while they stabilized broken bones on two scientists and treated Stephanie's burns, but that gave Captain Pao time to establish that *Clarke* was "floating, functional, and able to take us home," as she put it, in the opening remarks to the meeting. Besides the scientific and technical people, as many of the crew as did not have other duties were packed in to hear Nicole talk. The captain added, "When I took this job I wondered why a science ship was armoured and equipped like a nukeproof International Patrol disarmer, but I promise I'll never wonder again. We'll limp, but we'll limp clear to Cape Town. For the rest – Nicole?"

Nicole stood. "I think the first thing you're entitled to know is the answer to what everyone shouted during the burst: *what the hell was that?* So here goes. I think we've just confirmed one of the main hypotheses about why Martian and Europan life are so similar to Earthly life. The answer is what I called the 'upside-down trees,' what Stephanie calls the 'gasoline trees,' and what I just heard Captain Pao call the 'big rocket bush.' I think it's one path of panspermia – life spreading through space.

"The seed or spore of the gasoline tree arrived, perhaps, in a chunk of bone, tumbling through our air in a slow enough approach not to burn up or destroy the life it carried, sometime in the last half-billion years. It grew on the sea floor as slowly and coldly as stalactites on a cave ceiling. But now and then, a big meteor shower; or a cloud of interstellar dust; or the temporary capture of an asteroid inside Earth's Roche limit; or the right volcanic eruption, or perhaps the right impact on the moon, caused iron to rain down for a few decades, creating an immense bloom in the Southern Ocean, or one of its ancestor oceans. Or, in this case, the human race, in an increasingly warm soup of its own brewing, decided to clear out centuries of excess carbon dioxide in the air with rapid growth of phytoplankton.

"When such a bloom persists long enough to fill

the waters with life, the gasoline tree releases, or maybe synthesizes, the millions of species that make up the mat. The mat traps everything it can in that huge area of ocean, and drags it all to the centre, where some of the biomass is shredded and put in the bone cavities, and nearly all of it is oxidized for energy to fuel the construction of the bone towers, which are, just as Captain Pao said, rockets.

"Those rockets have just launched. A sampling of a few billion tons of Earthly life is on its way out beyond the solar system, to wherever it may come down; at a guess, the bone will crumble slowly into small pieces, each still pocketed with Earth life, and most of it will just continue through space forever, but some small fraction will rain down on many worlds as grains and bits, across perhaps as long as a billion years. On already-living worlds, Earth's genetic material will introduce new possibilities; on worlds not yet alive, it will provide many possible bases for a start. In any case, what we have just witnessed is as natural as the swarming of bees, the blowing of cottonwood fluff, or the sudden hatching of shrimp in dry salt lakes after a rainstorm fills them – just on such a long cycle that spring, or the rain, doesn't come very often. We may have similar events from time to time, here or elsewhere. Now –"

Lars asked, "And what must we do to prevent these eruptions?"

"What must we do to stop spring?" Nicole said. "Or continental drift? Or beaver pond succession? Lars, a natural process is a natural process; eventually we understand it and fit the way we live around it. Unless you want to go down in history with the people who controlled every forest fire, put levees on every river, and drained every estuary to create beachfronts. You remember how *that* worked out."

Letting the autorec pick up the rest of the meeting, Stephanie edited her main story. Her file of possible follow-on ideas grew and burgeoned like... *like the mat,* she thought. *Grab everything and throw it to the centre, wrap it up for others or use it for propellant.*

She didn't always understand Nicole's conversations with the scientists, but she realized Nicole had at least established her explanation of the gasoline trees as the one to beat.

Meanwhile, Lars, who had looked sick and old at the start of the meeting, seemed to awaken and youthen by the minute. He reminded Stephanie of the way she'd first seen him, down on the floor playing with her and the other children, on the television explaining the plan to cool the planet, defying mobs of protesters during his marriage to Nicole – like the return of the hero she had committed her life to.

Except maybe committing my life to a hero isn't what I want to do. Except it might be. Except...

The meeting wound down; on the way out, Nicole touched her shoulder, gently, and murmured, "As the more experienced wife-of-Lars, I want to suggest that you go straight to your cabin. He'll be in there fretting."

"Didn't take much experience to know that. And thanks for everything."

Back in the cabin, he was crying, big hard wracking sobs, and she was holding him before she had time to think what to do.

"I thought I'd lost you," he said. "I thought I'd lost you. Then afterward there wasn't a spare private second to tell you how glad I was you were alive."

She held him close. "You must be upset, too, that every plan you've made and everything you've done to tame the planet is undone now. You have to start all over."

He sank his pale fingers into her dark curls and guided her face close to his, as if afraid he'd lose sight of her. "Ten thousand interrelated things to put right, right away? Utter chaos where there needs to be order? What's not to like? I've been bored out of my mind ever since the Rapid Sequestration Initiative turned out to work. But I was so afraid I'd lost you. I didn't know what I could do with my life if you weren't there." He kissed her. "I'm declaring that there's nothing to be done until the science team reports, giving them six months, and ordering them to use it all. You and I are going somewhere, somehow, to celebrate the start of another lifetime of chaos and challenge, the best work there is." He kissed her again, slowly and tenderly, as if making sure he remembered. "So this might be our longest vacation for a decade to come. Where do you want to go? What do you want to do?"

"Surprise me," she said.

About the editor

Jonathan Strahan is editor of more than forty books, including *The New Space Opera* and *The New Space Opera 2* (with Gardner Dozois), *Eclipse Three*, *Life on Mars*, and *The Starry Rift*.

A three-time nominee for the prestigious Hugo Award and two-time nominee for the World Fantasy Award, he is also the editor of the *Best Science Fiction and Fantasy of the Year* and *Eclipse* anthology series, *Swords and Dark Magic* (with Lou Anders); *The Locus Awards* (with Charles Brown); *Mirror Kingdoms: The Best of Peter S. Beagle*; *Ascendancies: The Best of Bruce Sterling*; *The Best of Kim Stanley Robinson*; *Fritz Leiber: Essential Stories*; four volumes of work by Jack Vance; and many more.

Strahan has won the Locus Award twice, the Aurealis Award twice (he is the only person to win for Best Anthology), and the Ditmar Award six times. He is also a recipient of the Peter McNamara Award for contributions to Australian science fiction.

In the 1990s he cofounded the groundbreaking Australian semiprozine, *Eidolon*, and edited *The Year's Best Australian Science Fiction and Fantasy* anthology series. He has been reviews editor for *Locus: The Magazine of the Science Fiction and Fantasy Field* since 2002. He lives on the west coast of Australia with his wife and two daughters, and visits the United States regularly. His website is www.jonathanstrahan.com.au.

UK ISBN: 978 1 906735 66 1 • US ISBN: 978 1 906735 67 8 • £7.99/$7.99

A collection of near-future, optimistic SF stories where some of the genre's brightest stars and most exciting talents portray the possible roads to a better tomorrow. Definitely not a plethora of Pollyannas – but neither a barrage of dystopias – Shine *will show that positive change is far from being a foregone conclusion, but needs to be hard-fought, innovative, robust and imaginative. Let's make our tomorrows Shine.*

WWW.SOLARISBOOKS.COM

Follow us on Twitter! www.twitter.com/solarisbooks

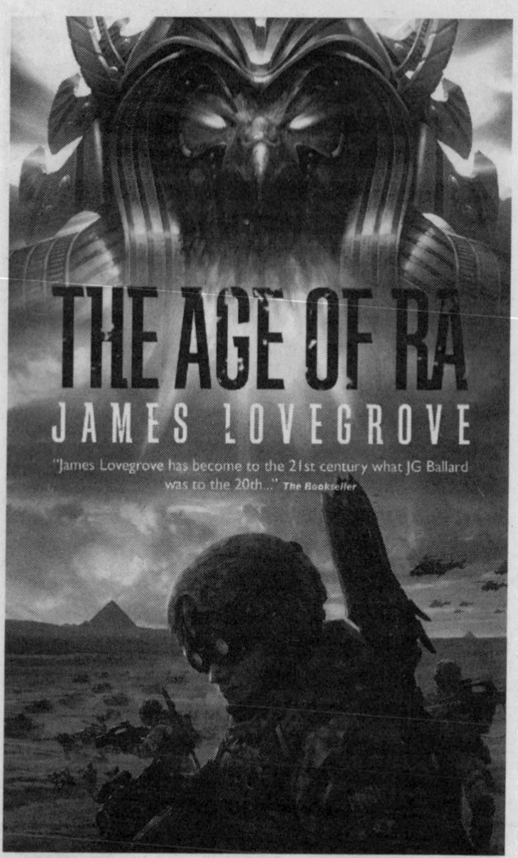

UK ISBN: 978 1 844167 46 3 • US ISBN: 978 1 844167 47 0 • £7.99/$7.99

The Ancient Egyptian gods have defeated all the other pantheons and divided the Earth into warring factions. Lt. David Westwynter, a British soldier, stumbles into Freegypt, the only place to have remained independent of the gods, and encounters the followers of a humanist freedom-fighter known as the Lightbringer. As the world heads towards an apocalyptic battle, there is far more to this leader than it seems...

WWW.SOLARISBOOKS.COM

Follow us on Twitter! www.twitter.com/solarisbooks

UK ISBN: 978 1 906735 68 5 • US ISBN: 978 1 906735 69 2 • £7.99/$7.99

The Olympians appeared a decade ago, living incarnations of the Ancient Greek gods, offering order and stability at the cost of placing humanity under the jackboot of divine oppression. Until former London police officer Sam Akehurst receives an invitation to join the Titans, the small band of battlesuited high-tech guerillas squaring off against the Olympians and their mythological monsters in a war they cannot all survive...

WWW.SOLARISBOOKS.COM

Follow us on Twitter! www.twitter.com/solarisbooks

UK ISBN: 978 1 907519 40 6 • US ISBN: 978 1 907519 41 3 • £7.99/$7.99

Gideon Coxall was a good soldier but bad at everything else, until a roadside explosive device leaves him with one deaf ear and a British Army half-pension. The Valhalla Project, recruiting useless soldiers like himself, no questions asked, seems like a dream, but the last thing Gid expects is to find himself fighting alongside ancient Viking gods. It seems Ragnarök *– the fabled final conflict of the Sagas – is looming.*

WWW.SOLARISBOOKS.COM

Follow us on Twitter! www.twitter.com/solarisbooks

UK ISBN: 978 1 906735 64 7 • US ISBN: 978 1 906735 65 4 • £7.99/$7.99

Philip Kaufman is on the brink of perfecting the long sought-after human/AI interface when a scandal from his past returns to haunt him and he is forced to flee, pursued by assassins and attacked in his own home. Black-ops specialist Jim Leyton is bewildered when he is diverted from his usual duties to hunt down a pirate vessel, The Noise Within. *Why this one obscure freebooter, in particular? Two very different lives are about to collide, changing everything forever...*

WWW.SOLARISBOOKS.COM

Follow us on Twitter! www.twitter.com/solarisbooks

UK ISBN: 978 1 907519 53 6 • US ISBN: 978 1 907519 54 3 • £7.99/$7.99

It is a time of change. While mankind is adjusting to its first ever encounter with an alien civilisation, Jim Leyton reluctantly allies himself with a stranger to rescue the woman he loves from his former employers at the United League of Allied Worlds. Philip Kaufman is discovering that there is more to Virtuality than he ever imagined, and some games have very real consequences. Both men begin to suspect that, behind the so-called "First Contact," a sinister con is being perpetrated on the whole human race...

WWW.SOLARISBOOKS.COM

Follow us on Twitter! www.twitter.com/solarisbooks